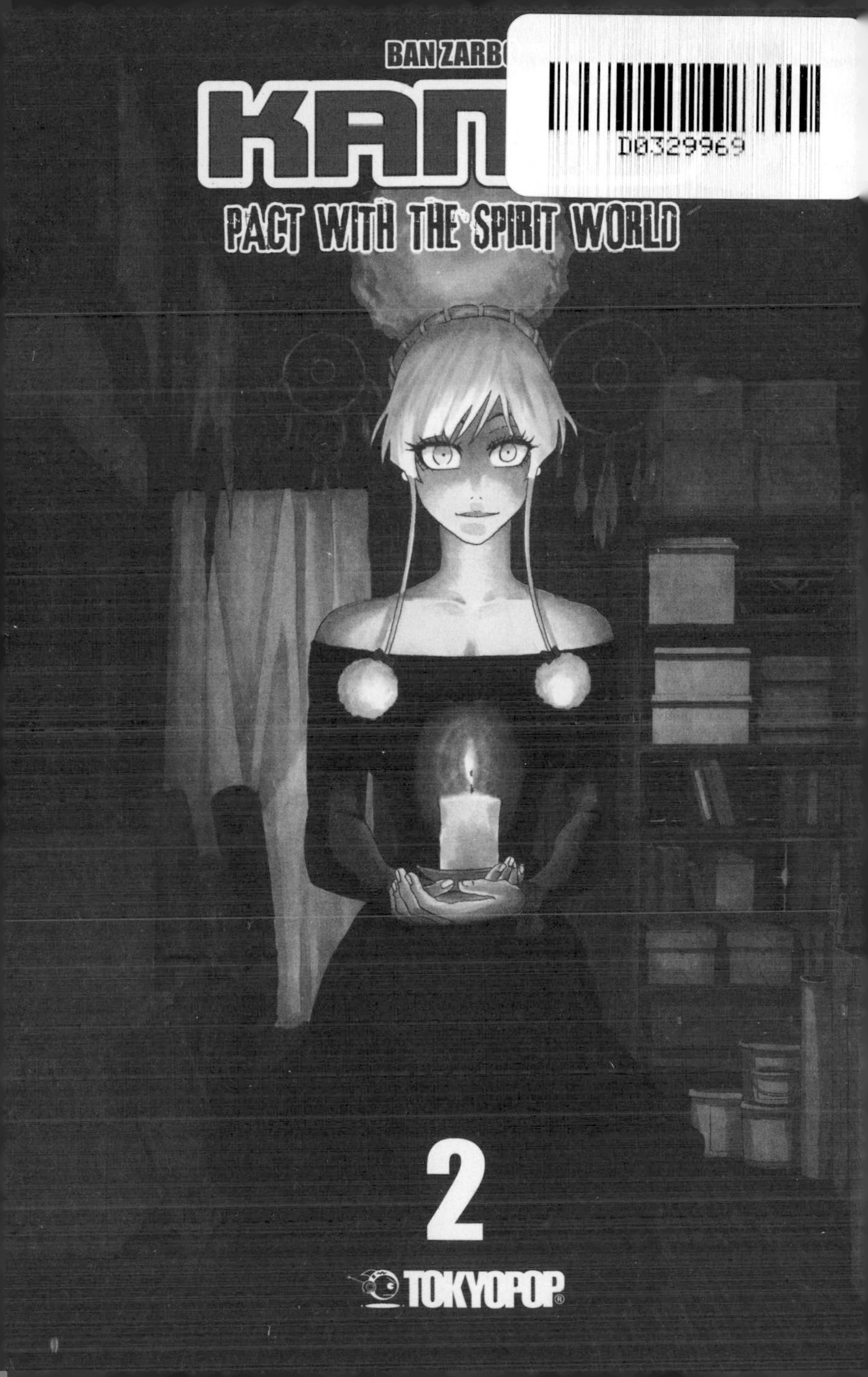
BAN ZARBO
PACT WITH THE SPIRIT WORLD
2
TOKYOPOP

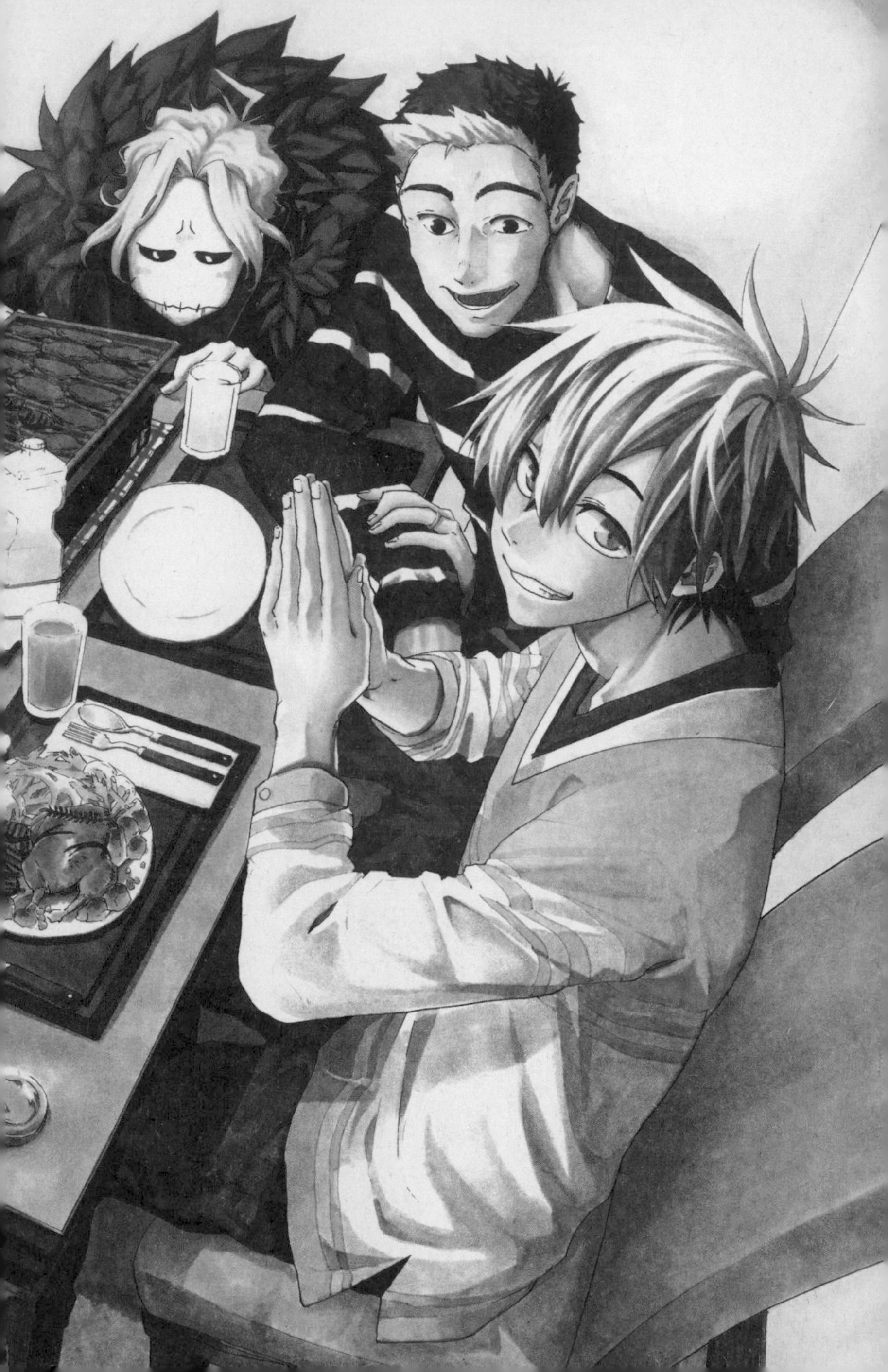

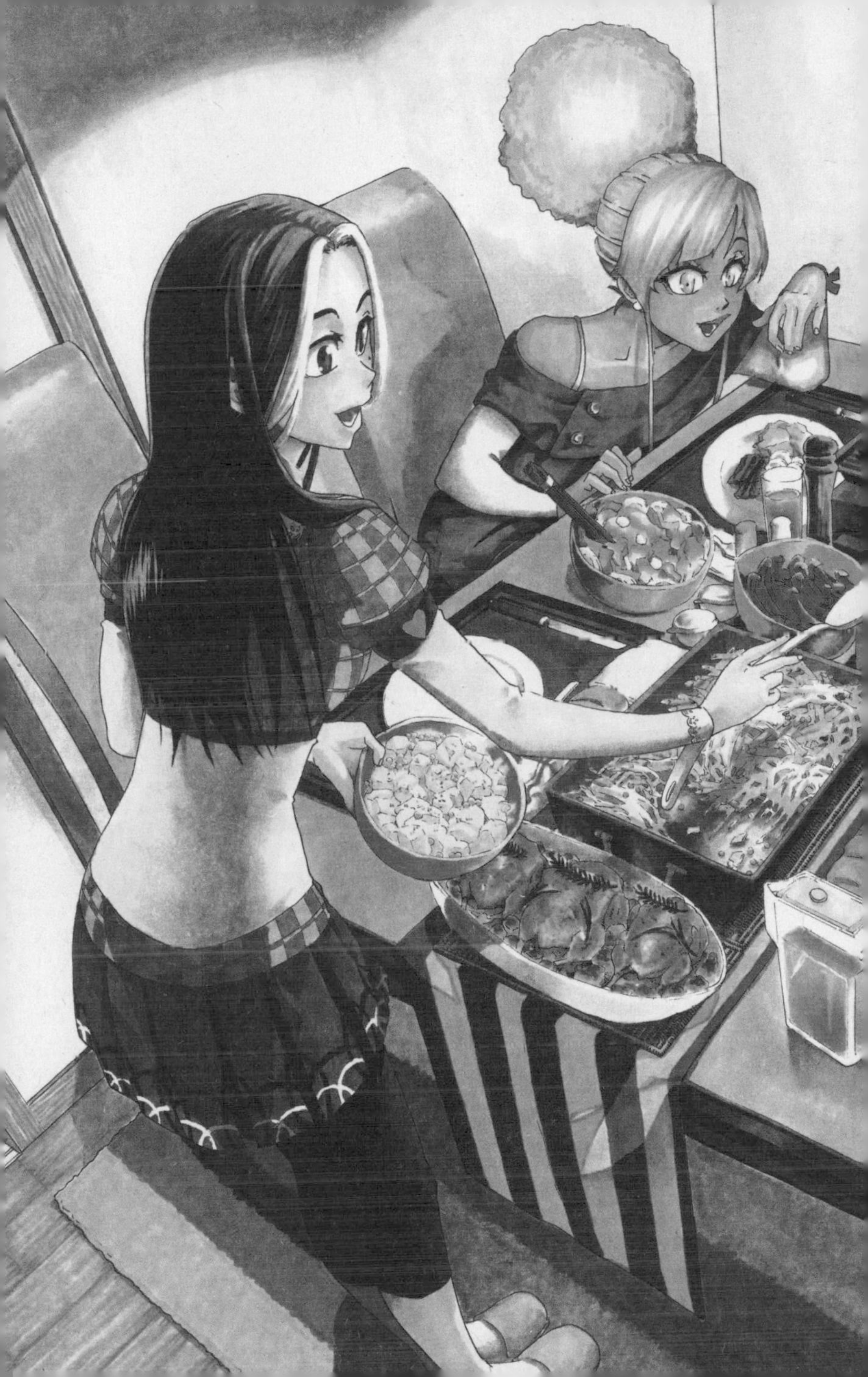

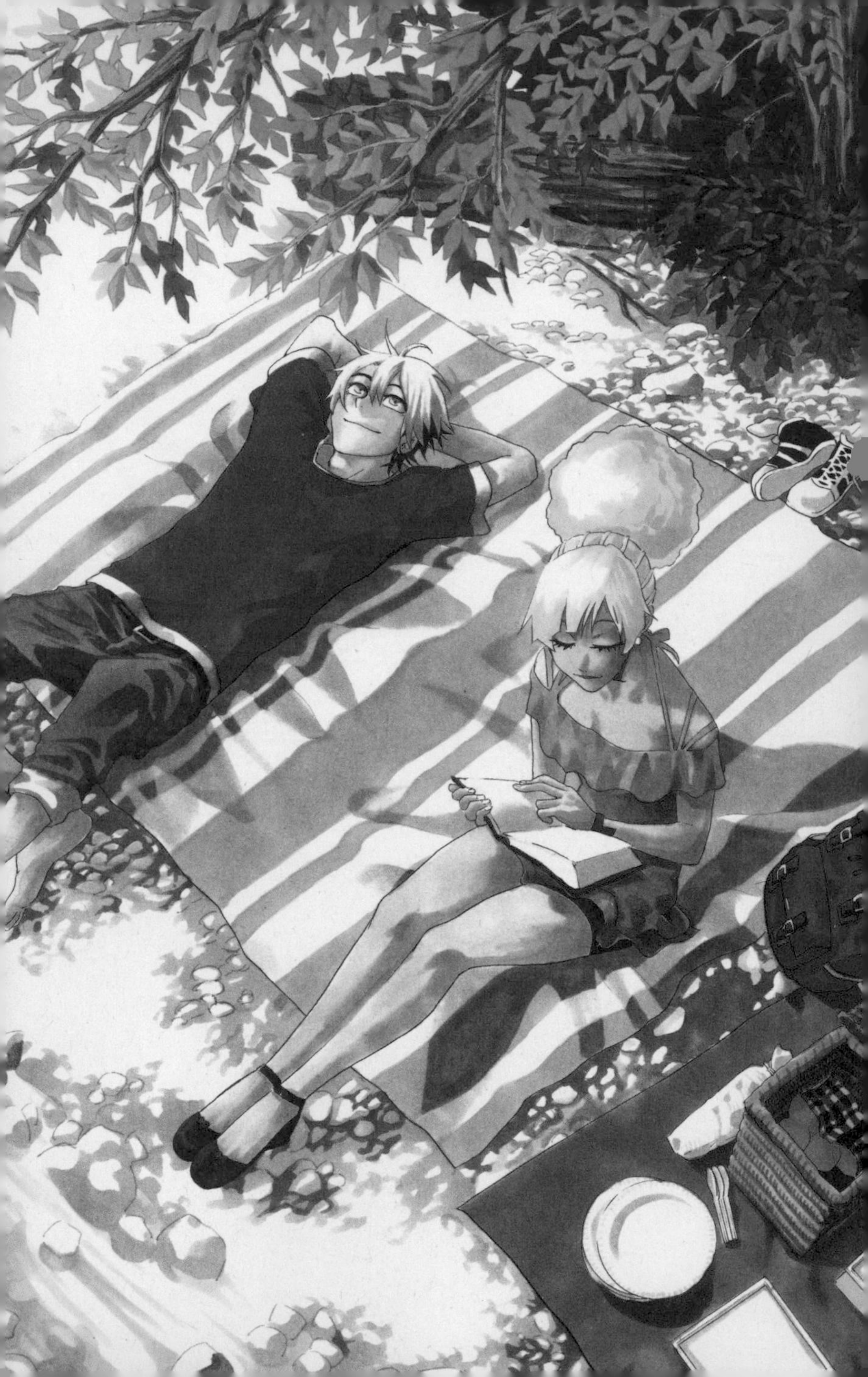

THE STORY SO FAR

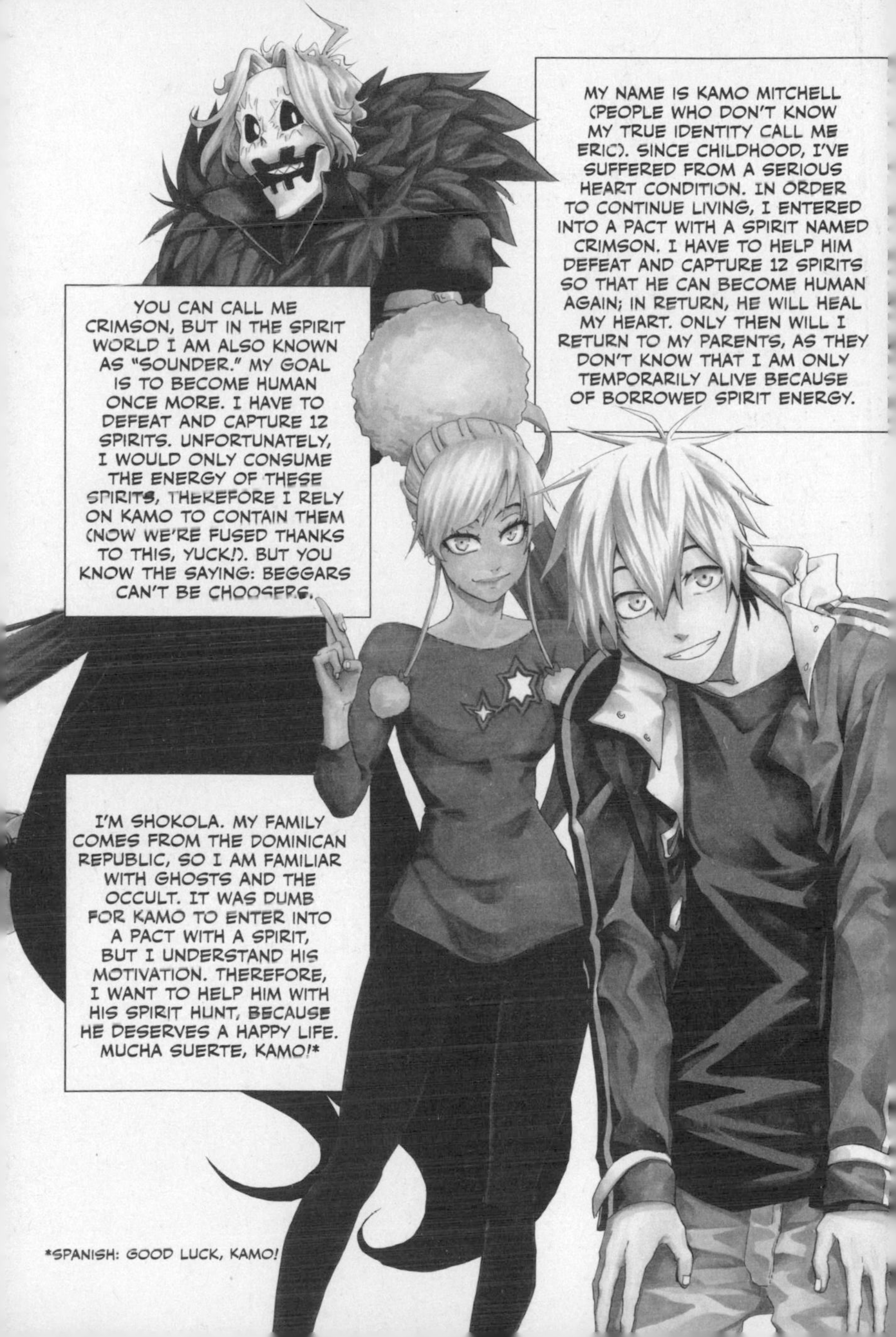
MY NAME IS KAMO MITCHELL (PEOPLE WHO DON'T KNOW MY TRUE IDENTITY CALL ME ERIC). SINCE CHILDHOOD, I'VE SUFFERED FROM A SERIOUS HEART CONDITION. IN ORDER TO CONTINUE LIVING, I ENTERED INTO A PACT WITH A SPIRIT NAMED CRIMSON. I HAVE TO HELP HIM DEFEAT AND CAPTURE 12 SPIRITS SO THAT HE CAN BECOME HUMAN AGAIN; IN RETURN, HE WILL HEAL MY HEART. ONLY THEN WILL I RETURN TO MY PARENTS, AS THEY DON'T KNOW THAT I AM ONLY TEMPORARILY ALIVE BECAUSE OF BORROWED SPIRIT ENERGY.
YOU CAN CALL ME CRIMSON, BUT IN THE SPIRIT WORLD I AM ALSO KNOWN AS "SOUNDER." MY GOAL IS TO BECOME HUMAN ONCE MORE. I HAVE TO DEFEAT AND CAPTURE 12 SPIRITS. UNFORTUNATELY, I WOULD ONLY CONSUME THE ENERGY OF THESE SPIRITS, THEREFORE I RELY ON KAMO TO CONTAIN THEM (NOW WE'RE FUSED THANKS TO THIS, YUCK!). BUT YOU KNOW THE SAYING: BEGGARS CAN'T BE CHOOSERS.
I'M SHOKOLA. MY FAMILY COMES FROM THE DOMINICAN REPUBLIC, SO I AM FAMILIAR WITH GHOSTS AND THE OCCULT. IT WAS DUMB FOR KAMO TO ENTER INTO A PACT WITH A SPIRIT, BUT I UNDERSTAND HIS MOTIVATION. THEREFORE, I WANT TO HELP HIM WITH HIS SPIRIT HUNT, BECAUSE HE DESERVES A HAPPY LIFE. MUCHA SUERTE, KAMO!*

*SPANISH: GOOD LUCK, KAMO!

CONTENTS

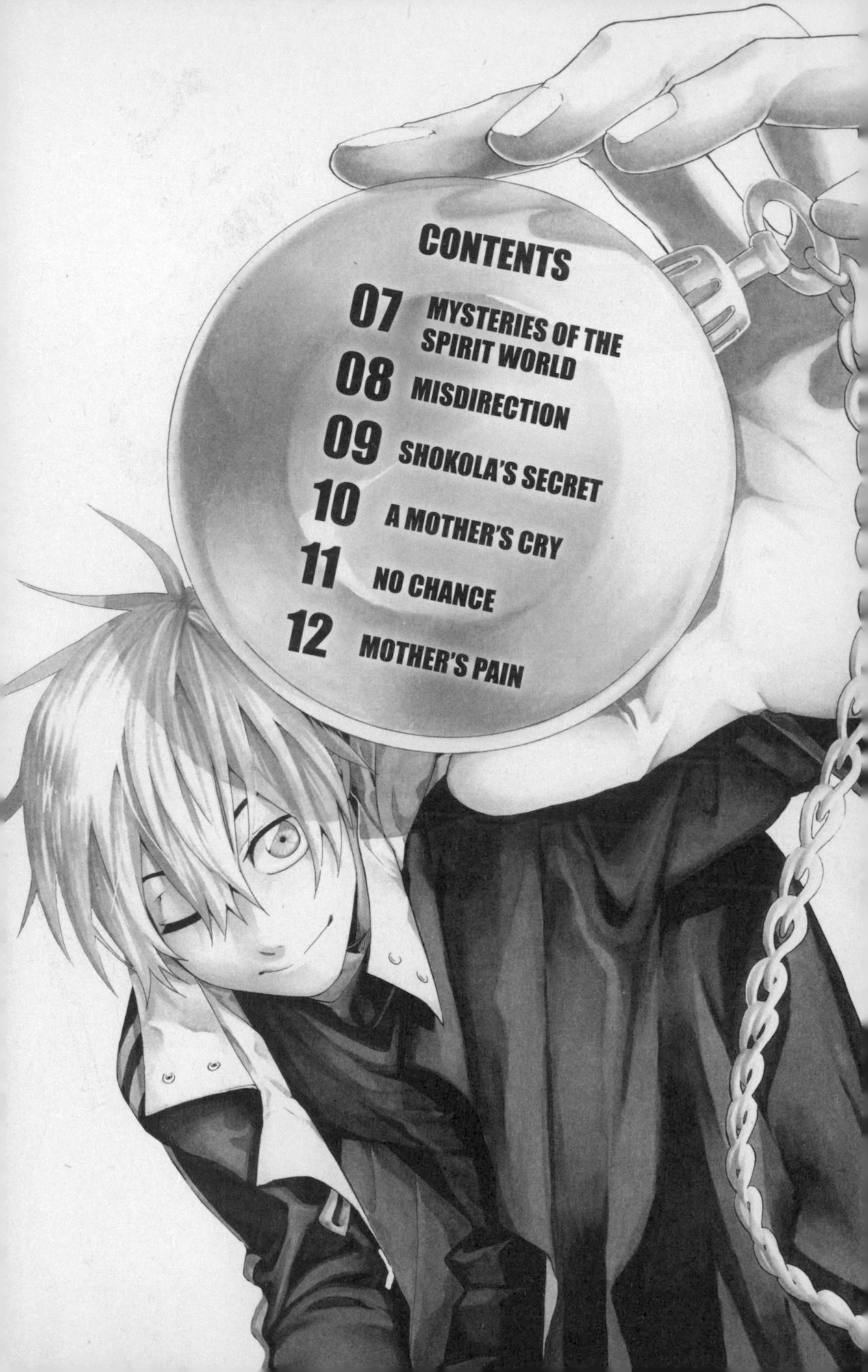

07
MYSTERIES OF THE SPIRIT WORLD

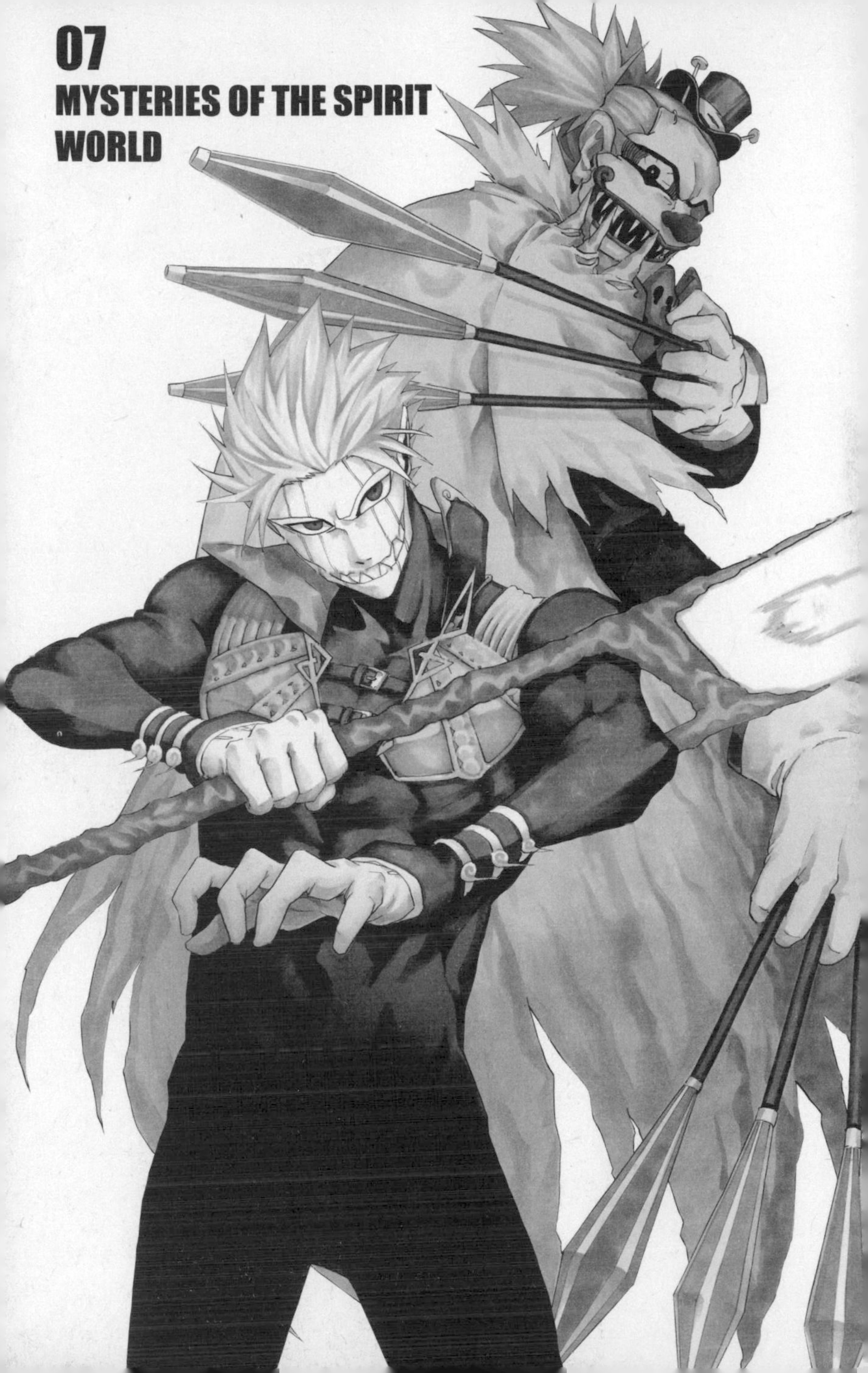

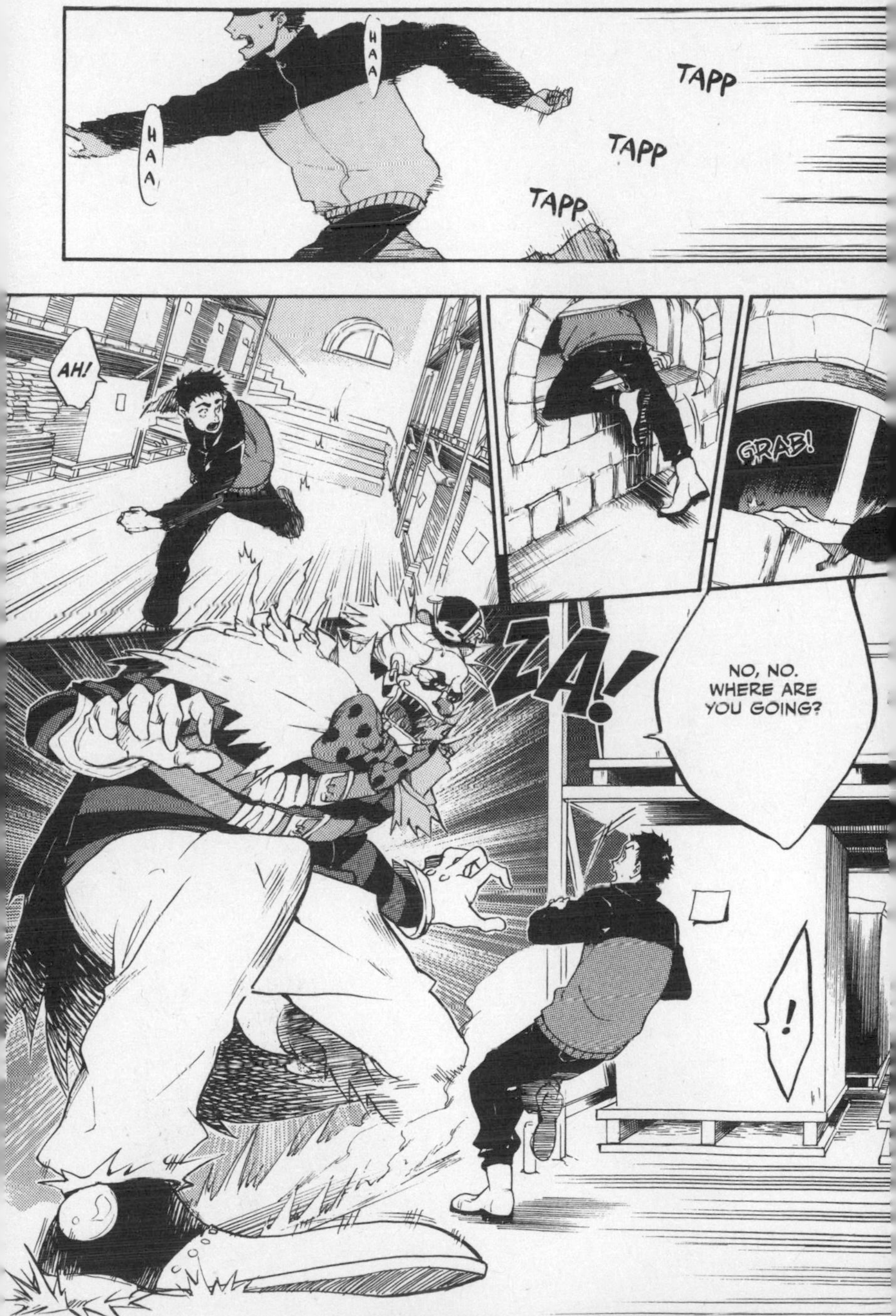
TAPP
TAPP
TAPP
HAA
HAA
GRAB!
AH!
NO, NO. WHERE ARE YOU GOING?
ZA!
!

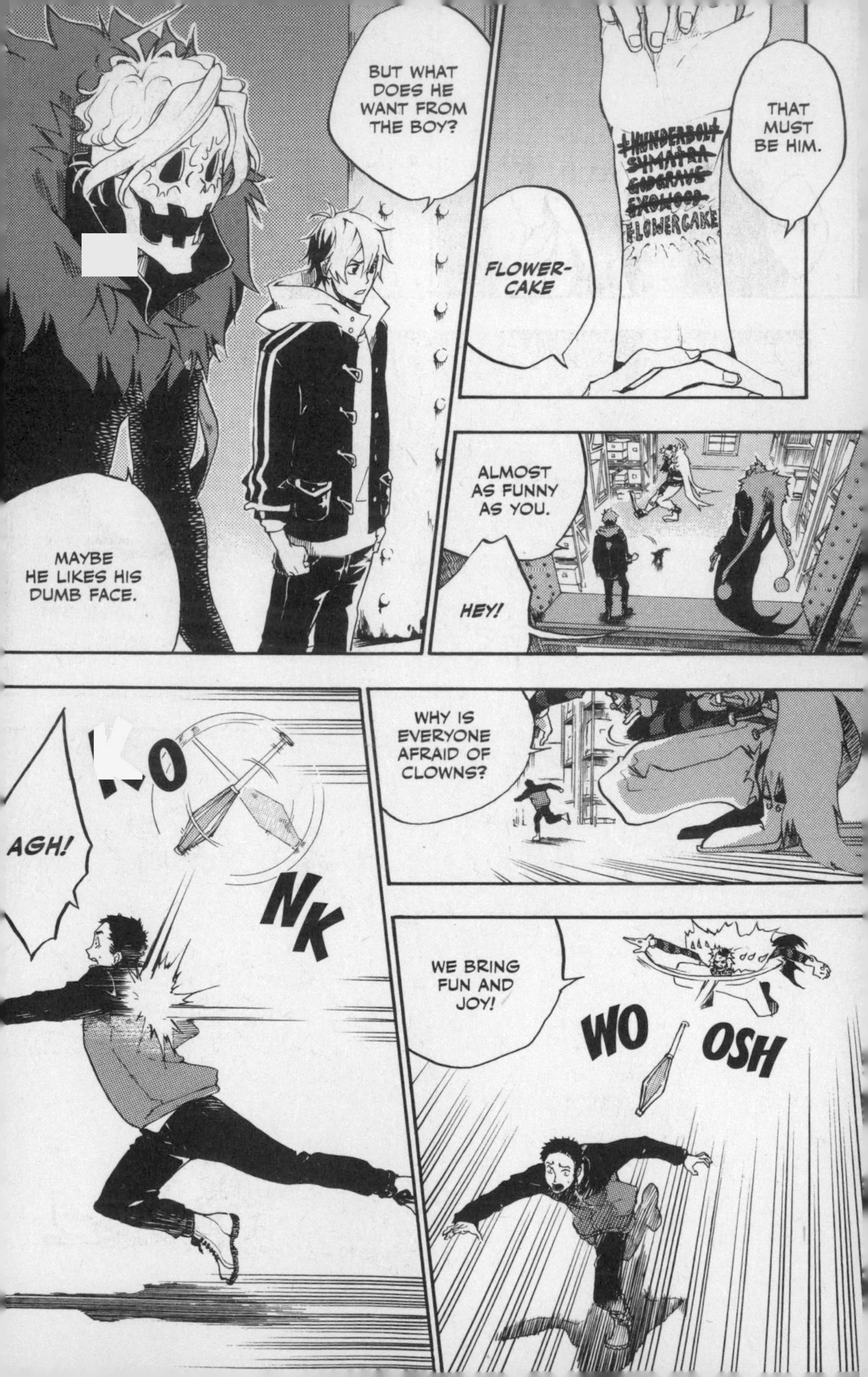
THUNDERBOLT
SUMATRA
GODGRAVE
EXOHOOD
FLOWERCAKE
THAT MUST BE HIM.
FLOWER-CAKE
ALMOST AS FUNNY AS YOU.
HEY!
BUT WHAT DOES HE WANT FROM THE BOY?
MAYBE HE LIKES HIS DUMB FACE.
WHY IS EVERYONE AFRAID OF CLOWNS?
WE BRING FUN AND JOY!
WOOSH
KONK
AGH!

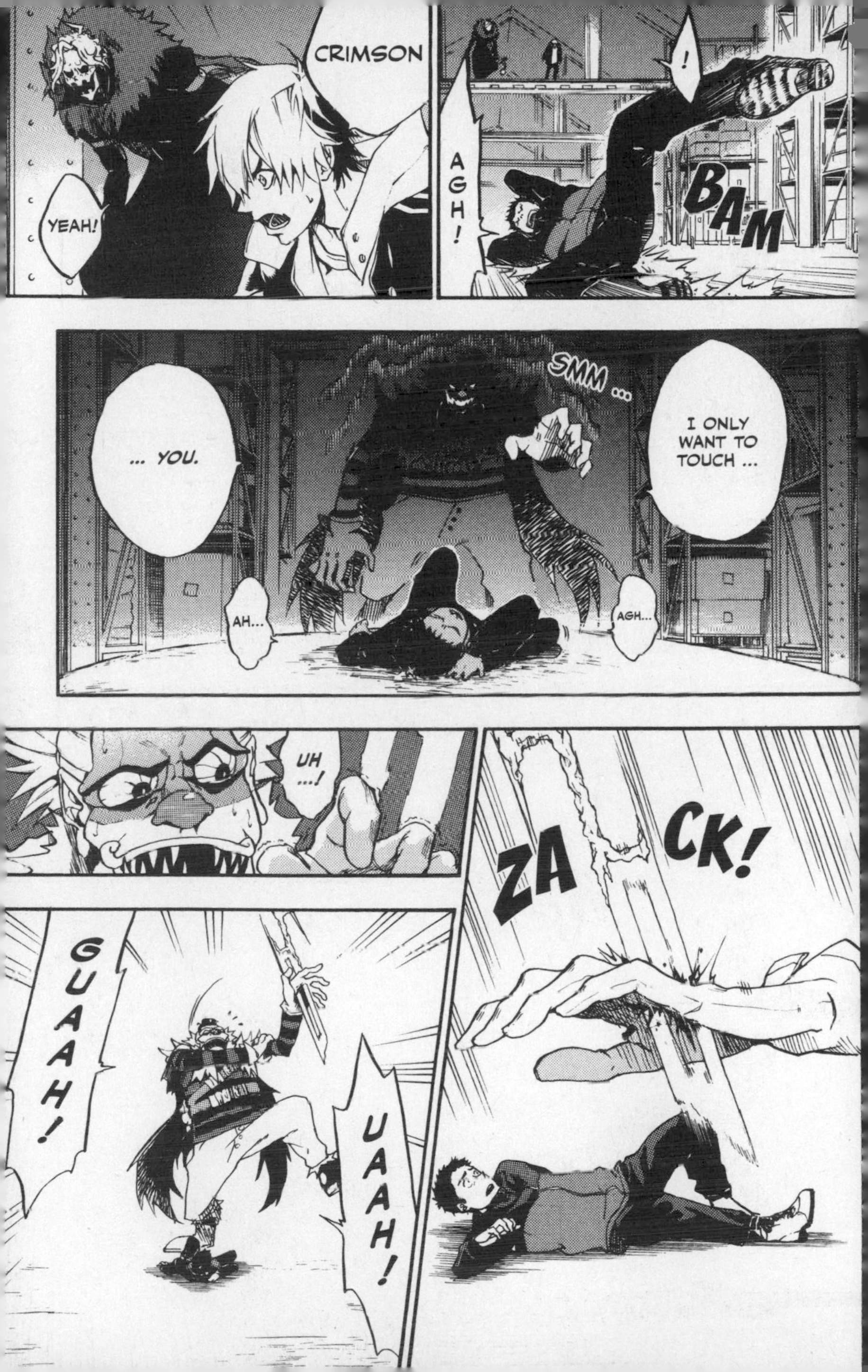
!
AGH!
BAM
CRIMSON
YEAH!
I ONLY WANT TO TOUCH ...
SMM ...
... YOU.
AGH...
AH...
ZACK!
UH ...!
UAAH!
GUAAAH!

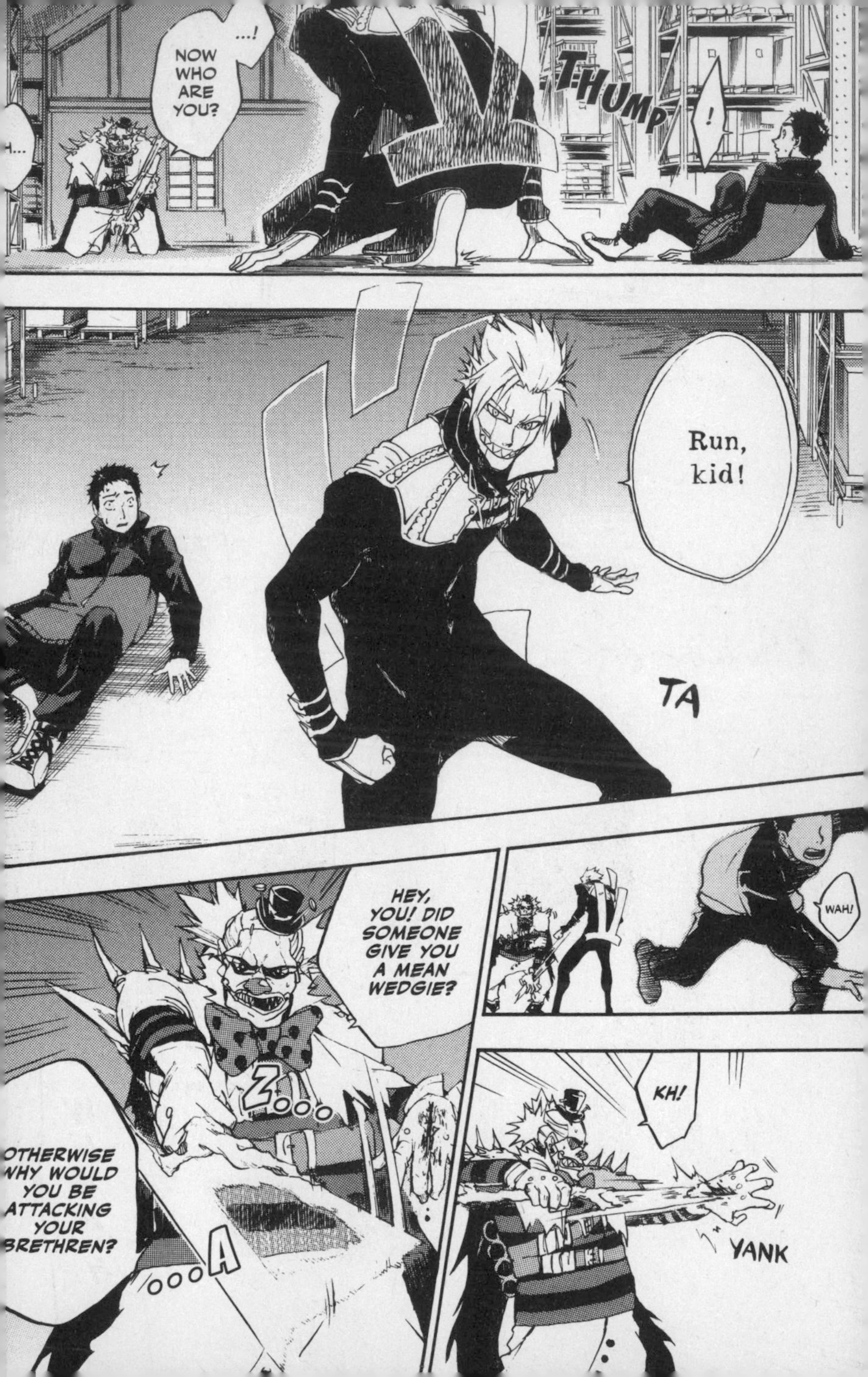
THUMP
!
...! NOW WHO ARE YOU?
H...
Run, kid!
TA
WAH!
KH!
YANK
HEY, YOU! DID SOMEONE GIVE YOU A MEAN WEDGIE?
ZOOOO
OTHERWISE WHY WOULD YOU BE ATTACKING YOUR BRETHREN?
OOOA

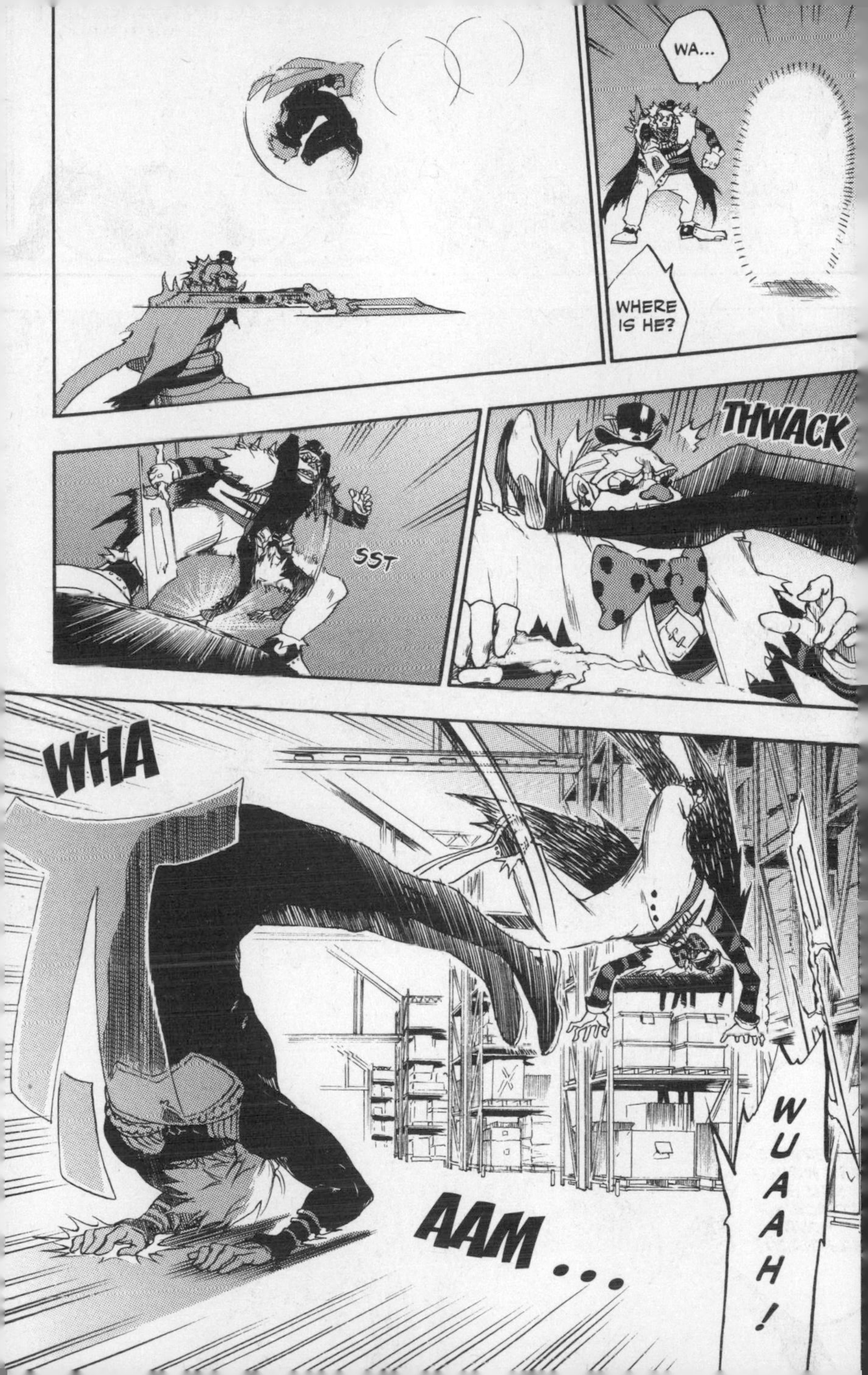
WA...
WHERE IS HE?
THWACK
SST
WUAAAH!
WHA
AAM...

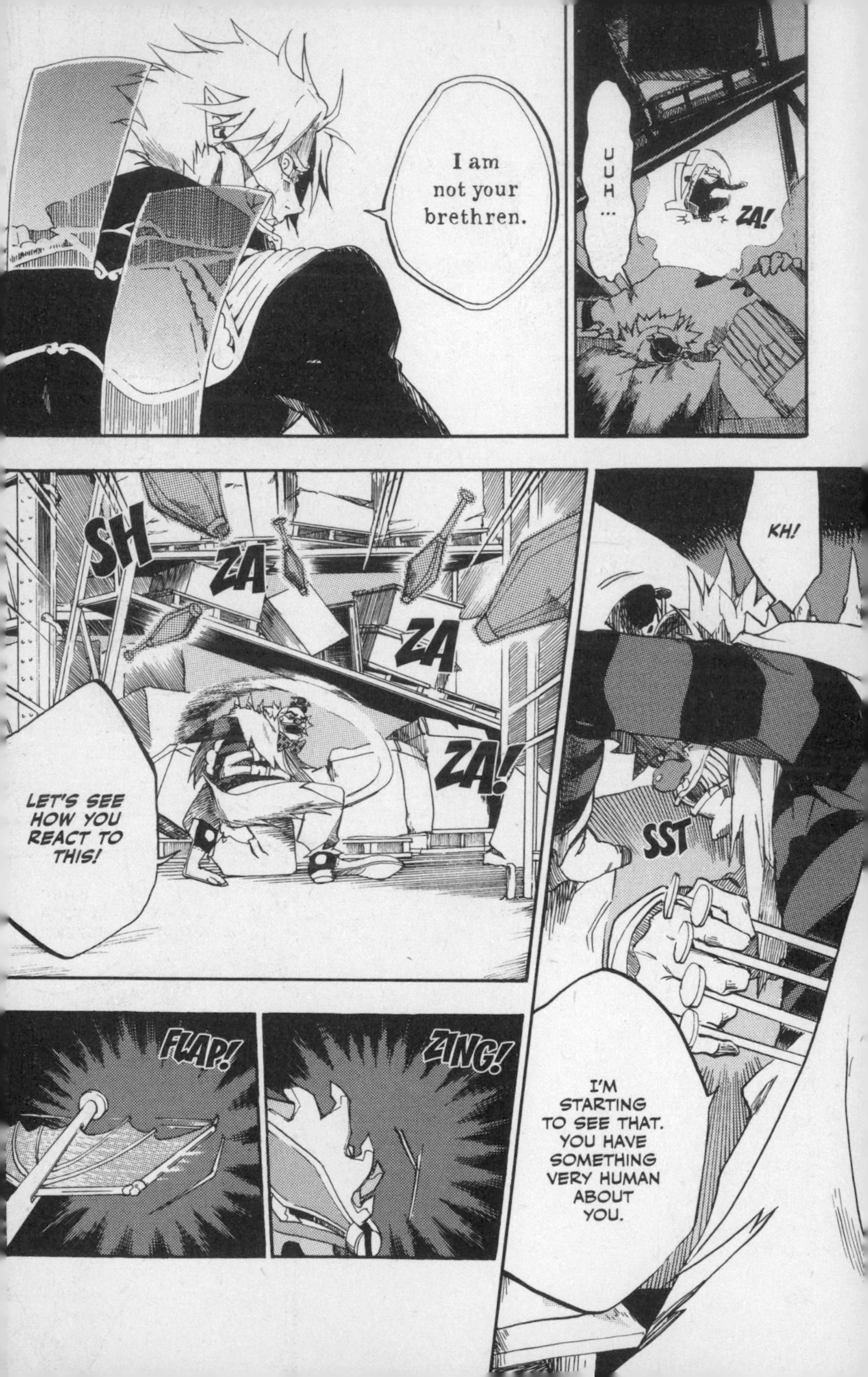
UUH ...
ZA!
I am not your brethren.
KH!
SST
I'M STARTING TO SEE THAT. YOU HAVE SOMETHING VERY HUMAN ABOUT YOU.
SH
ZA
ZA
ZA!
LET'S SEE HOW YOU REACT TO THIS!
ZING!
FLAP!

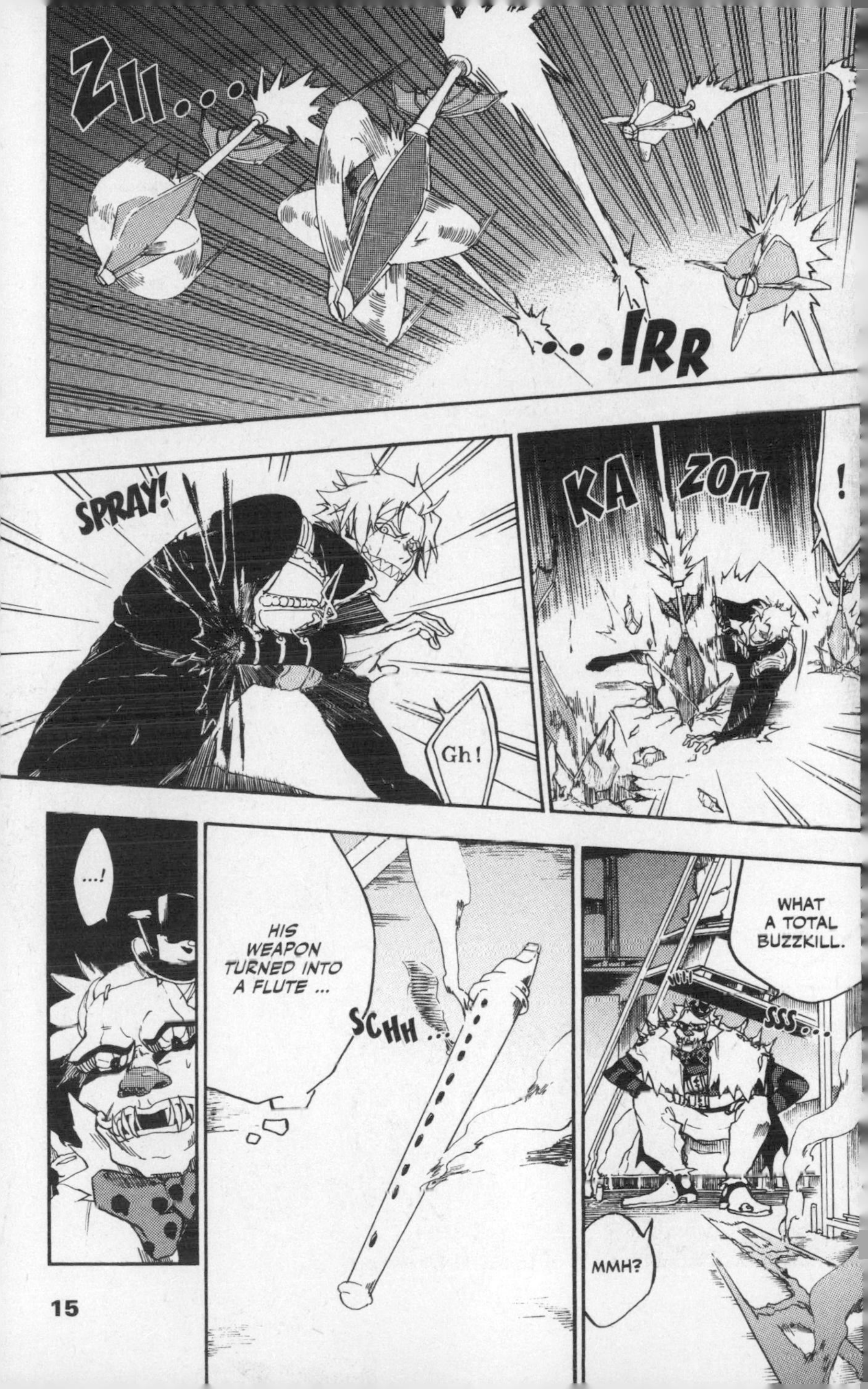
ZII...
...IRR
KA
ZOM
!
SPRAY!
Gh!
WHAT A TOTAL BUZZKILL.
SSS...
MMH?
HIS WEAPON TURNED INTO A FLUTE ...
SCHH...
...!

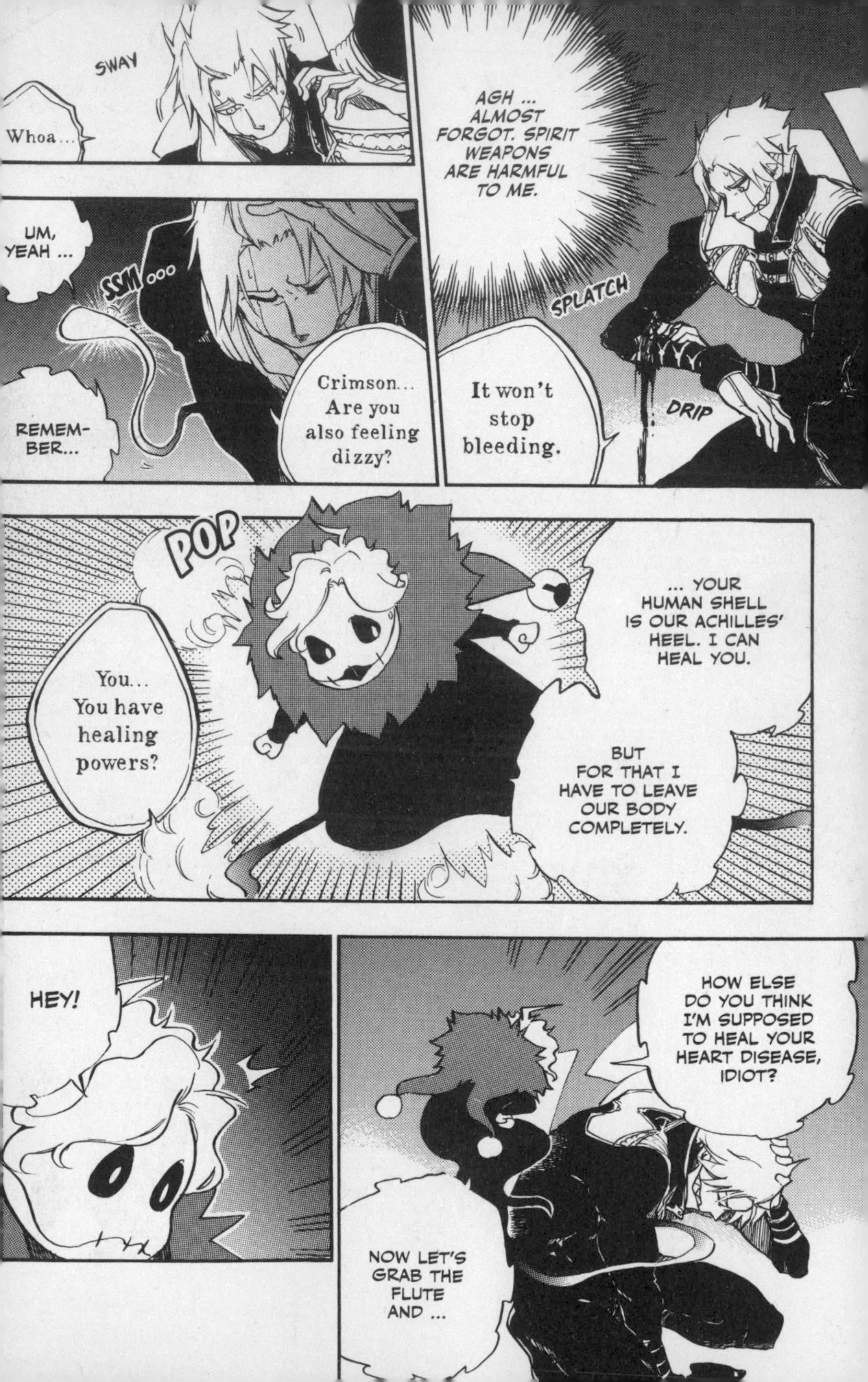

SWAY
Whoa...
AGH ... ALMOST FORGOT. SPIRIT WEAPONS ARE HARMFUL TO ME.
SPLATCH
DRIP
It won't stop bleeding.
Crimson... Are you also feeling dizzy?
UM, YEAH ...
SSM ooo
REMEM-BER...
POP
... YOUR HUMAN SHELL IS OUR ACHILLES' HEEL. I CAN HEAL YOU.
You... You have healing powers?
BUT FOR THAT I HAVE TO LEAVE OUR BODY COMPLETELY.
HEY!
HOW ELSE DO YOU THINK I'M SUPPOSED TO HEAL YOUR HEART DISEASE, IDIOT?
NOW LET'S GRAB THE FLUTE AND ...

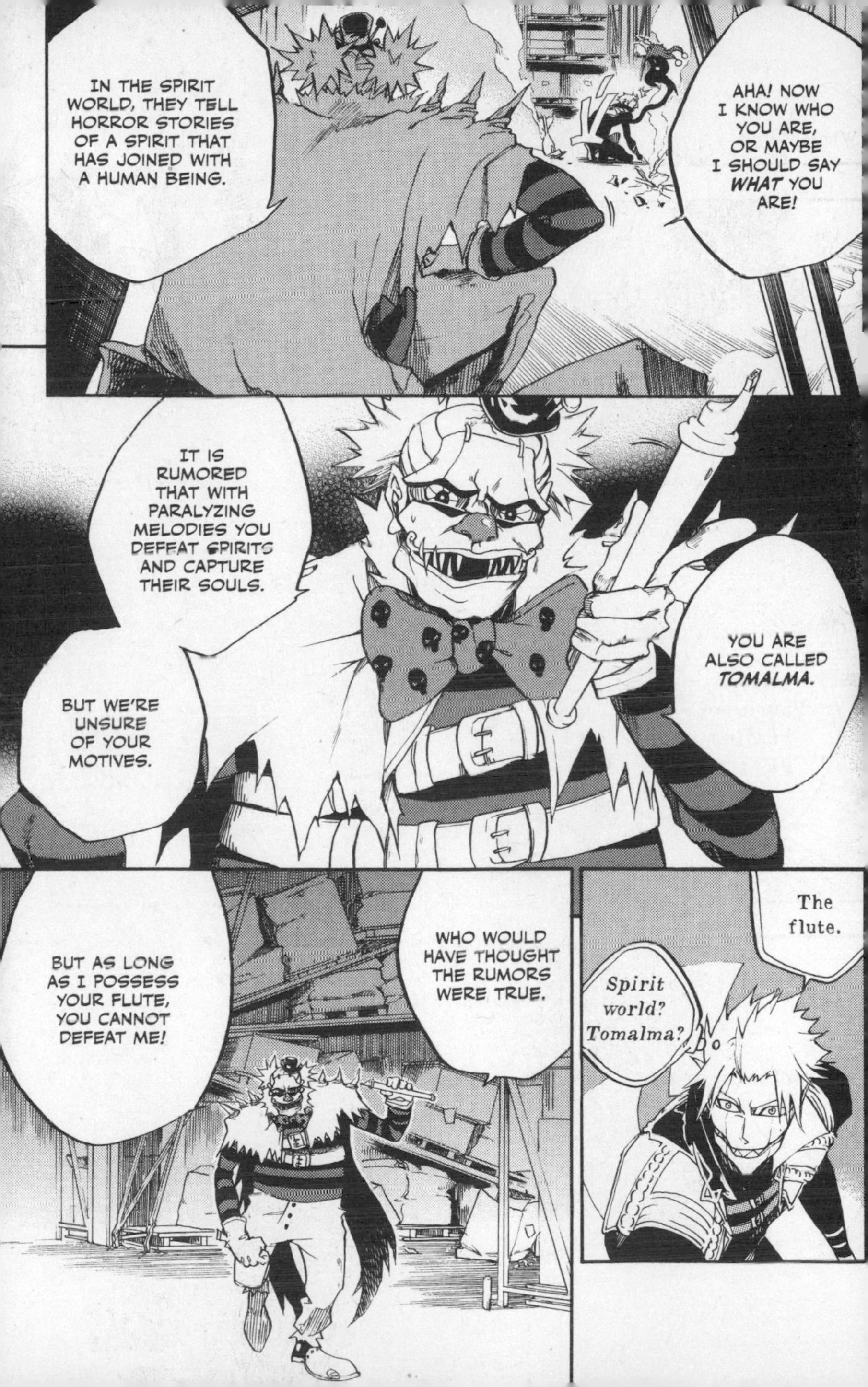
AHA! NOW I KNOW WHO YOU ARE, OR MAYBE I SHOULD SAY *WHAT* YOU ARE!
IN THE SPIRIT WORLD, THEY TELL HORROR STORIES OF A SPIRIT THAT HAS JOINED WITH A HUMAN BEING.
YOU ARE ALSO CALLED *TOMALMA.*
IT IS RUMORED THAT WITH PARALYZING MELODIES YOU DEFEAT SPIRITS AND CAPTURE THEIR SOULS.
BUT WE'RE UNSURE OF YOUR MOTIVES.
The flute.
Spirit world? Tomalma?
WHO WOULD HAVE THOUGHT THE RUMORS WERE TRUE.
BUT AS LONG AS I POSSESS YOUR FLUTE, YOU CANNOT DEFEAT ME!

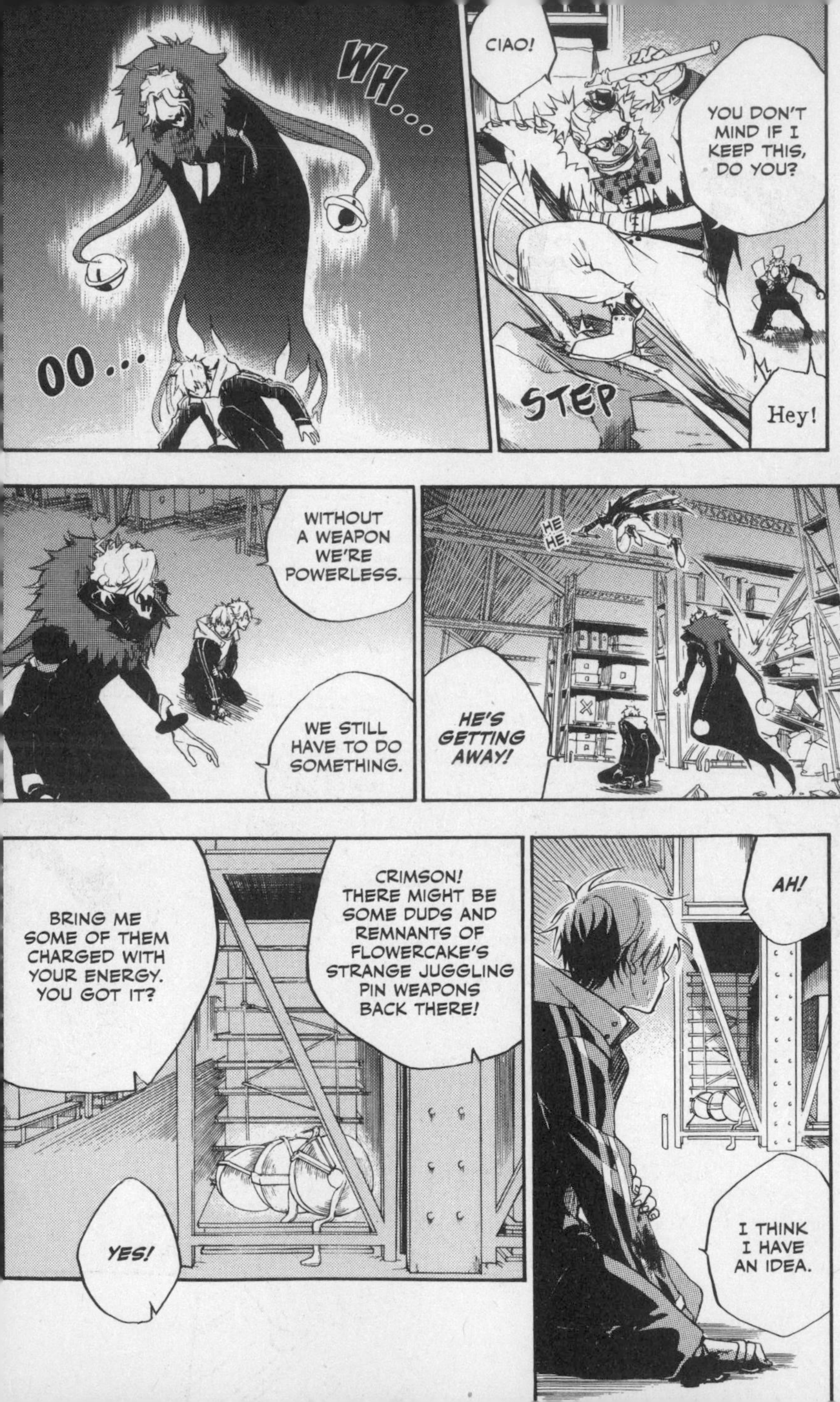
CIAO!
YOU DON'T MIND IF I KEEP THIS, DO YOU?
STEP
Hey!
WH...
OO...
HE HE.
HE'S GETTING AWAY!
WITHOUT A WEAPON WE'RE POWERLESS.
WE STILL HAVE TO DO SOMETHING.
AH!
I THINK I HAVE AN IDEA.
CRIMSON! THERE MIGHT BE SOME DUDS AND REMNANTS OF FLOWERCAKE'S STRANGE JUGGLING PIN WEAPONS BACK THERE!
BRING ME SOME OF THEM CHARGED WITH YOUR ENERGY. YOU GOT IT?
YES!

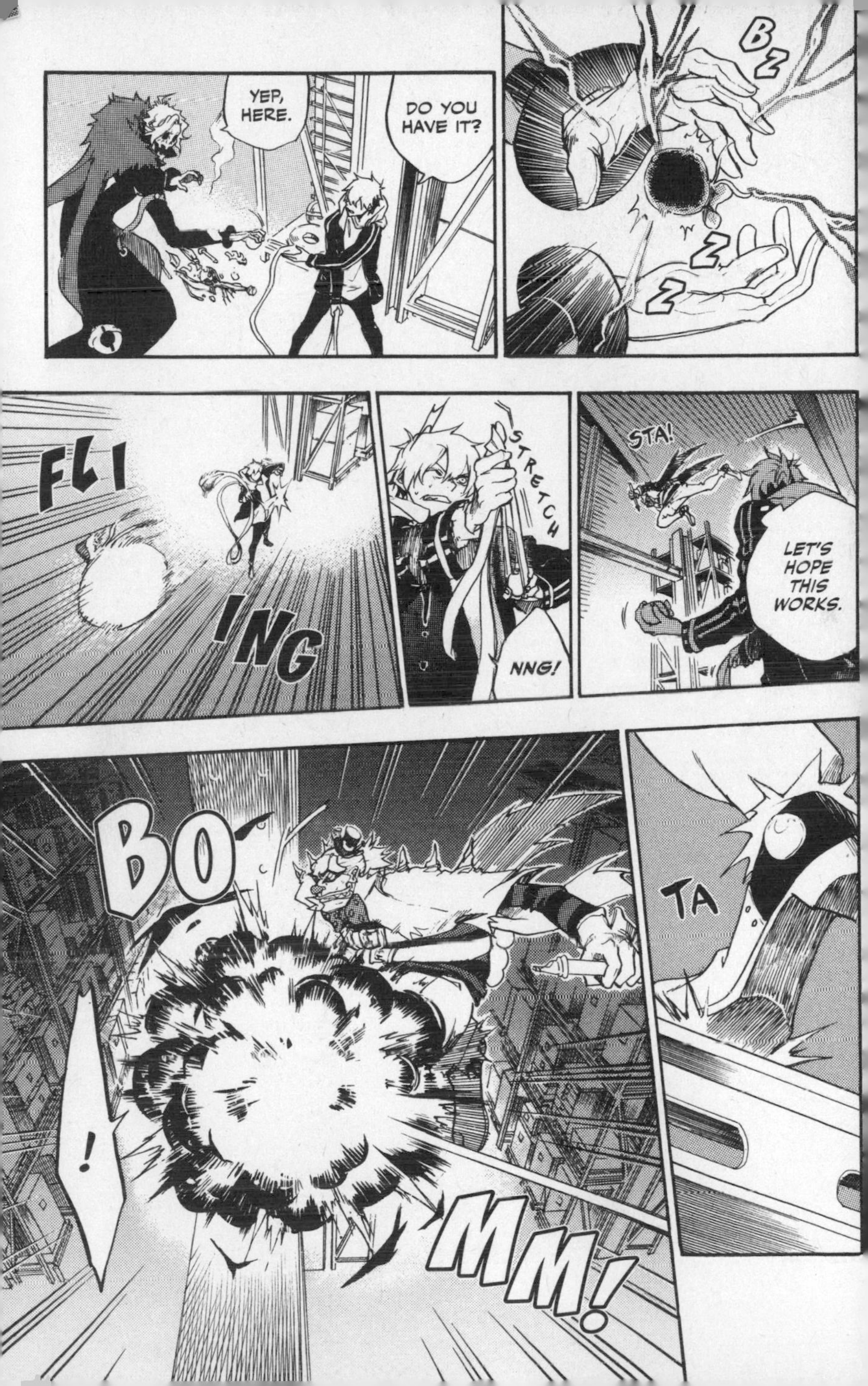
BZ
Z
Z
DO YOU HAVE IT?
YEP, HERE.
STA!
LET'S HOPE THIS WORKS.
STRETCH
NNG!
FLI
ING
TA
BO
!
MM!

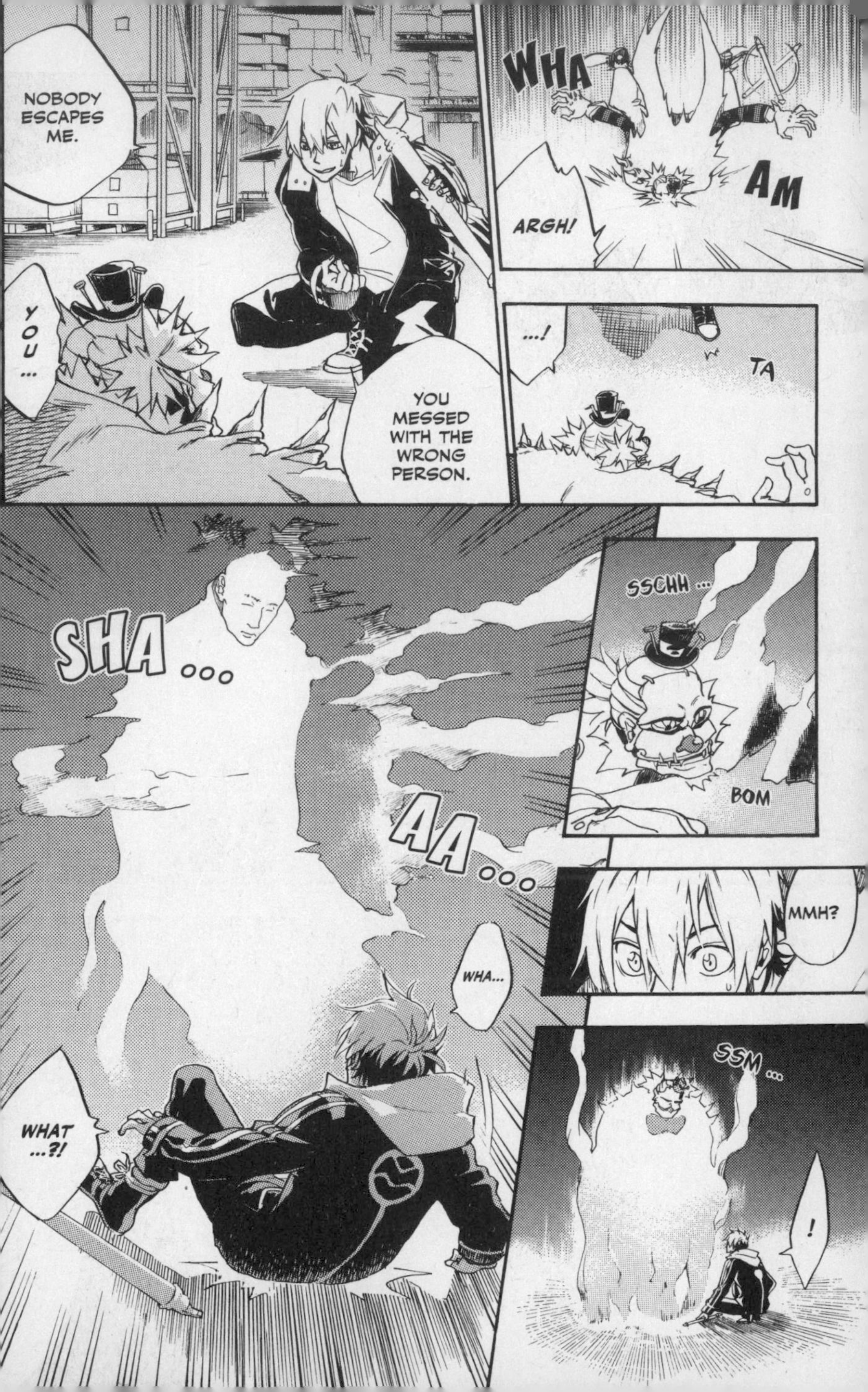
WHA
AM
ARGH!
...!
TA
YOU ...
NOBODY ESCAPES ME.
YOU MESSED WITH THE WRONG PERSON.
SSCHH ...
BOM
MMH?
SSM ...
!
SHA ooo
AA ooo
WHA...
WHAT ...?!

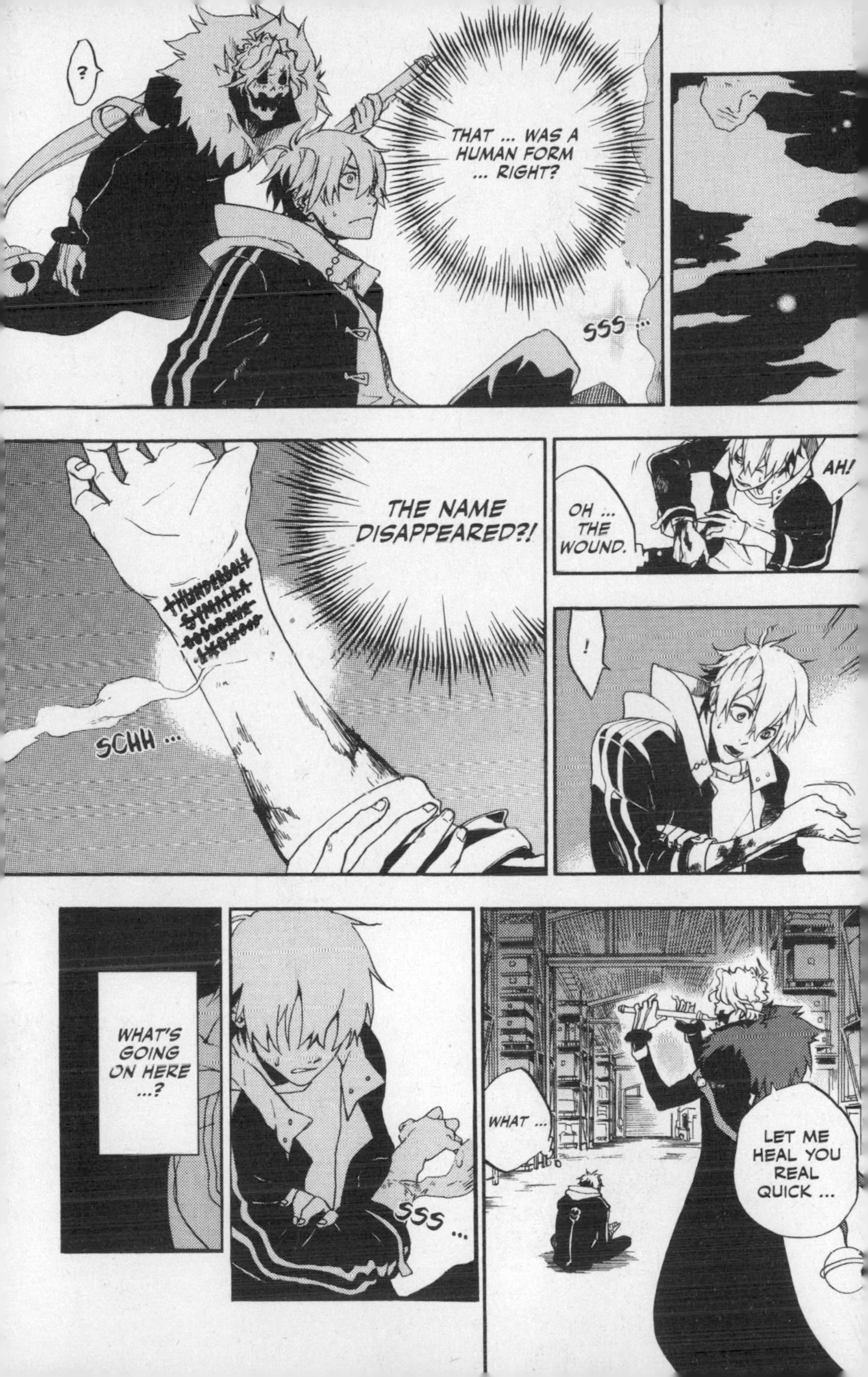
THAT ... WAS A HUMAN FORM ... RIGHT?
?
SSS ...
AH!
OH ... THE WOUND.
!
THE NAME DISAPPEARED?!
SCHH ...
LET ME HEAL YOU REAL QUICK ...
WHAT ...
SSS ...
WHAT'S GOING ON HERE ...?

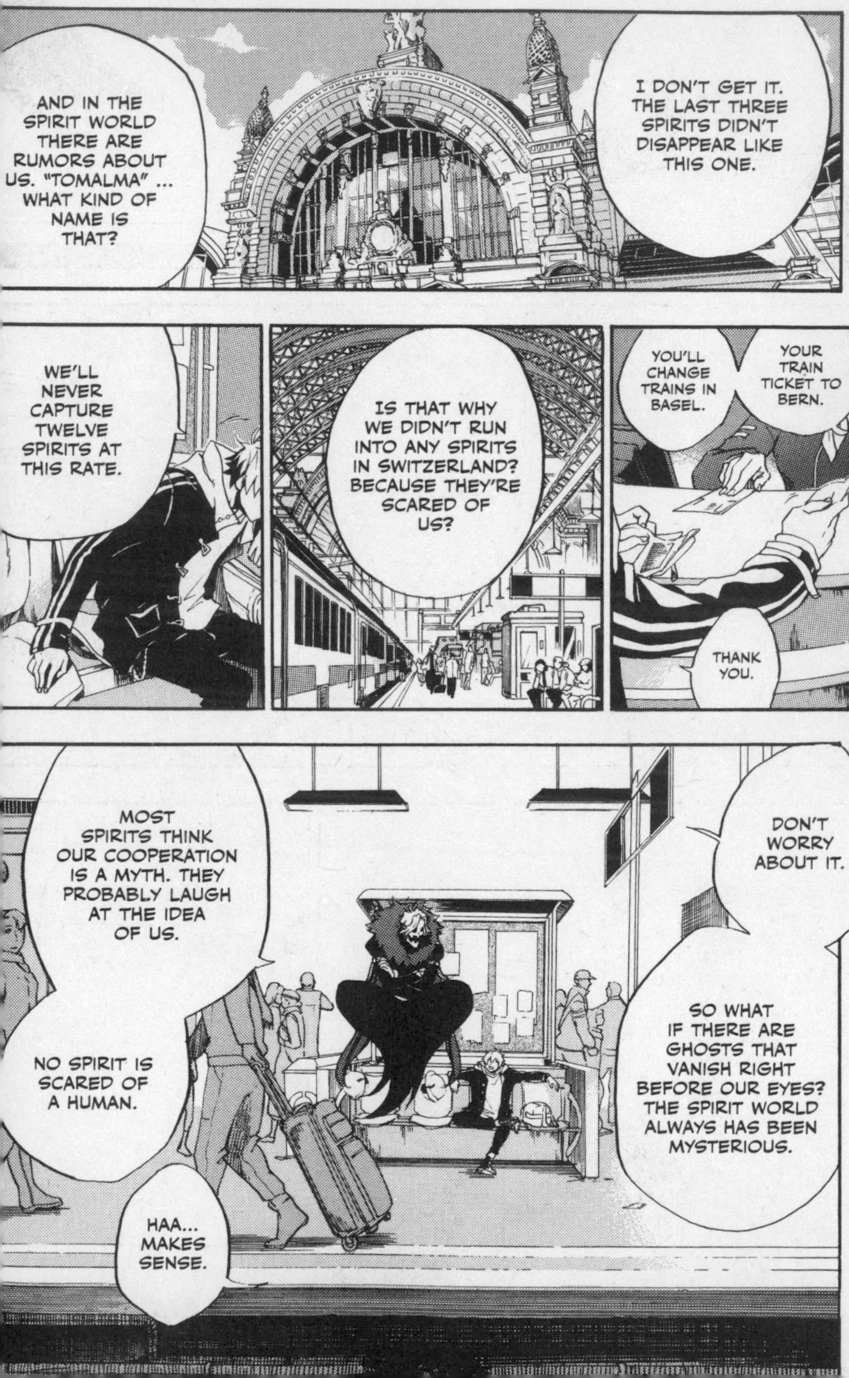
I DON'T GET IT. THE LAST THREE SPIRITS DIDN'T DISAPPEAR LIKE THIS ONE.
AND IN THE SPIRIT WORLD THERE ARE RUMORS ABOUT US. "TOMALMA" ... WHAT KIND OF NAME IS THAT?
YOUR TRAIN TICKET TO BERN.
YOU'LL CHANGE TRAINS IN BASEL.
THANK YOU.
IS THAT WHY WE DIDN'T RUN INTO ANY SPIRITS IN SWITZERLAND? BECAUSE THEY'RE SCARED OF US?
WE'LL NEVER CAPTURE TWELVE SPIRITS AT THIS RATE.
DON'T WORRY ABOUT IT.
SO WHAT IF THERE ARE GHOSTS THAT VANISH RIGHT BEFORE OUR EYES? THE SPIRIT WORLD ALWAYS HAS BEEN MYSTERIOUS.
MOST SPIRITS THINK OUR COOPERATION IS A MYTH. THEY PROBABLY LAUGH AT THE IDEA OF US.
NO SPIRIT IS SCARED OF A HUMAN.
HAA... MAKES SENSE.

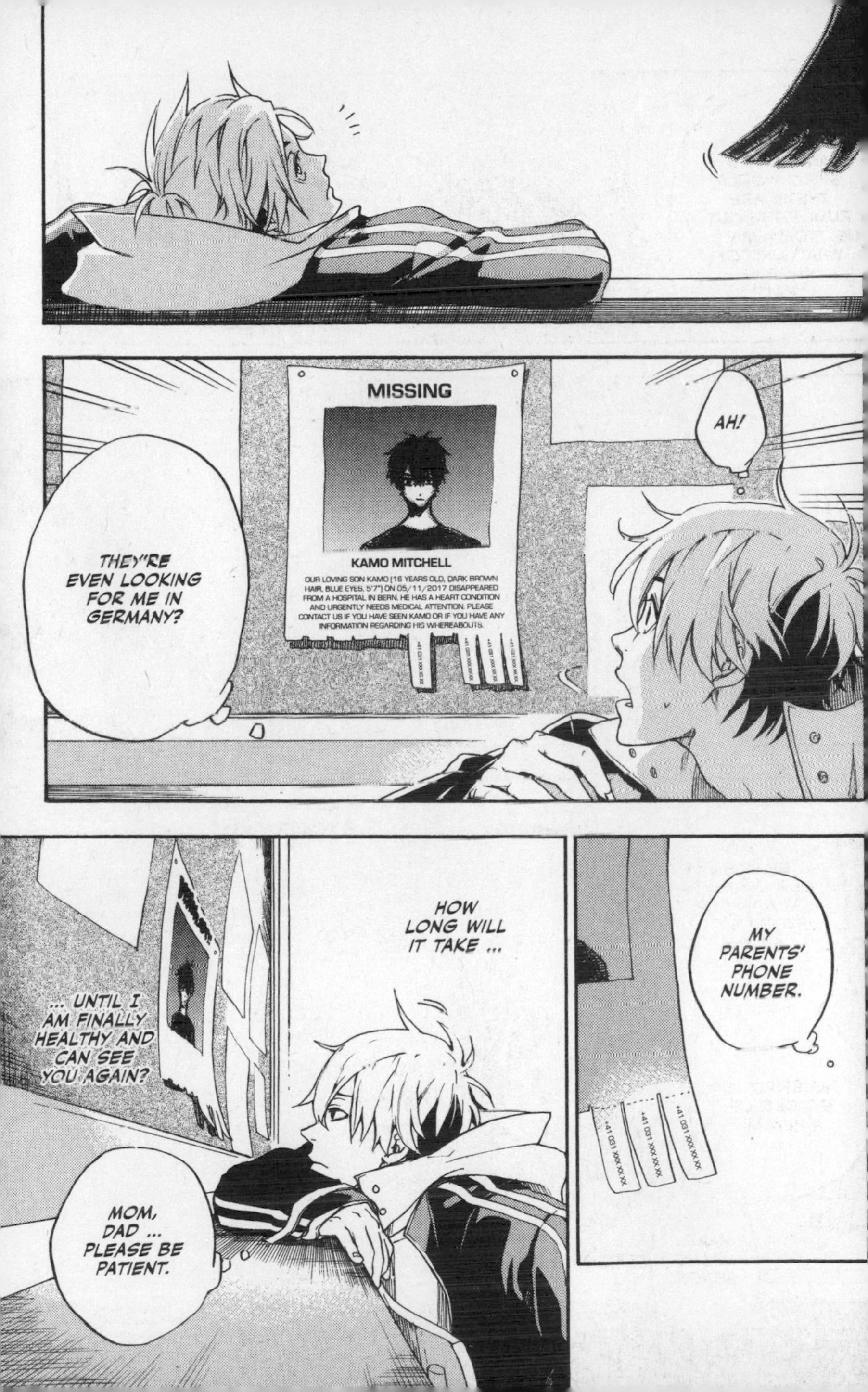
AH!
MISSING
KAMO MITCHELL
OUR LOVING SON KAMO (16 YEARS OLD, DARK BROWN HAIR, BLUE EYES, 5'7") ON 05/11/2017 DISAPPEARED FROM A HOSPITAL IN BERN. HE HAS A HEART CONDITION AND URGENTLY NEEDS MEDICAL ATTENTION. PLEASE CONTACT US IF YOU HAVE SEEN KAMO OR IF YOU HAVE ANY INFORMATION REGARDING HIS WHEREABOUTS.
THEY'RE EVEN LOOKING FOR ME IN GERMANY?
MY PARENTS' PHONE NUMBER.
HOW LONG WILL IT TAKE ...
... UNTIL I AM FINALLY HEALTHY AND CAN SEE YOU AGAIN?
MOM, DAD ... PLEASE BE PATIENT.

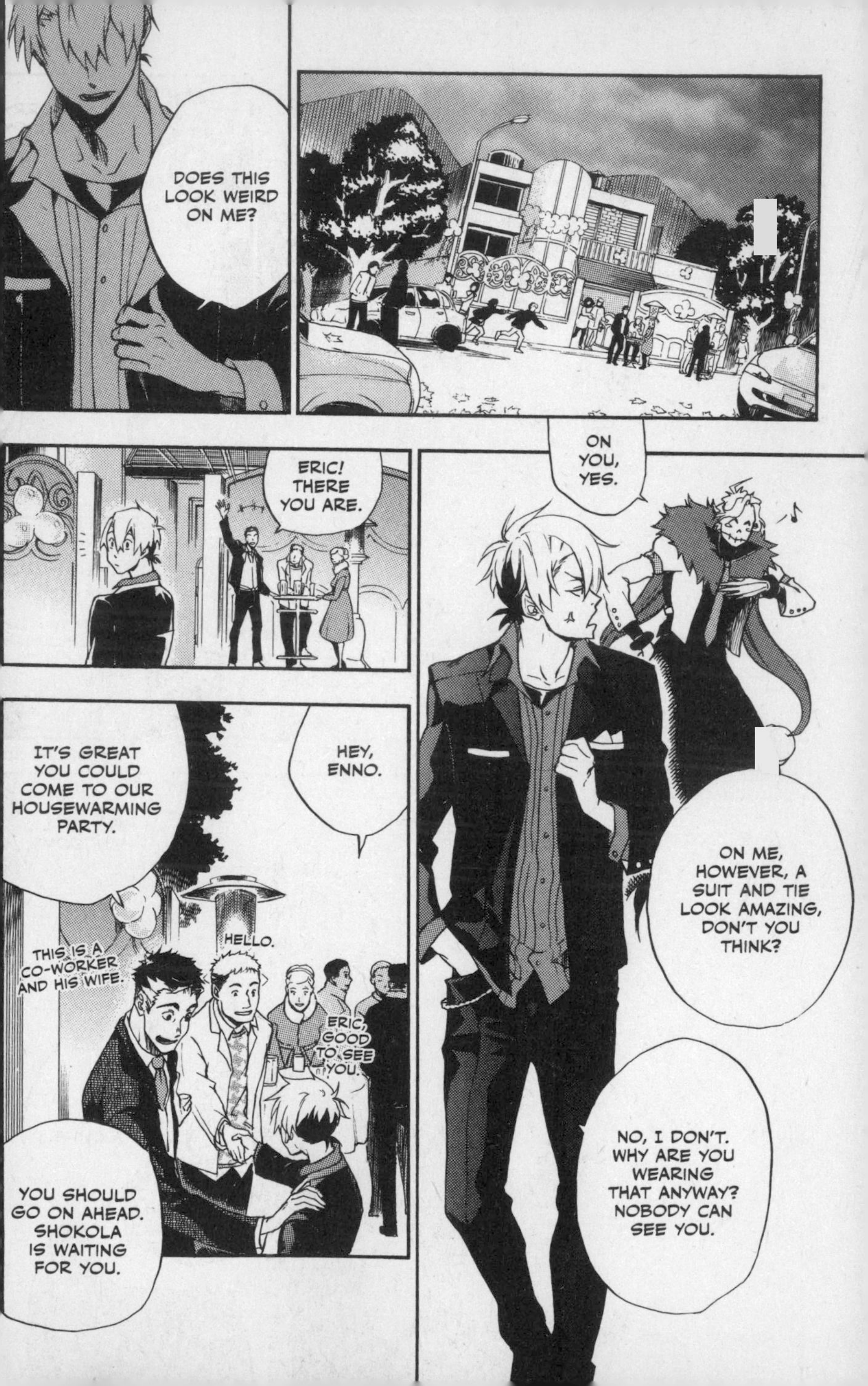
DOES THIS LOOK WEIRD ON ME?
ON YOU, YES.
ON ME, HOWEVER, A SUIT AND TIE LOOK AMAZING, DON'T YOU THINK?
NO, I DON'T. WHY ARE YOU WEARING THAT ANYWAY? NOBODY CAN SEE YOU.
ERIC! THERE YOU ARE.
HEY, ENNO.
IT'S GREAT YOU COULD COME TO OUR HOUSEWARMING PARTY.
HELLO.
THIS IS A CO-WORKER AND HIS WIFE.
ERIC, GOOD TO SEE YOU.
YOU SHOULD GO ON AHEAD. SHOKOLA IS WAITING FOR YOU.

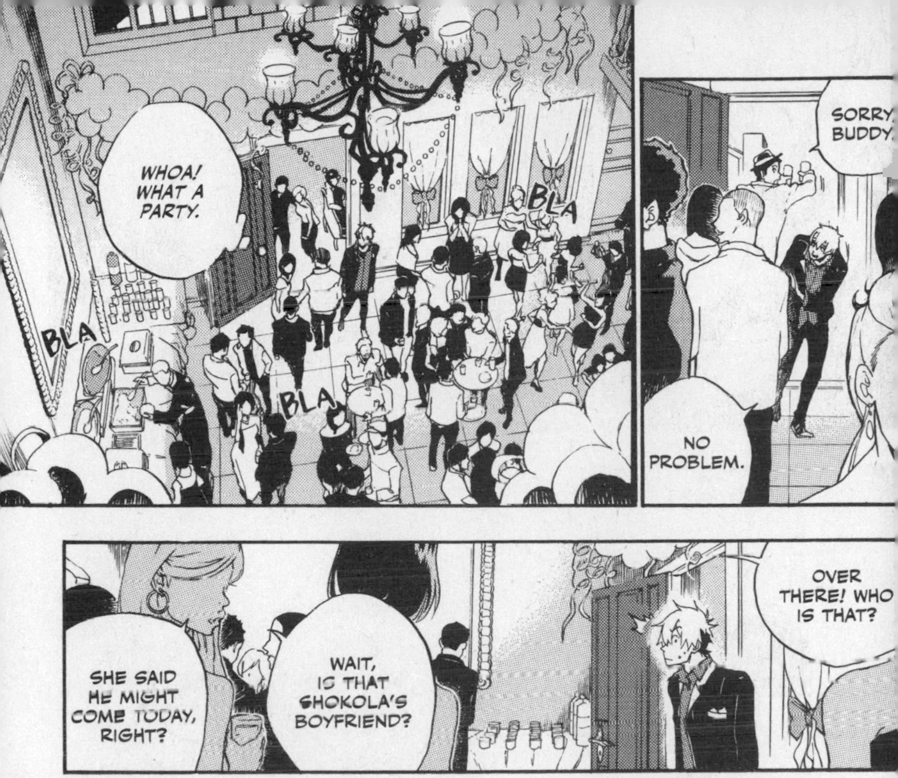
SORRY, BUDDY.
NO PROBLEM.
WHOA! WHAT A PARTY.
BLA
BLA
BLA
OVER THERE! WHO IS THAT?
WAIT, IS THAT SHOKOLA'S BOYFRIEND?
SHE SAID HE MIGHT COME TODAY, RIGHT?

*SPANISH: GO

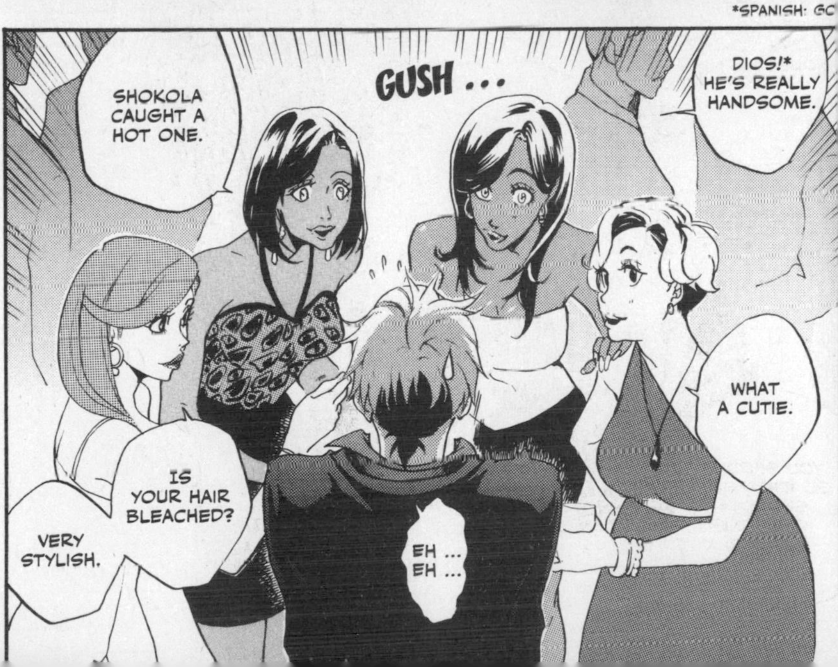
DIOS!* HE'S REALLY HANDSOME.
GUSH ...
SHOKOLA CAUGHT A HOT ONE.
WHAT A CUTIE.
EH ... EH ...
IS YOUR HAIR BLEACHED?
VERY STYLISH.

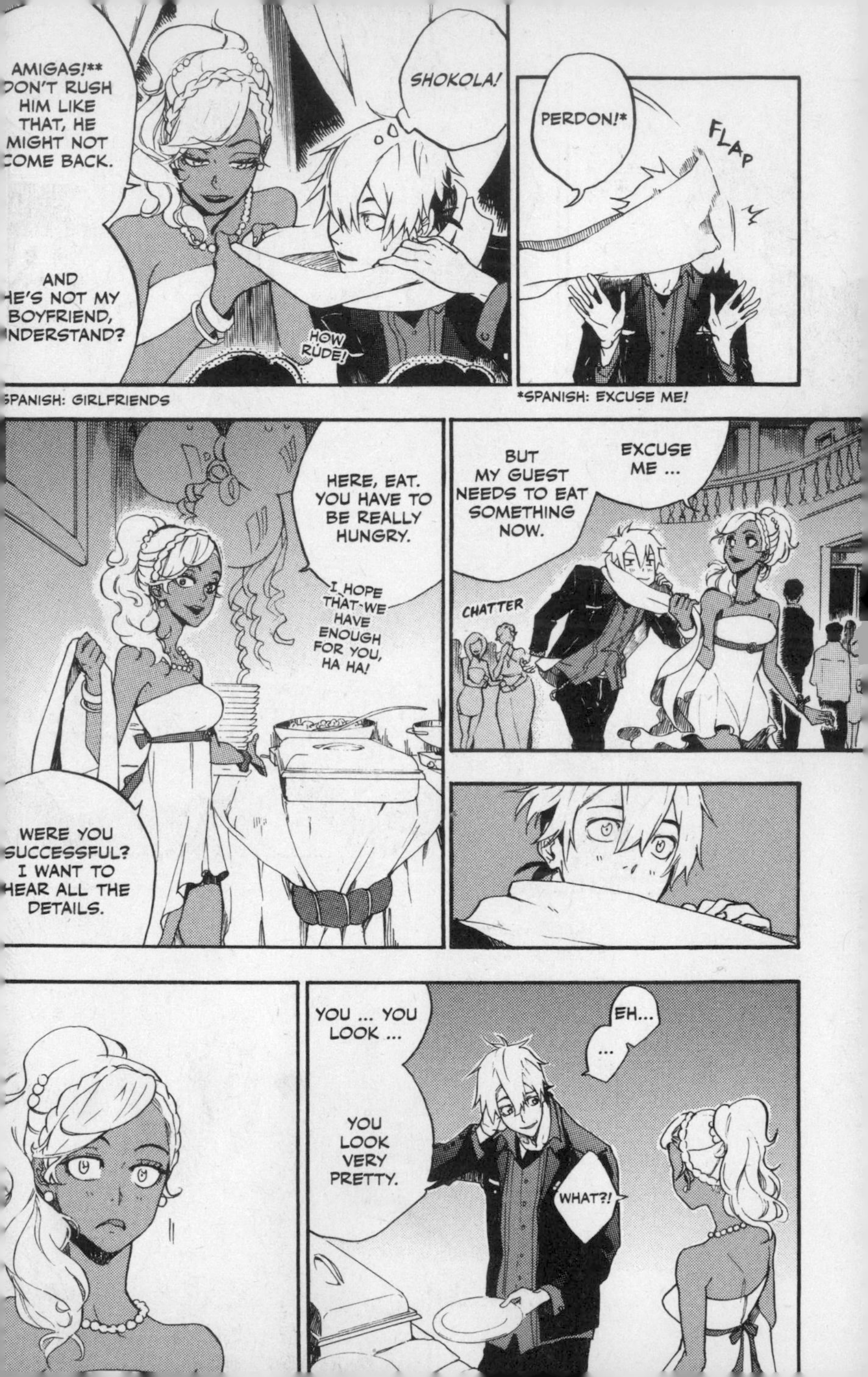
PERDON!*
FLAP
SHOKOLA!
AMIGAS!** DON'T RUSH HIM LIKE THAT, HE MIGHT NOT COME BACK.
HOW RUDE!
AND HE'S NOT MY BOYFRIEND, UNDERSTAND?
*SPANISH: EXCUSE ME!
**SPANISH: GIRLFRIENDS
EXCUSE ME ...
BUT MY GUEST NEEDS TO EAT SOMETHING NOW.
CHATTER
HERE, EAT. YOU HAVE TO BE REALLY HUNGRY.
I HOPE THAT WE HAVE ENOUGH FOR YOU, HA HA!
WERE YOU SUCCESSFUL? I WANT TO HEAR ALL THE DETAILS.
EH... ...
YOU ... YOU LOOK ...
YOU LOOK VERY PRETTY.
WHAT?!

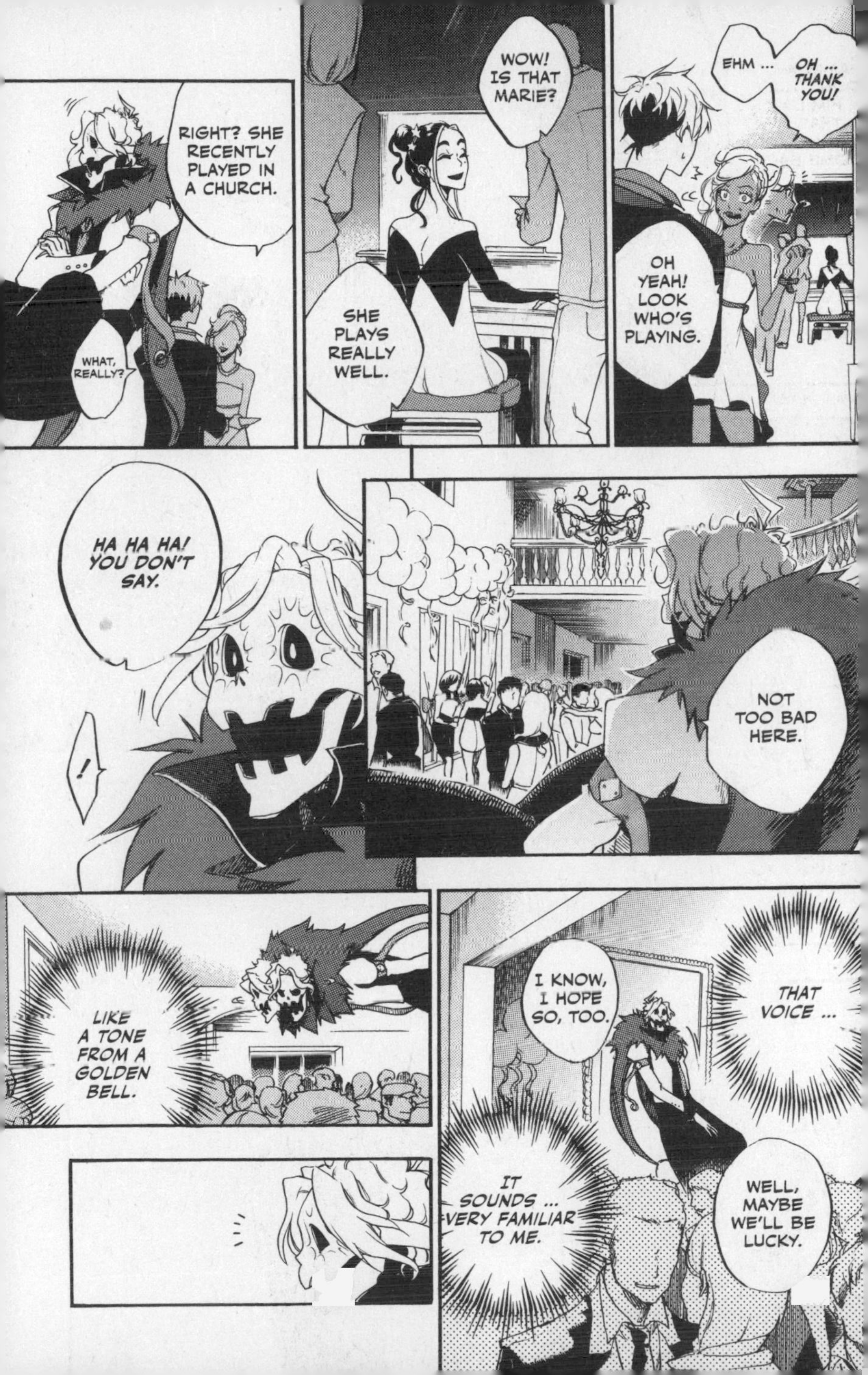
EHM ... OH ... THANK YOU!
OH YEAH! LOOK WHO'S PLAYING.
WOW! IS THAT MARIE?
SHE PLAYS REALLY WELL.
RIGHT? SHE RECENTLY PLAYED IN A CHURCH.
WHAT, REALLY?
NOT TOO BAD HERE.
HA HA HA! YOU DON'T SAY.
!
THAT VOICE ...
I KNOW, I HOPE SO, TOO.
WELL, MAYBE WE'LL BE LUCKY.
IT SOUNDS ... VERY FAMILIAR TO ME.
LIKE A TONE FROM A GOLDEN BELL.

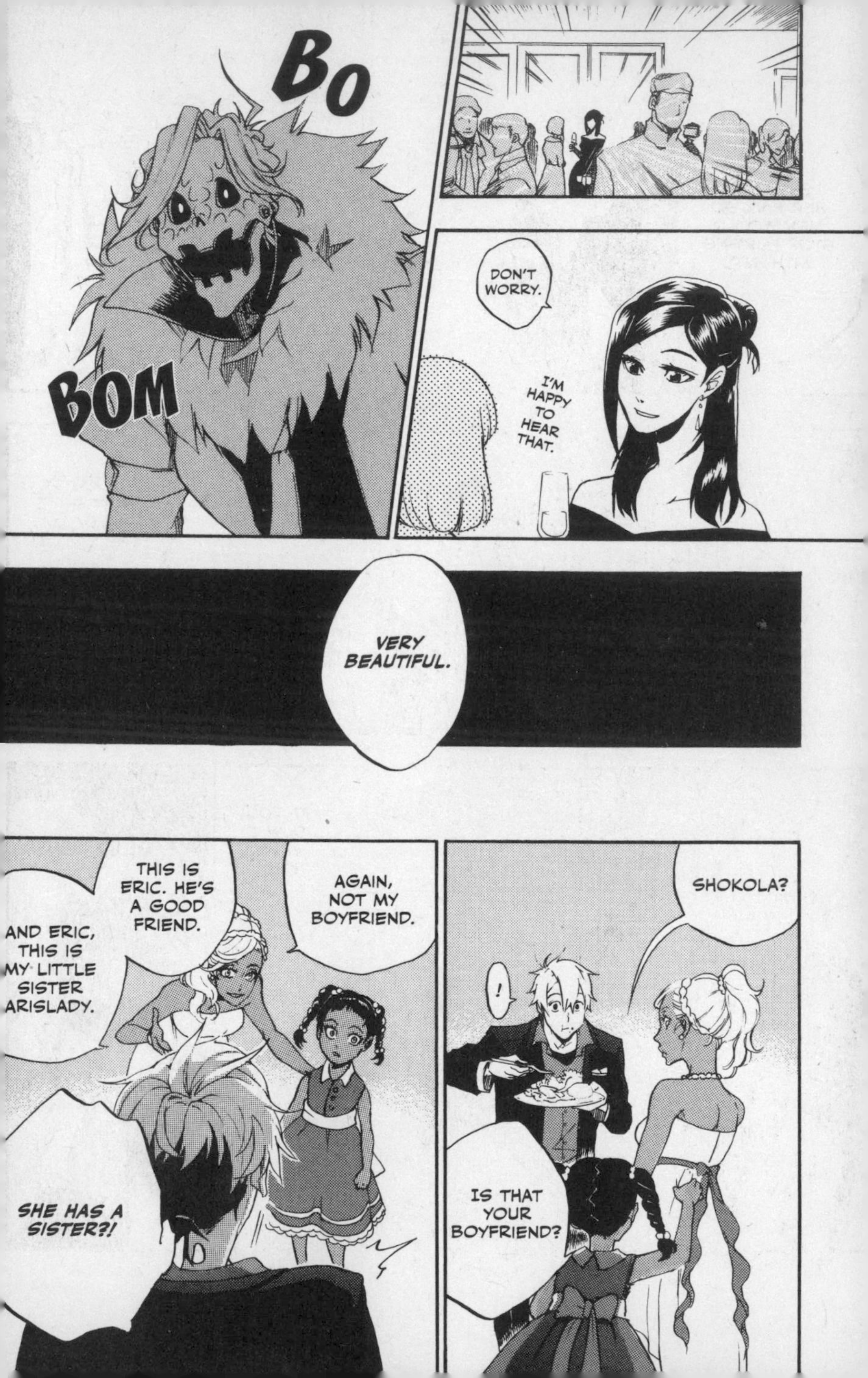
DON'T WORRY.
I'M HAPPY TO HEAR THAT.
BO
BOM
VERY BEAUTIFUL.
SHOKOLA?
!
IS THAT YOUR BOYFRIEND?
AGAIN, NOT MY BOYFRIEND.
THIS IS ERIC. HE'S A GOOD FRIEND.
AND ERIC, THIS IS MY LITTLE SISTER ARISLADY.
SHE HAS A SISTER?!

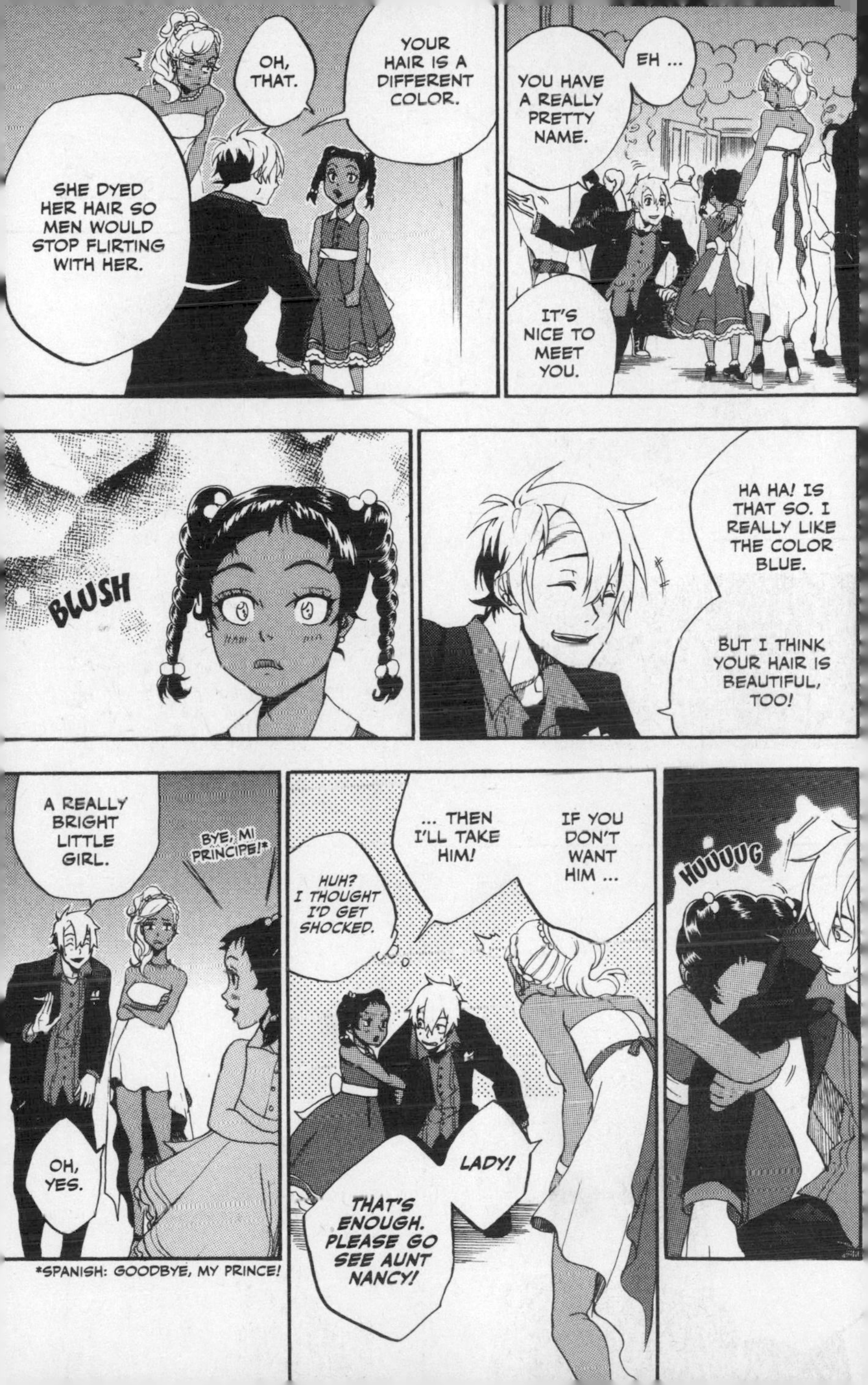
EH ...
YOU HAVE A REALLY PRETTY NAME.
IT'S NICE TO MEET YOU.
YOUR HAIR IS A DIFFERENT COLOR.
OH, THAT.
SHE DYED HER HAIR SO MEN WOULD STOP FLIRTING WITH HER.
HA HA! IS THAT SO. I REALLY LIKE THE COLOR BLUE.
BUT I THINK YOUR HAIR IS BEAUTIFUL, TOO!
BLUSH
HUUUUG
IF YOU DON'T WANT HIM ...
... THEN I'LL TAKE HIM!
HUH? I THOUGHT I'D GET SHOCKED.
LADY!
THAT'S ENOUGH. PLEASE GO SEE AUNT NANCY!
A REALLY BRIGHT LITTLE GIRL.
BYE, MI PRINCIPE!*
OH, YES.
*SPANISH: GOODBYE, MY PRINCE!

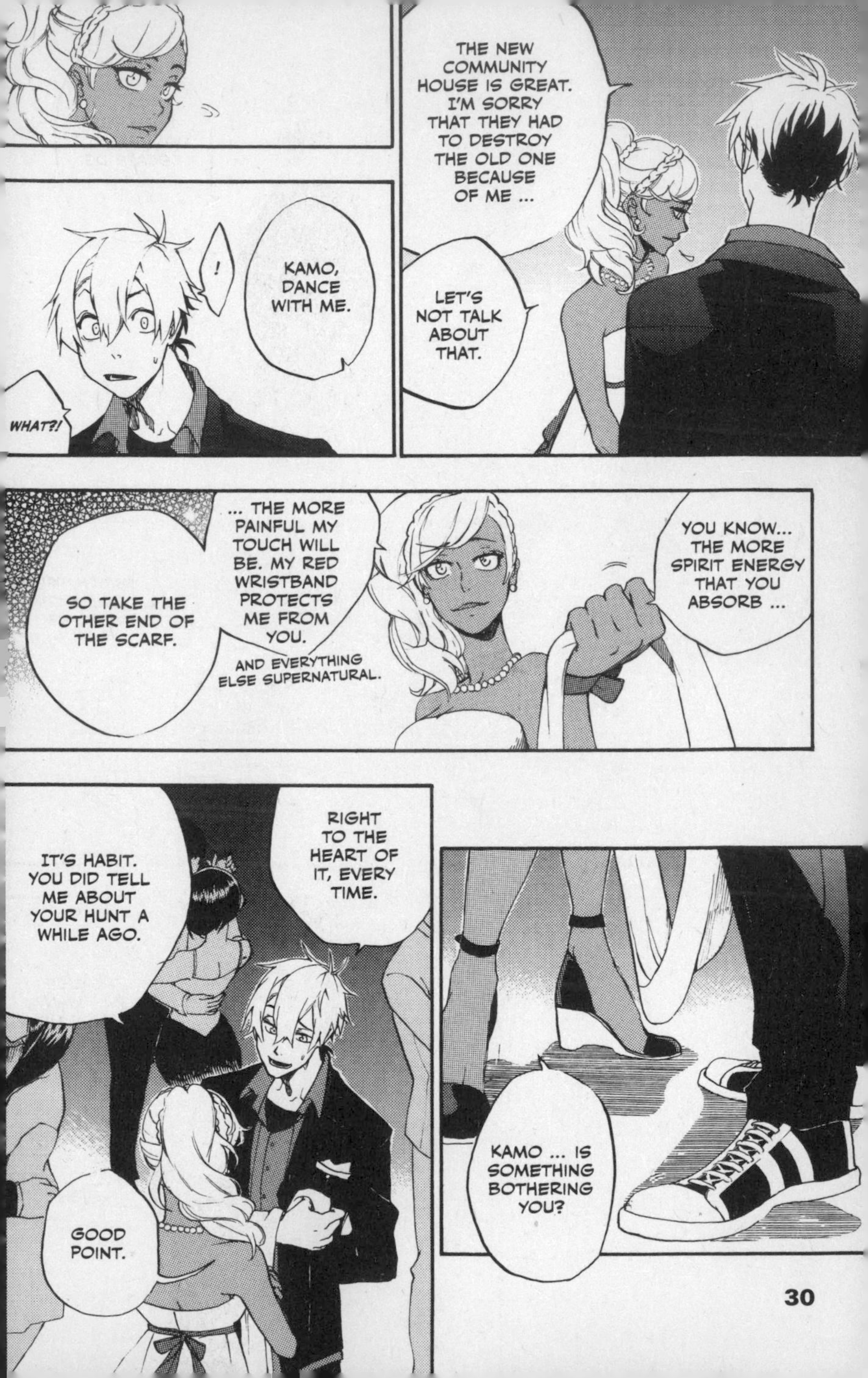
THE NEW COMMUNITY HOUSE IS GREAT. I'M SORRY THAT THEY HAD TO DESTROY THE OLD ONE BECAUSE OF ME ...
LET'S NOT TALK ABOUT THAT.
KAMO, DANCE WITH ME.
!
WHAT?!
YOU KNOW... THE MORE SPIRIT ENERGY THAT YOU ABSORB ...
... THE MORE PAINFUL MY TOUCH WILL BE. MY RED WRISTBAND PROTECTS ME FROM YOU.
AND EVERYTHING ELSE SUPERNATURAL.
SO TAKE THE OTHER END OF THE SCARF.
KAMO ... IS SOMETHING BOTHERING YOU?
RIGHT TO THE HEART OF IT, EVERY TIME.
IT'S HABIT. YOU DID TELL ME ABOUT YOUR HUNT A WHILE AGO.
GOOD POINT.

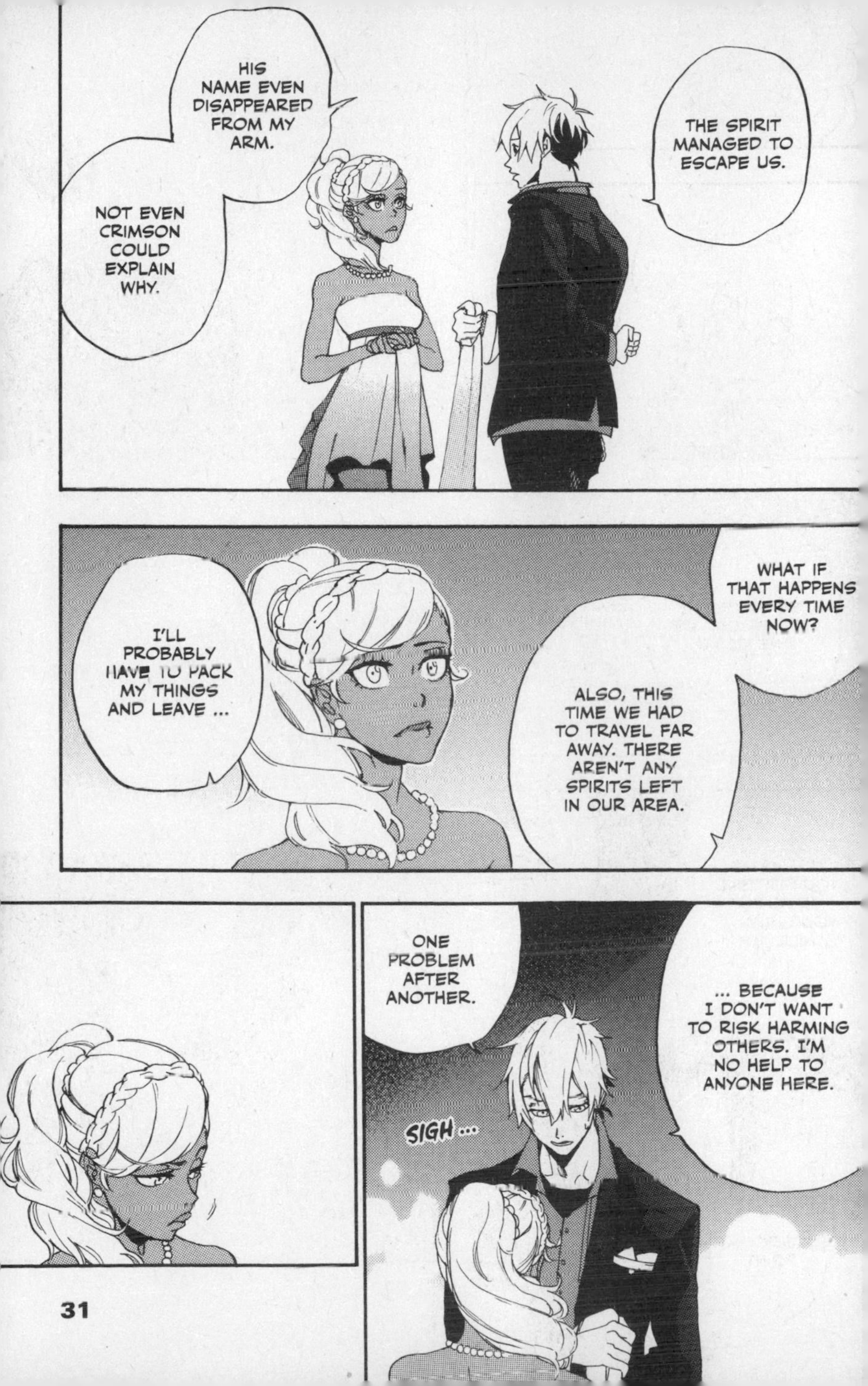
THE SPIRIT MANAGED TO ESCAPE US.
HIS NAME EVEN DISAPPEARED FROM MY ARM.
NOT EVEN CRIMSON COULD EXPLAIN WHY.
WHAT IF THAT HAPPENS EVERY TIME NOW?
ALSO, THIS TIME WE HAD TO TRAVEL FAR AWAY. THERE AREN'T ANY SPIRITS LEFT IN OUR AREA.
I'LL PROBABLY HAVE TO PACK MY THINGS AND LEAVE ...
... BECAUSE I DON'T WANT TO RISK HARMING OTHERS. I'M NO HELP TO ANYONE HERE.
ONE PROBLEM AFTER ANOTHER.
SIGH ...

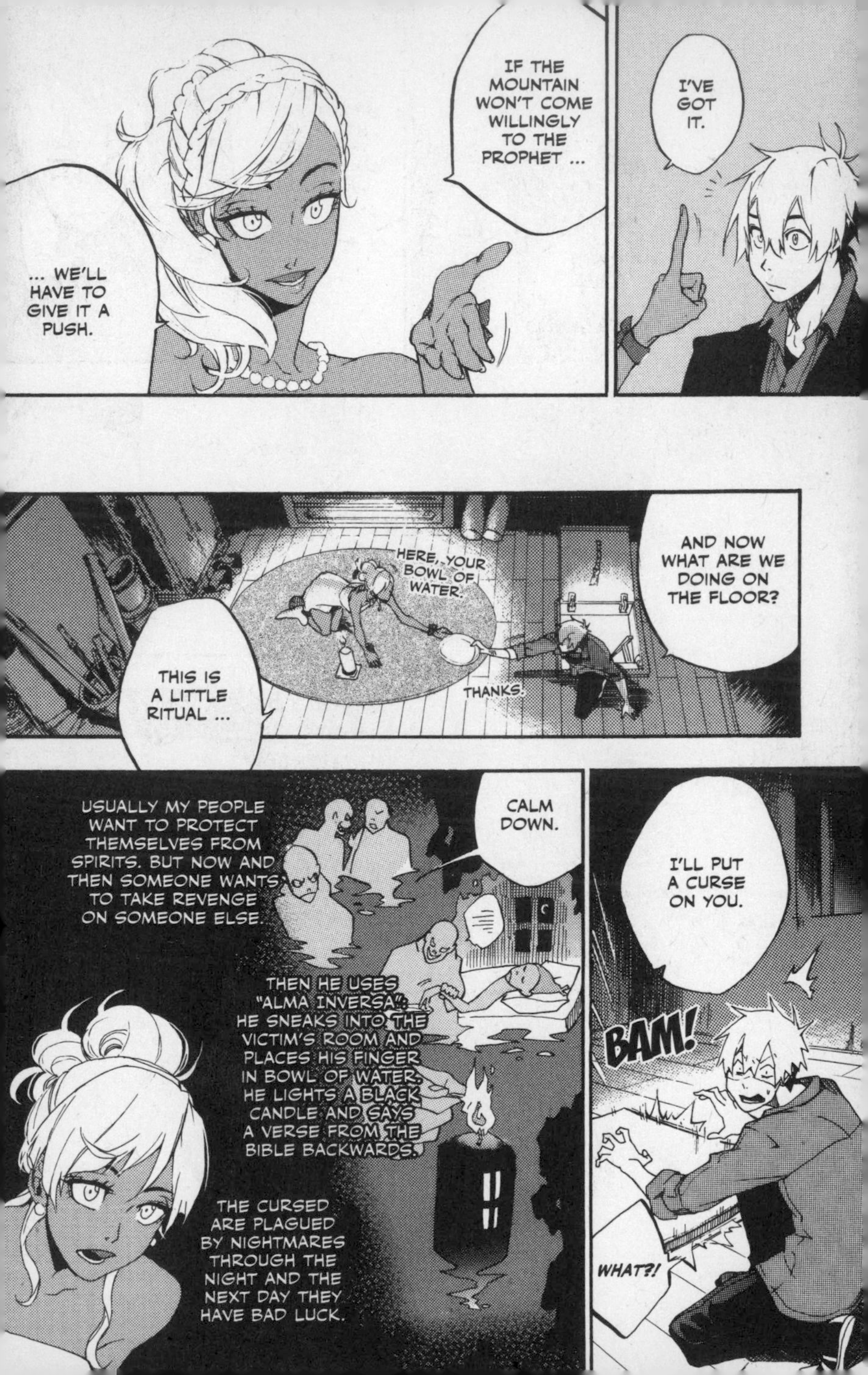
IF THE MOUNTAIN WON'T COME WILLINGLY TO THE PROPHET ...
... WE'LL HAVE TO GIVE IT A PUSH.
I'VE GOT IT.
HERE, YOUR BOWL OF WATER.
THANKS.
AND NOW WHAT ARE WE DOING ON THE FLOOR?
THIS IS A LITTLE RITUAL ...
USUALLY MY PEOPLE WANT TO PROTECT THEMSELVES FROM SPIRITS. BUT NOW AND THEN SOMEONE WANTS TO TAKE REVENGE ON SOMEONE ELSE.
THEN HE USES "ALMA INVERSA": HE SNEAKS INTO THE VICTIM'S ROOM AND PLACES HIS FINGER IN BOWL OF WATER. HE LIGHTS A BLACK CANDLE AND SAYS A VERSE FROM THE BIBLE BACKWARDS.
THE CURSED ARE PLAGUED BY NIGHTMARES THROUGH THE NIGHT AND THE NEXT DAY THEY HAVE BAD LUCK.
CALM DOWN.
I'LL PUT A CURSE ON YOU.
BAM!
WHAT?!

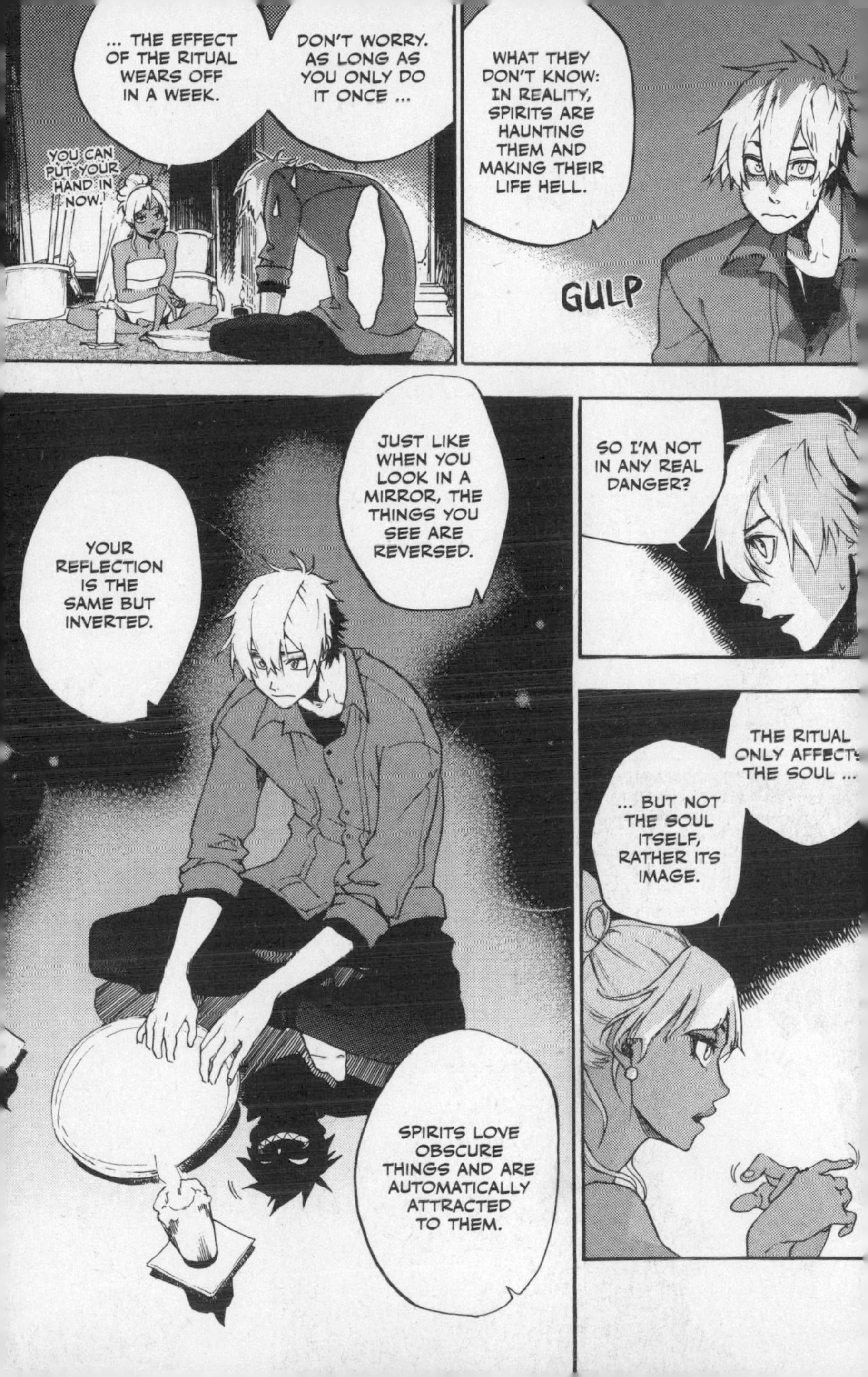
WHAT THEY DON'T KNOW: IN REALITY, SPIRITS ARE HAUNTING THEM AND MAKING THEIR LIFE HELL.
GULP
DON'T WORRY. AS LONG AS YOU ONLY DO IT ONCE ...
... THE EFFECT OF THE RITUAL WEARS OFF IN A WEEK.
YOU CAN PUT YOUR HAND IN NOW.
SO I'M NOT IN ANY REAL DANGER?
THE RITUAL ONLY AFFECTS THE SOUL ...
... BUT NOT THE SOUL ITSELF, RATHER ITS IMAGE.
JUST LIKE WHEN YOU LOOK IN A MIRROR, THE THINGS YOU SEE ARE REVERSED.
YOUR REFLECTION IS THE SAME BUT INVERTED.
SPIRITS LOVE OBSCURE THINGS AND ARE AUTOMATICALLY ATTRACTED TO THEM.

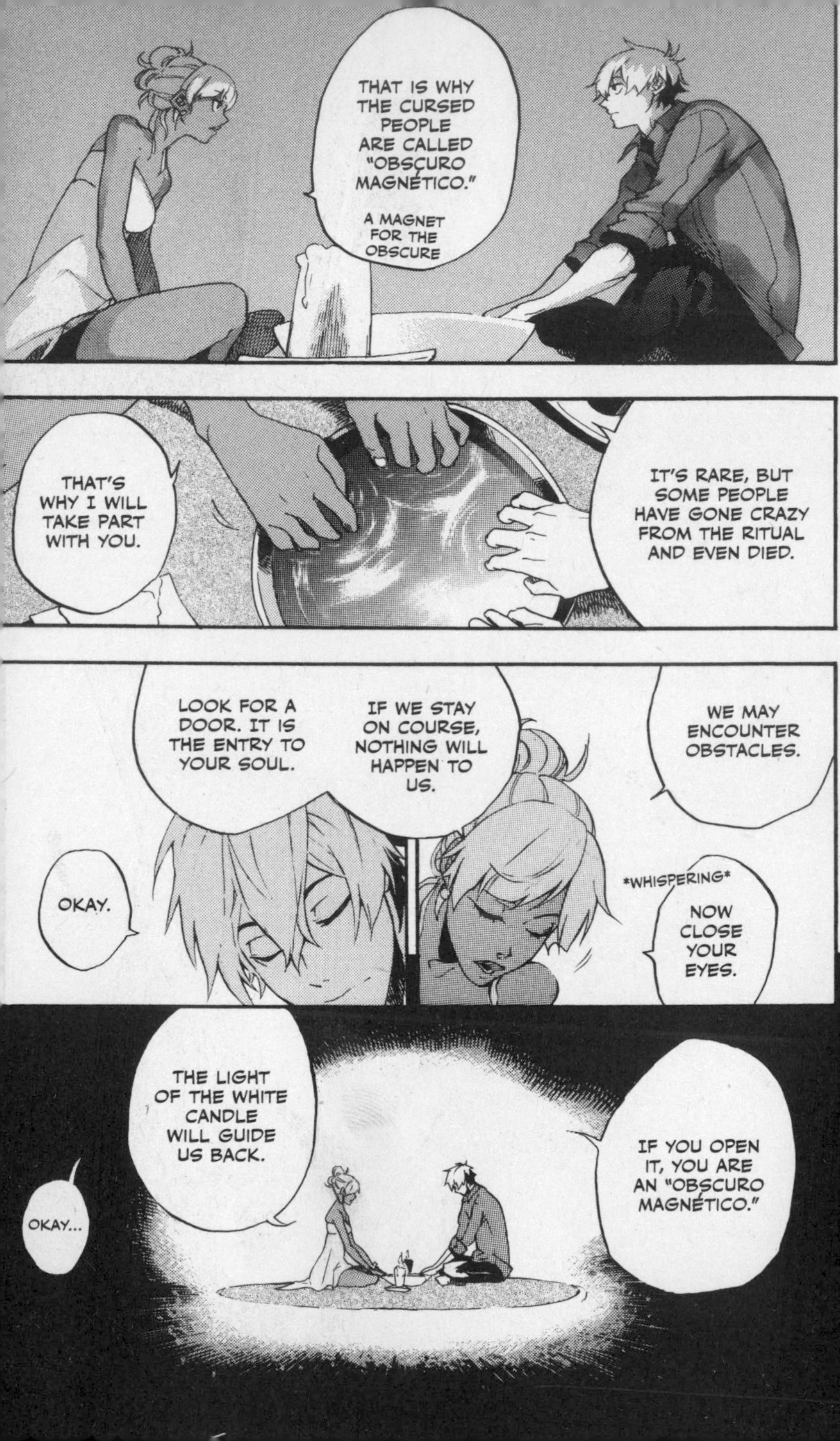
THAT IS WHY THE CURSED PEOPLE ARE CALLED "OBSCURO MAGNÉTICO."
A MAGNET FOR THE OBSCURE
IT'S RARE, BUT SOME PEOPLE HAVE GONE CRAZY FROM THE RITUAL AND EVEN DIED.
THAT'S WHY I WILL TAKE PART WITH YOU.
WE MAY ENCOUNTER OBSTACLES.
IF WE STAY ON COURSE, NOTHING WILL HAPPEN TO US.
LOOK FOR A DOOR. IT IS THE ENTRY TO YOUR SOUL.
WHISPERING
NOW CLOSE YOUR EYES.
OKAY.
IF YOU OPEN IT, YOU ARE AN "OBSCURO MAGNÉTICO."
THE LIGHT OF THE WHITE CANDLE WILL GUIDE US BACK.
OKAY...

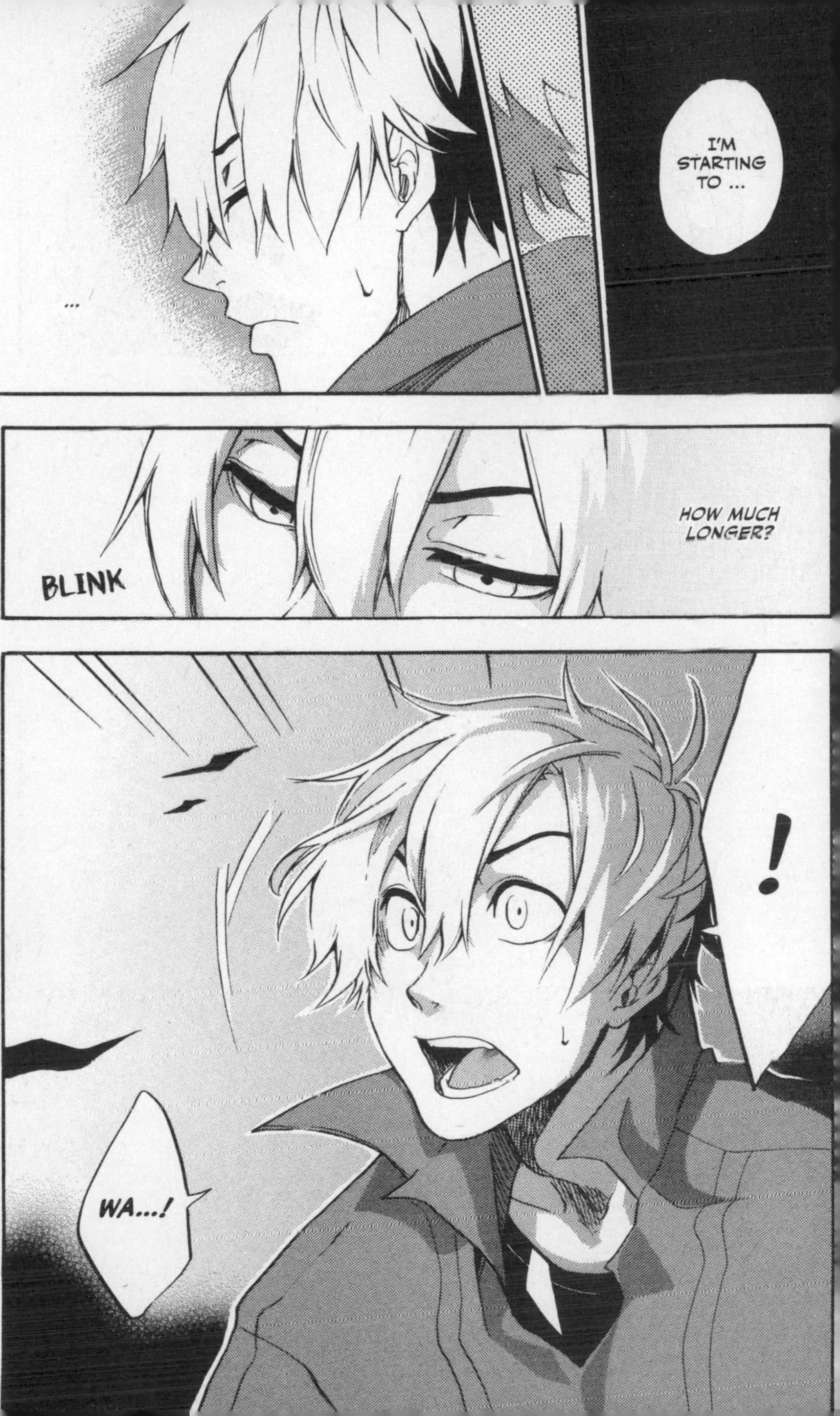
I'M STARTING TO ...
...
HOW MUCH LONGER?
BLINK
!
WA...!

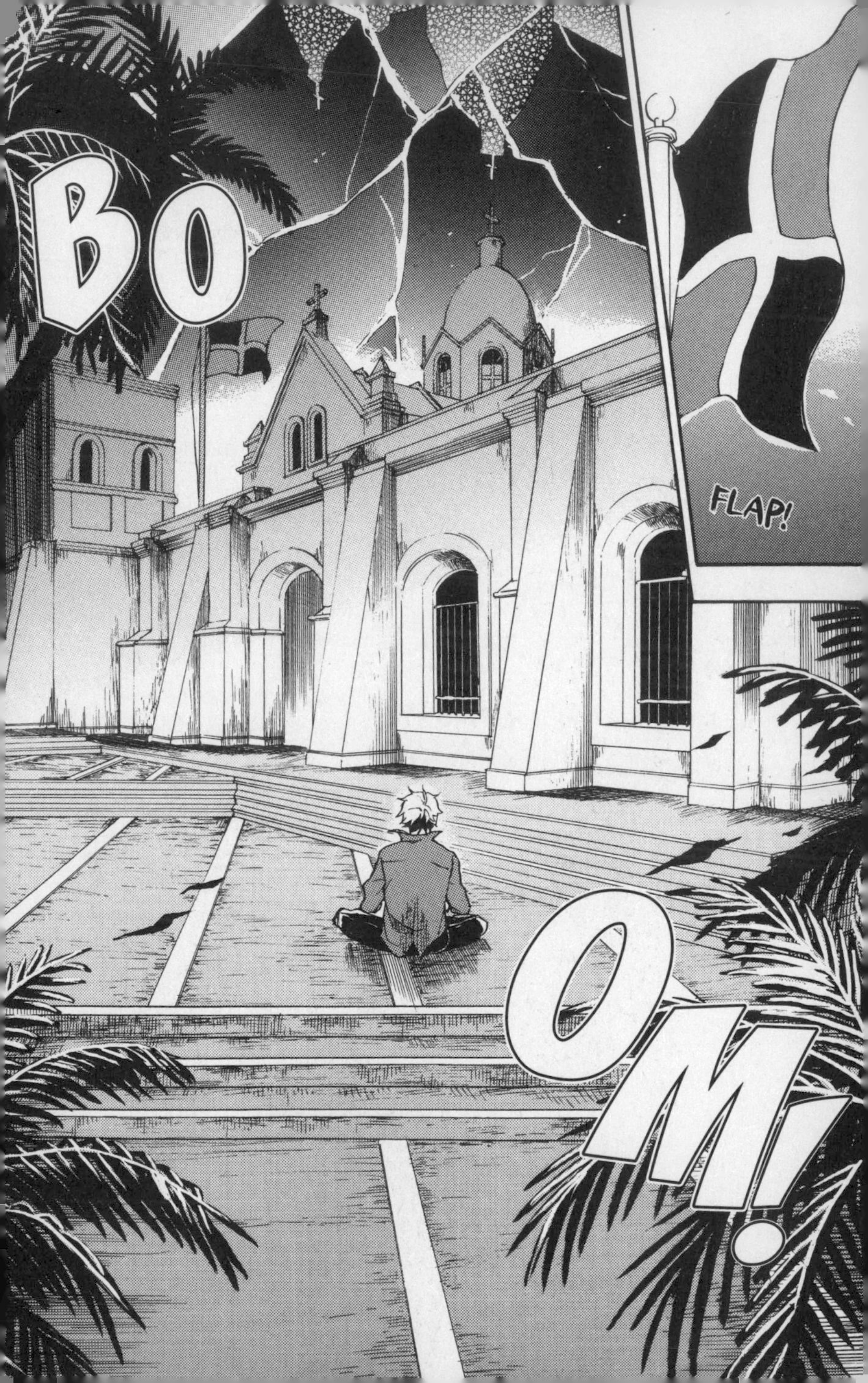
FLAP!
BO
OM!

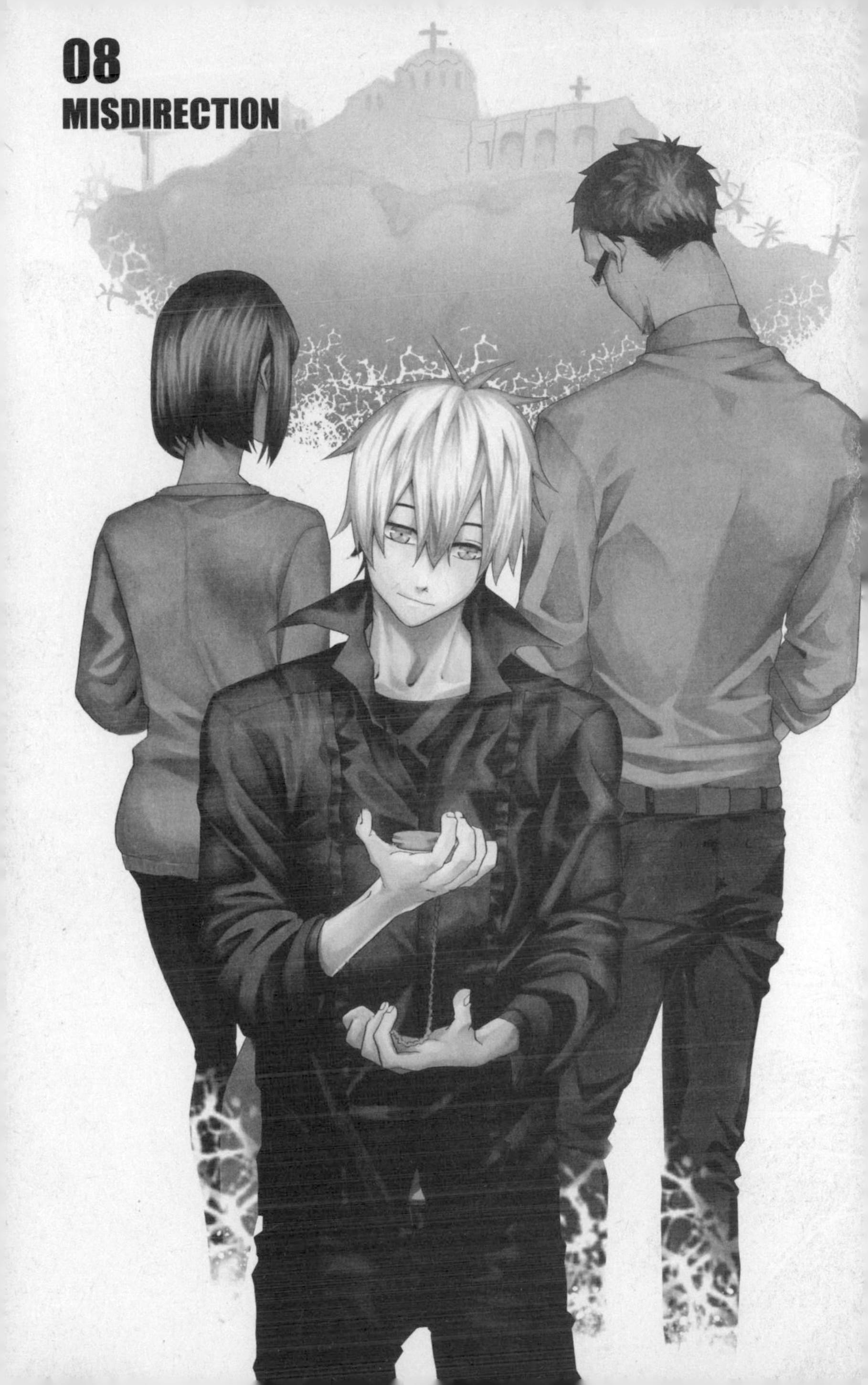
08
MISDIRECTION

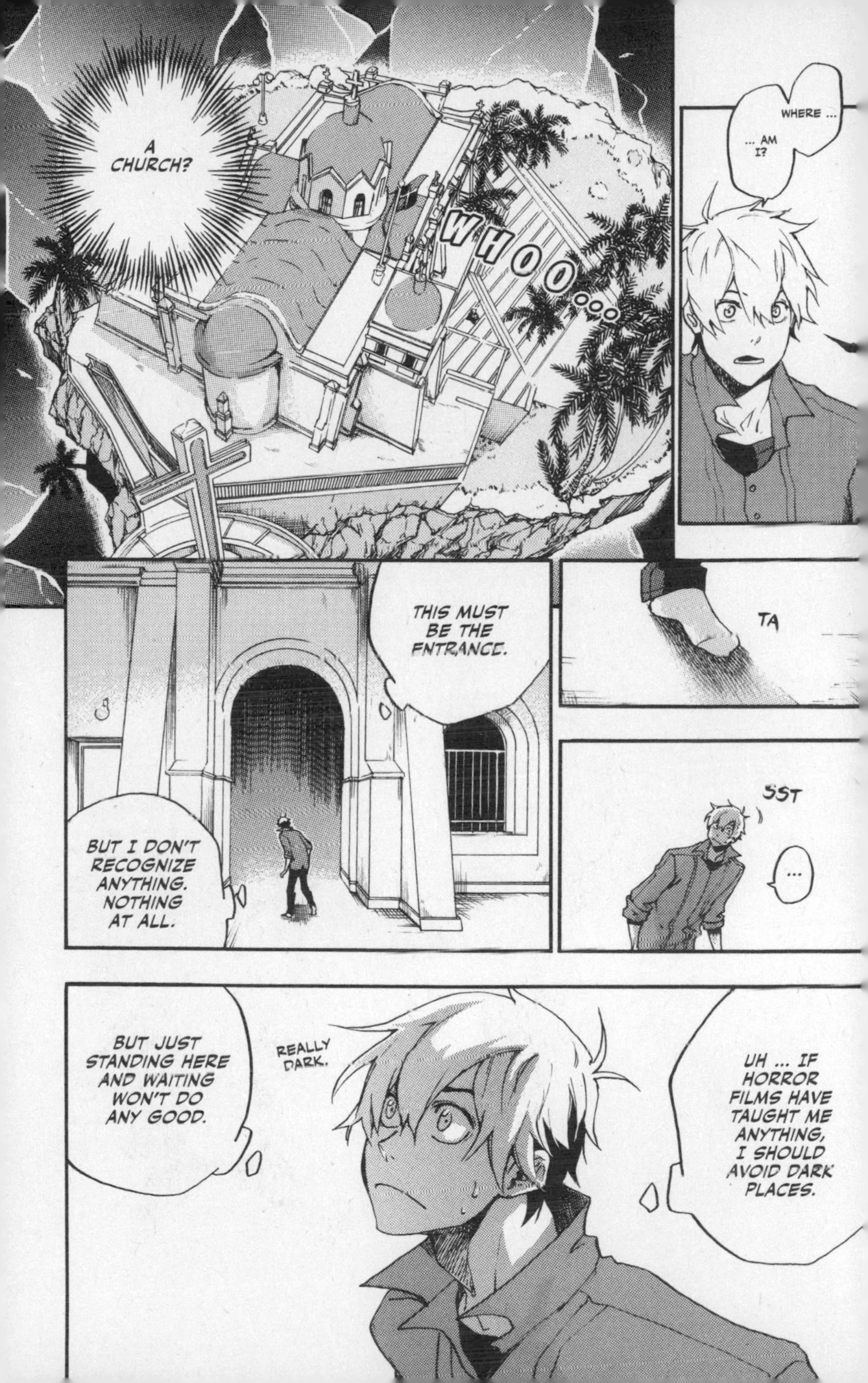
WHERE ... ... AM I?
A CHURCH?
WHOO...
TA
SST
...
THIS MUST BE THE ENTRANCE.
BUT I DON'T RECOGNIZE ANYTHING. NOTHING AT ALL.
UH ... IF HORROR FILMS HAVE TAUGHT ME ANYTHING, I SHOULD AVOID DARK PLACES.
REALLY DARK.
BUT JUST STANDING HERE AND WAITING WON'T DO ANY GOOD.

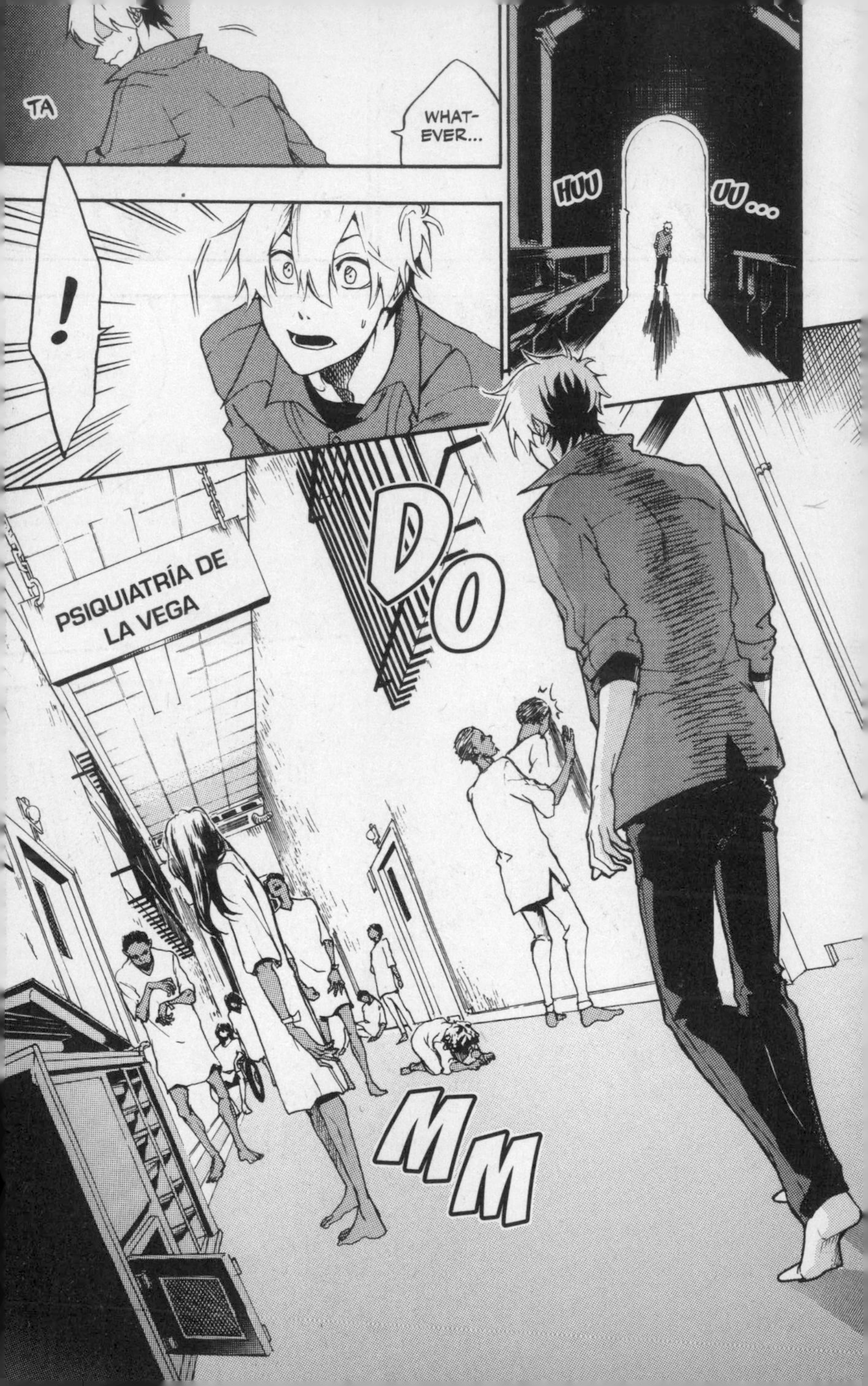
HUU
UU...
TA
WHAT-EVER...
!
PSIQUIATRÍA DE LA VEGA
DO
MM

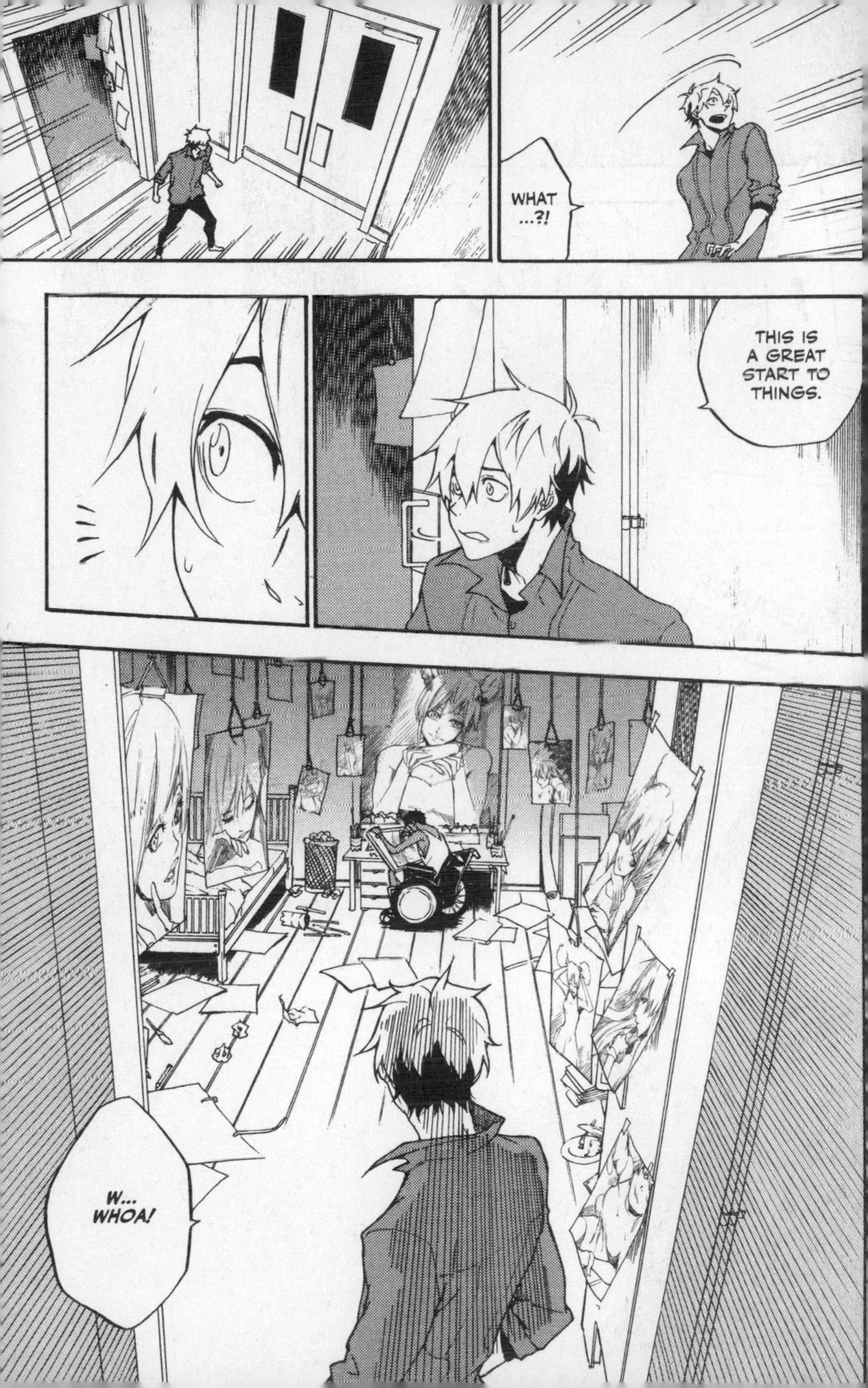
WHAT ...?!
THIS IS A GREAT START TO THINGS.
W... WHOA!

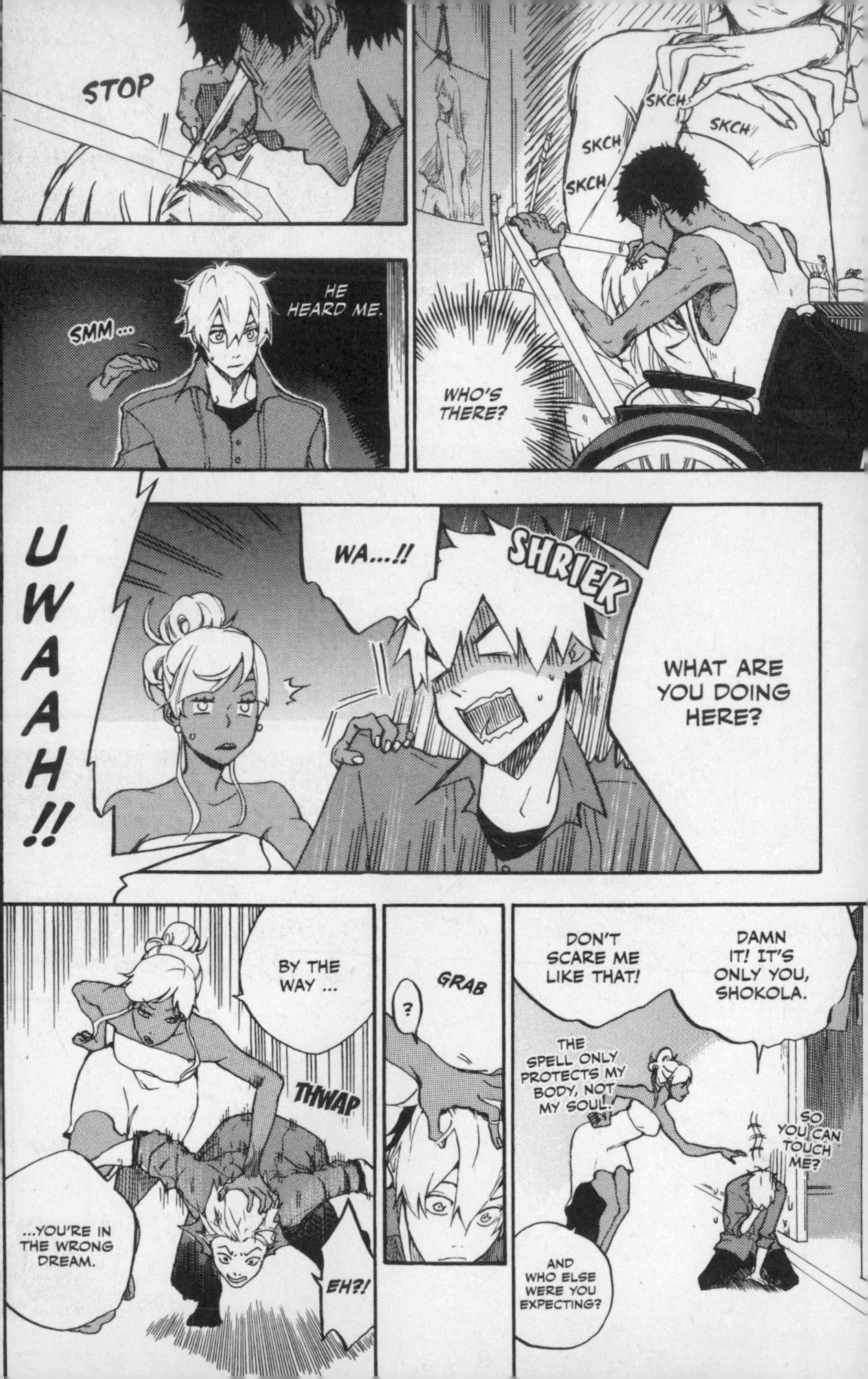
SKCH
SKCH
SKCH
SKCH
STOP
WHO'S THERE?
HE HEARD ME.
SMM ...
SHRIEK
WHAT ARE YOU DOING HERE?
WA...!!
UWAAAH!!
DAMN IT! IT'S ONLY YOU, SHOKOLA.
DON'T SCARE ME LIKE THAT!
SO YOU CAN TOUCH ME?
THE SPELL ONLY PROTECTS MY BODY, NOT MY SOUL.
AND WHO ELSE WERE YOU EXPECTING?
GRAB
?
BY THE WAY ...
THWAP
EH?!
...YOU'RE IN THE WRONG DREAM.

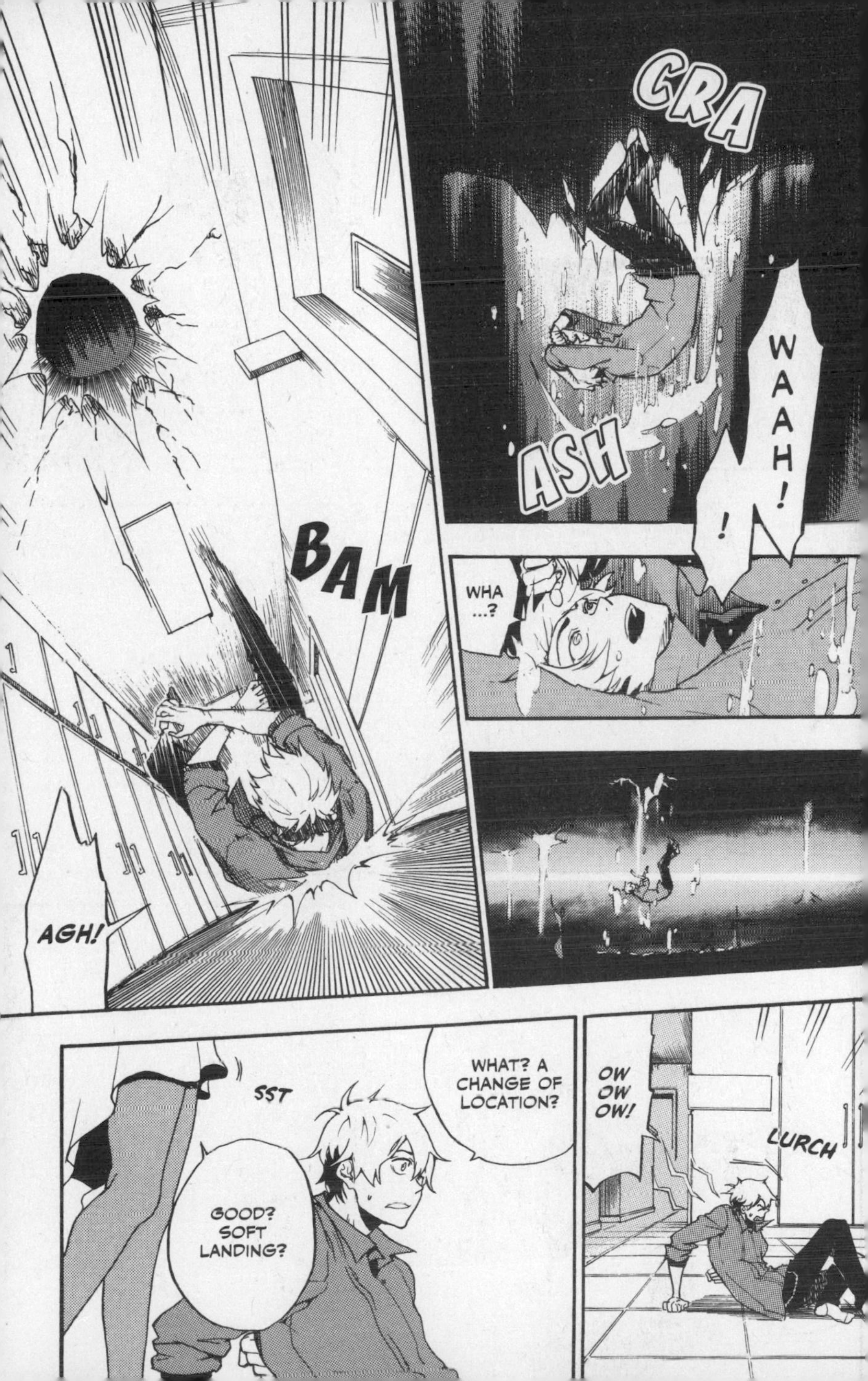
CRA
ASH
WAAH!!
WHA ...?
BAM
AGH!
OW OW OW!
LURCH
WHAT? A CHANGE OF LOCATION?
SST
GOOD? SOFT LANDING?

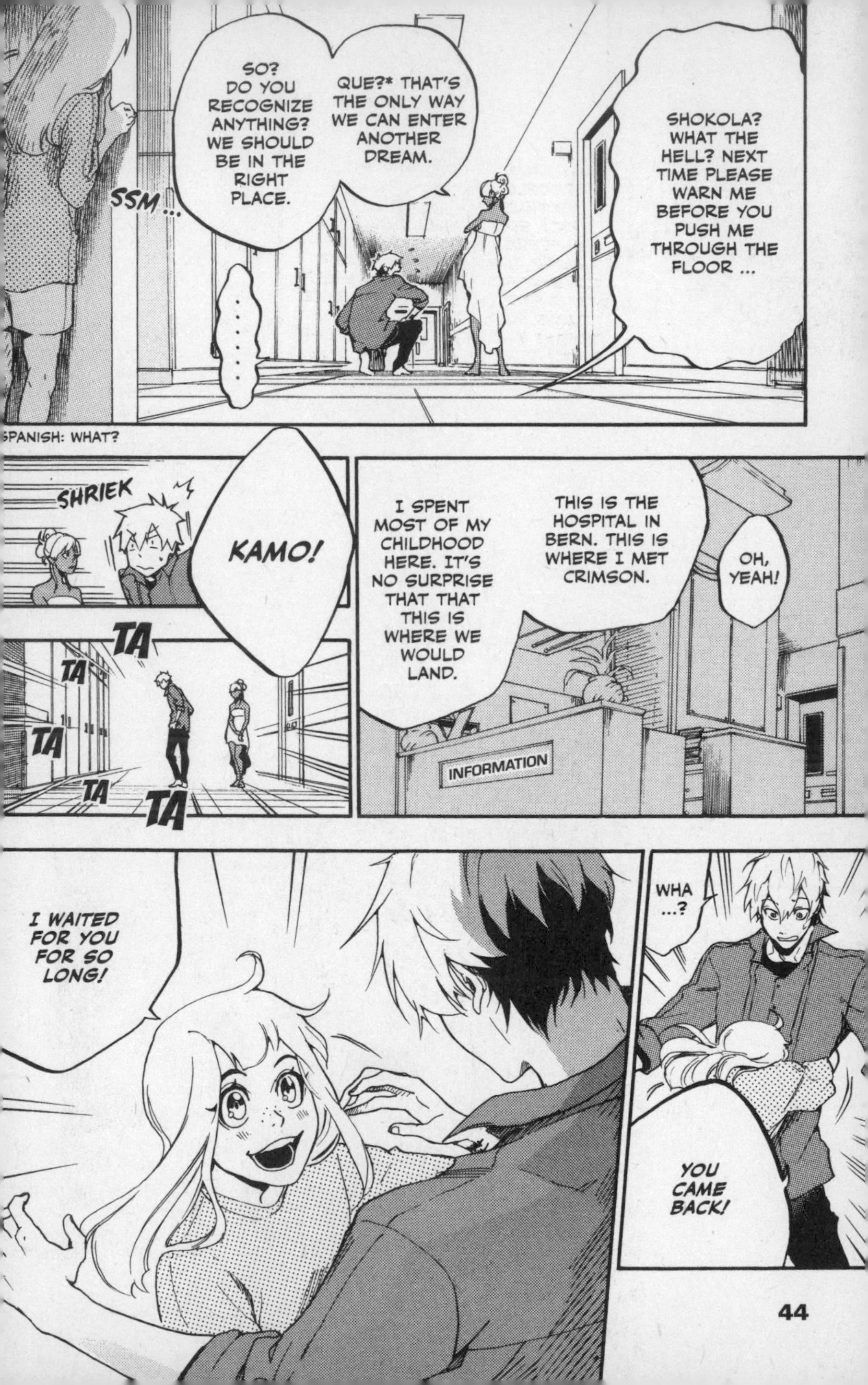
SHOKOLA? WHAT THE HELL? NEXT TIME PLEASE WARN ME BEFORE YOU PUSH ME THROUGH THE FLOOR ...
QUE?* THAT'S THE ONLY WAY WE CAN ENTER ANOTHER DREAM.
SO? DO YOU RECOGNIZE ANYTHING? WE SHOULD BE IN THE RIGHT PLACE.
SSM ...
......
OH, YEAH!
THIS IS THE HOSPITAL IN BERN. THIS IS WHERE I MET CRIMSON.
I SPENT MOST OF MY CHILDHOOD HERE. IT'S NO SURPRISE THAT THAT THIS IS WHERE WE WOULD LAND.
INFORMATION
SHRIEK
KAMO!
TA
TA
TA
TA
TA
WHA ...?
YOU CAME BACK!
I WAITED FOR YOU FOR SO LONG!

*SPANISH: WHAT?

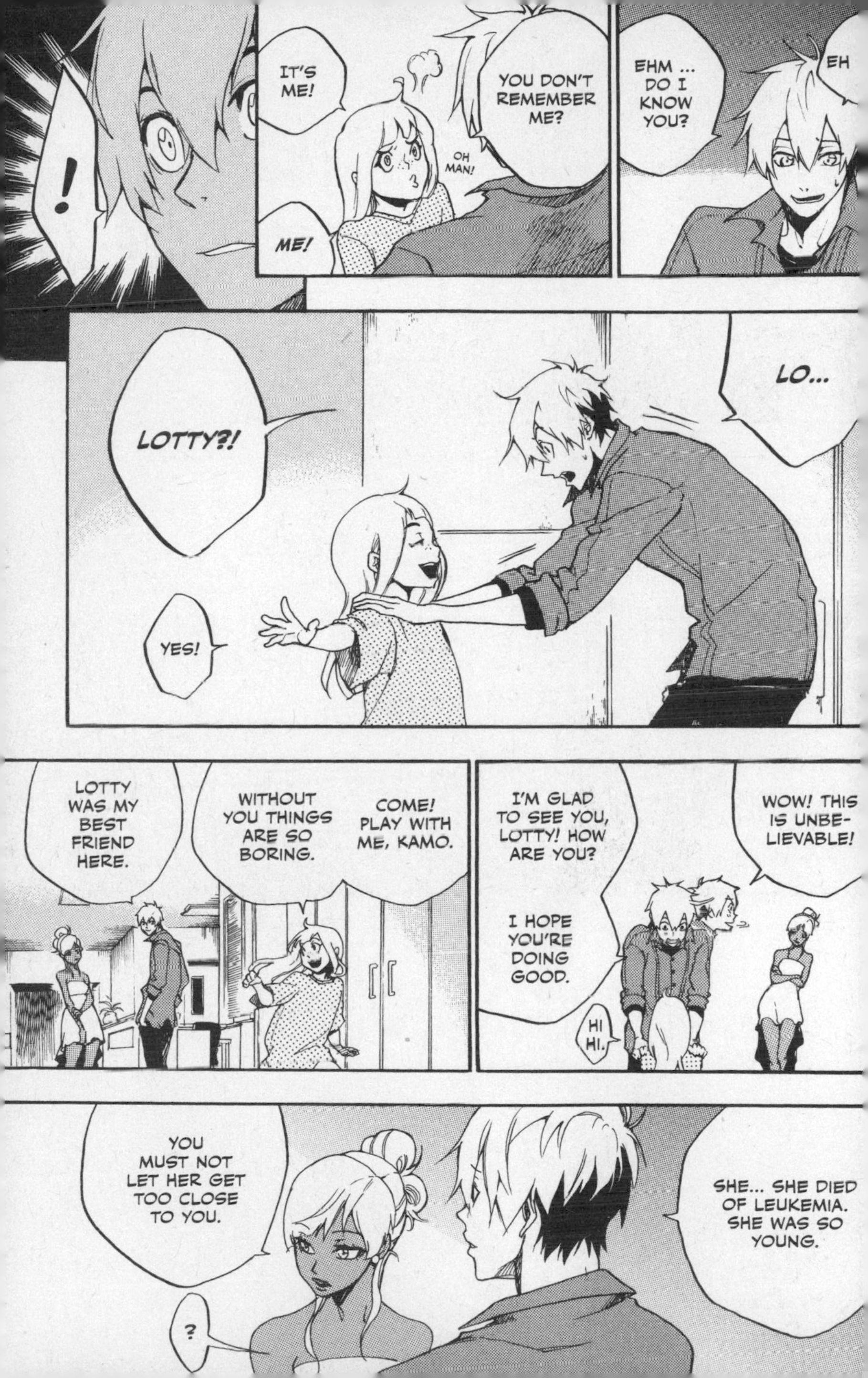
EH
EHM ... DO I KNOW YOU?
YOU DON'T REMEMBER ME?
IT'S ME!
OH MAN!
ME!
!
LO...
LOTTY?!
YES!
WOW! THIS IS UNBE-LIEVABLE!
I'M GLAD TO SEE YOU, LOTTY! HOW ARE YOU?
I HOPE YOU'RE DOING GOOD.
HI HI.
COME! PLAY WITH ME, KAMO.
WITHOUT YOU THINGS ARE SO BORING.
LOTTY WAS MY BEST FRIEND HERE.
SHE... SHE DIED OF LEUKEMIA. SHE WAS SO YOUNG.
YOU MUST NOT LET HER GET TOO CLOSE TO YOU.
?

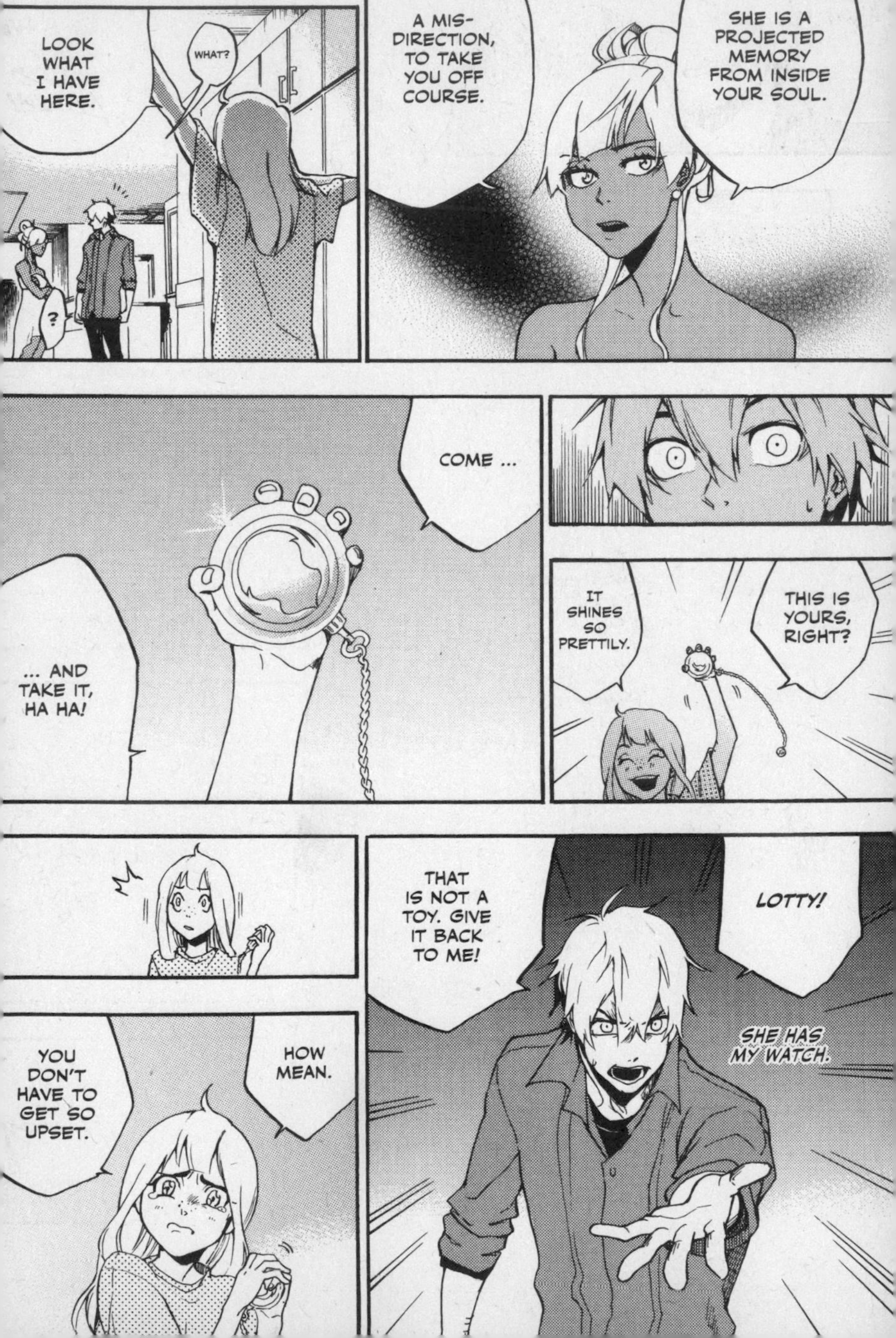
SHE IS A PROJECTED MEMORY FROM INSIDE YOUR SOUL.
A MIS-DIRECTION, TO TAKE YOU OFF COURSE.
WHAT?
LOOK WHAT I HAVE HERE.
?
THIS IS YOURS, RIGHT?
IT SHINES SO PRETTILY.
COME ...
... AND TAKE IT, HA HA!
LOTTY!
THAT IS NOT A TOY. GIVE IT BACK TO ME!
SHE HAS MY WATCH.
HOW MEAN.
YOU DON'T HAVE TO GET SO UPSET.

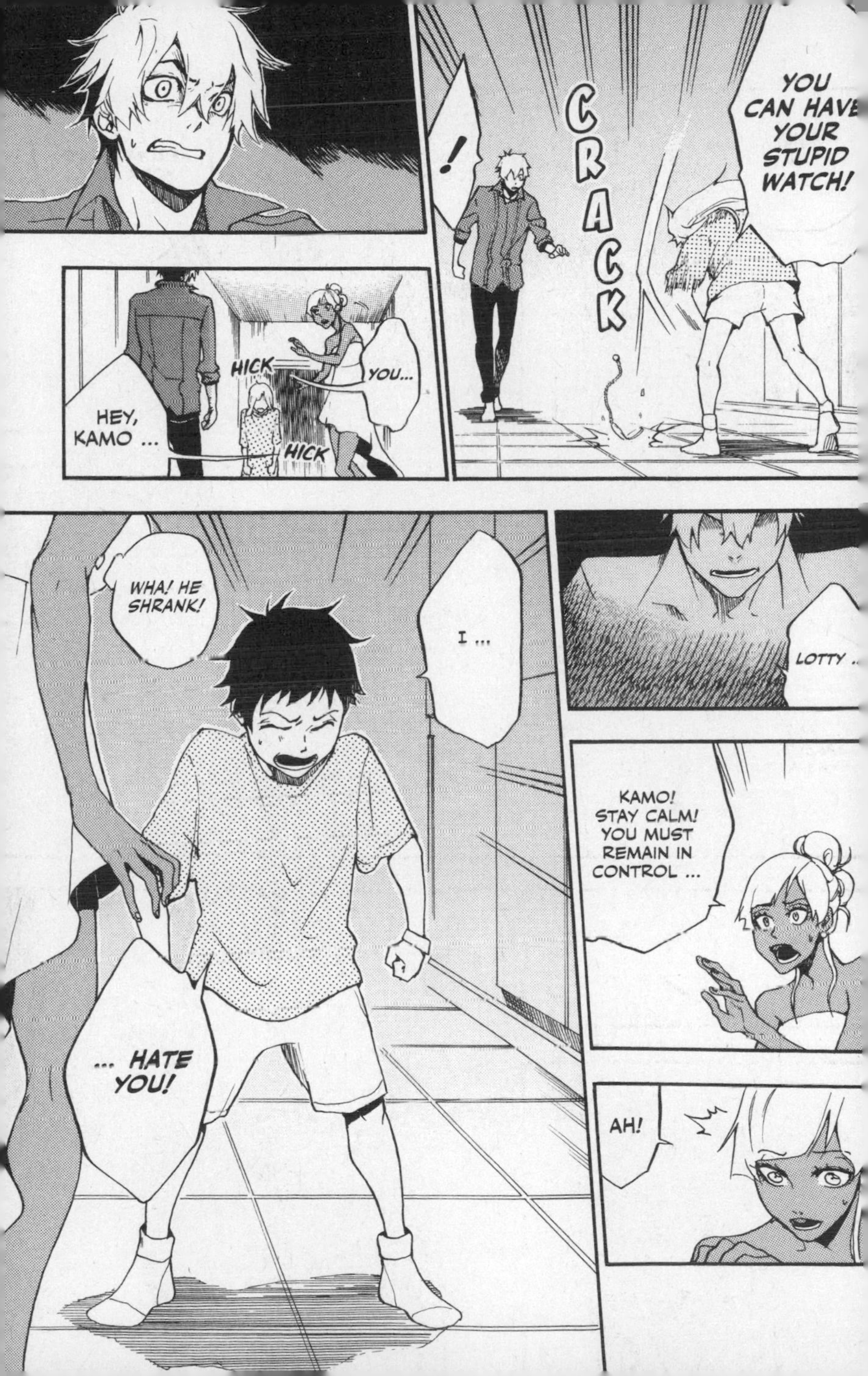
YOU CAN HAVE YOUR STUPID WATCH!
CRACK
!
YOU...
HICK
HICK
HEY, KAMO ...
LOTTY ...
KAMO! STAY CALM! YOU MUST REMAIN IN CONTROL ...
AH!
I ...
WHA! HE SHRANK!
... HATE YOU!

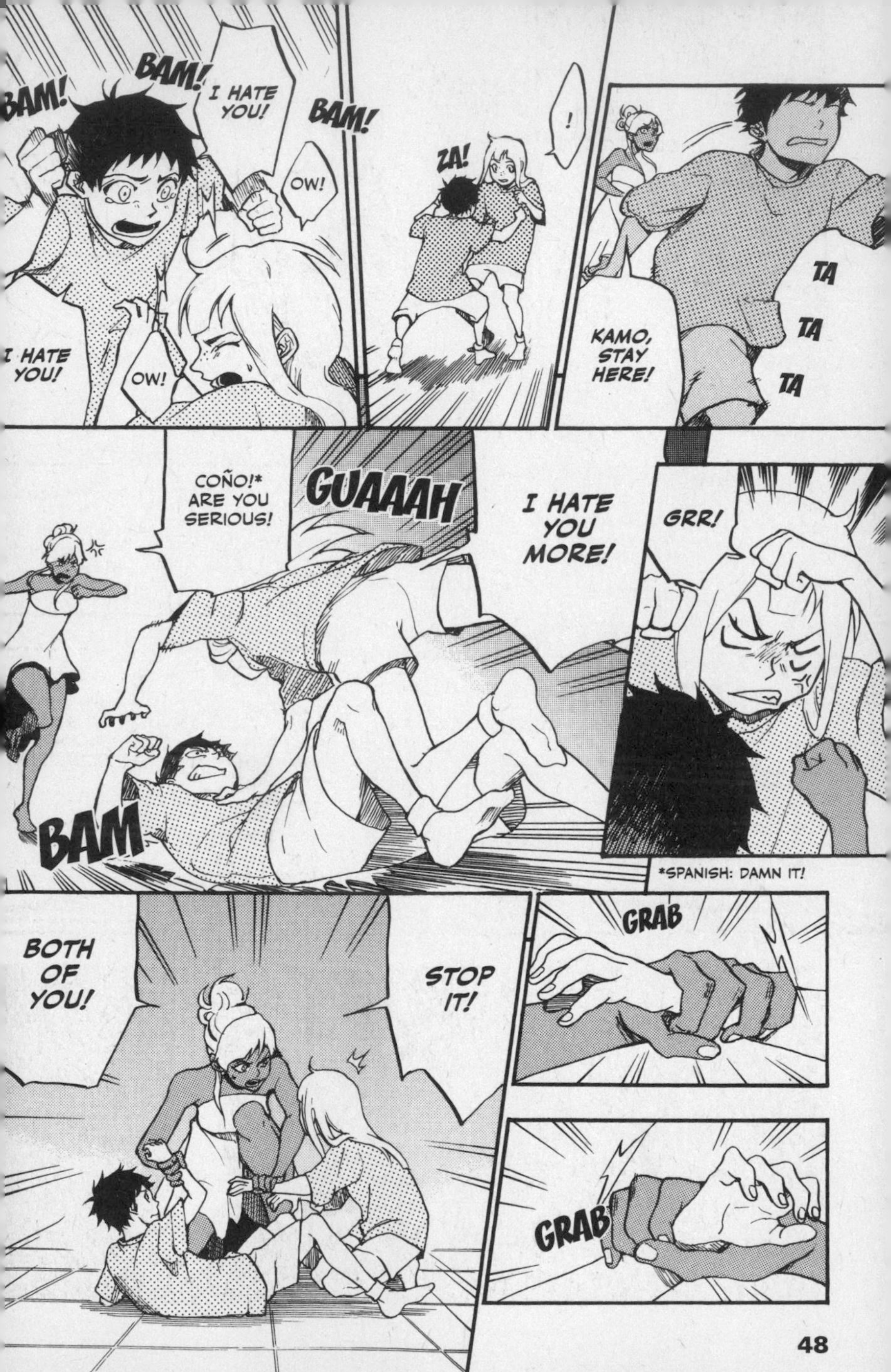
KAMO, STAY HERE!
TA
TA
TA
!
ZA!
BAM!
BAM!
I HATE YOU!
BAM!
OW!
I HATE YOU!
OW!
GRR!
I HATE YOU MORE!
GUAAAH
COÑO!* ARE YOU SERIOUS!
BAM
*SPANISH: DAMN IT!
GRAB
GRAB
BOTH OF YOU!
STOP IT!

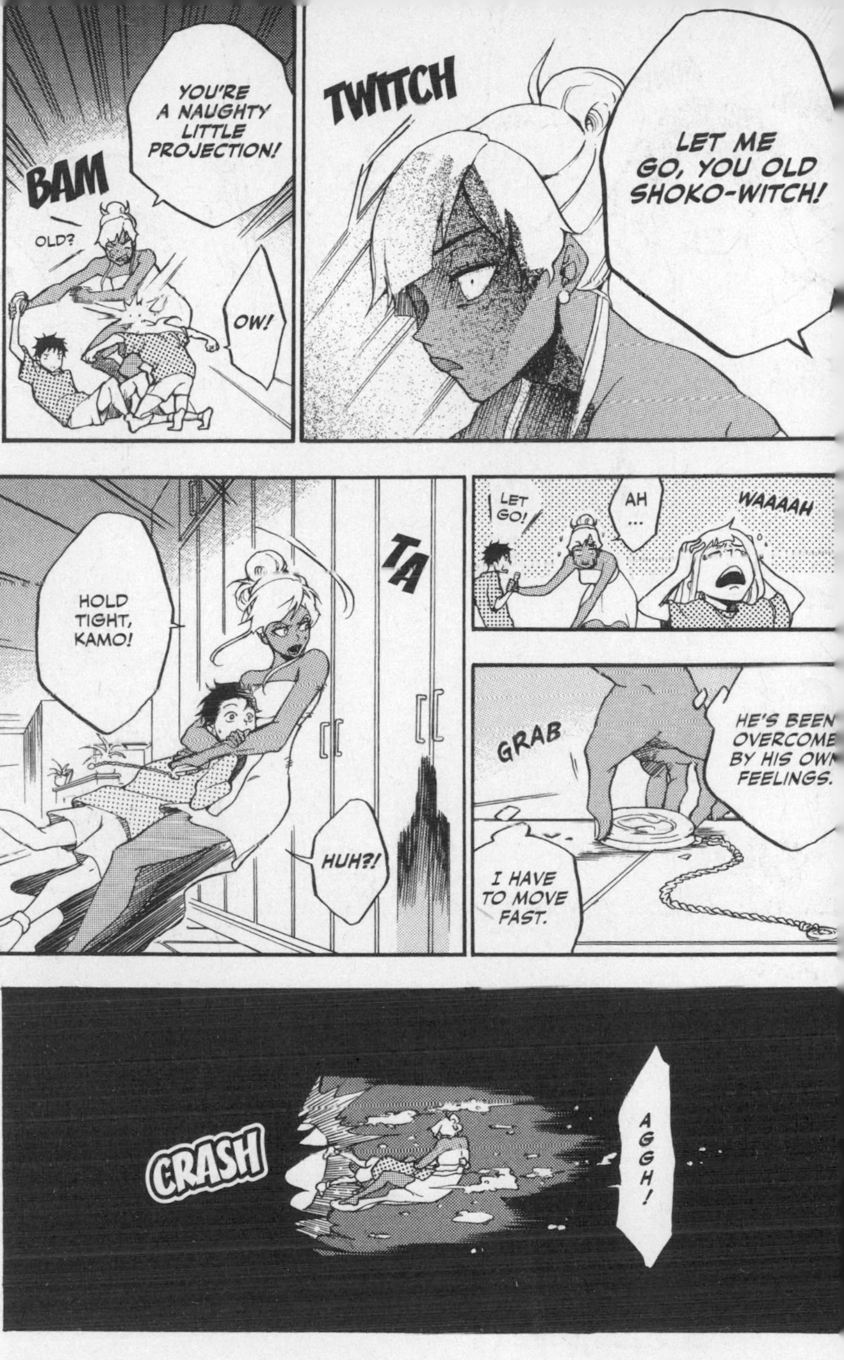
LET ME GO, YOU OLD SHOKO-WITCH!
TWITCH
YOU'RE A NAUGHTY LITTLE PROJECTION!
BAM
OLD?
OW!
WAAAAH
AH ...
LET GO!
HE'S BEEN OVERCOME BY HIS OWN FEELINGS.
GRAB
I HAVE TO MOVE FAST.
TA
HOLD TIGHT, KAMO!
HUH?!
AGGH!
CRASH

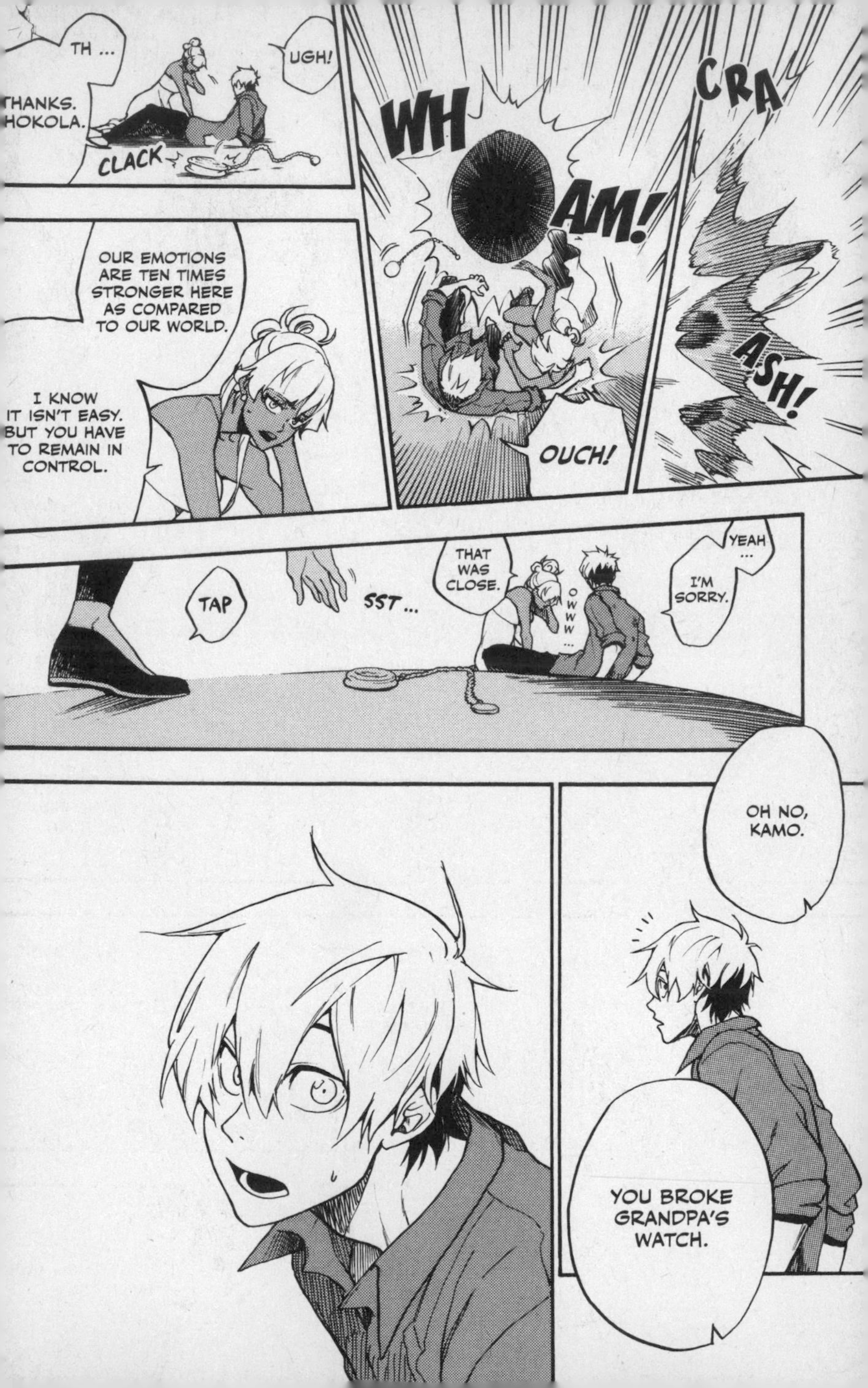
UGH!
TH ...
THANKS. HOKOLA.
CLACK
CRA
ASH!
WH
AM!
OUCH!
OUR EMOTIONS ARE TEN TIMES STRONGER HERE AS COMPARED TO OUR WORLD.
I KNOW IT ISN'T EASY. BUT YOU HAVE TO REMAIN IN CONTROL.
YEAH ...
I'M SORRY.
OWWW ...
THAT WAS CLOSE.
SST ...
TAP
OH NO, KAMO.
YOU BROKE GRANDPA'S WATCH.

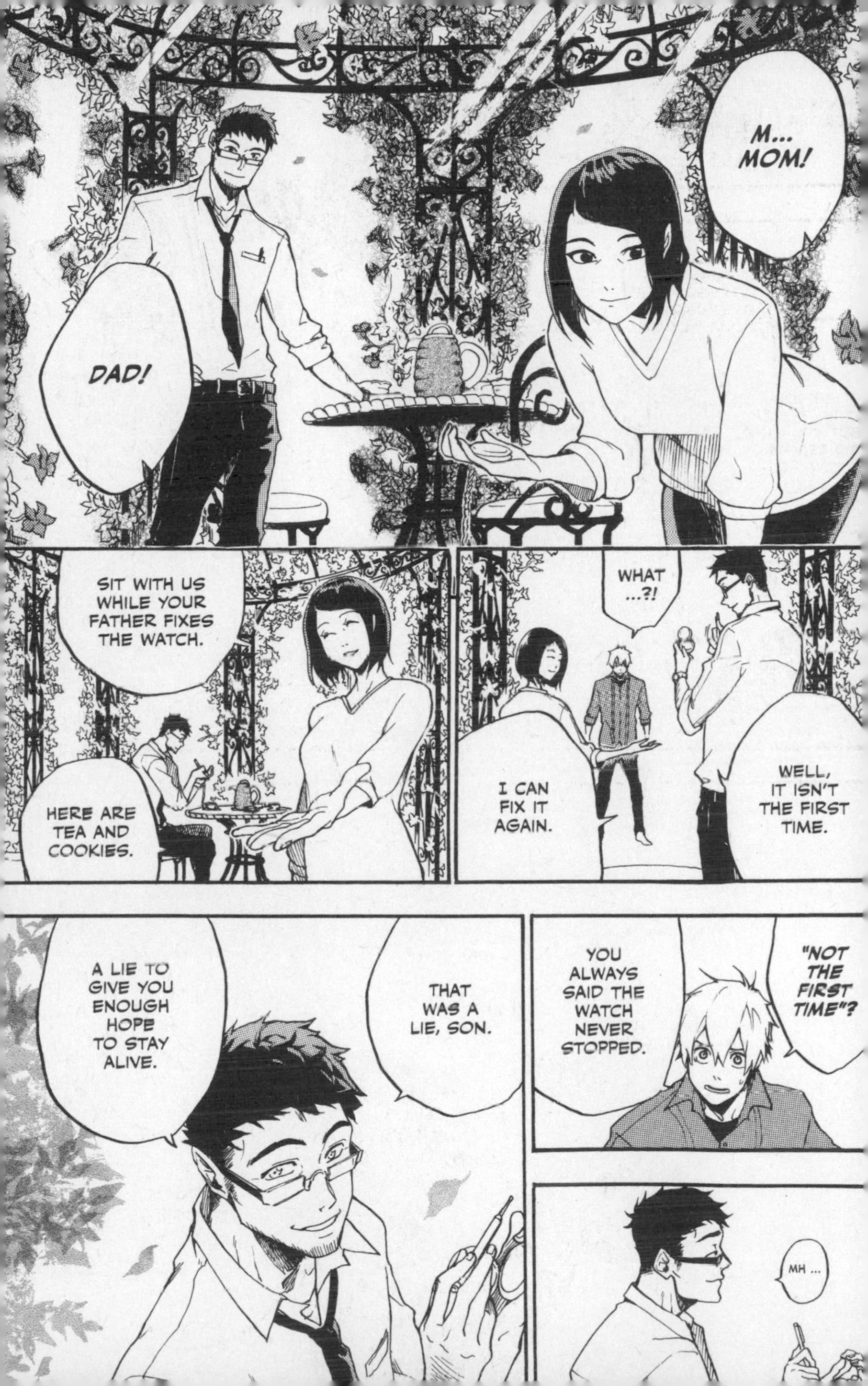
M... MOM!
DAD!
WHAT ...?!
WELL, IT ISN'T THE FIRST TIME.
I CAN FIX IT AGAIN.
SIT WITH US WHILE YOUR FATHER FIXES THE WATCH.
HERE ARE TEA AND COOKIES.
"NOT THE FIRST TIME"?
YOU ALWAYS SAID THE WATCH NEVER STOPPED.
MH ...
THAT WAS A LIE, SON.
A LIE TO GIVE YOU ENOUGH HOPE TO STAY ALIVE.

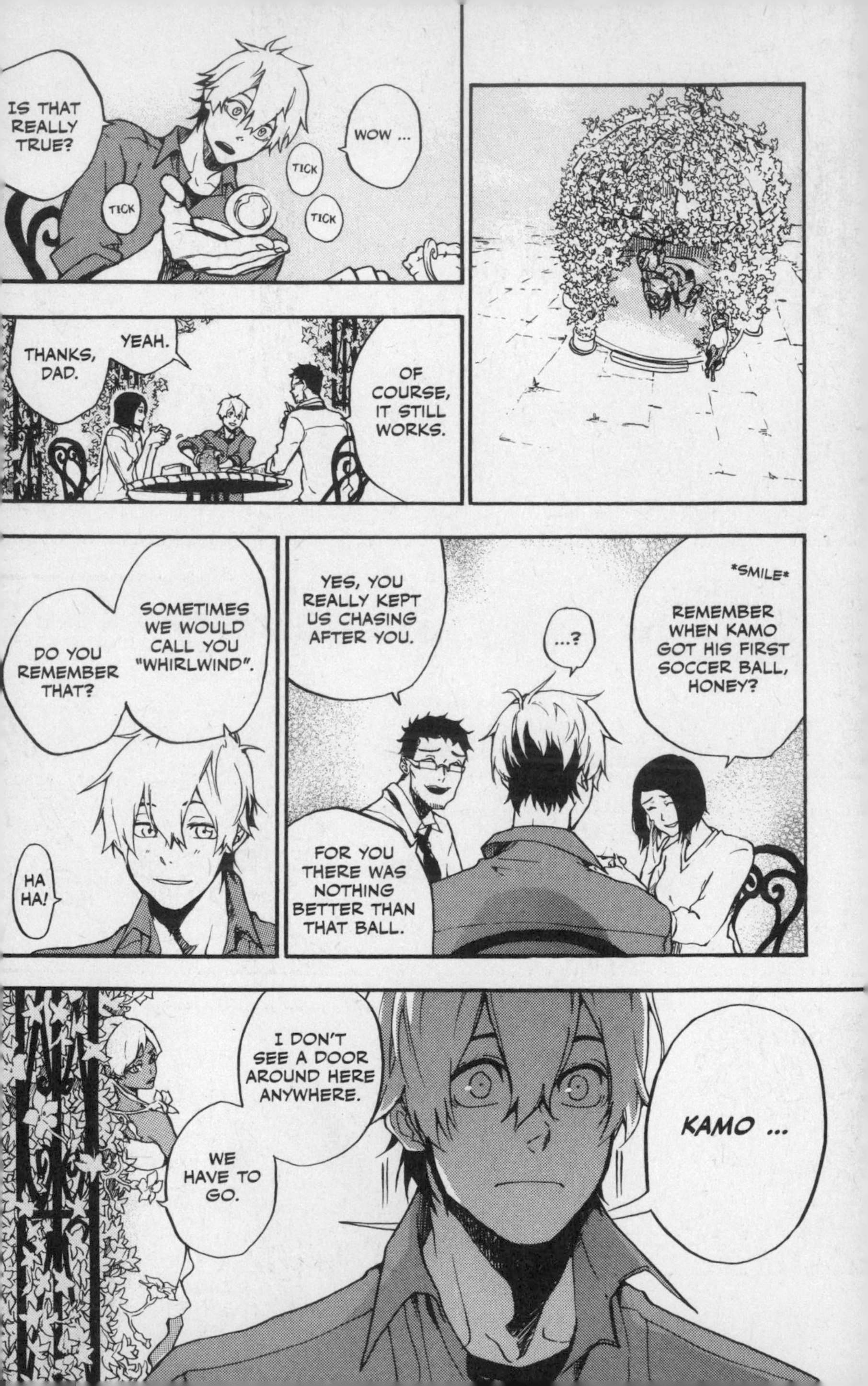
WOW ...
TICK
TICK
TICK
IS THAT REALLY TRUE?
OF COURSE, IT STILL WORKS.
YEAH.
THANKS, DAD.
SMILE
REMEMBER WHEN KAMO GOT HIS FIRST SOCCER BALL, HONEY?
...?
YES, YOU REALLY KEPT US CHASING AFTER YOU.
FOR YOU THERE WAS NOTHING BETTER THAN THAT BALL.
SOMETIMES WE WOULD CALL YOU "WHIRLWIND".
DO YOU REMEMBER THAT?
HA HA!
KAMO ...
I DON'T SEE A DOOR AROUND HERE ANYWHERE.
WE HAVE TO GO.

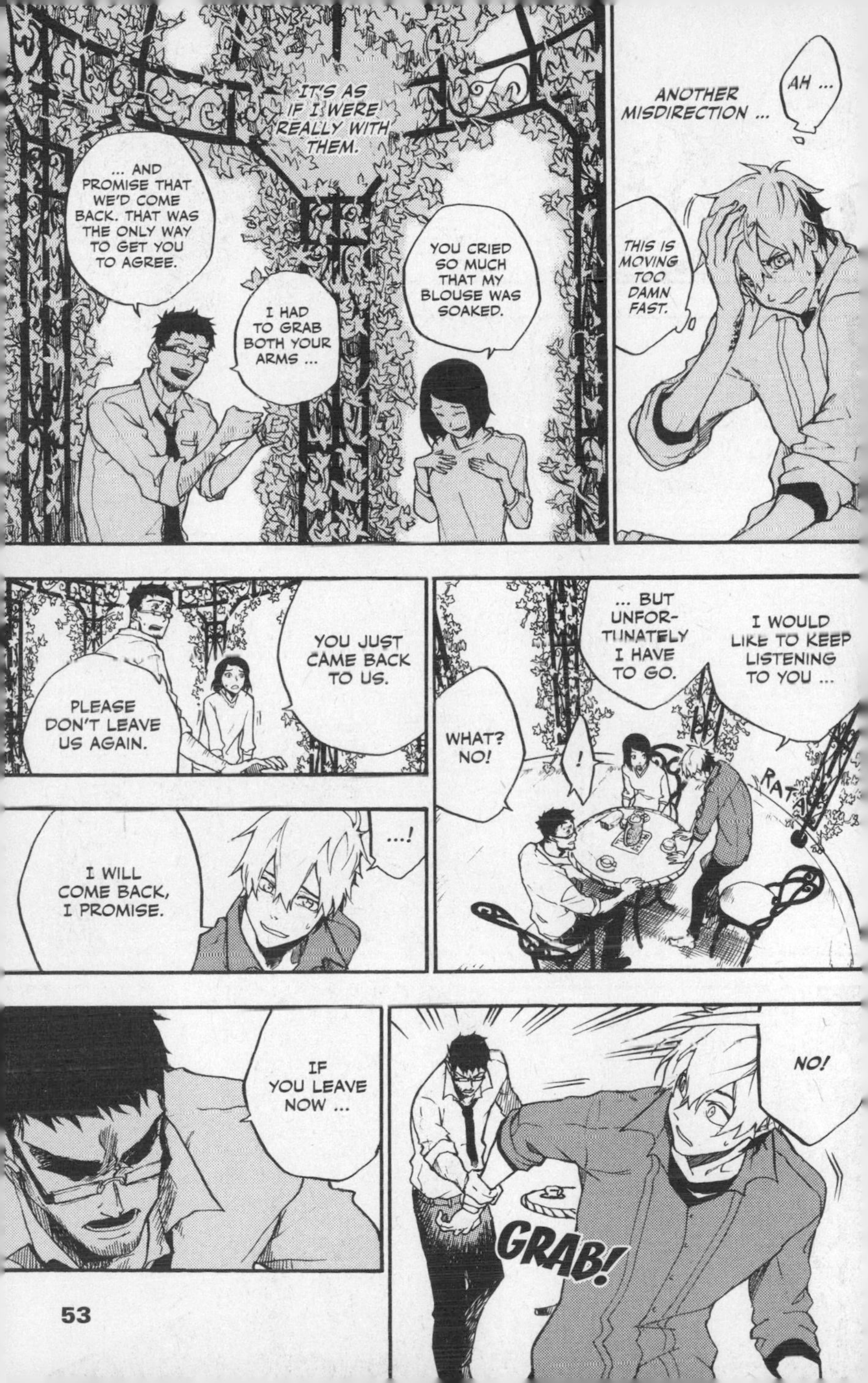
AH ...
ANOTHER MISDIRECTION ...
THIS IS MOVING TOO DAMN FAST.
IT'S AS IF I WERE REALLY WITH THEM.
YOU CRIED SO MUCH THAT MY BLOUSE WAS SOAKED.
I HAD TO GRAB BOTH YOUR ARMS ...
... AND PROMISE THAT WE'D COME BACK. THAT WAS THE ONLY WAY TO GET YOU TO AGREE.
I WOULD LIKE TO KEEP LISTENING TO YOU ...
... BUT UNFORTUNATELY I HAVE TO GO.
RATA
!
WHAT? NO!
YOU JUST CAME BACK TO US.
PLEASE DON'T LEAVE US AGAIN.
...!
I WILL COME BACK, I PROMISE.
NO!
GRAB!
IF YOU LEAVE NOW ...

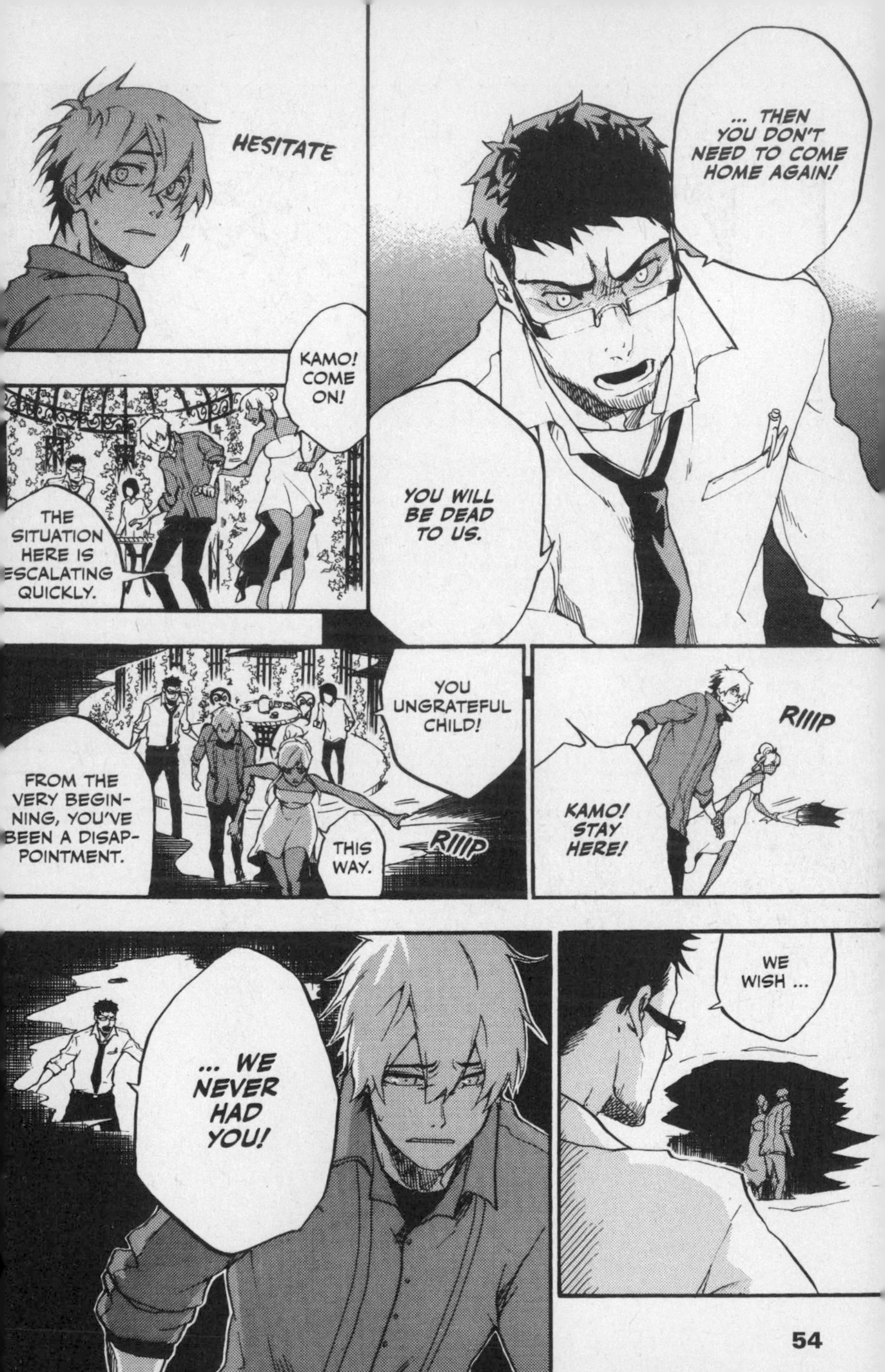

... THEN YOU DON'T NEED TO COME HOME AGAIN!
YOU WILL BE DEAD TO US.
HESITATE
KAMO! COME ON!
THE SITUATION HERE IS ESCALATING QUICKLY.
RIIIP
KAMO! STAY HERE!
YOU UNGRATEFUL CHILD!
FROM THE VERY BEGINNING, YOU'VE BEEN A DISAPPOINTMENT.
THIS WAY.
RIIIP
WE WISH ...
... WE NEVER HAD YOU!

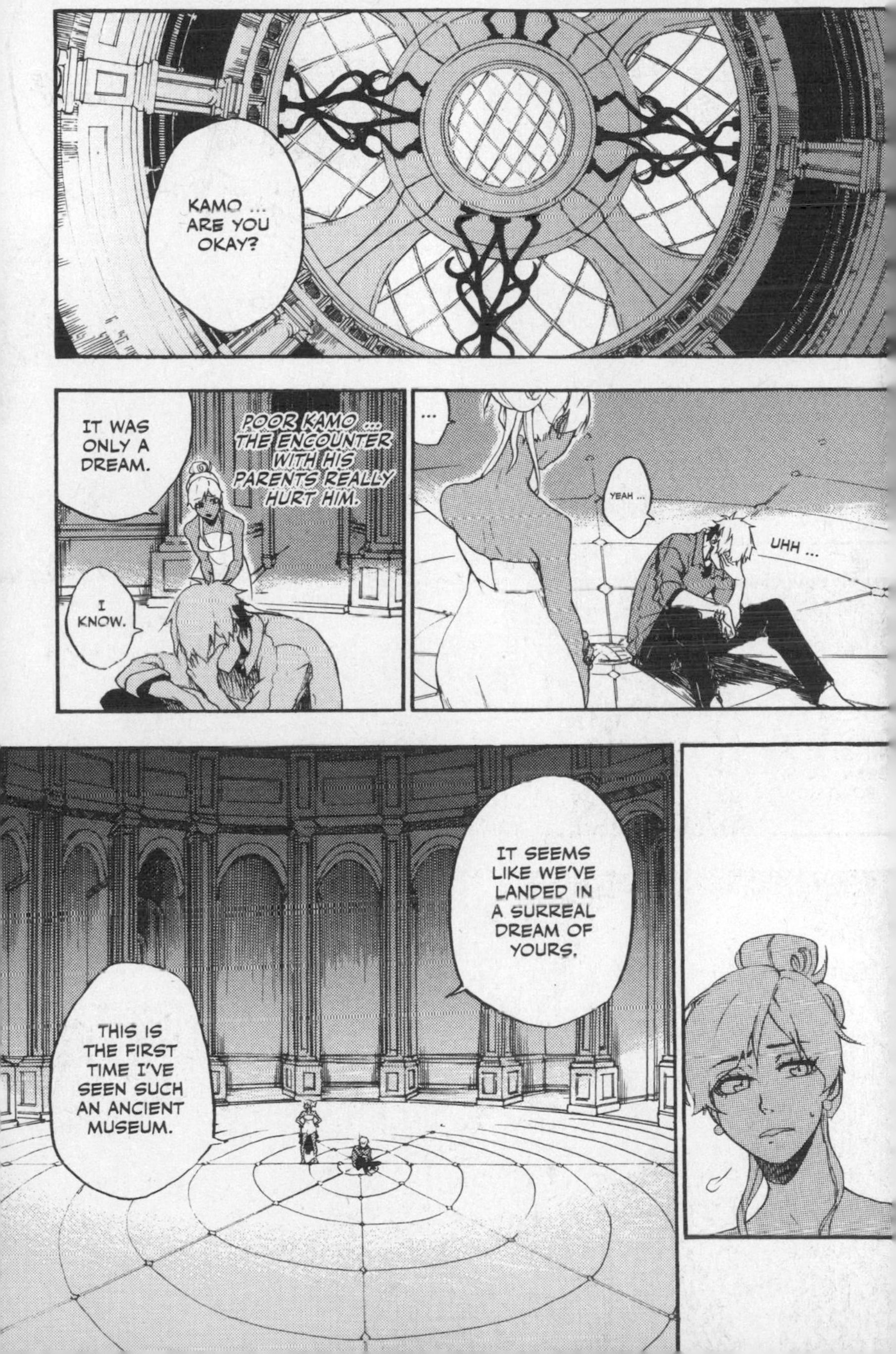
KAMO ... ARE YOU OKAY?
...
YEAH ...
UHH ...
IT WAS ONLY A DREAM.
POOR KAMO ... THE ENCOUNTER WITH HIS PARENTS REALLY HURT HIM.
I KNOW.
IT SEEMS LIKE WE'VE LANDED IN A SURREAL DREAM OF YOURS.
THIS IS THE FIRST TIME I'VE SEEN SUCH AN ANCIENT MUSEUM.

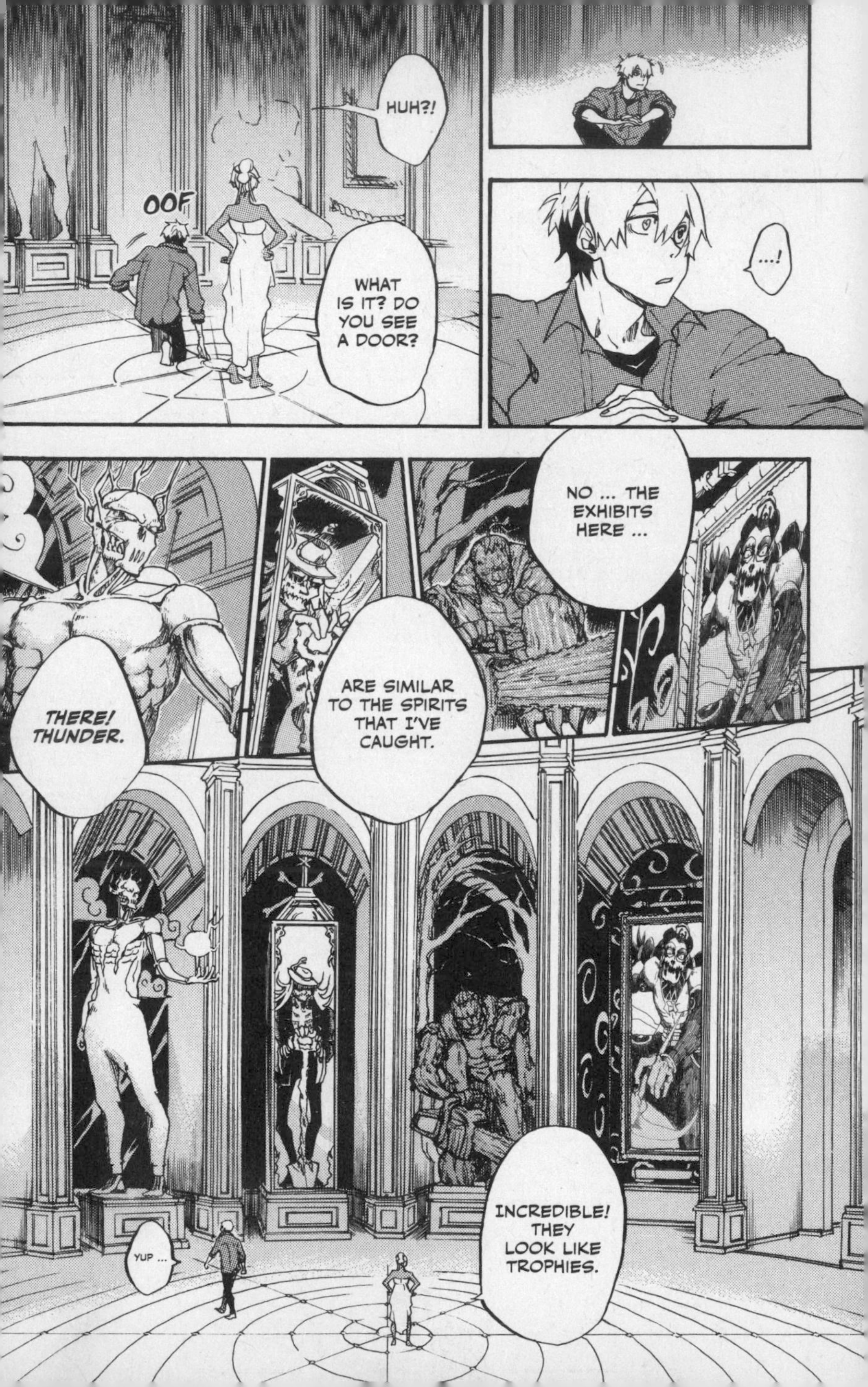
...!
HUH?!
OOF
WHAT IS IT? DO YOU SEE A DOOR?
NO ... THE EXHIBITS HERE ...
ARE SIMILAR TO THE SPIRITS THAT I'VE CAUGHT.
THERE! THUNDER.
INCREDIBLE! THEY LOOK LIKE TROPHIES.
YUP ...

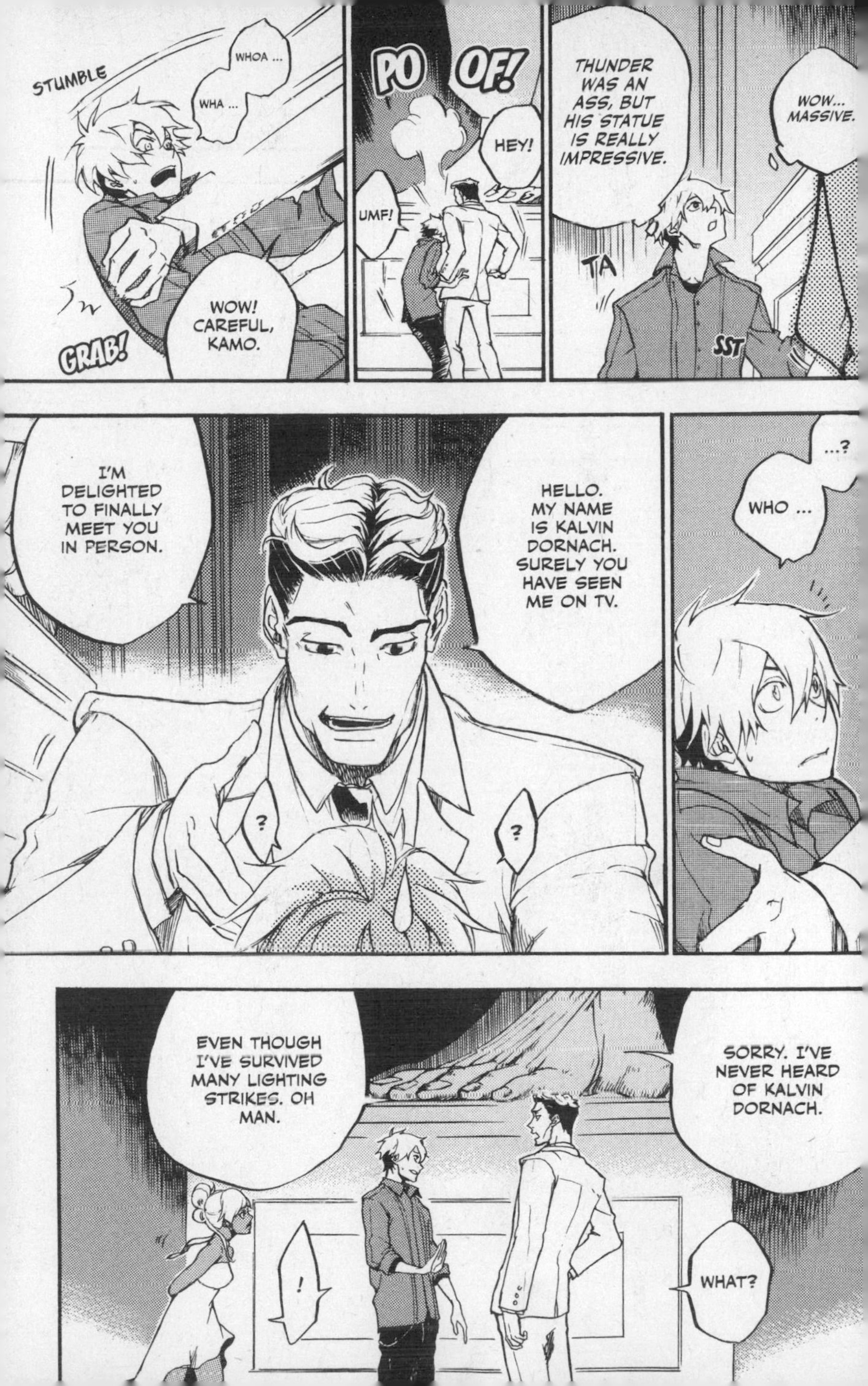
THUNDER WAS AN ASS, BUT HIS STATUE IS REALLY IMPRESSIVE.
WOW... MASSIVE.
TA
SST
PO OF!
HEY!
UMF!
WHOA ...
STUMBLE
WHA ...
WOW! CAREFUL, KAMO.
GRAB!
...?
WHO ...
HELLO. MY NAME IS KALVIN DORNACH. SURELY YOU HAVE SEEN ME ON TV.
I'M DELIGHTED TO FINALLY MEET YOU IN PERSON.
?
?
SORRY. I'VE NEVER HEARD OF KALVIN DORNACH.
WHAT?
!
EVEN THOUGH I'VE SURVIVED MANY LIGHTING STRIKES. OH MAN.

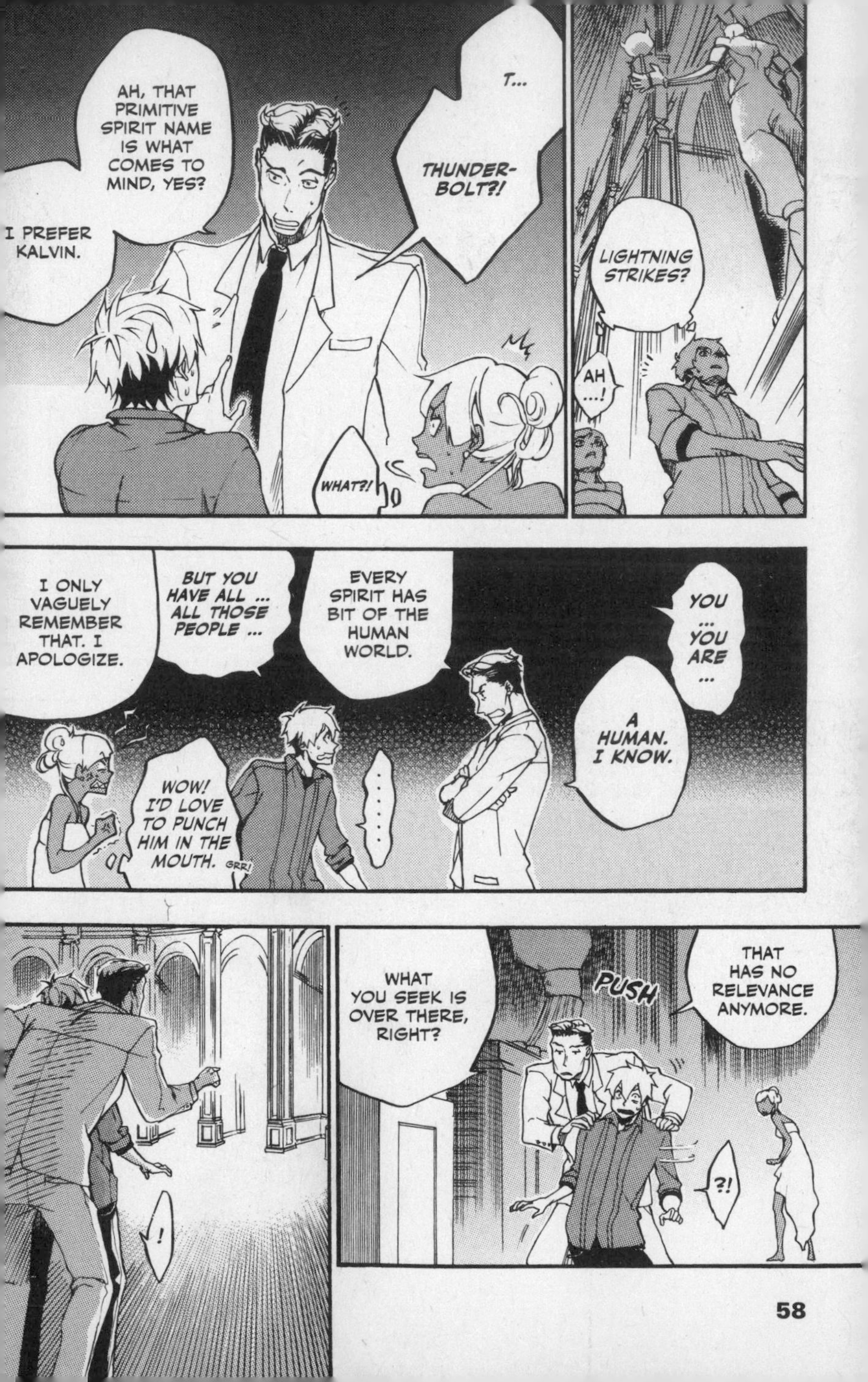
LIGHTNING STRIKES?
AH ...!
T...
THUNDER-BOLT?!
AH, THAT PRIMITIVE SPIRIT NAME IS WHAT COMES TO MIND, YES?
I PREFER KALVIN.
WHAT?!
YOU ... YOU ARE ...
A HUMAN. I KNOW.
EVERY SPIRIT HAS BIT OF THE HUMAN WORLD.
BUT YOU HAVE ALL ... ALL THOSE PEOPLE ...
I ONLY VAGUELY REMEMBER THAT. I APOLOGIZE.
......
WOW! I'D LOVE TO PUNCH HIM IN THE MOUTH.
GRR!
THAT HAS NO RELEVANCE ANYMORE.
PUSH
WHAT YOU SEEK IS OVER THERE, RIGHT?
?!
!

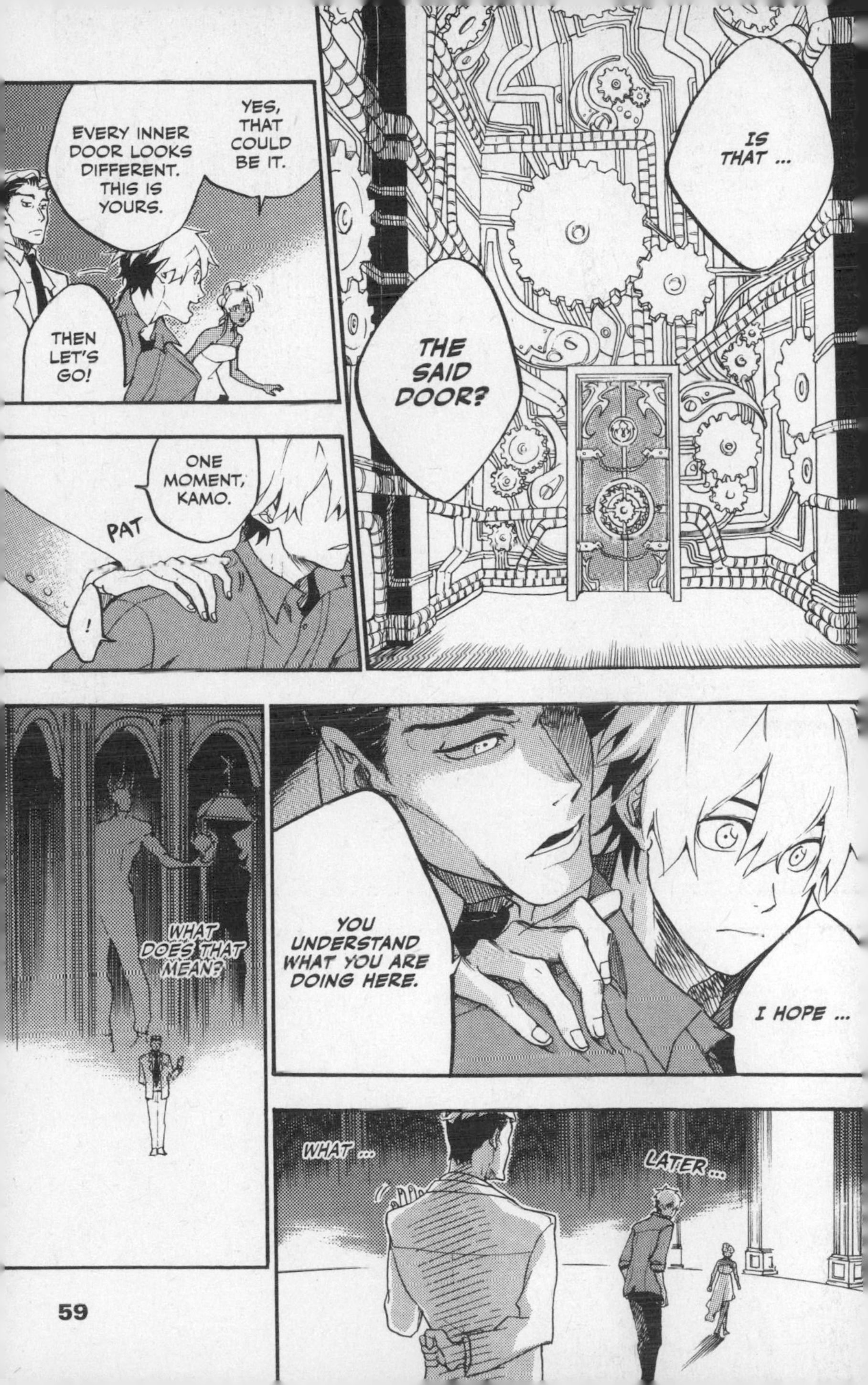
IS THAT ...
THE SAID DOOR?
YES, THAT COULD BE IT.
EVERY INNER DOOR LOOKS DIFFERENT. THIS IS YOURS.
THEN LET'S GO!
ONE MOMENT, KAMO.
PAT
!
I HOPE ...
YOU UNDERSTAND WHAT YOU ARE DOING HERE.
LATER ...
WHAT ...
WHAT DOES THAT MEAN?

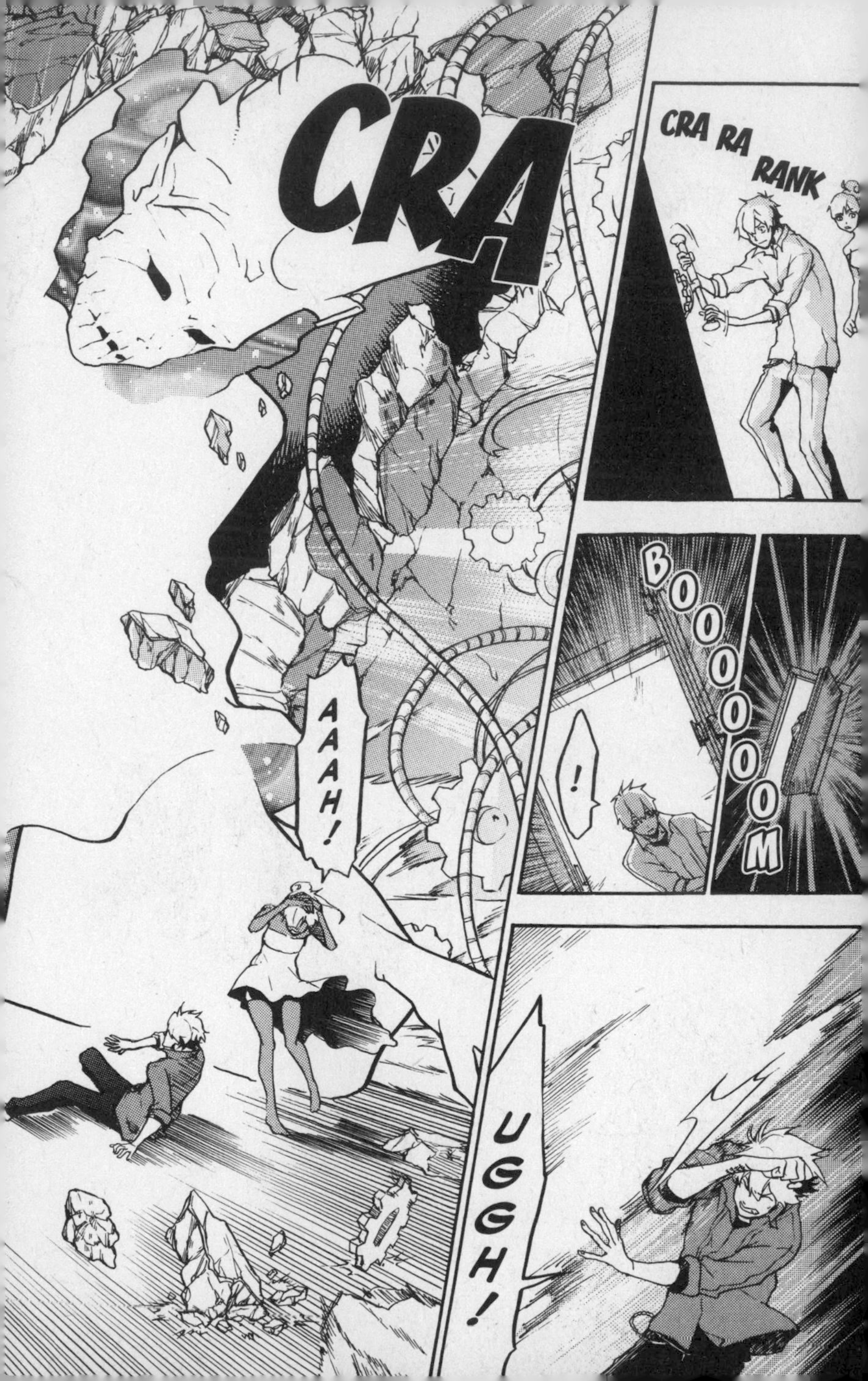
CRA RA RANK
BOOOOOOM
!
UGGH!
CRA
AAAH!

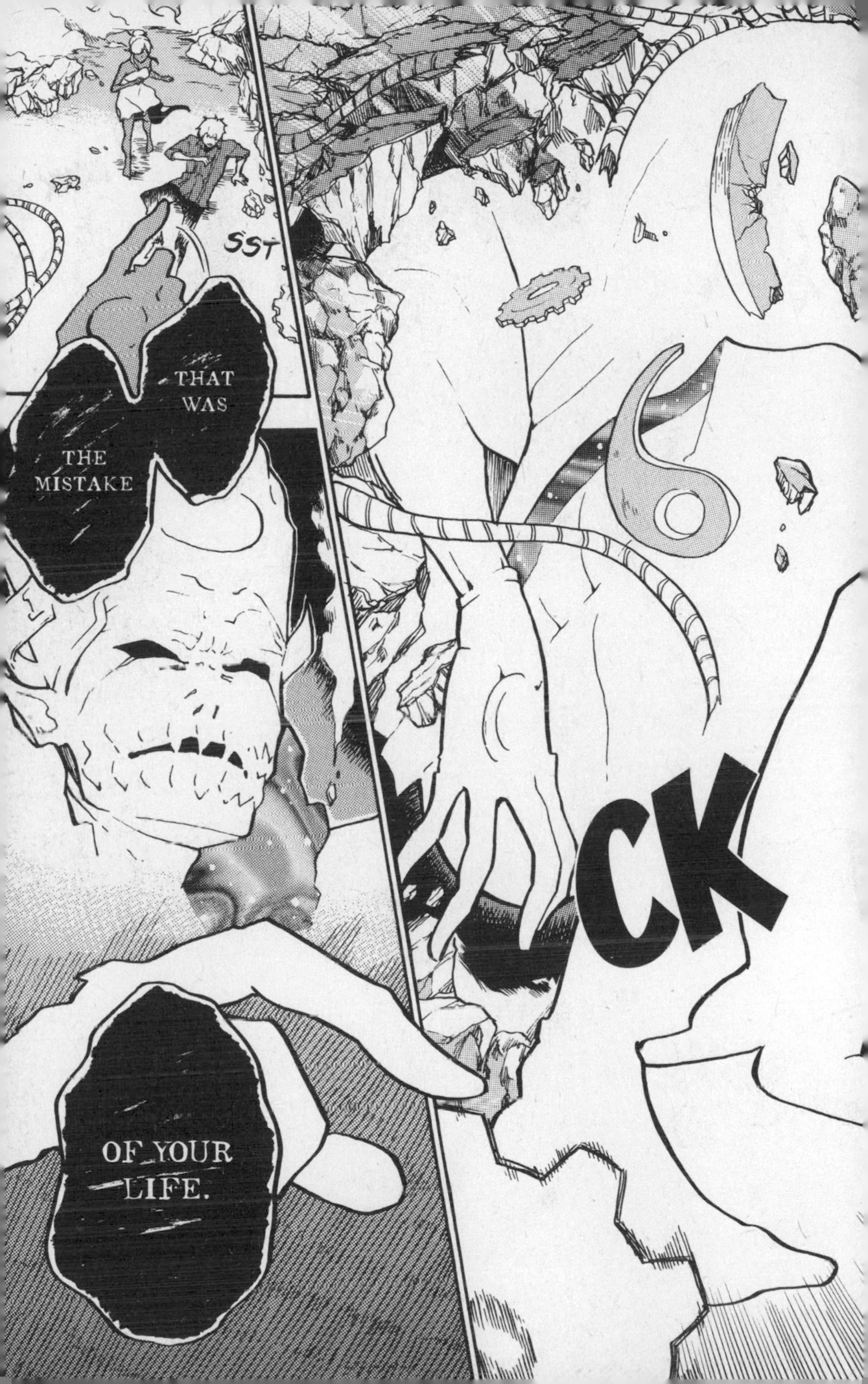
SST
THAT WAS
THE MISTAKE
OF YOUR LIFE.
CK

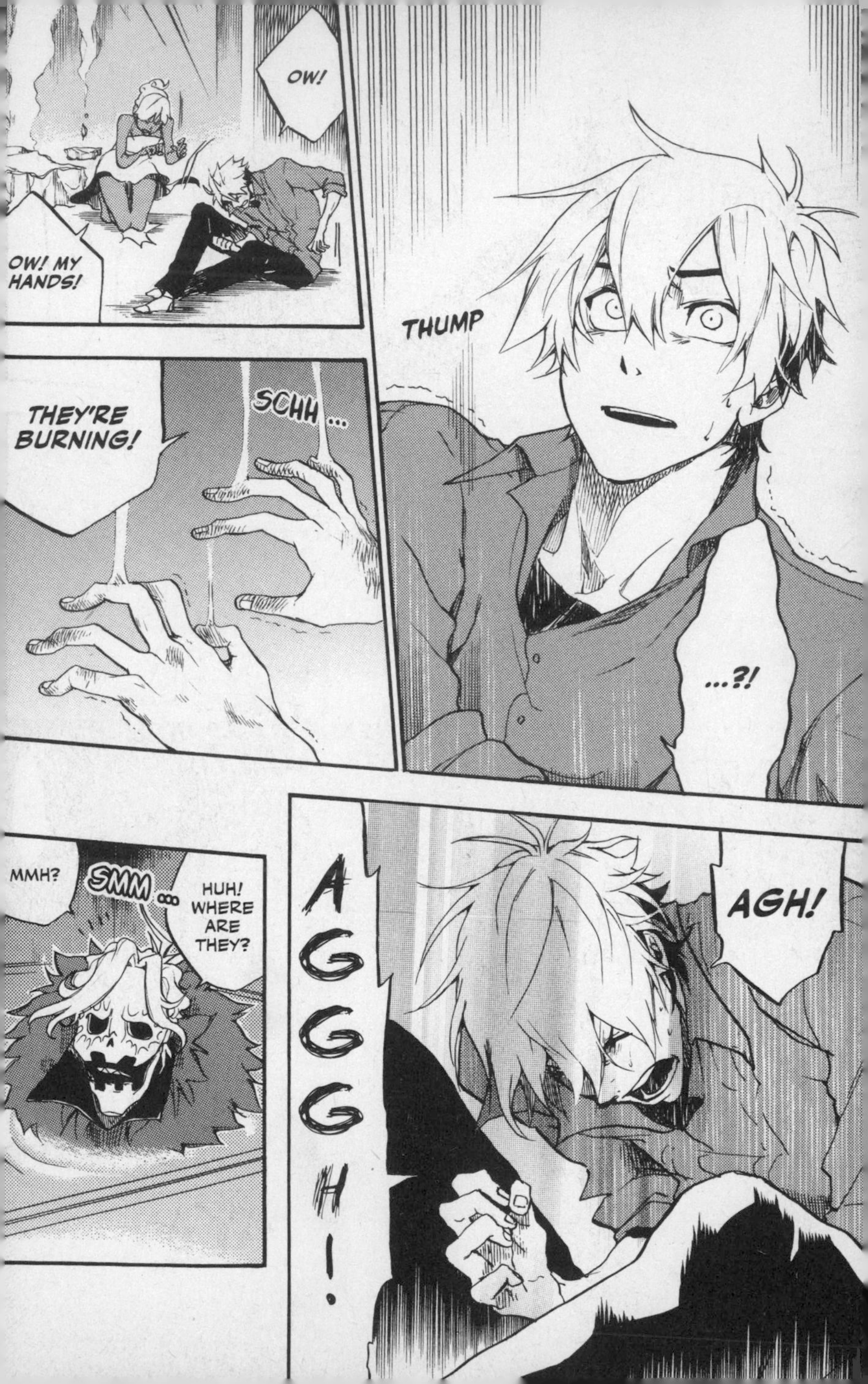
THUMP
...?!
OW!
OW! MY HANDS!
SCHH...
THEY'RE BURNING!
AGH!
AGGGH!
HUH! WHERE ARE THEY?
SMM...
MMH?

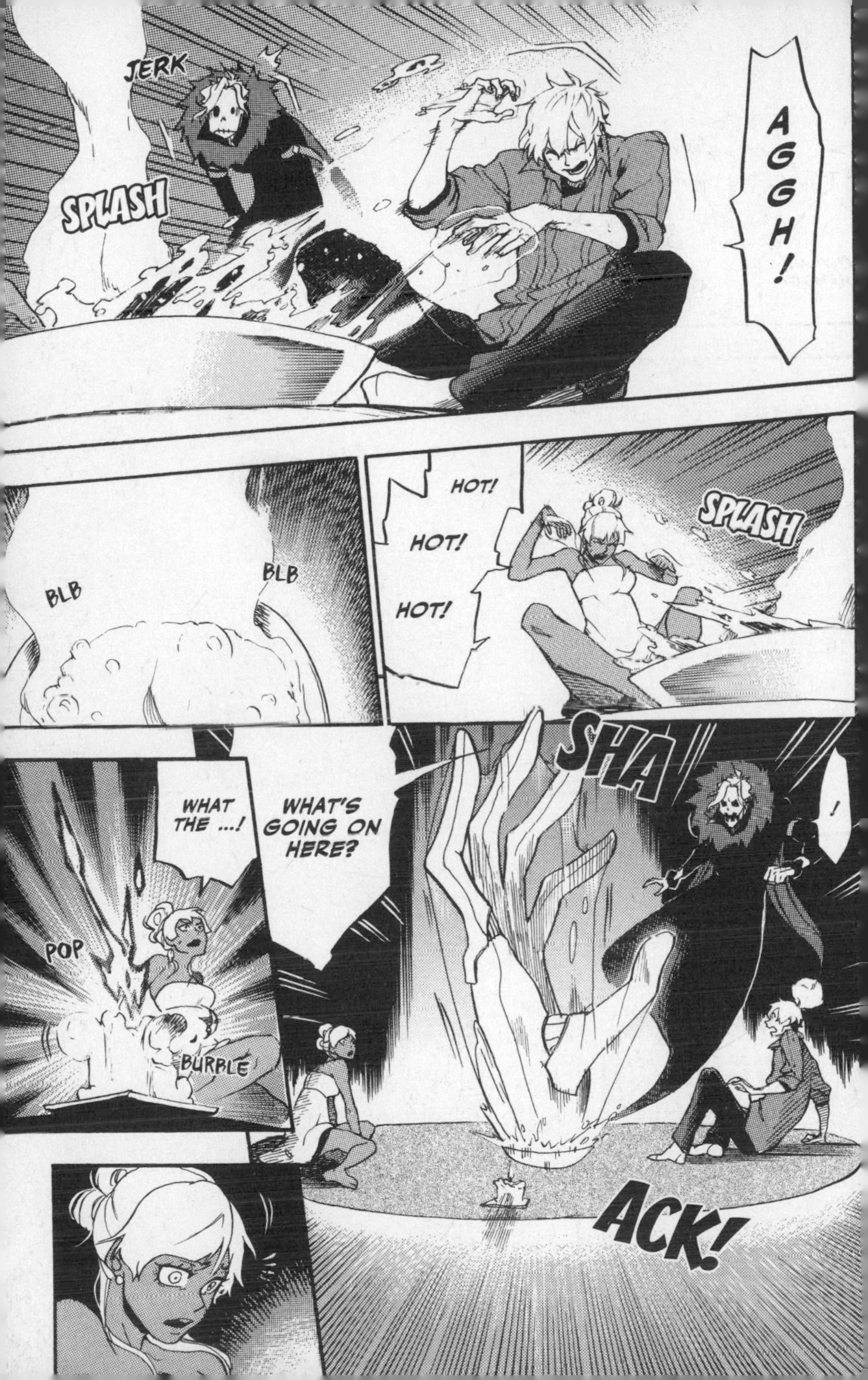
AGGH!
JERK
SPLASH
SPLASH
HOT!
HOT!
HOT!
BLB
BLB
SHA
!
WHAT'S GOING ON HERE?
WHAT THE ...!
POP
BURBLE
ACK!

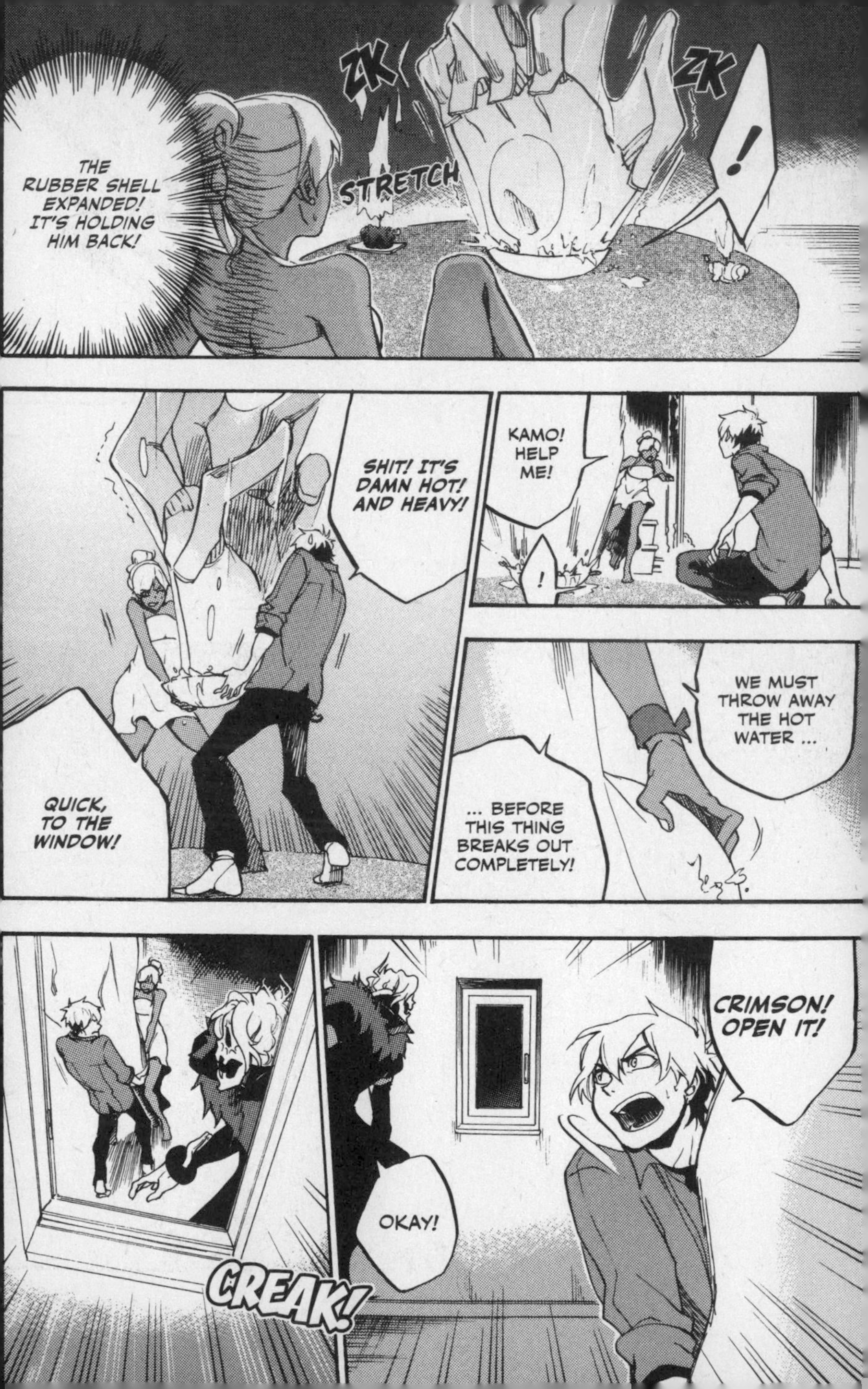
ZK
!
ZK
STRETCH
THE RUBBER SHELL EXPANDED! IT'S HOLDING HIM BACK!
KAMO! HELP ME!
!
WE MUST THROW AWAY THE HOT WATER ...
... BEFORE THIS THING BREAKS OUT COMPLETELY!
SHIT! IT'S DAMN HOT! AND HEAVY!
QUICK, TO THE WINDOW!
CRIMSON! OPEN IT!
OKAY!
CREAK!

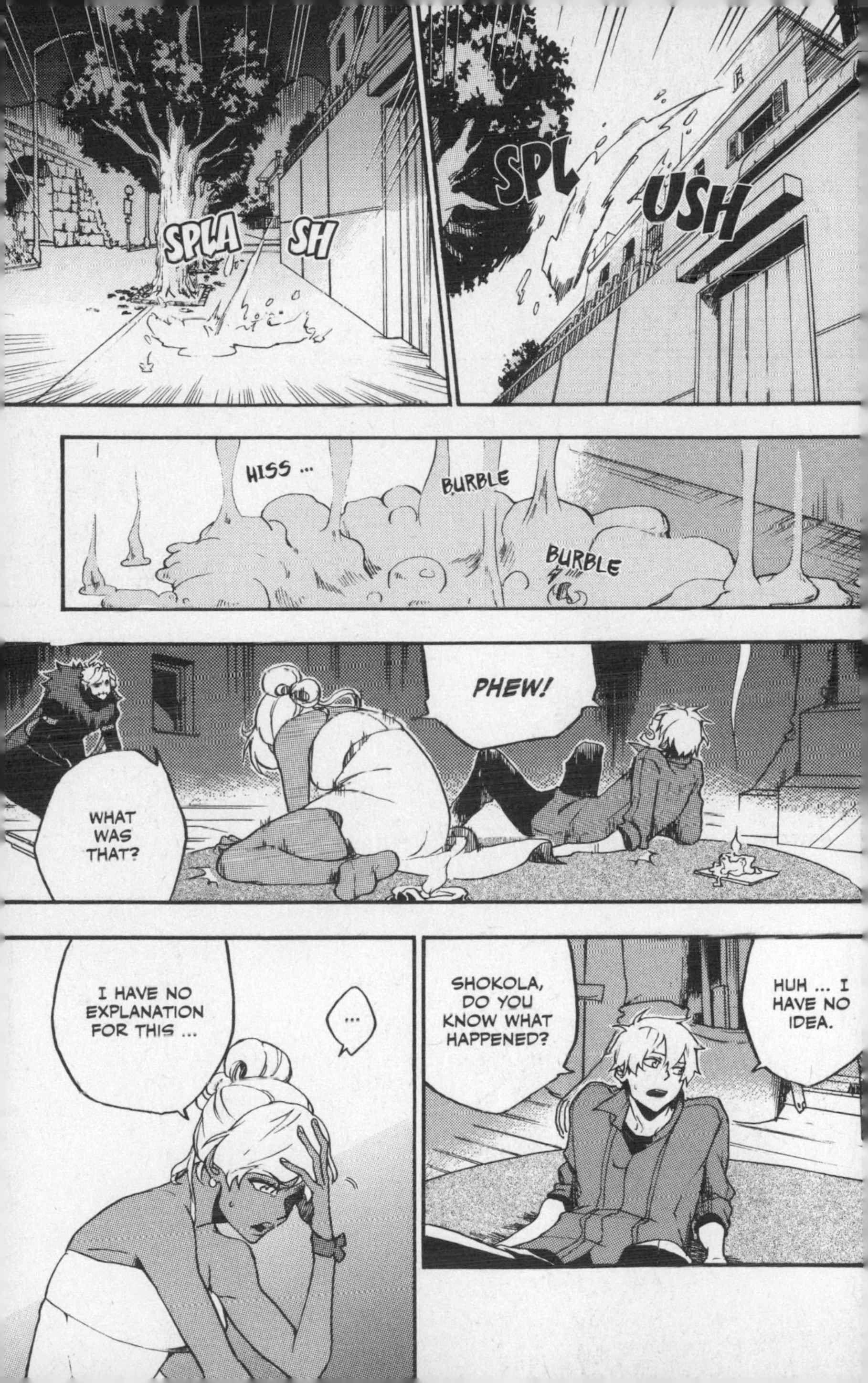
SPL USH
SPLA SH
HISS ...
BURBLE
BURBLE
PHEW!
WHAT WAS THAT?
SHOKOLA, DO YOU KNOW WHAT HAPPENED?
HUH ... I HAVE NO IDEA.
...
I HAVE NO EXPLANATION FOR THIS ...

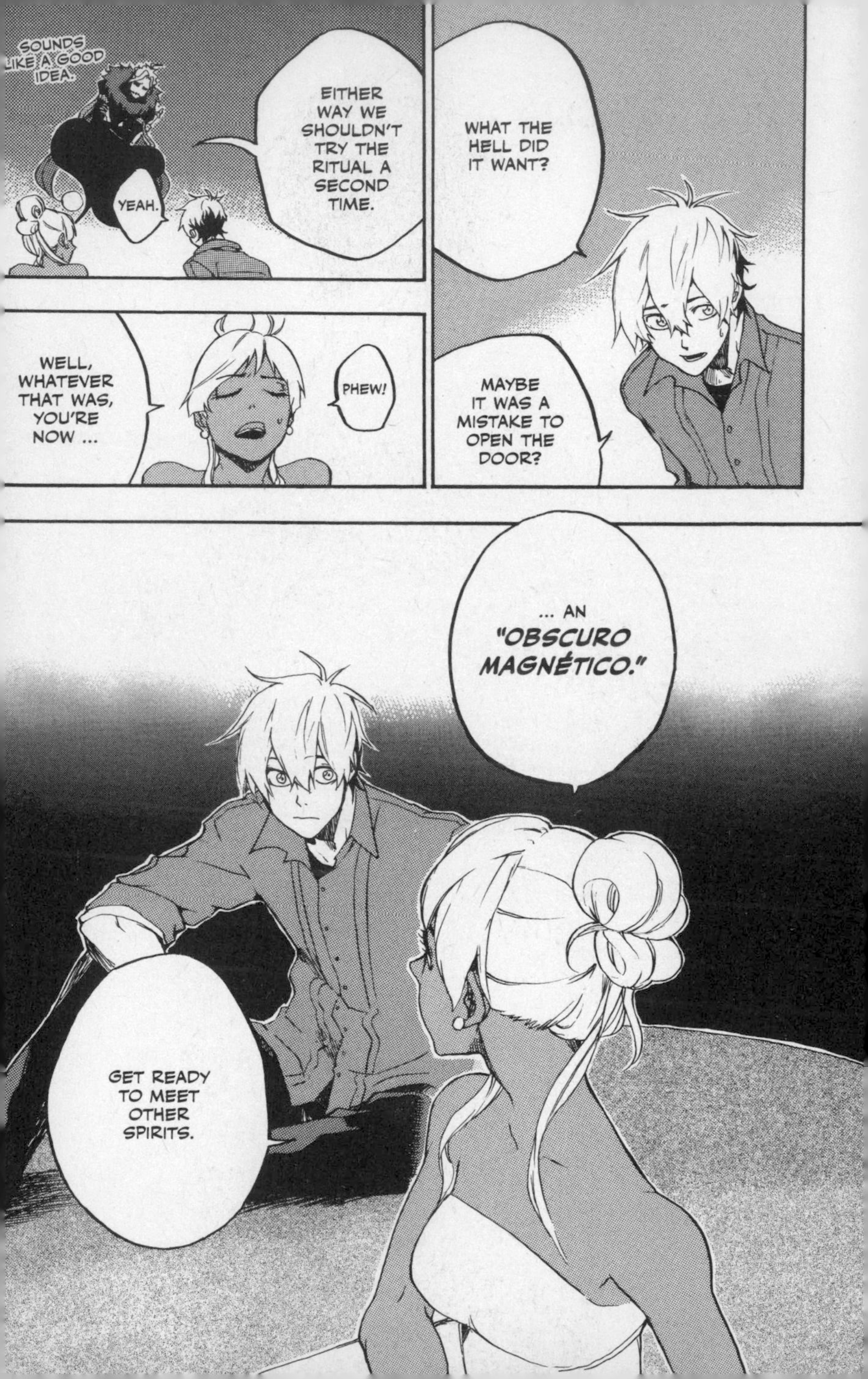
WHAT THE HELL DID IT WANT?
MAYBE IT WAS A MISTAKE TO OPEN THE DOOR?
EITHER WAY WE SHOULDN'T TRY THE RITUAL A SECOND TIME.
YEAH.
SOUNDS LIKE A GOOD IDEA.
PHEW!
WELL, WHATEVER THAT WAS, YOU'RE NOW ...
... AN "OBSCURO MAGNÉTICO."
GET READY TO MEET OTHER SPIRITS.

09
SHOKOLA'S SECRET

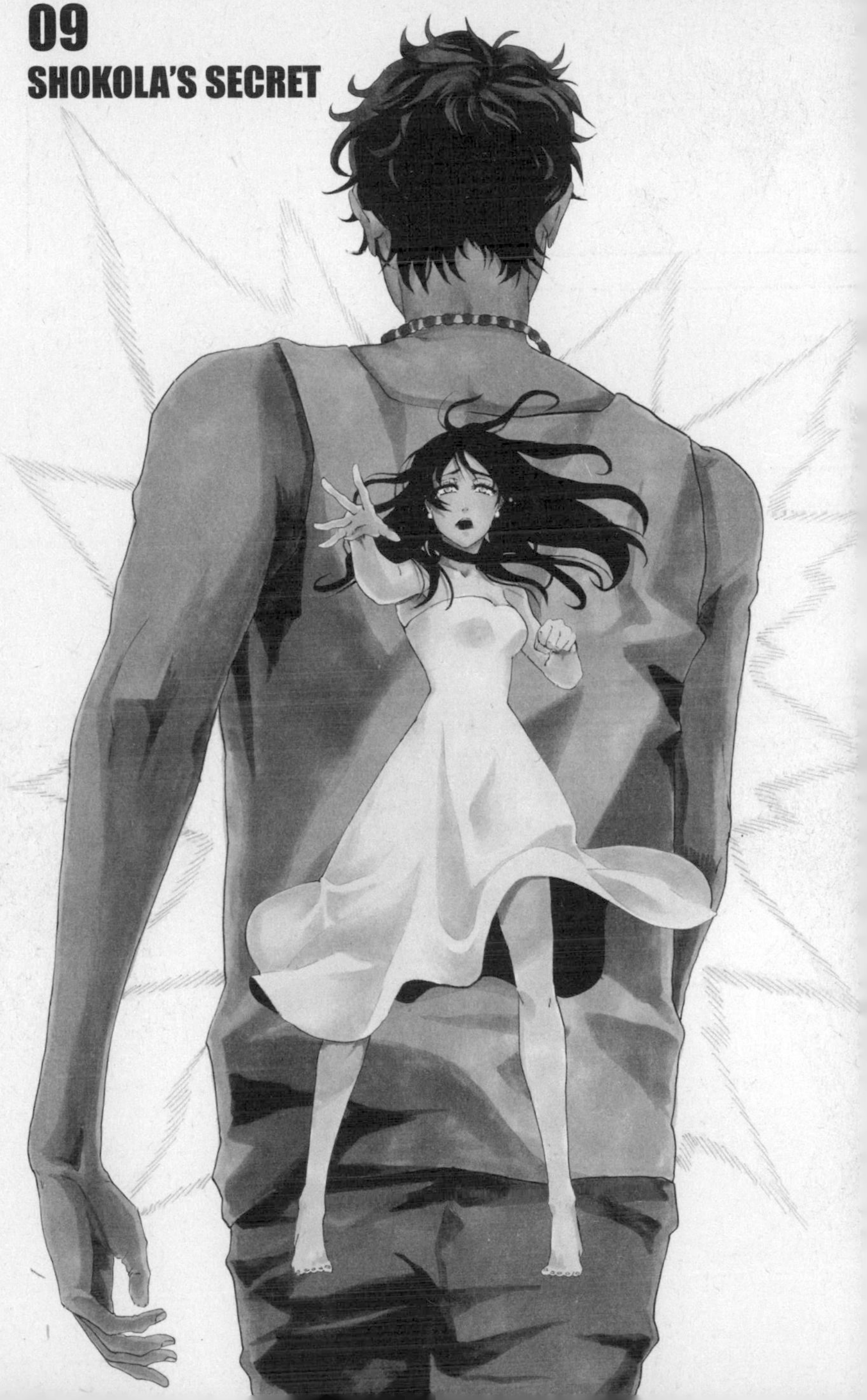

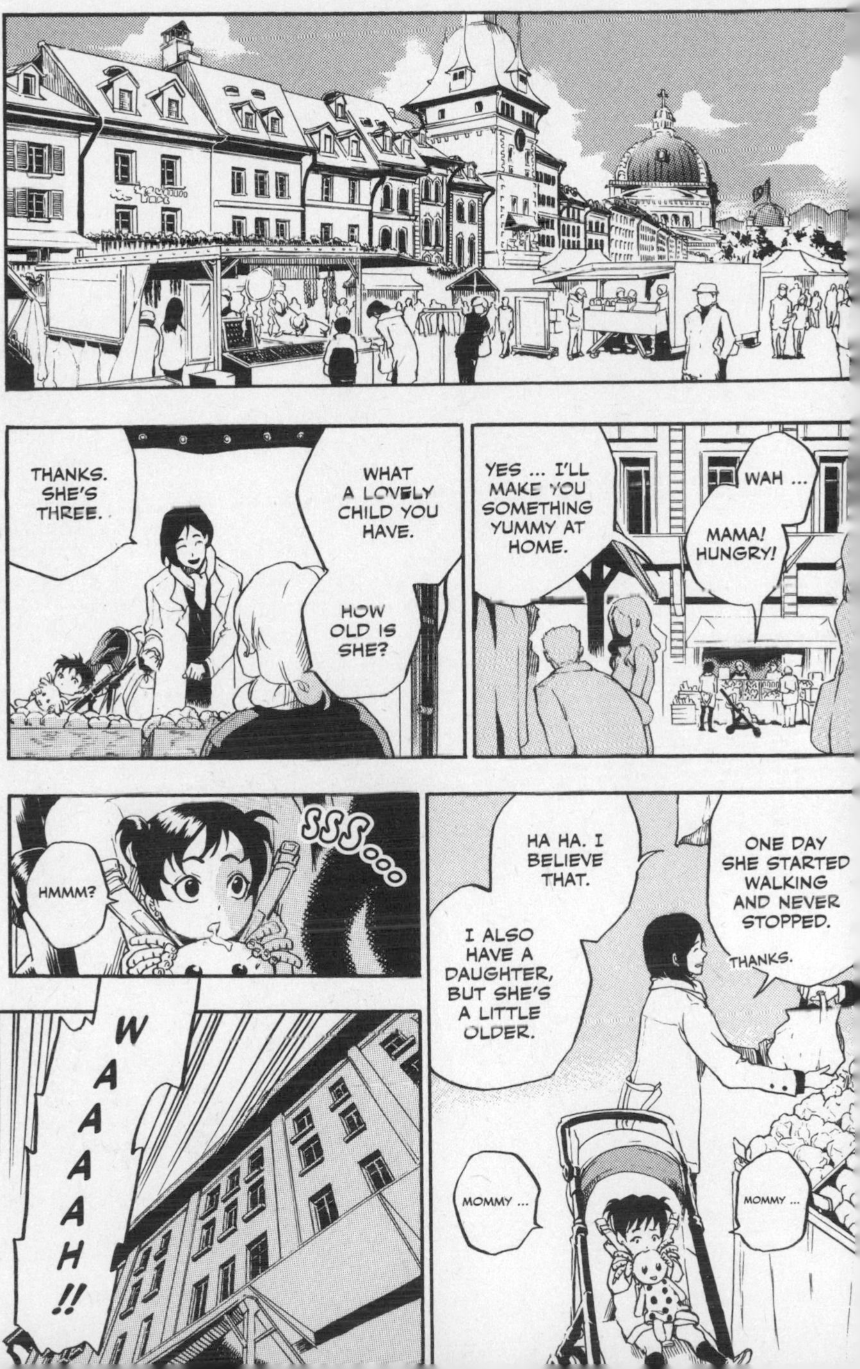
WAH ...
MAMA! HUNGRY!
YES ... I'LL MAKE YOU SOMETHING YUMMY AT HOME.
WHAT A LOVELY CHILD YOU HAVE.
HOW OLD IS SHE?
THANKS. SHE'S THREE.
ONE DAY SHE STARTED WALKING AND NEVER STOPPED.
HA HA. I BELIEVE THAT.
I ALSO HAVE A DAUGHTER, BUT SHE'S A LITTLE OLDER.
THANKS.
MOMMY ...
MOMMY ...
SSSooo
HMMM?
WAAAAAH!!

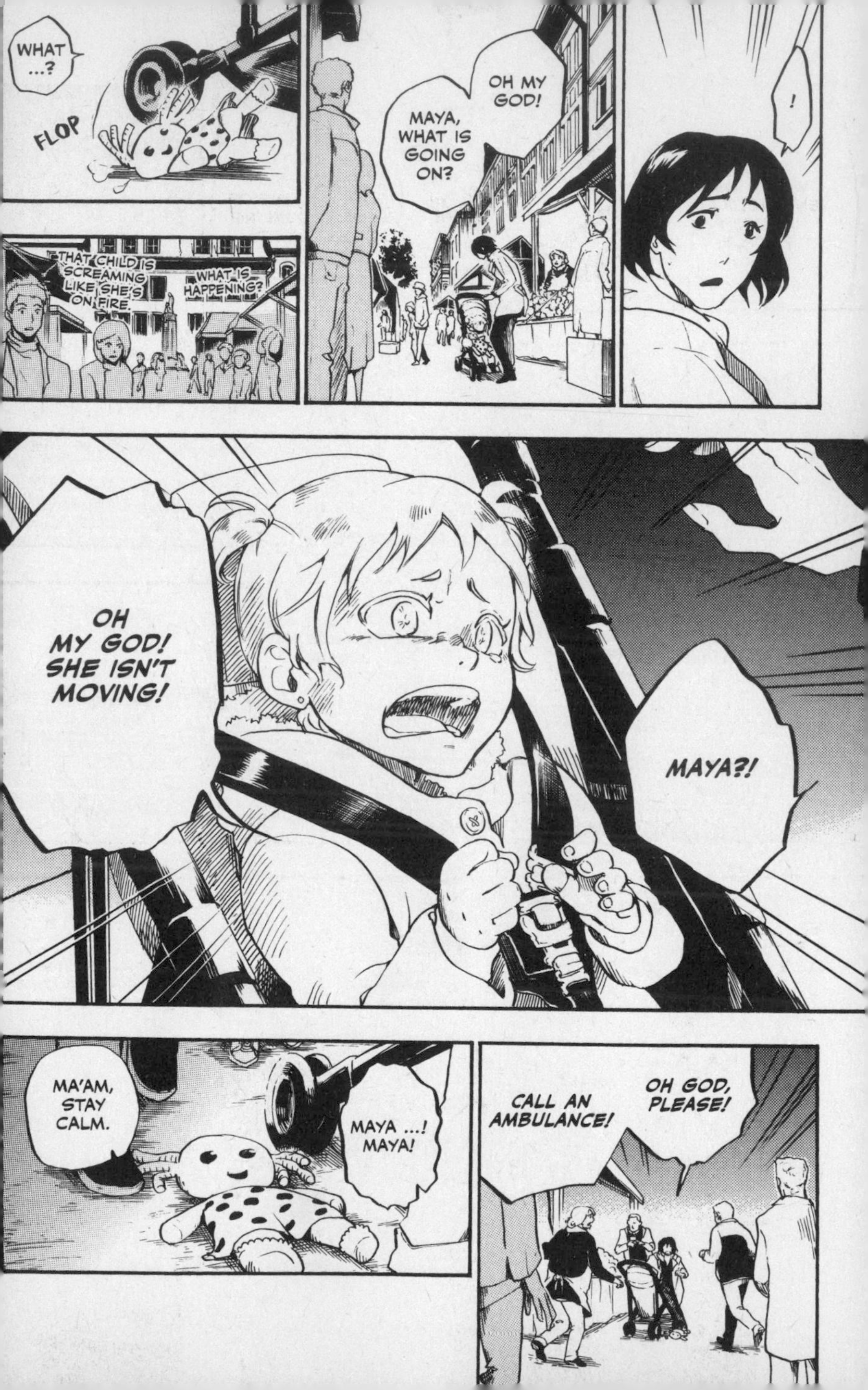
!
OH MY GOD!
MAYA, WHAT IS GOING ON?
WHAT ...?
FLOP
WHAT IS HAPPENING?
THAT CHILD IS SCREAMING LIKE SHE'S ON FIRE.
MAYA?!
OH MY GOD! SHE ISN'T MOVING!
OH GOD, PLEASE!
CALL AN AMBULANCE!
MAYA ...! MAYA!
MA'AM, STAY CALM.

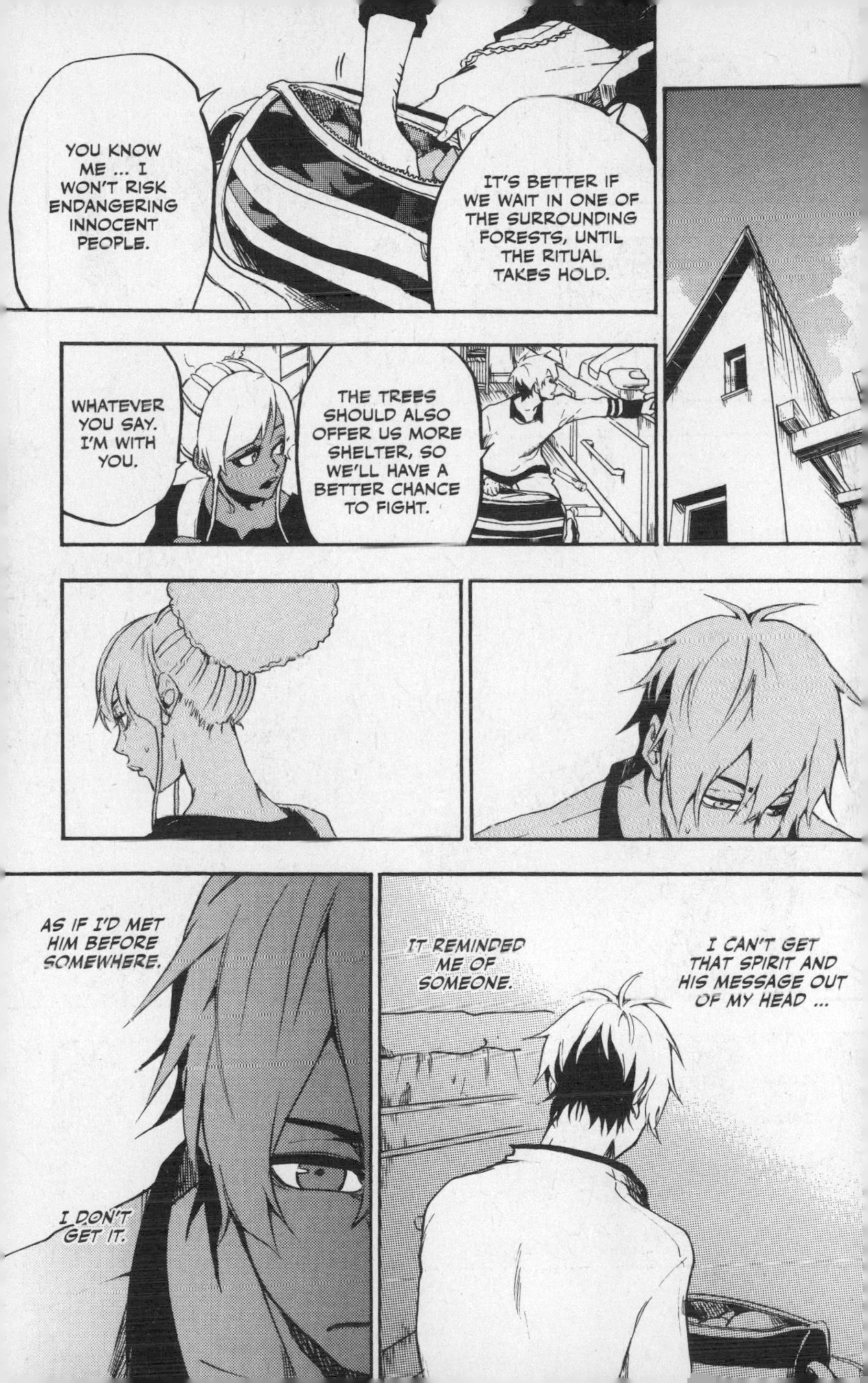
YOU KNOW ME ... I WON'T RISK ENDANGERING INNOCENT PEOPLE.
IT'S BETTER IF WE WAIT IN ONE OF THE SURROUNDING FORESTS, UNTIL THE RITUAL TAKES HOLD.
THE TREES SHOULD ALSO OFFER US MORE SHELTER, SO WE'LL HAVE A BETTER CHANCE TO FIGHT.
WHATEVER YOU SAY. I'M WITH YOU.
I CAN'T GET THAT SPIRIT AND HIS MESSAGE OUT OF MY HEAD ...
IT REMINDED ME OF SOMEONE.
AS IF I'D MET HIM BEFORE SOMEWHERE.
I DON'T GET IT.

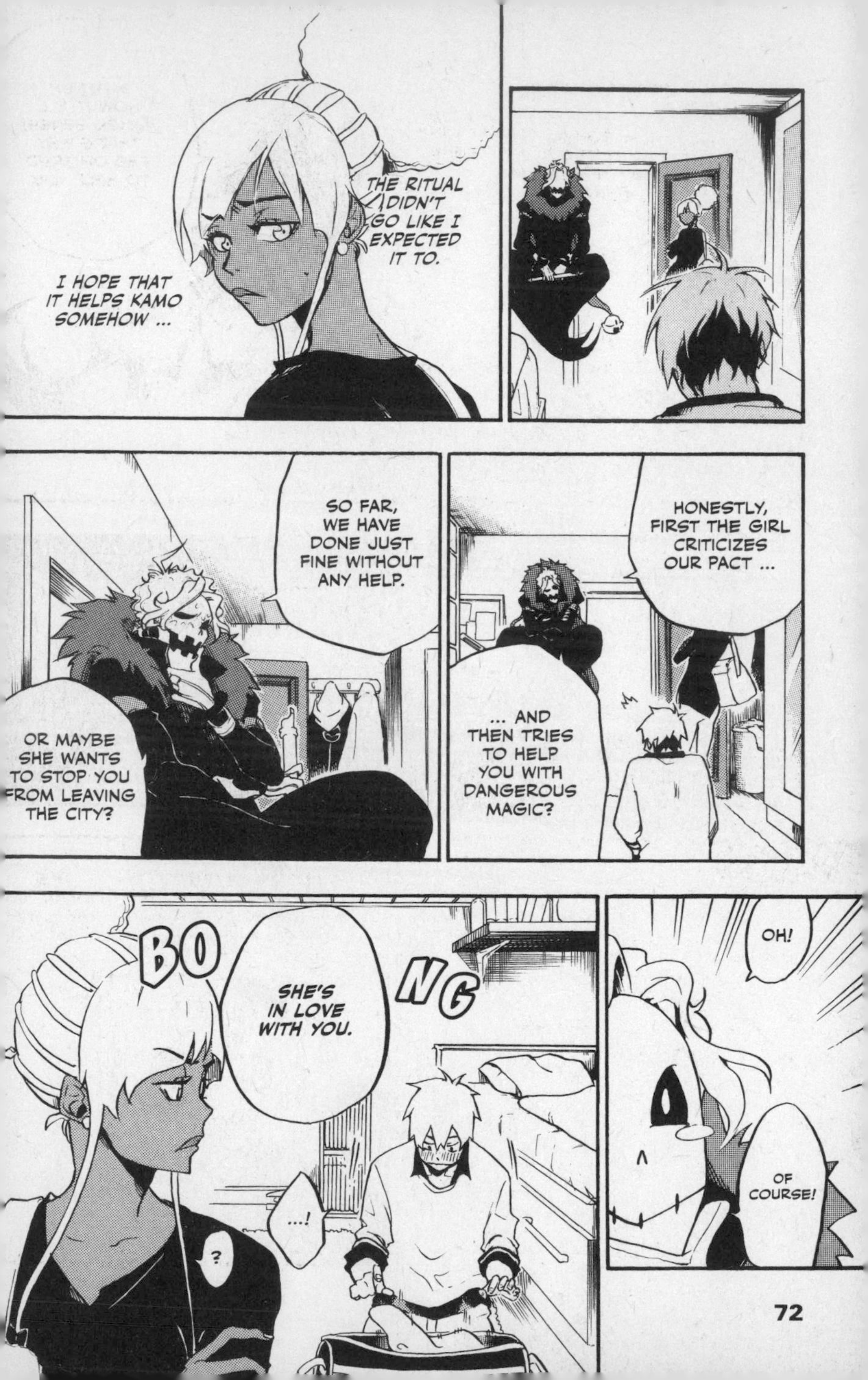
THE RITUAL DIDN'T GO LIKE I EXPECTED IT TO.
I HOPE THAT IT HELPS KAMO SOMEHOW ...
HONESTLY, FIRST THE GIRL CRITICIZES OUR PACT ...
... AND THEN TRIES TO HELP YOU WITH DANGEROUS MAGIC?
SO FAR, WE HAVE DONE JUST FINE WITHOUT ANY HELP.
OR MAYBE SHE WANTS TO STOP YOU FROM LEAVING THE CITY?
OH!
OF COURSE!
BONG
SHE'S IN LOVE WITH YOU.
...!
?

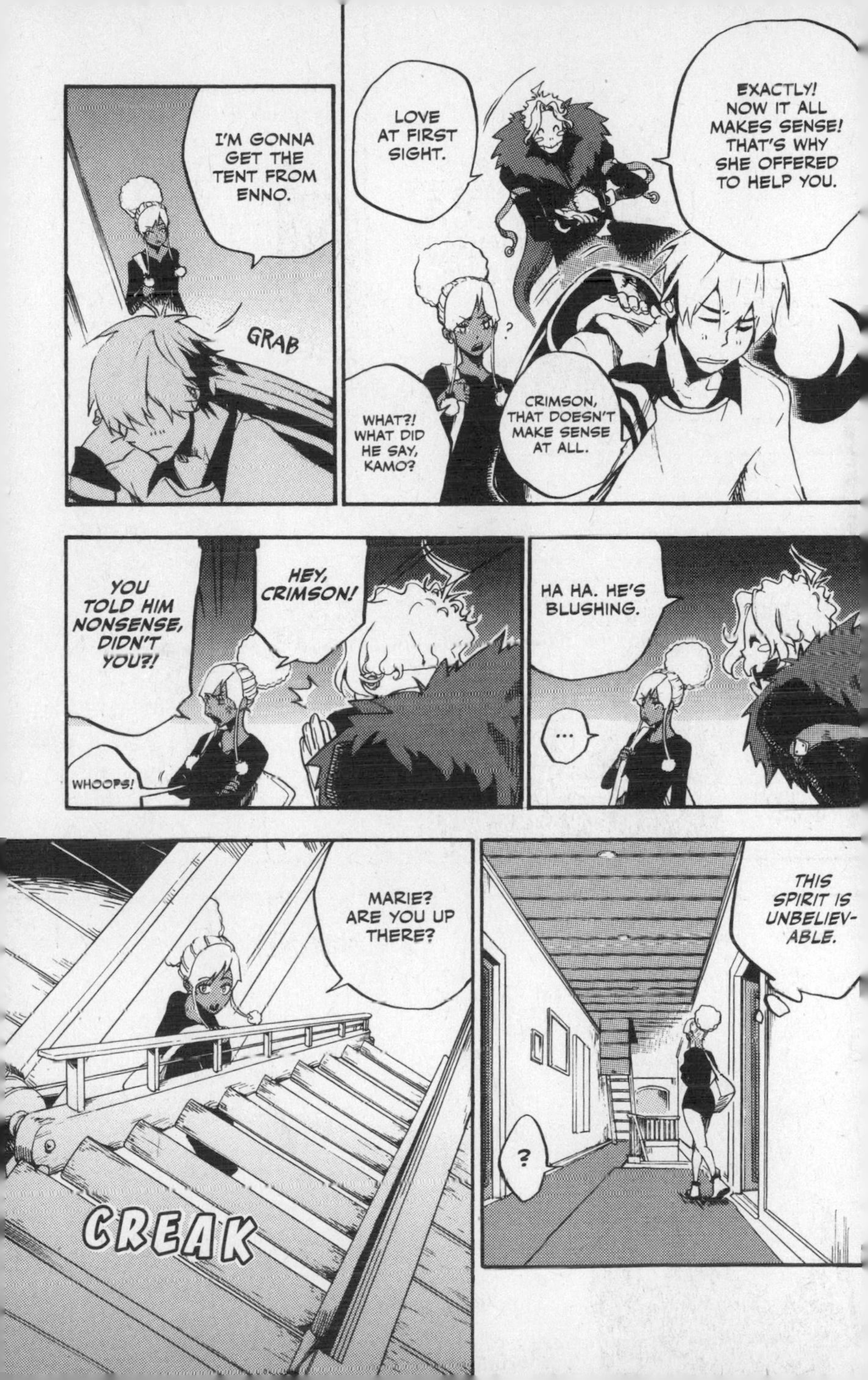
LOVE AT FIRST SIGHT.
EXACTLY! NOW IT ALL MAKES SENSE! THAT'S WHY SHE OFFERED TO HELP YOU.
WHAT?! WHAT DID HE SAY, KAMO?
CRIMSON, THAT DOESN'T MAKE SENSE AT ALL.
I'M GONNA GET THE TENT FROM ENNO.
GRAB
HA HA. HE'S BLUSHING.
...
HEY, CRIMSON!
YOU TOLD HIM NONSENSE, DIDN'T YOU?!
WHOOPS!
THIS SPIRIT IS UNBELIEV-ABLE.
?
MARIE? ARE YOU UP THERE?
CREAK

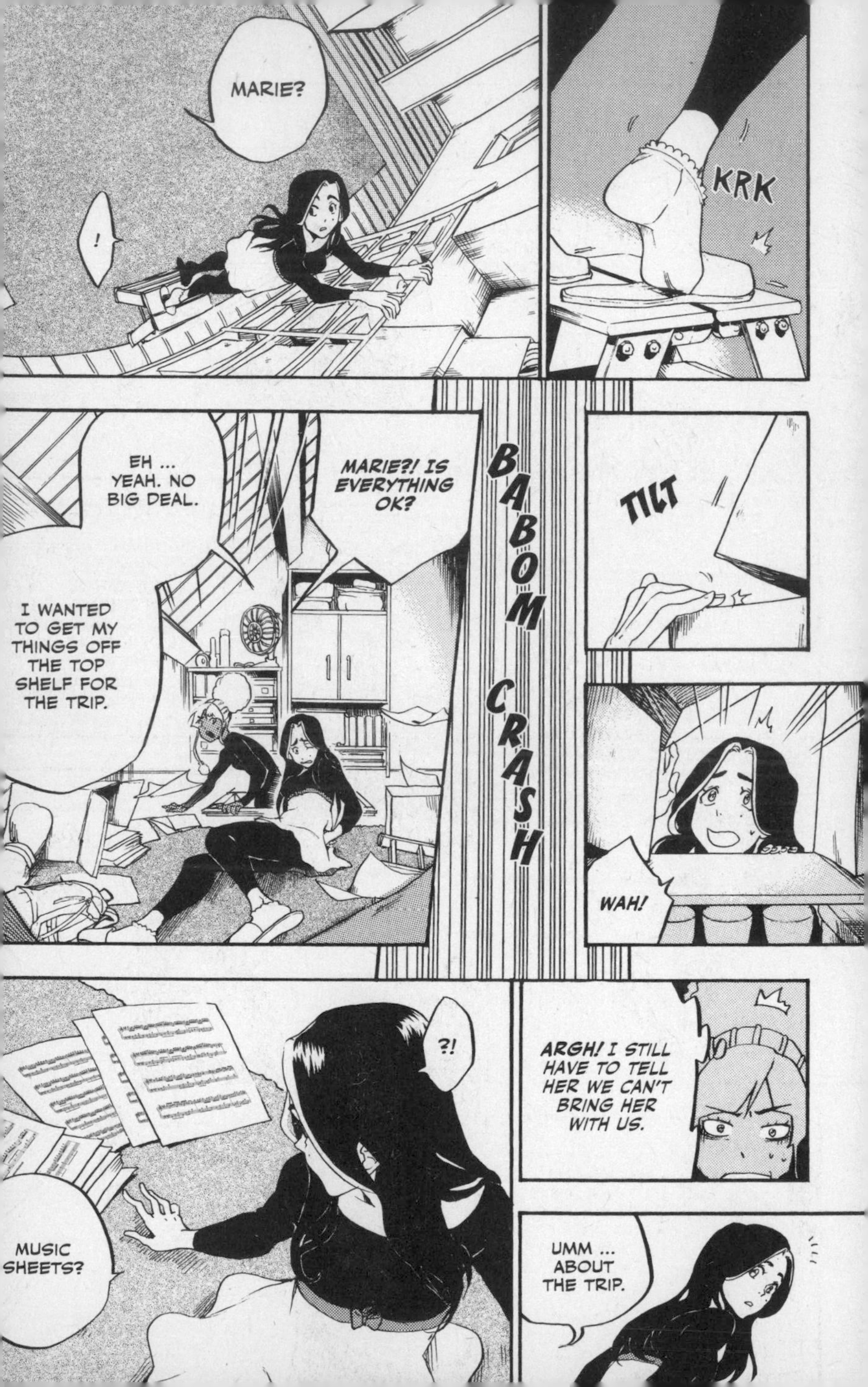
KRK
MARIE?
!
TILT
WAH!
BABOM
CRASH
MARIE?! IS EVERYTHING OK?
EH ... YEAH. NO BIG DEAL.
I WANTED TO GET MY THINGS OFF THE TOP SHELF FOR THE TRIP.
ARGH! I STILL HAVE TO TELL HER WE CAN'T BRING HER WITH US.
UMM ... ABOUT THE TRIP.
?!
MUSIC SHEETS?

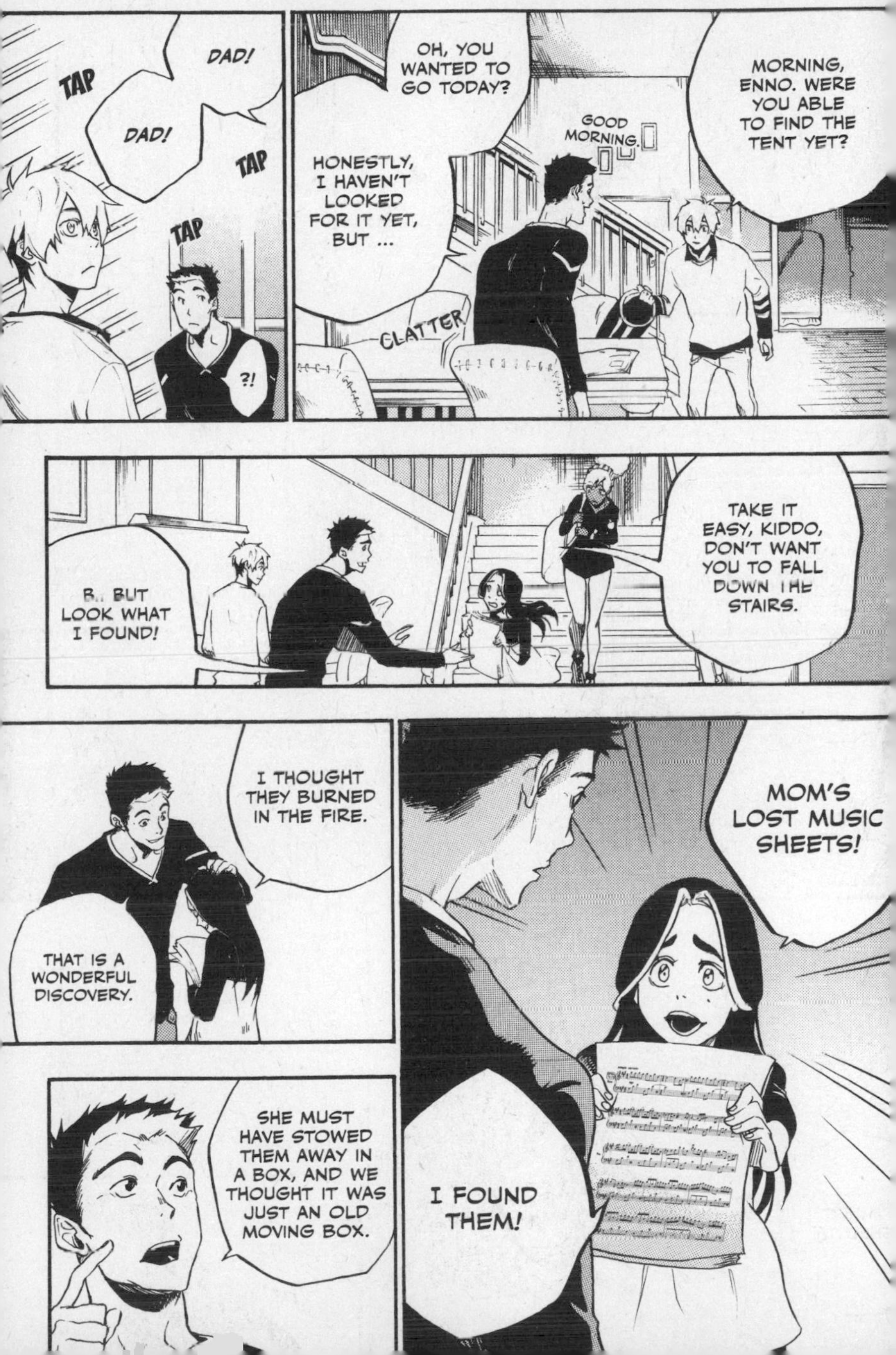
MORNING, ENNO. WERE YOU ABLE TO FIND THE TENT YET?
GOOD MORNING.
OH, YOU WANTED TO GO TODAY?
HONESTLY, I HAVEN'T LOOKED FOR IT YET, BUT ...
CLATTER
DAD!
TAP
DAD!
TAP
TAP
?!
TAKE IT EASY, KIDDO, DON'T WANT YOU TO FALL DOWN THE STAIRS.
B.. BUT LOOK WHAT I FOUND!
MOM'S LOST MUSIC SHEETS!
I FOUND THEM!
I THOUGHT THEY BURNED IN THE FIRE.
THAT IS A WONDERFUL DISCOVERY.
SHE MUST HAVE STOWED THEM AWAY IN A BOX, AND WE THOUGHT IT WAS JUST AN OLD MOVING BOX.

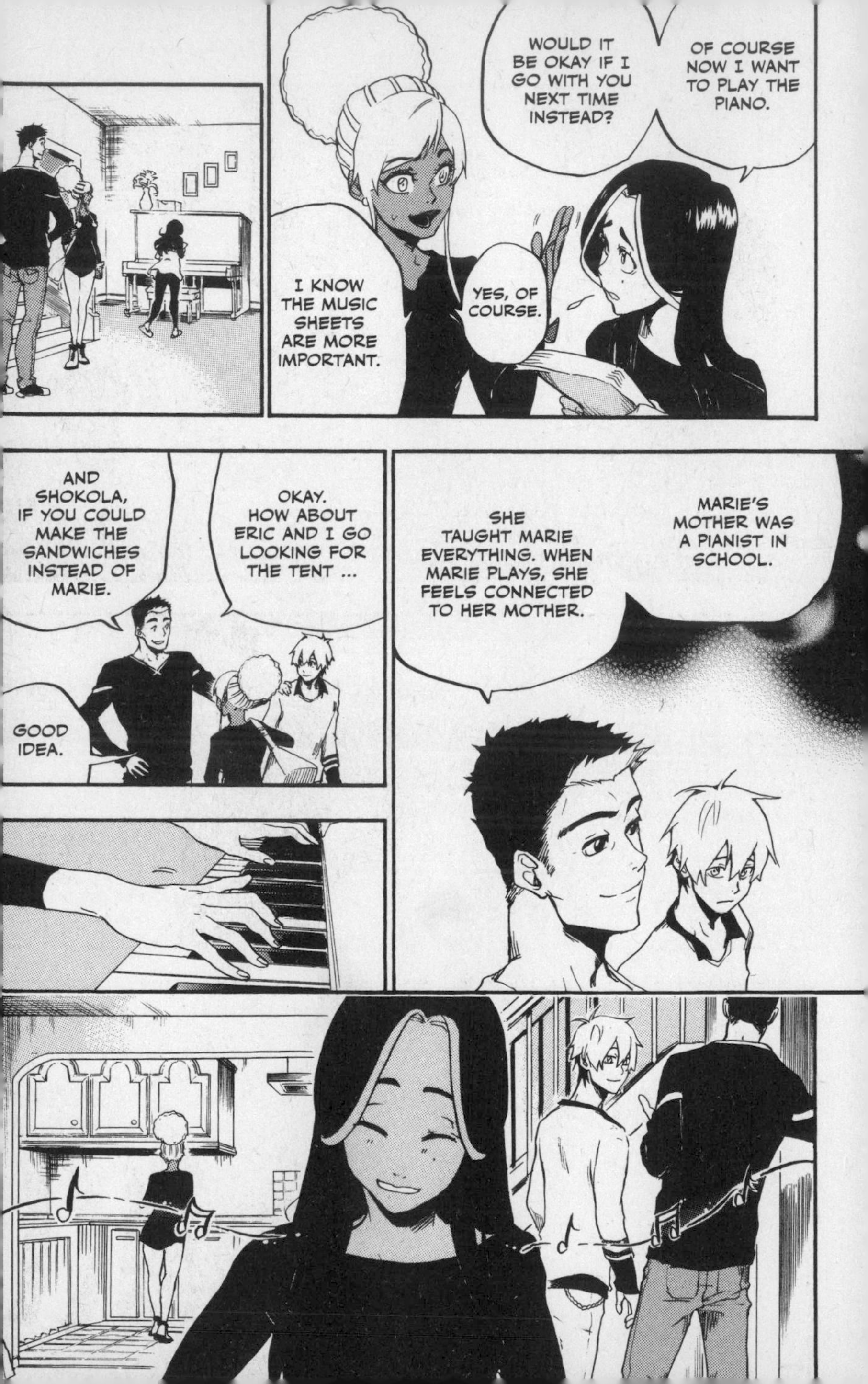
OF COURSE NOW I WANT TO PLAY THE PIANO.
WOULD IT BE OKAY IF I GO WITH YOU NEXT TIME INSTEAD?
YES, OF COURSE.
I KNOW THE MUSIC SHEETS ARE MORE IMPORTANT.
MARIE'S MOTHER WAS A PIANIST IN SCHOOL.
SHE TAUGHT MARIE EVERYTHING. WHEN MARIE PLAYS, SHE FEELS CONNECTED TO HER MOTHER.
OKAY. HOW ABOUT ERIC AND I GO LOOKING FOR THE TENT ...
AND SHOKOLA, IF YOU COULD MAKE THE SANDWICHES INSTEAD OF MARIE.
GOOD IDEA.

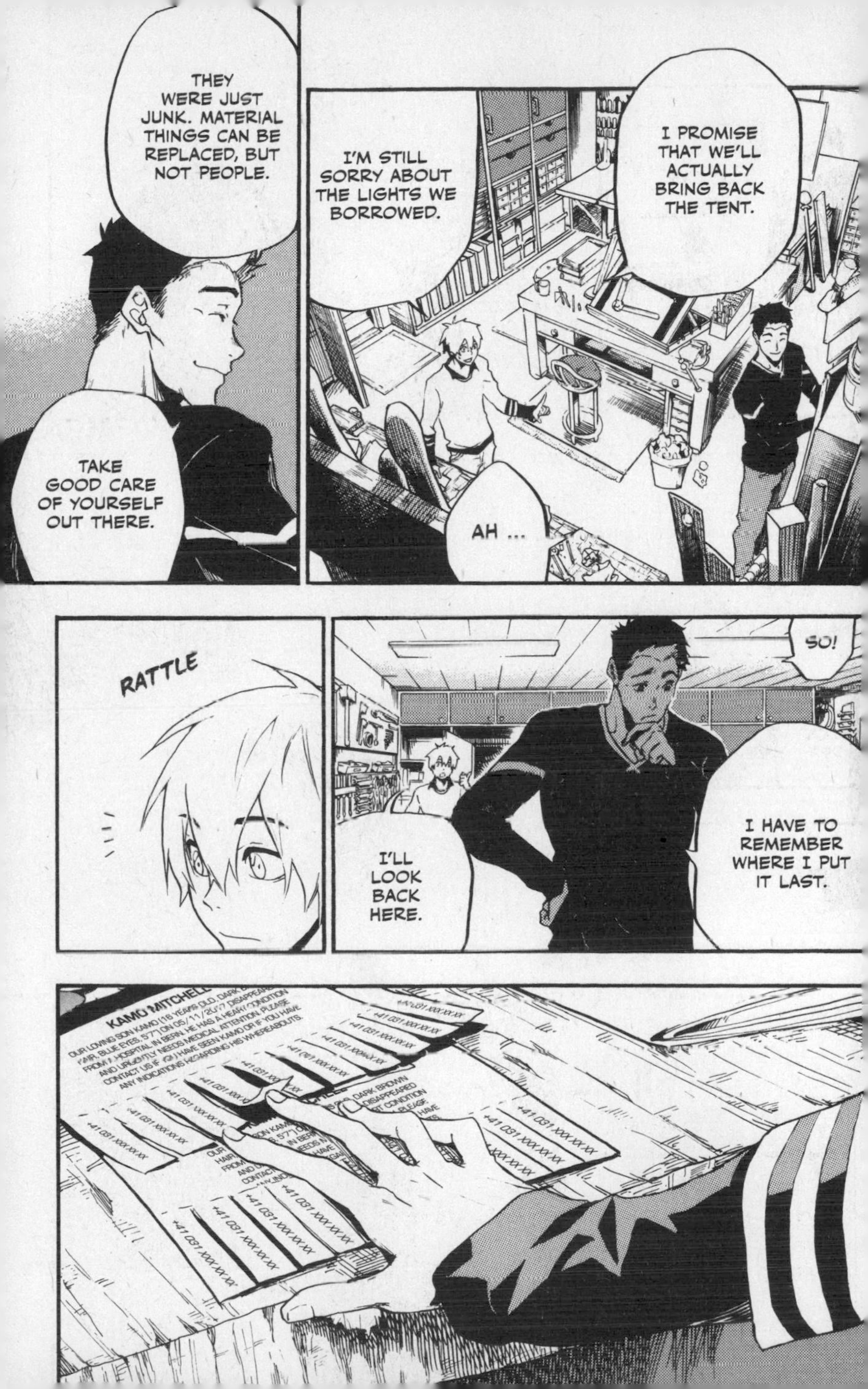
I'M STILL SORRY ABOUT THE LIGHTS WE BORROWED.
I PROMISE THAT WE'LL ACTUALLY BRING BACK THE TENT.
AH ...
THEY WERE JUST JUNK. MATERIAL THINGS CAN BE REPLACED, BUT NOT PEOPLE.
TAKE GOOD CARE OF YOURSELF OUT THERE.
SO!
I HAVE TO REMEMBER WHERE I PUT IT LAST.
I'LL LOOK BACK HERE.
RATTLE
KAMO MITCHELL
OUR LOVING SON KAMO (16 YEARS OLD, DARK
HAIR, BLUE EYES, 5'7") ON 05/11/2017 DISAPPEARED
FROM A HOSPITAL IN BERN. HE HAS A HEART CONDITION
AND URGENTLY NEEDS MEDICAL ATTENTION. PLEASE
CONTACT US IF YOU HAVE SEEN KAMO OR IF YOU HAVE
ANY INDICATIONS REGARDING HIS WHEREABOUTS.
+41 031 XXX XX XX

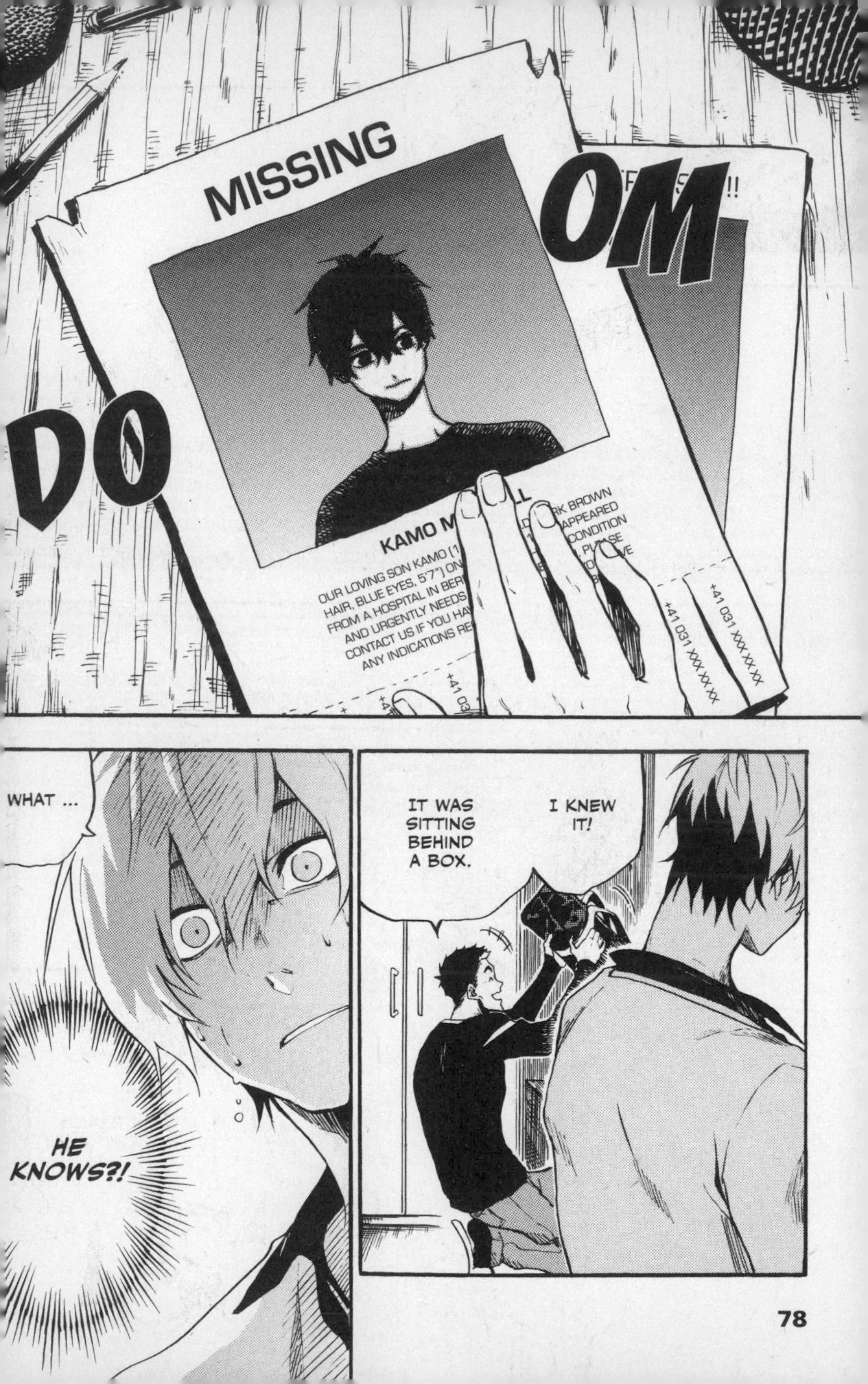
MISSING
DO
OM
I KNEW IT!
IT WAS SITTING BEHIND A BOX.
WHAT ...
HE KNOWS?!

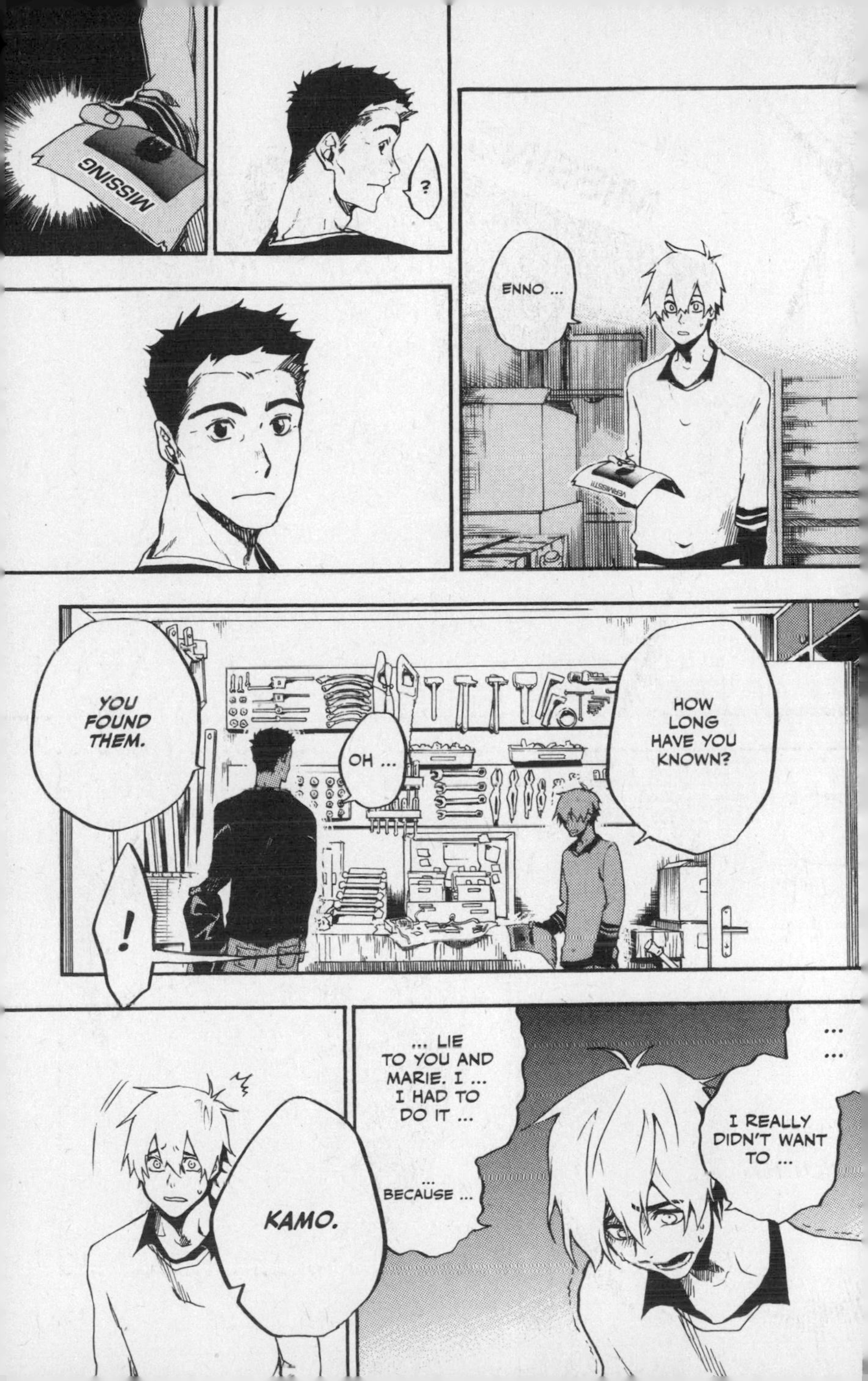
ENNO ...
VERMISST!
?
MISSING
HOW LONG HAVE YOU KNOWN?
OH ...
YOU FOUND THEM.
!
... ...
I REALLY DIDN'T WANT TO ...
... LIE TO YOU AND MARIE. I ... I HAD TO DO IT ...
... BECAUSE ...
KAMO.

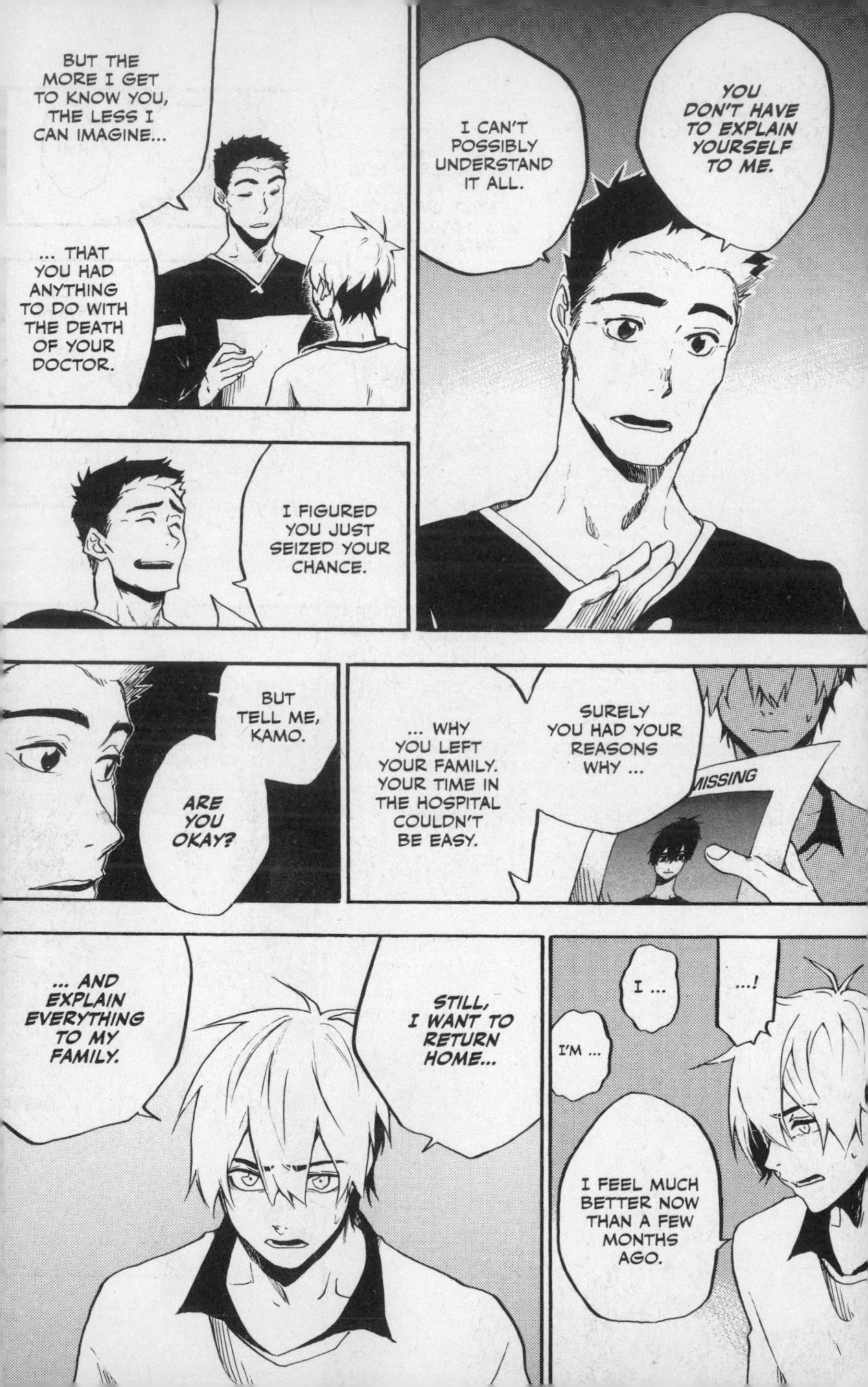
YOU DON'T HAVE TO EXPLAIN YOURSELF TO ME.
I CAN'T POSSIBLY UNDERSTAND IT ALL.
BUT THE MORE I GET TO KNOW YOU, THE LESS I CAN IMAGINE...
... THAT YOU HAD ANYTHING TO DO WITH THE DEATH OF YOUR DOCTOR.
I FIGURED YOU JUST SEIZED YOUR CHANCE.
MISSING
SURELY YOU HAD YOUR REASONS WHY ...
... WHY YOU LEFT YOUR FAMILY. YOUR TIME IN THE HOSPITAL COULDN'T BE EASY.
BUT TELL ME, KAMO.
ARE YOU OKAY?
...!
I ...
I'M ...
I FEEL MUCH BETTER NOW THAN A FEW MONTHS AGO.
STILL, I WANT TO RETURN HOME...
... AND EXPLAIN EVERYTHING TO MY FAMILY.

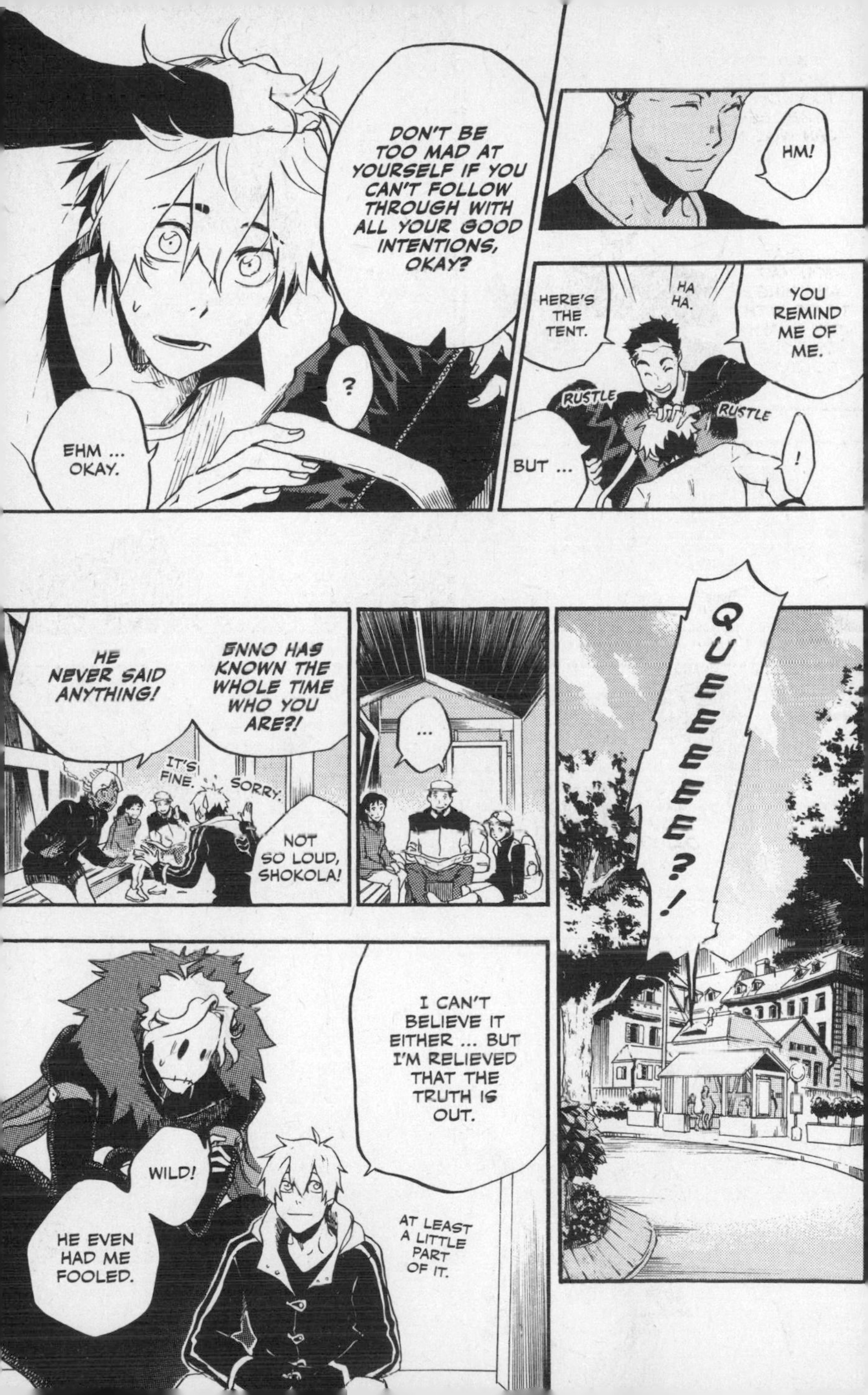
HM!
HA HA.
YOU REMIND ME OF ME.
HERE'S THE TENT.
RUSTLE
RUSTLE
!
BUT ...
DON'T BE TOO MAD AT YOURSELF IF YOU CAN'T FOLLOW THROUGH WITH ALL YOUR GOOD INTENTIONS, OKAY?
?
EHM ... OKAY.
QUEEEEEE?!
...
ENNO HAS KNOWN THE WHOLE TIME WHO YOU ARE?!
HE NEVER SAID ANYTHING!
NOT SO LOUD, SHOKOLA!
SORRY.
IT'S FINE.
I CAN'T BELIEVE IT EITHER ... BUT I'M RELIEVED THAT THE TRUTH IS OUT.
AT LEAST A LITTLE PART OF IT.
WILD!
HE EVEN HAD ME FOOLED.

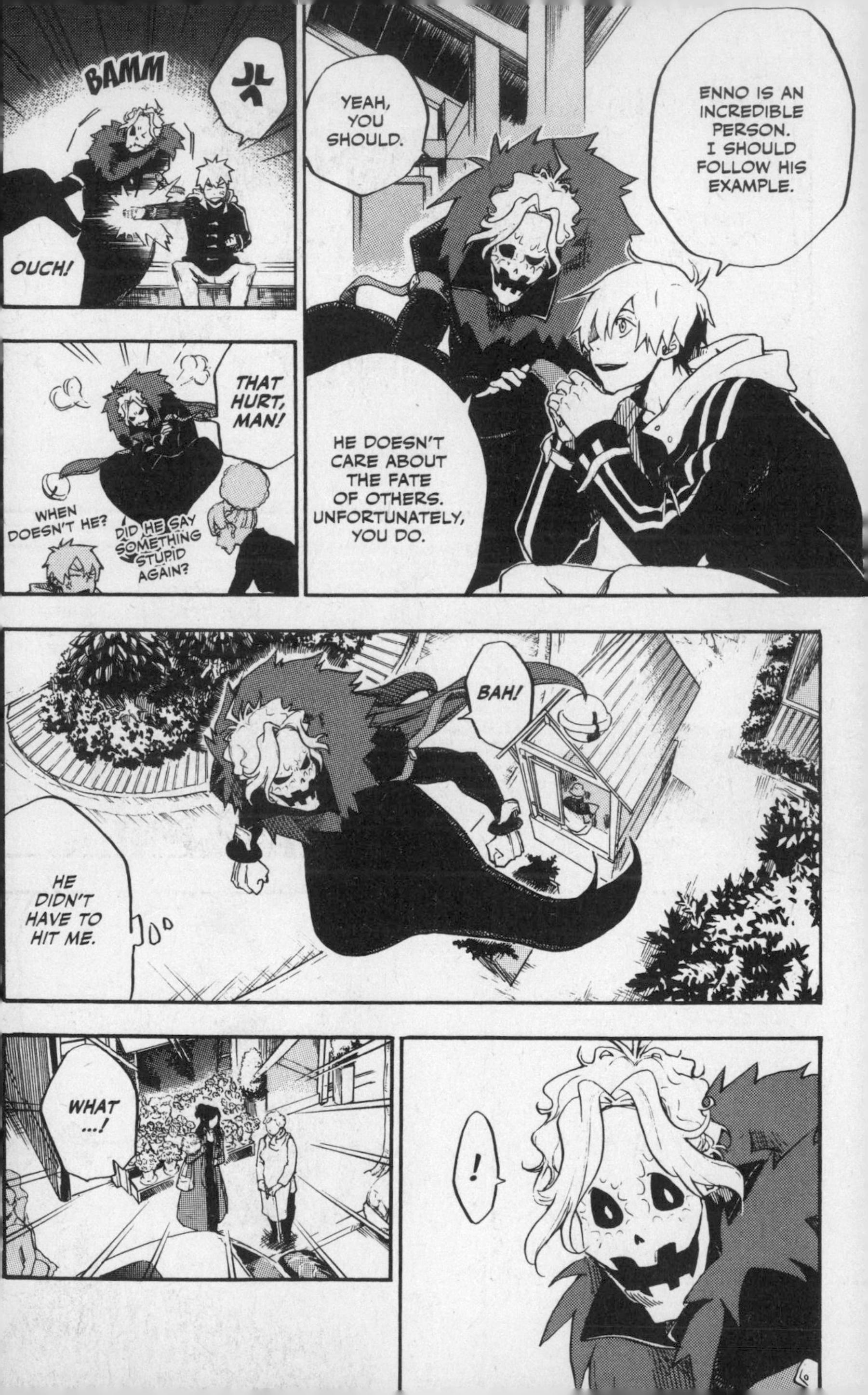
ENNO IS AN INCREDIBLE PERSON. I SHOULD FOLLOW HIS EXAMPLE.
YEAH, YOU SHOULD.
HE DOESN'T CARE ABOUT THE FATE OF OTHERS. UNFORTUNATELY, YOU DO.
BAMM
OUCH!
THAT HURT, MAN!
DID HE SAY SOMETHING STUPID AGAIN?
WHEN DOESN'T HE?
BAH!
HE DIDN'T HAVE TO HIT ME.
!
WHAT ...!

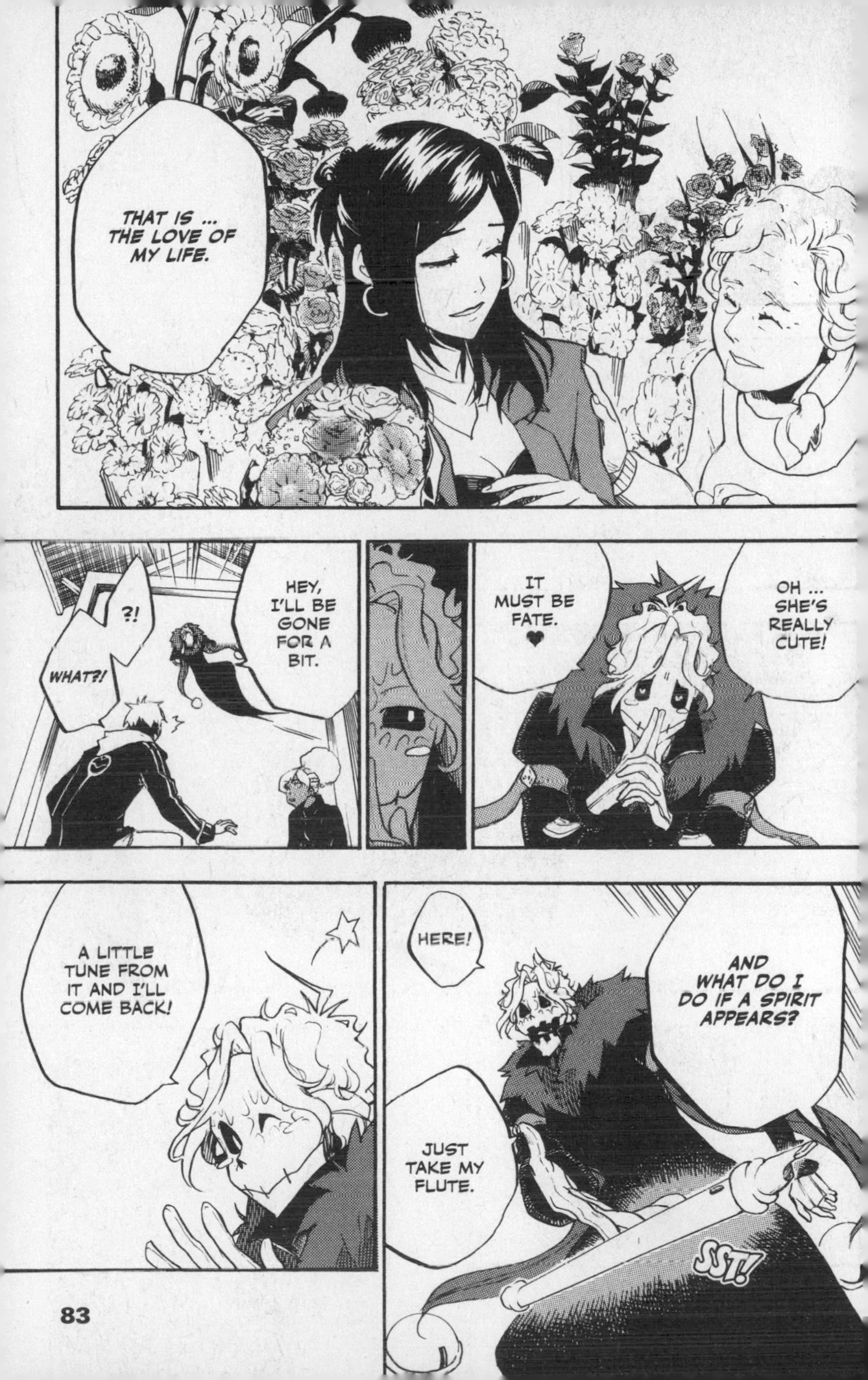
THAT IS ... THE LOVE OF MY LIFE.
OH ... SHE'S REALLY CUTE!
IT MUST BE FATE. ♥
HEY, I'LL BE GONE FOR A BIT.
?!
WHAT?!
AND WHAT DO I DO IF A SPIRIT APPEARS?
HERE!
JUST TAKE MY FLUTE.
SST!
A LITTLE TUNE FROM IT AND I'LL COME BACK!

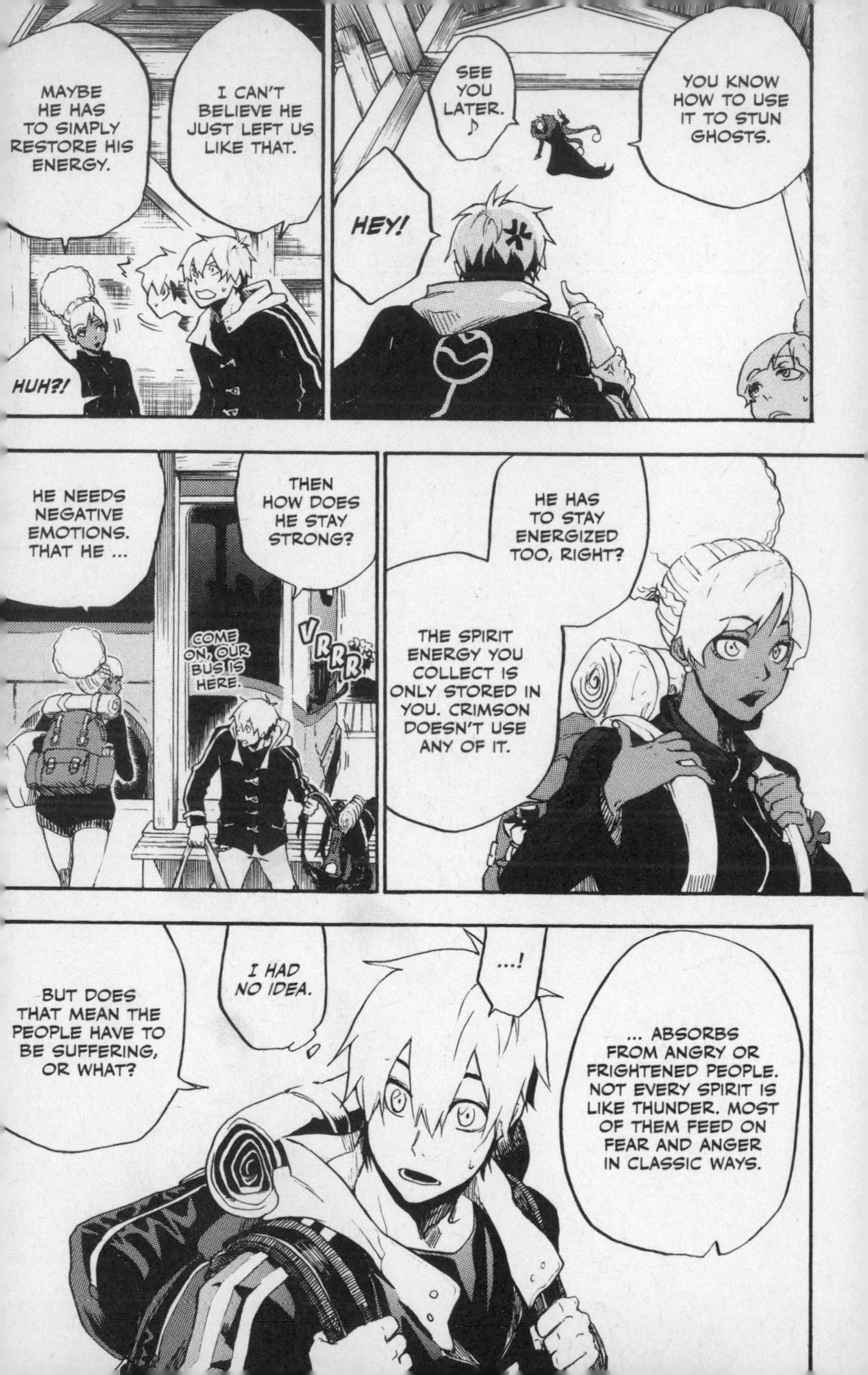
YOU KNOW HOW TO USE IT TO STUN GHOSTS.
SEE YOU LATER. ♪
HEY!
I CAN'T BELIEVE HE JUST LEFT US LIKE THAT.
MAYBE HE HAS TO SIMPLY RESTORE HIS ENERGY.
HUH?!
HE HAS TO STAY ENERGIZED TOO, RIGHT?
THE SPIRIT ENERGY YOU COLLECT IS ONLY STORED IN YOU. CRIMSON DOESN'T USE ANY OF IT.
THEN HOW DOES HE STAY STRONG?
HE NEEDS NEGATIVE EMOTIONS. THAT HE ...
VRRR
COME ON, OUR BUS IS HERE.
... ABSORBS FROM ANGRY OR FRIGHTENED PEOPLE. NOT EVERY SPIRIT IS LIKE THUNDER. MOST OF THEM FEED ON FEAR AND ANGER IN CLASSIC WAYS.
...!
I HAD NO IDEA.
BUT DOES THAT MEAN THE PEOPLE HAVE TO BE SUFFERING, OR WHAT?

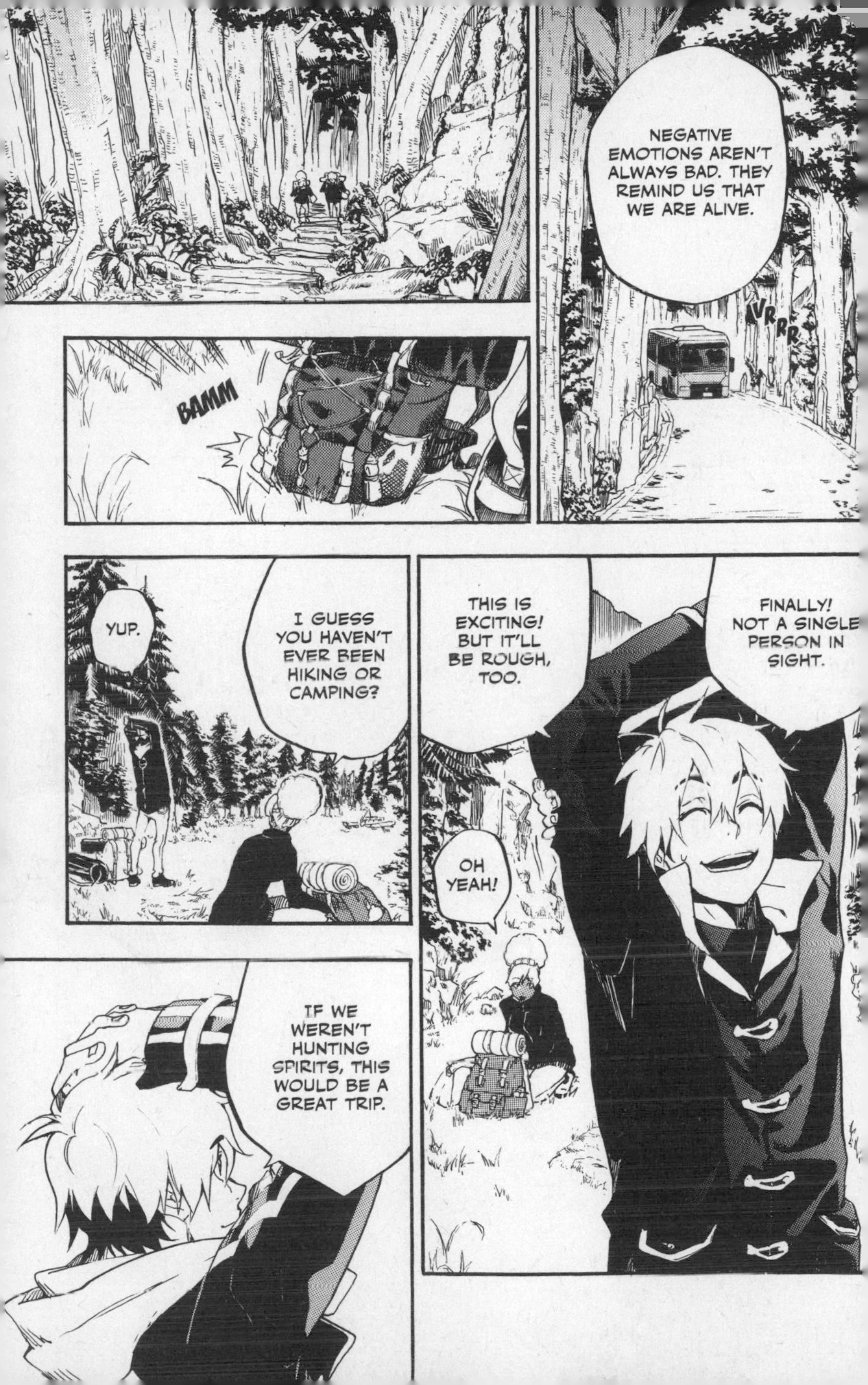
NEGATIVE EMOTIONS AREN'T ALWAYS BAD. THEY REMIND US THAT WE ARE ALIVE.
VRRR
BAMM
FINALLY! NOT A SINGLE PERSON IN SIGHT.
THIS IS EXCITING! BUT IT'LL BE ROUGH, TOO.
OH YEAH!
I GUESS YOU HAVEN'T EVER BEEN HIKING OR CAMPING?
YUP.
IF WE WEREN'T HUNTING SPIRITS, THIS WOULD BE A GREAT TRIP.

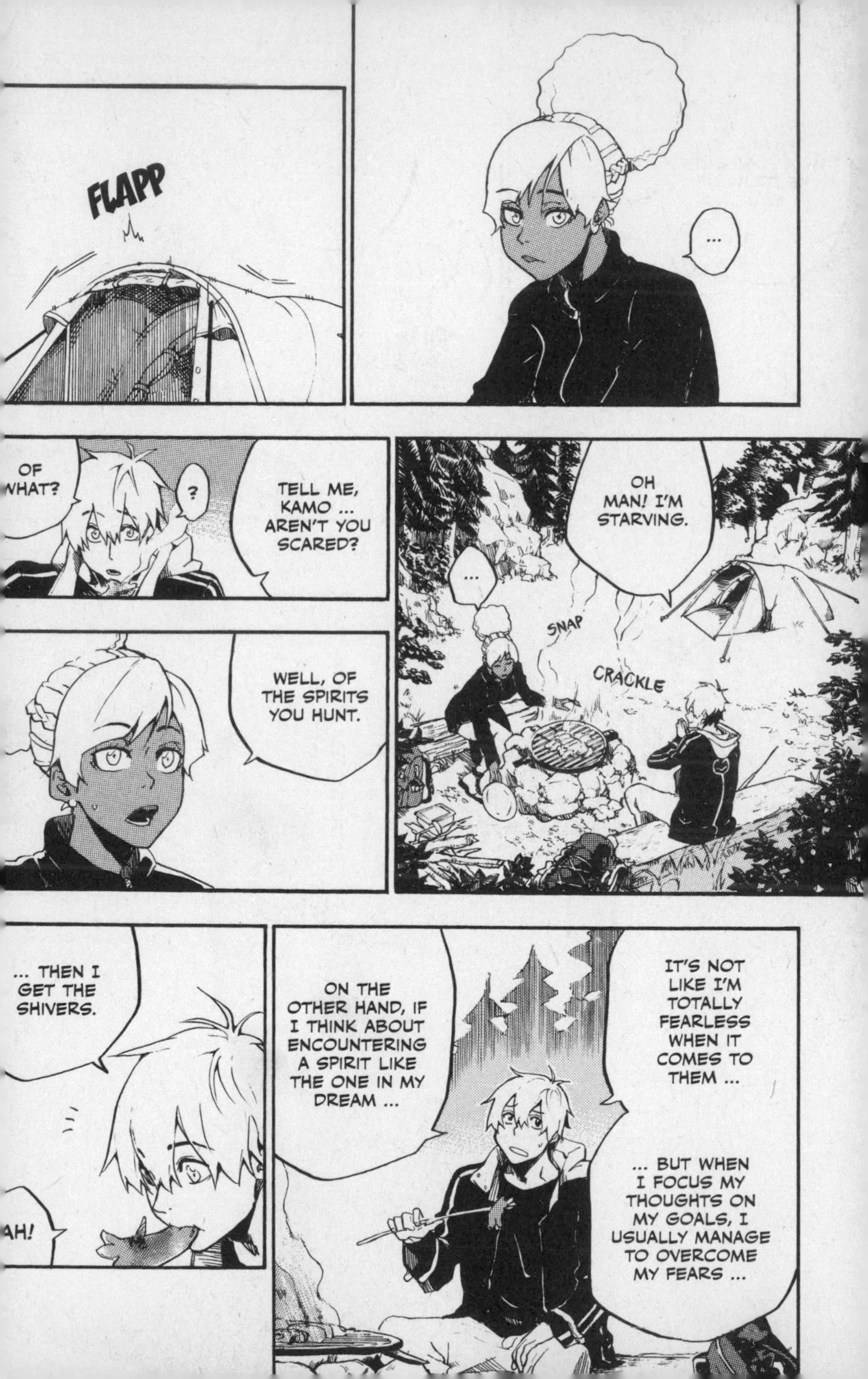
...
FLAPP
OH MAN! I'M STARVING.
...
SNAP
CRACKLE
TELL ME, KAMO ... AREN'T YOU SCARED?
?
OF WHAT?
WELL, OF THE SPIRITS YOU HUNT.
IT'S NOT LIKE I'M TOTALLY FEARLESS WHEN IT COMES TO THEM ...
... BUT WHEN I FOCUS MY THOUGHTS ON MY GOALS, I USUALLY MANAGE TO OVERCOME MY FEARS ...
ON THE OTHER HAND, IF I THINK ABOUT ENCOUNTERING A SPIRIT LIKE THE ONE IN MY DREAM ...
... THEN I GET THE SHIVERS.
AH!

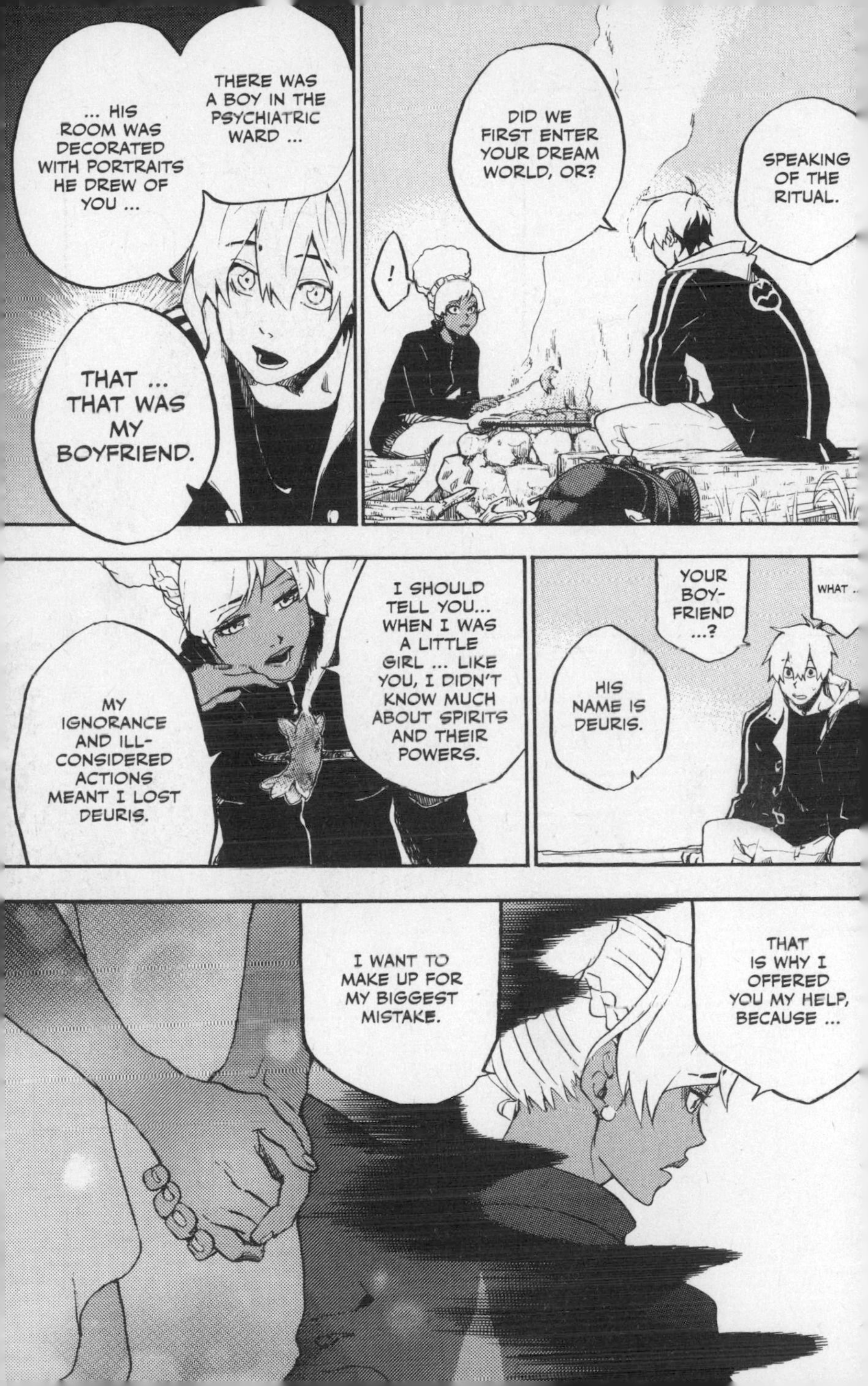
SPEAKING OF THE RITUAL.
DID WE FIRST ENTER YOUR DREAM WORLD, OR?
!
THERE WAS A BOY IN THE PSYCHIATRIC WARD ...
... HIS ROOM WAS DECORATED WITH PORTRAITS HE DREW OF YOU ...
THAT ... THAT WAS MY BOYFRIEND.
WHAT ...
YOUR BOY-FRIEND ...?
HIS NAME IS DEURIS.
I SHOULD TELL YOU... WHEN I WAS A LITTLE GIRL ... LIKE YOU, I DIDN'T KNOW MUCH ABOUT SPIRITS AND THEIR POWERS.
MY IGNORANCE AND ILL-CONSIDERED ACTIONS MEANT I LOST DEURIS.
THAT IS WHY I OFFERED YOU MY HELP, BECAUSE ...
I WANT TO MAKE UP FOR MY BIGGEST MISTAKE.

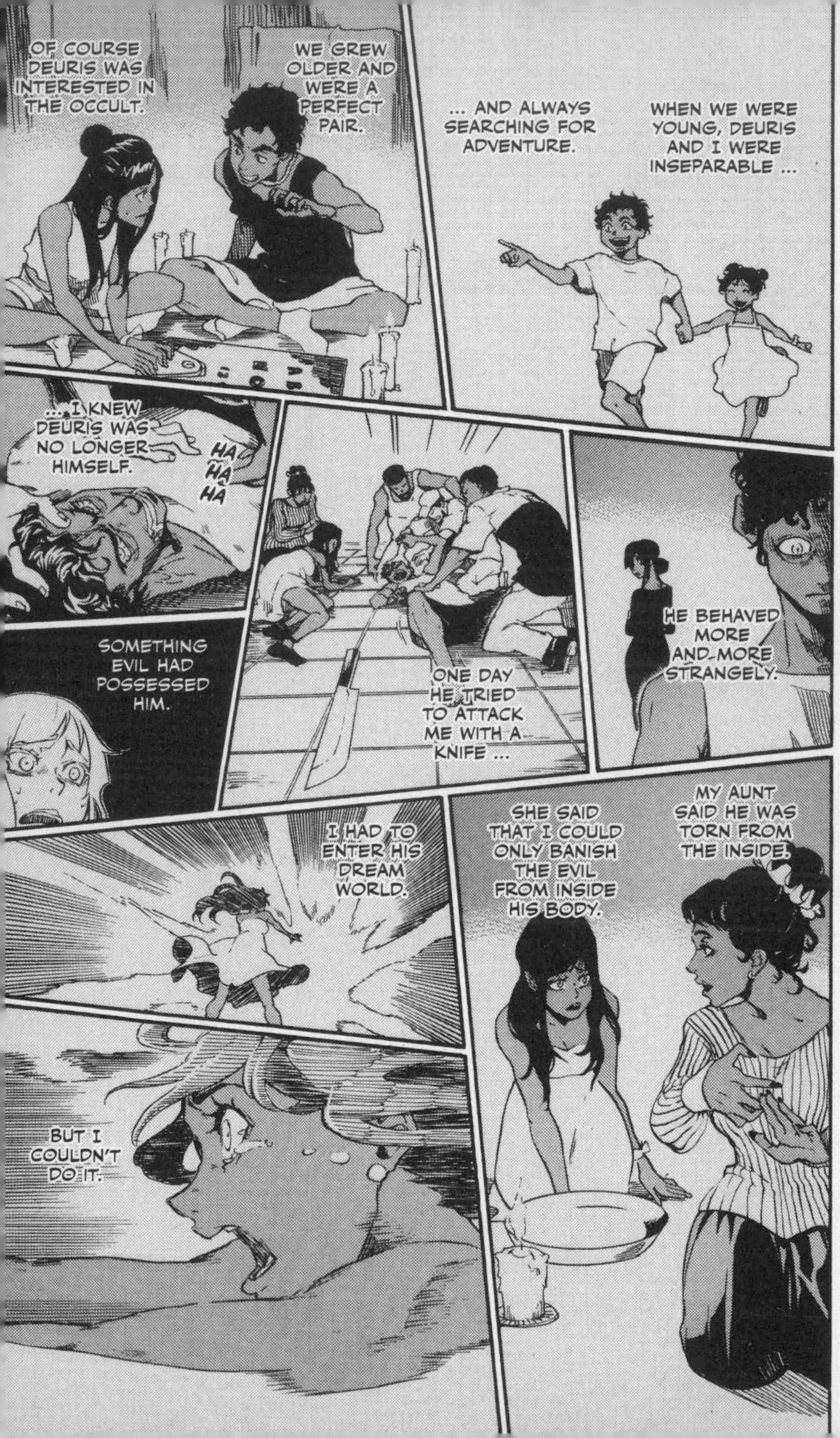
WHEN WE WERE YOUNG, DEURIS AND I WERE INSEPARABLE ...
... AND ALWAYS SEARCHING FOR ADVENTURE.
WE GREW OLDER AND WERE A PERFECT PAIR.
OF COURSE DEURIS WAS INTERESTED IN THE OCCULT.
HE BEHAVED MORE AND MORE STRANGELY.
ONE DAY HE TRIED TO ATTACK ME WITH A KNIFE ...
... I KNEW DEURIS WAS NO LONGER HIMSELF.
HA HA HA
SOMETHING EVIL HAD POSSESSED HIM.
MY AUNT SAID HE WAS TORN FROM THE INSIDE.
SHE SAID THAT I COULD ONLY BANISH THE EVIL FROM INSIDE HIS BODY.
I HAD TO ENTER HIS DREAM WORLD.
BUT I COULDN'T DO IT.

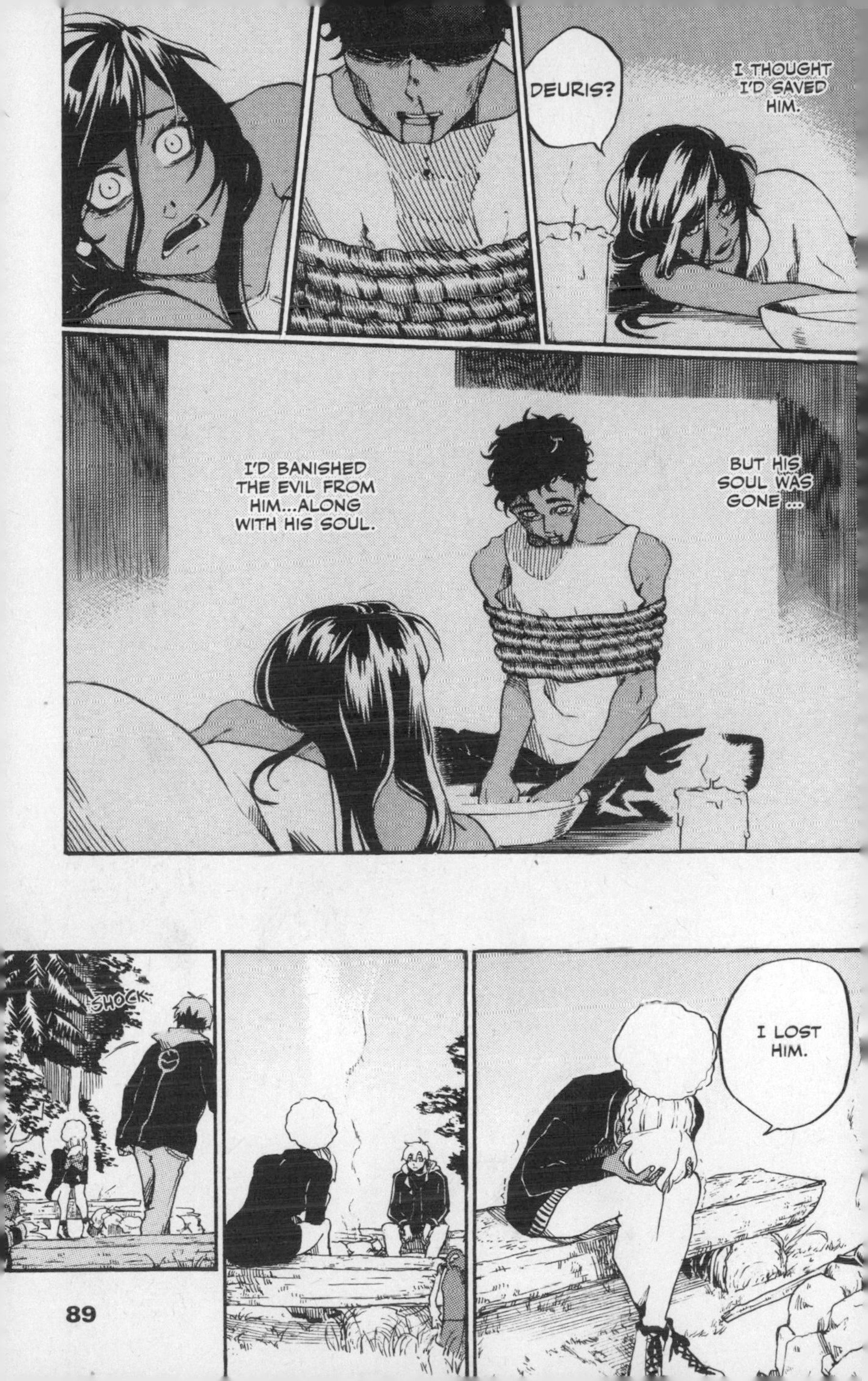
DEURIS?
I THOUGHT I'D SAVED HIM.
I'D BANISHED THE EVIL FROM HIM...ALONG WITH HIS SOUL.
BUT HIS SOUL WAS GONE ...
SHOCK
I LOST HIM.

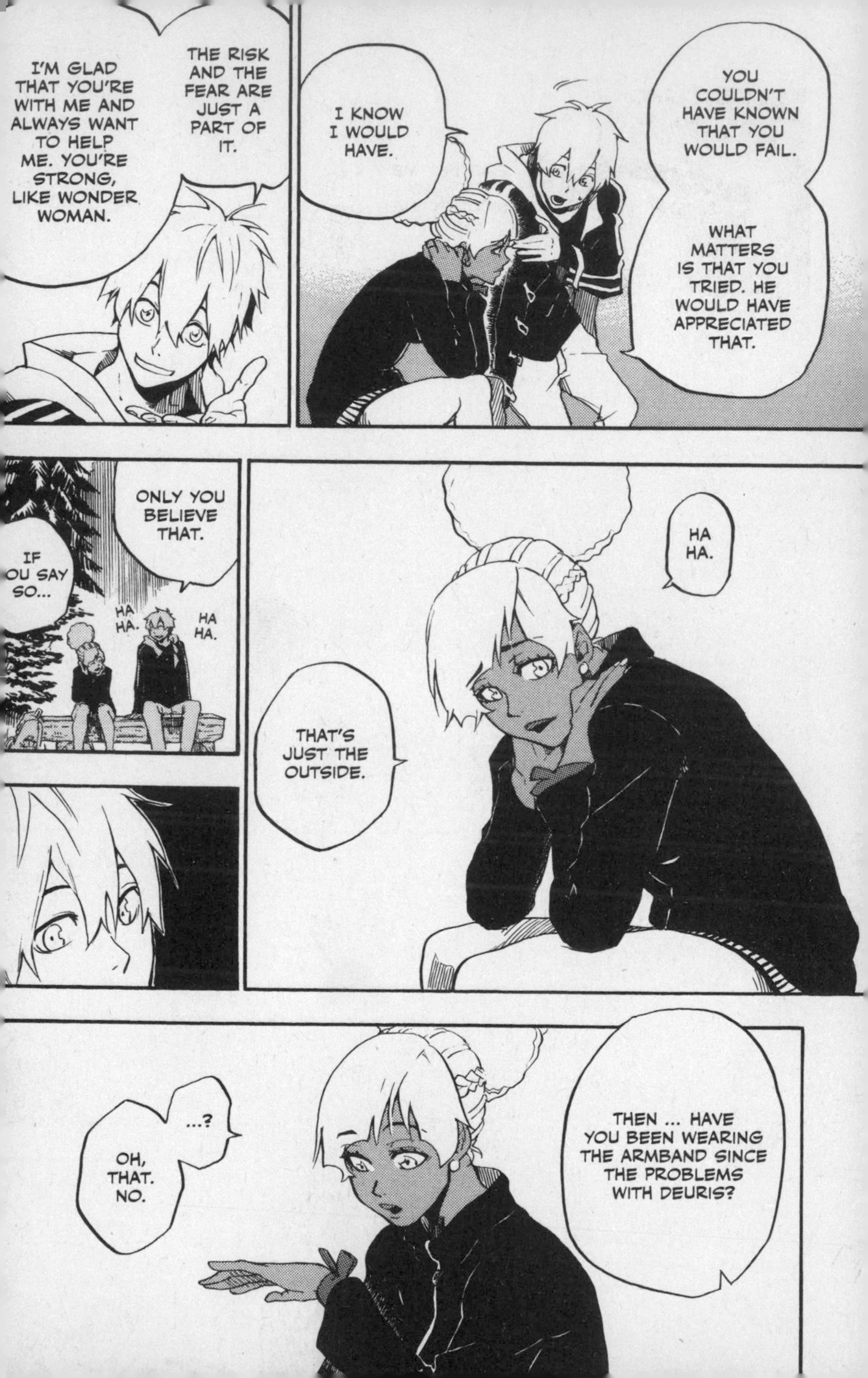
YOU COULDN'T HAVE KNOWN THAT YOU WOULD FAIL.
I KNOW I WOULD HAVE.
WHAT MATTERS IS THAT YOU TRIED. HE WOULD HAVE APPRECIATED THAT.
THE RISK AND THE FEAR ARE JUST A PART OF IT.
I'M GLAD THAT YOU'RE WITH ME AND ALWAYS WANT TO HELP ME. YOU'RE STRONG, LIKE WONDER WOMAN.
HA HA.
THAT'S JUST THE OUTSIDE.
ONLY YOU BELIEVE THAT.
IF
OU SAY SO...
HA HA.
HA HA.
THEN ... HAVE YOU BEEN WEARING THE ARMBAND SINCE THE PROBLEMS WITH DEURIS?
...?
OH, THAT. NO.

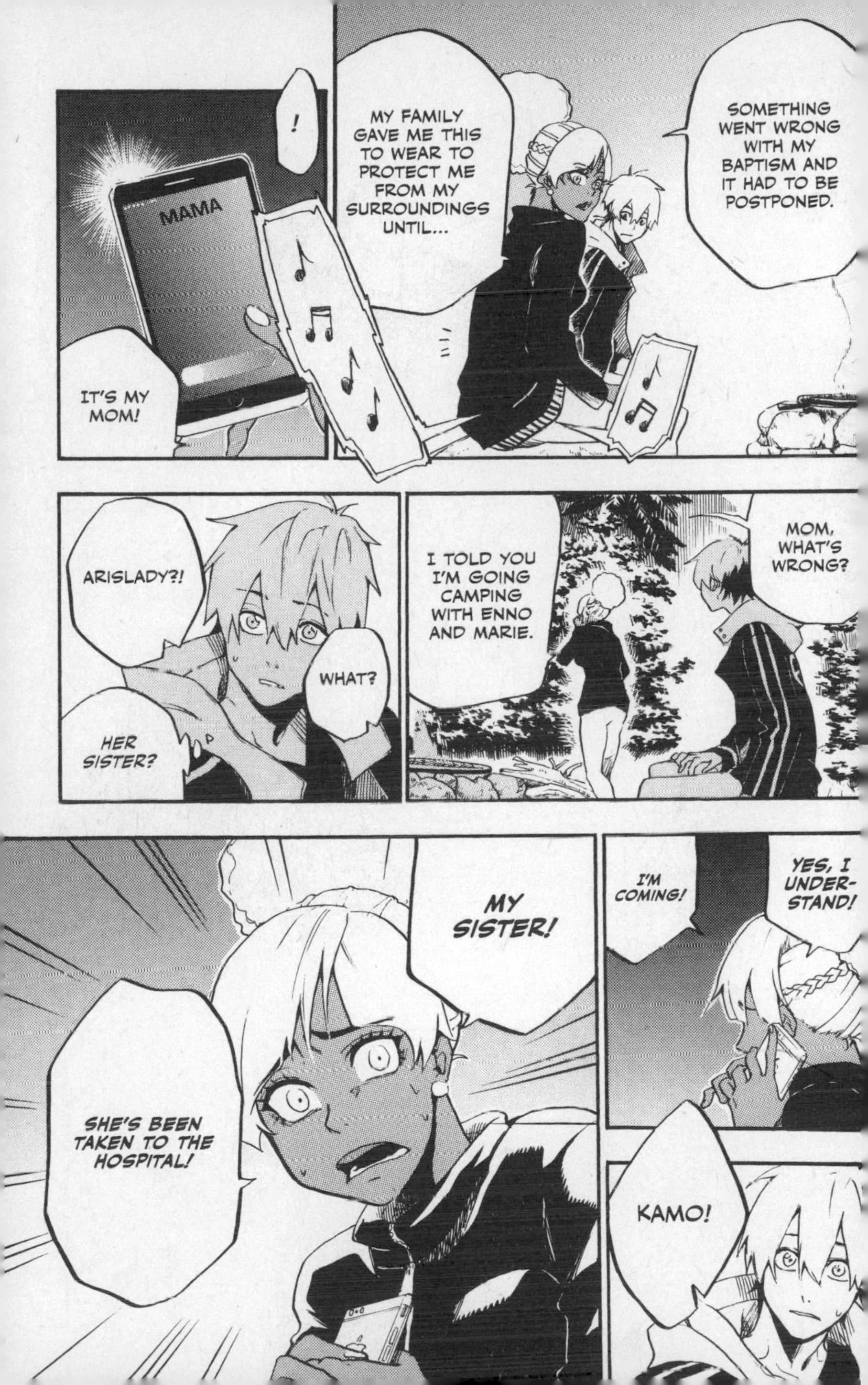
SOMETHING WENT WRONG WITH MY BAPTISM AND IT HAD TO BE POSTPONED.
MY FAMILY GAVE ME THIS TO WEAR TO PROTECT ME FROM MY SURROUNDINGS UNTIL...
!
MAMA
IT'S MY MOM!
MOM, WHAT'S WRONG?
I TOLD YOU I'M GOING CAMPING WITH ENNO AND MARIE.
ARISLADY?!
WHAT?
HER SISTER?
YES, I UNDERSTAND!
I'M COMING!
KAMO!
MY SISTER!
SHE'S BEEN TAKEN TO THE HOSPITAL!

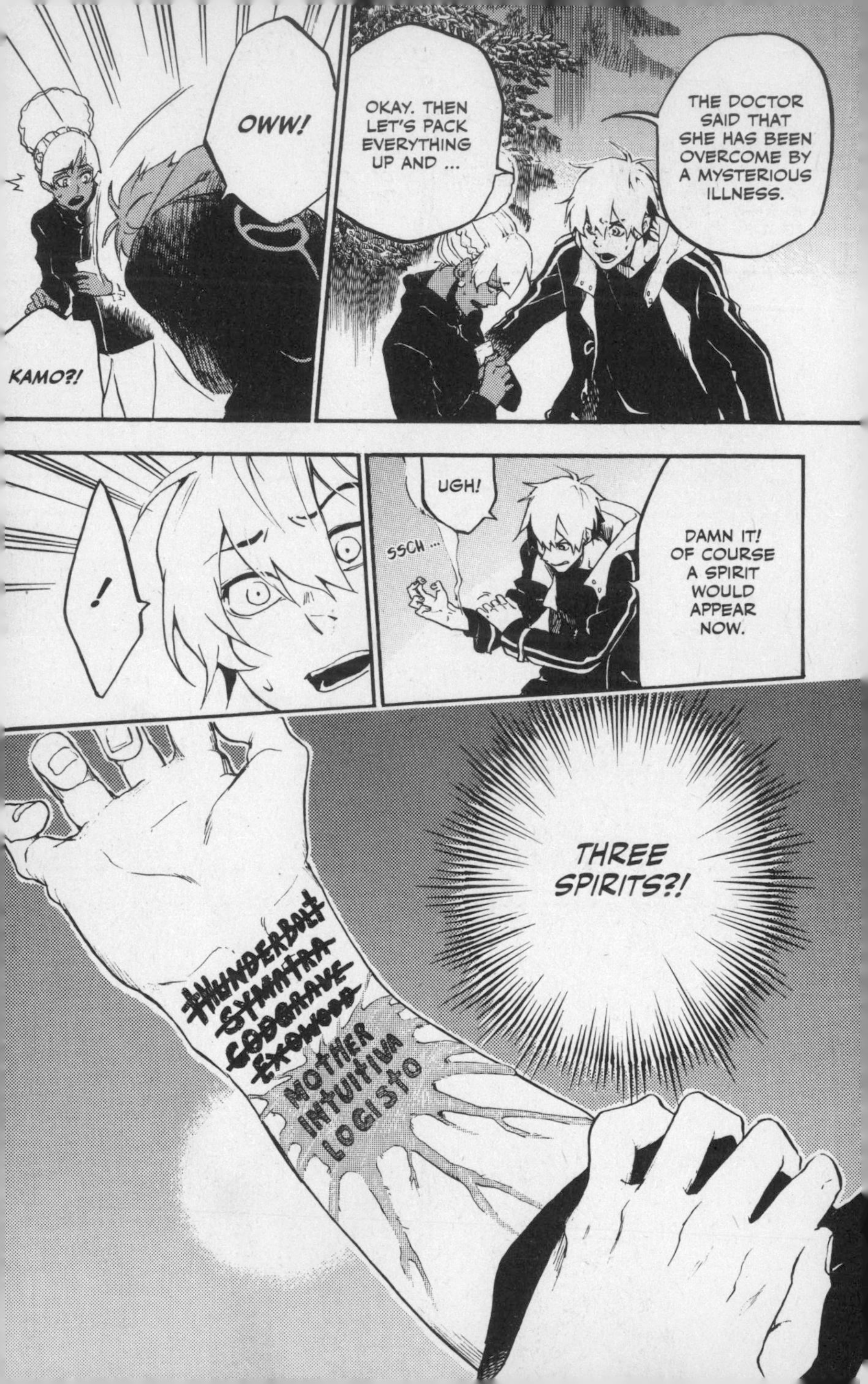
THE DOCTOR SAID THAT SHE HAS BEEN OVERCOME BY A MYSTERIOUS ILLNESS.
OKAY. THEN LET'S PACK EVERYTHING UP AND ...
OWW!
KAMO?!
DAMN IT! OF COURSE A SPIRIT WOULD APPEAR NOW.
UGH!
SSCH ...
!
THREE SPIRITS?!
MOTHER
INTUITIVA
LOGISTO

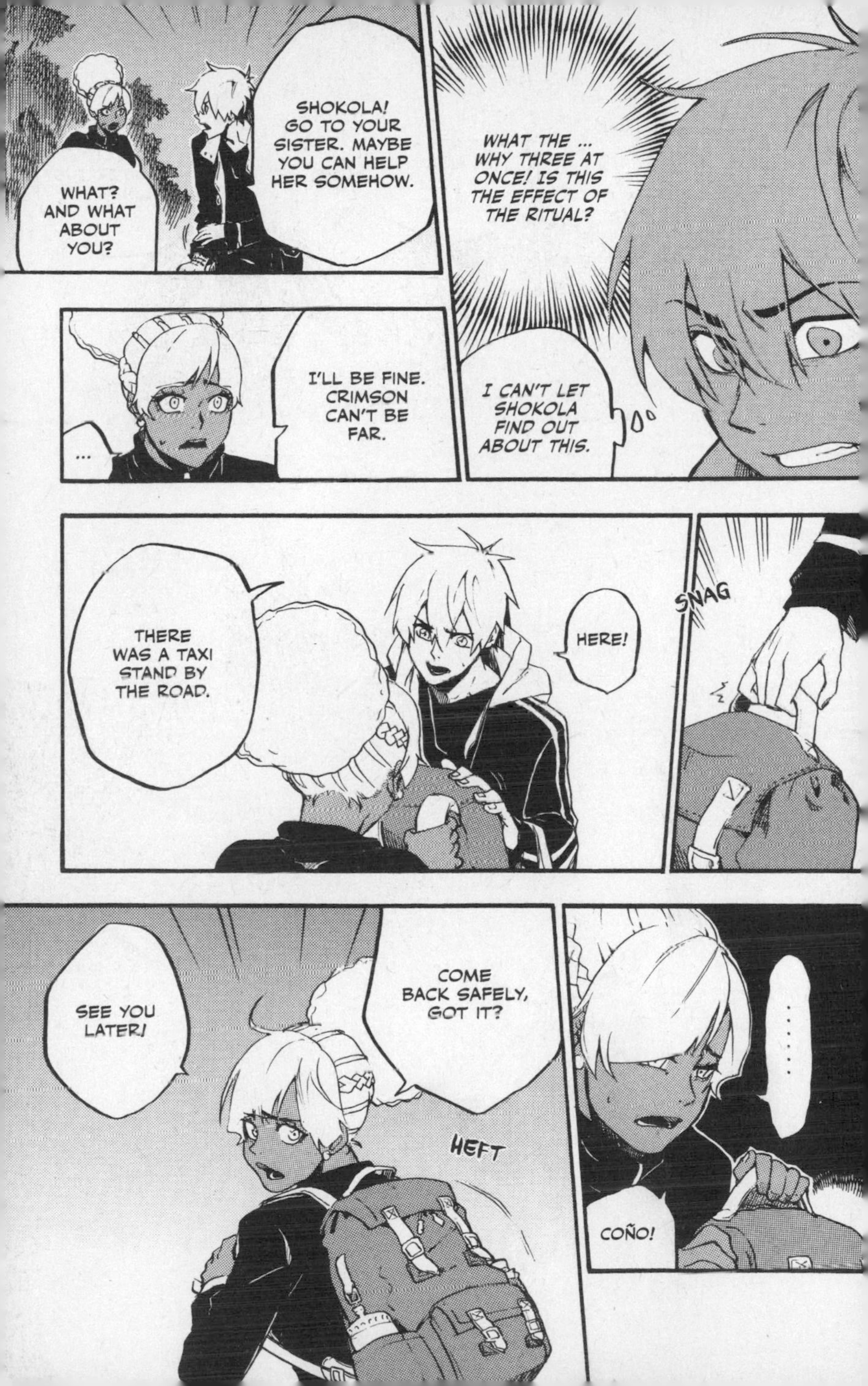
WHAT THE ... WHY THREE AT ONCE! IS THIS THE EFFECT OF THE RITUAL?
I CAN'T LET SHOKOLA FIND OUT ABOUT THIS.
SHOKOLA! GO TO YOUR SISTER. MAYBE YOU CAN HELP HER SOMEHOW.
WHAT? AND WHAT ABOUT YOU?
I'LL BE FINE. CRIMSON CAN'T BE FAR.
...
SNAG
HERE!
THERE WAS A TAXI STAND BY THE ROAD.
......
COÑO!
COME BACK SAFELY, GOT IT?
SEE YOU LATER!
HEFT

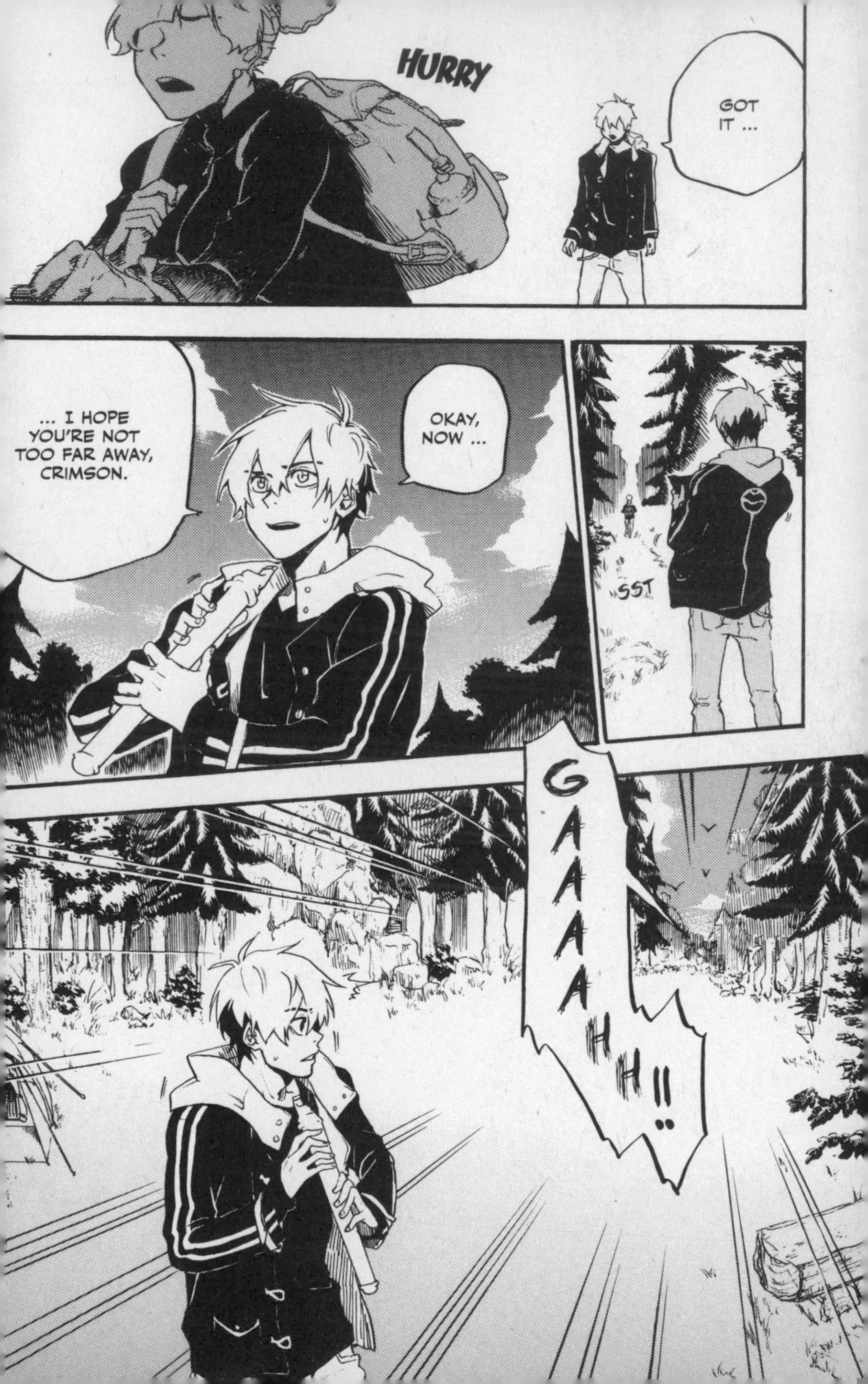
HURRY
GOT IT ...
SST
OKAY, NOW ...
... I HOPE YOU'RE NOT TOO FAR AWAY, CRIMSON.
GAAAAAHH!!

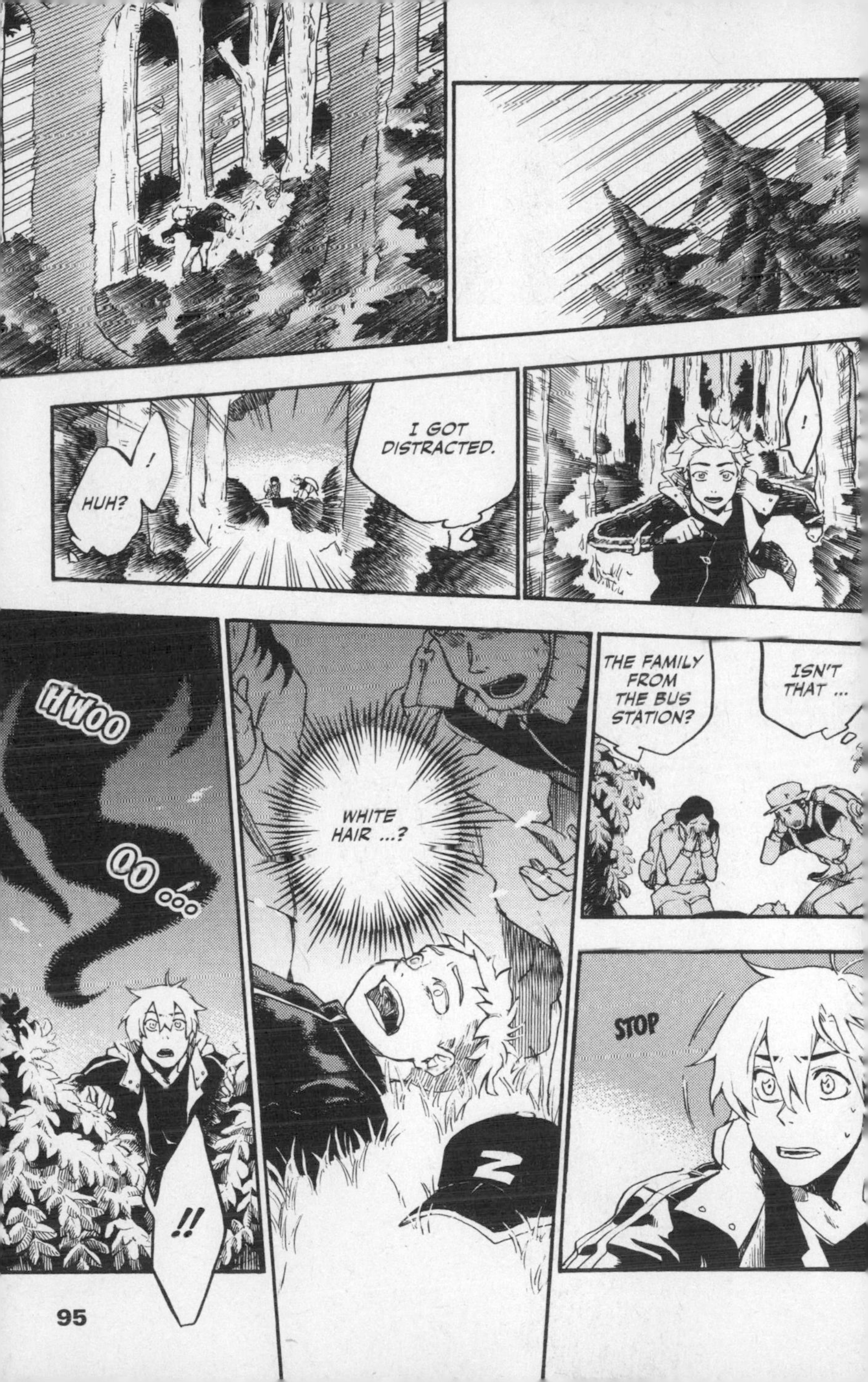

!
I GOT DISTRACTED.
!
HUH?
ISN'T THAT ...
THE FAMILY FROM THE BUS STATION?
STOP
WHITE HAIR ...?
HWOO
OO ...
!!

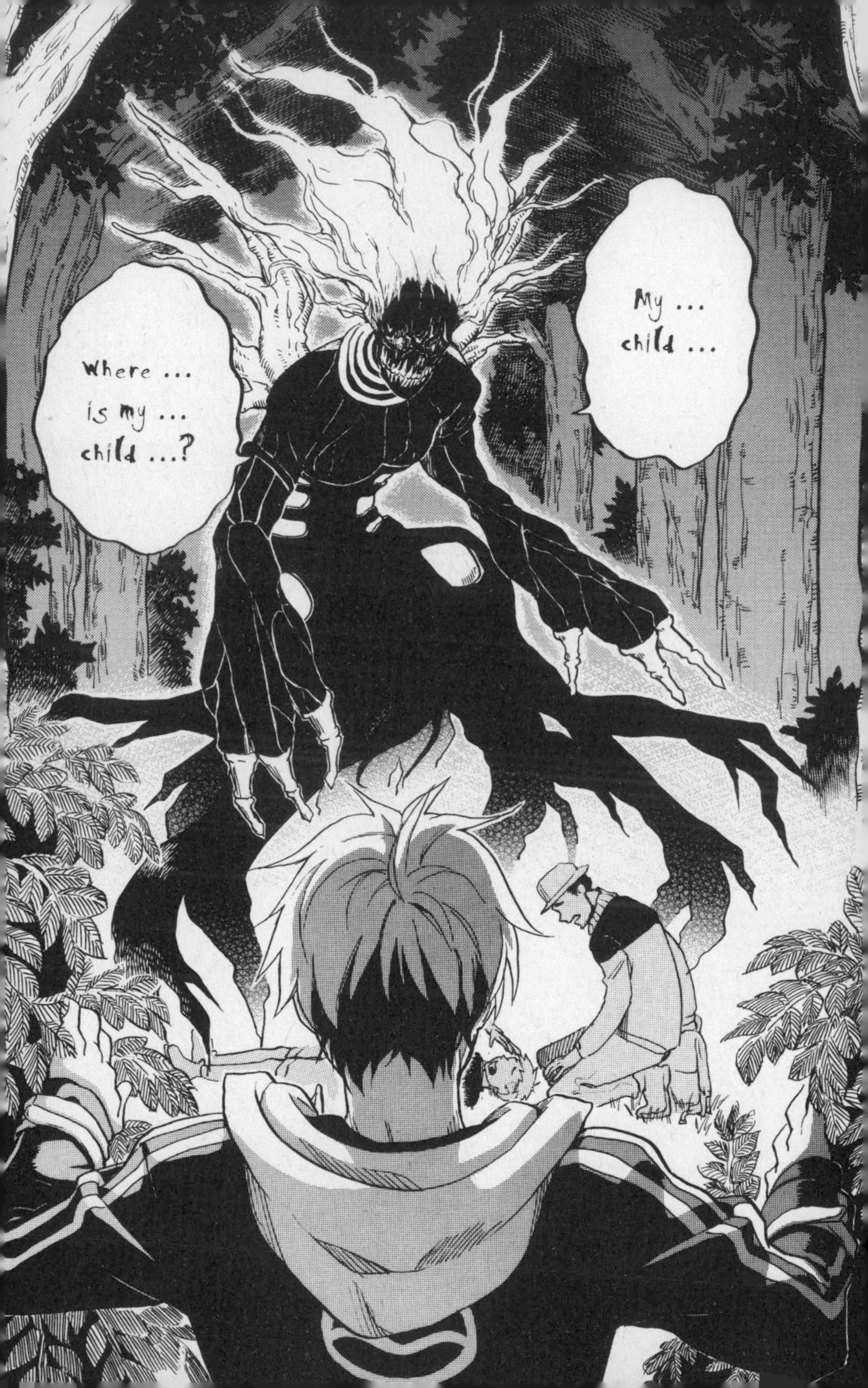
My ... child ...
Where ... is my ... child ...?

10

A MOTHER'S CRY

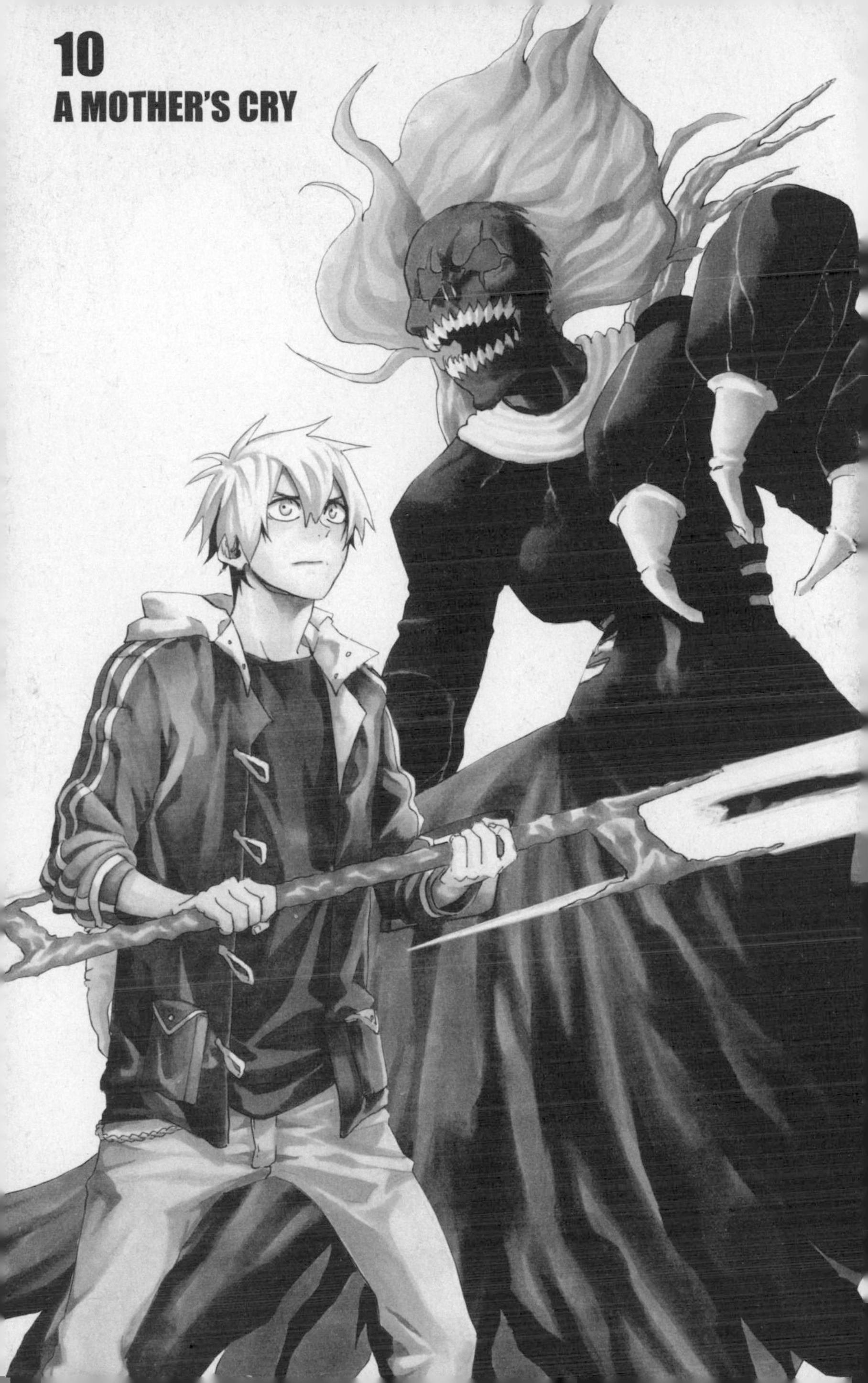

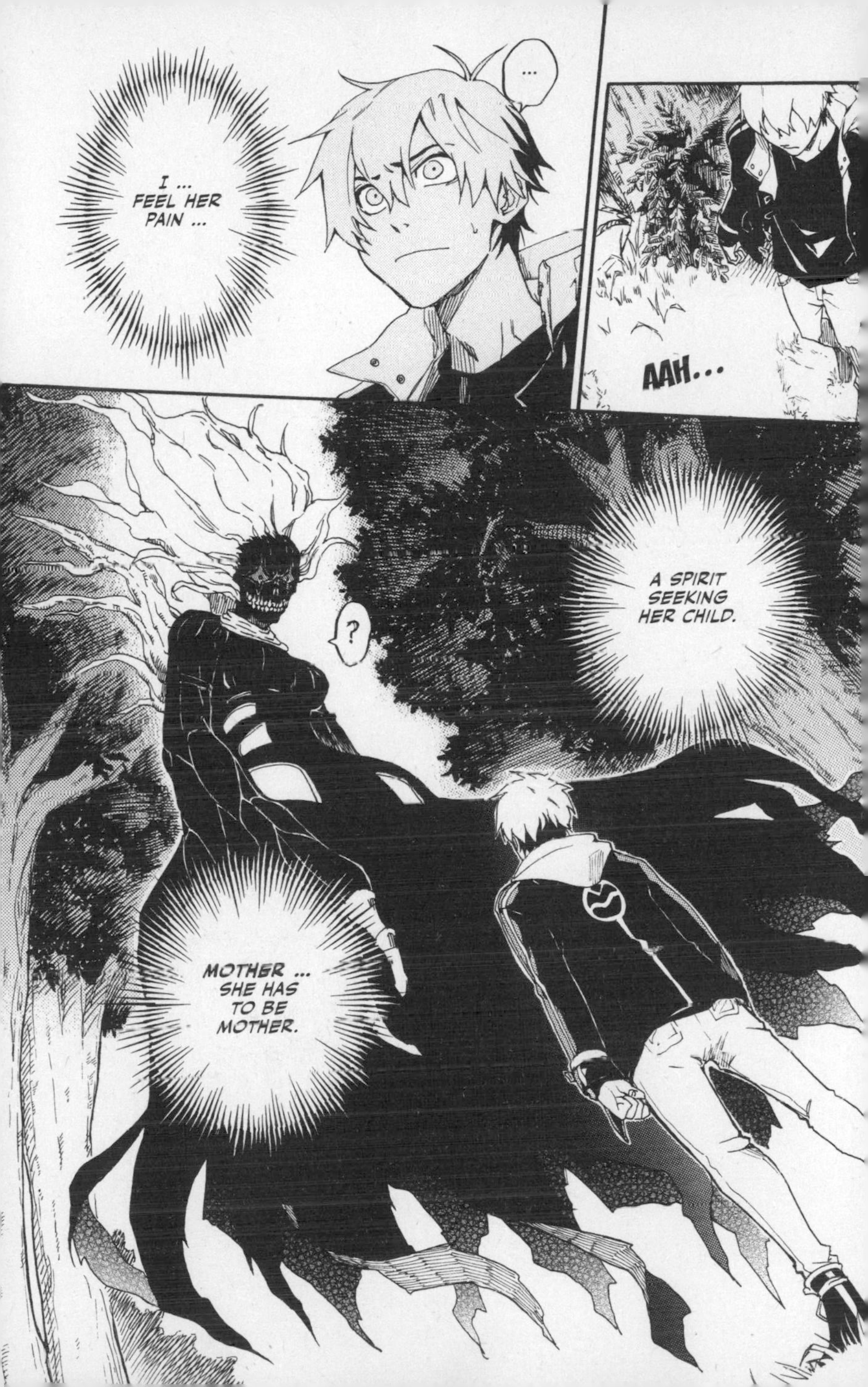
AAH...
...
I ... FEEL HER PAIN ...
A SPIRIT SEEKING HER CHILD.
?
MOTHER ... SHE HAS TO BE MOTHER.

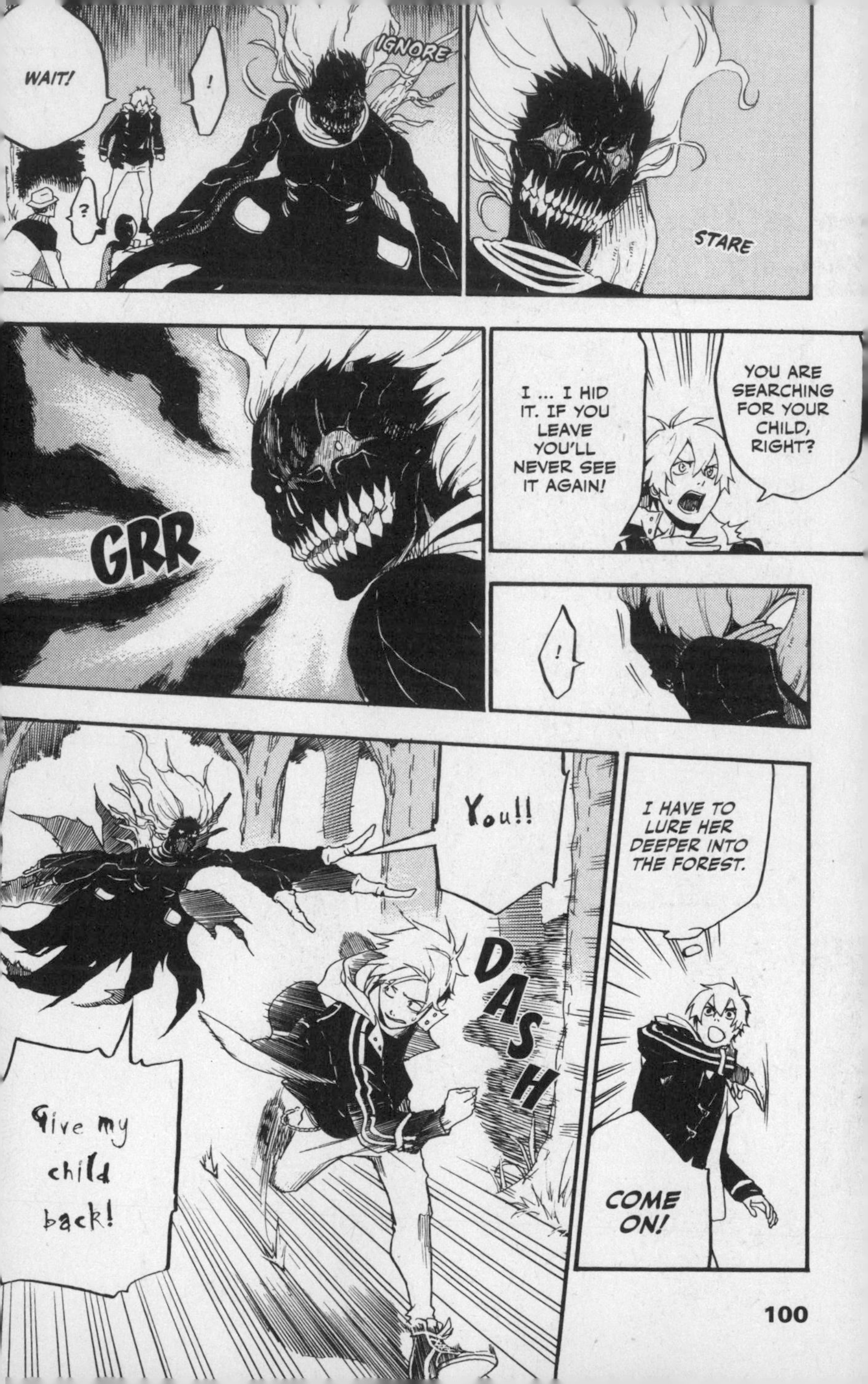
STARE
IGNORE
!
WAIT!
?
YOU ARE SEARCHING FOR YOUR CHILD, RIGHT?
I ... I HID IT. IF YOU LEAVE YOU'LL NEVER SEE IT AGAIN!
!
GRR
I HAVE TO LURE HER DEEPER INTO THE FOREST.
COME ON!
You!!
DASH
Give my child back!

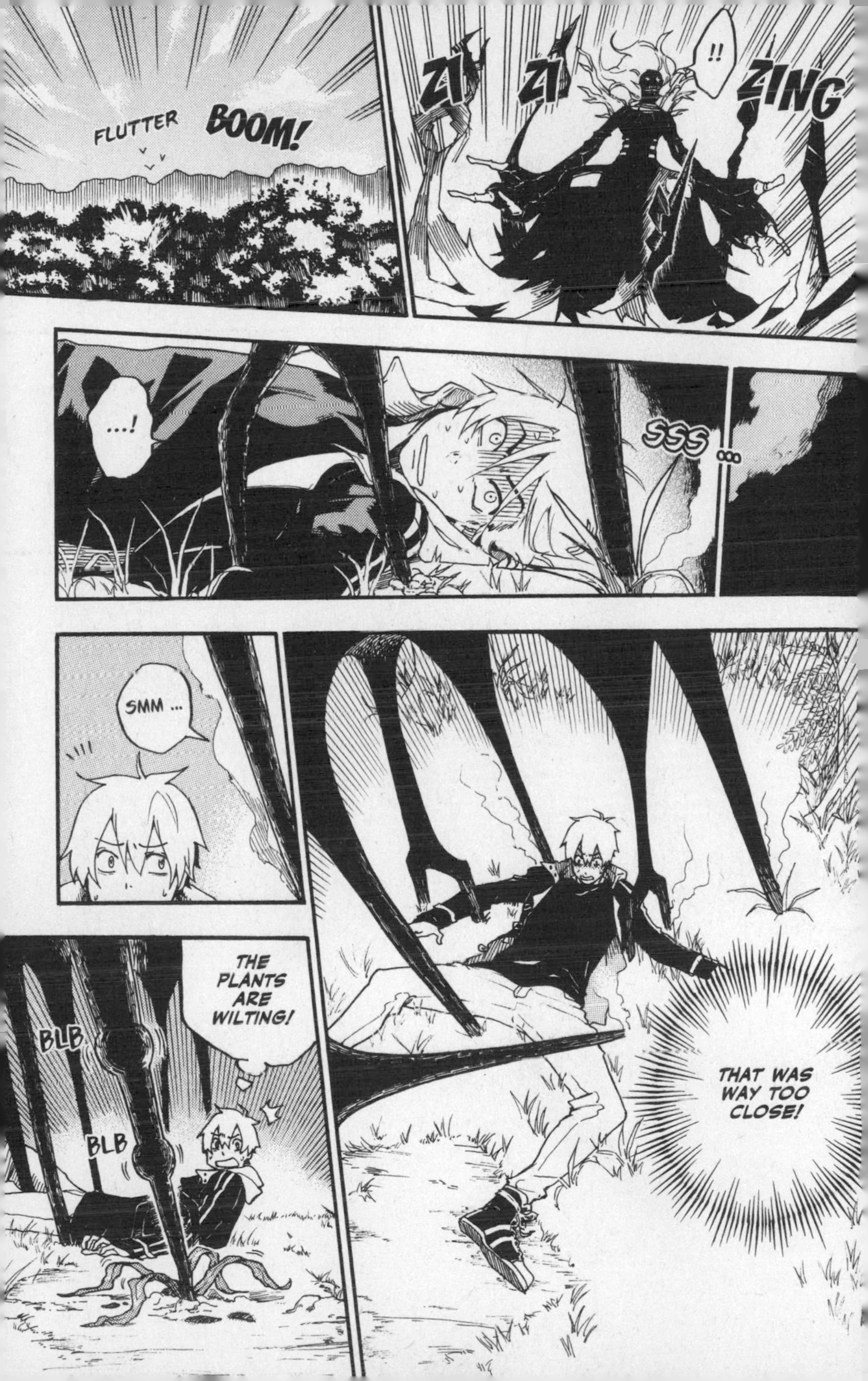
!!
ZING
ZI
ZI
BOOM!
FLUTTER
SSS...
...!
THAT WAS WAY TOO CLOSE!
SMM ...
THE PLANTS ARE WILTING!
BLB
BLB

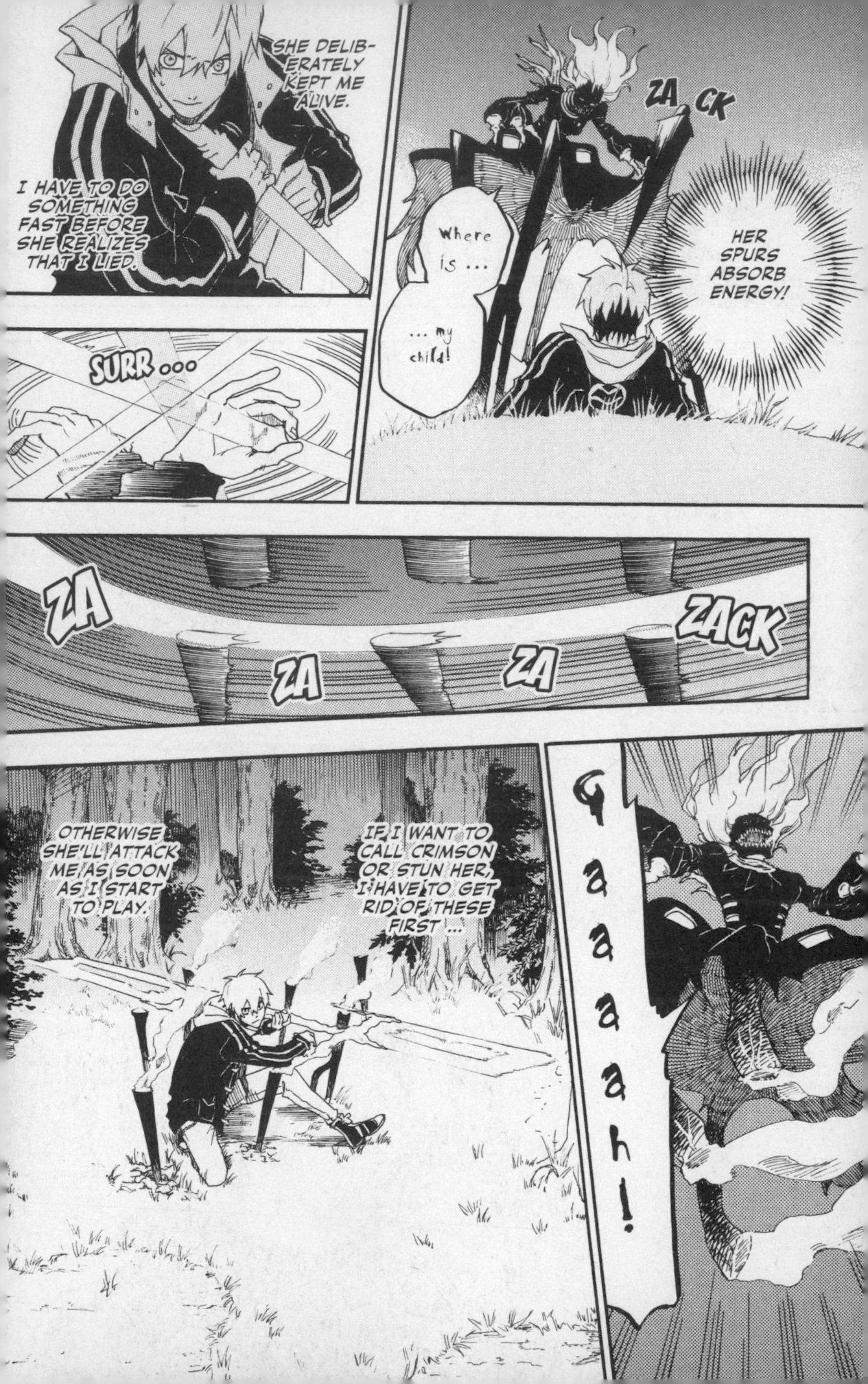
ZA CK
Where is ...
... my child!
HER SPURS ABSORB ENERGY!
SHE DELIBERATELY KEPT ME ALIVE.
I HAVE TO DO SOMETHING FAST BEFORE SHE REALIZES THAT I LIED.
SURR ooo
ZACK
ZA
ZA
ZA
Gaaaah!
IF I WANT TO CALL CRIMSON OR STUN HER, I HAVE TO GET RID OF THESE FIRST ...
OTHERWISE SHE'LL ATTACK ME AS SOON AS I START TO PLAY.

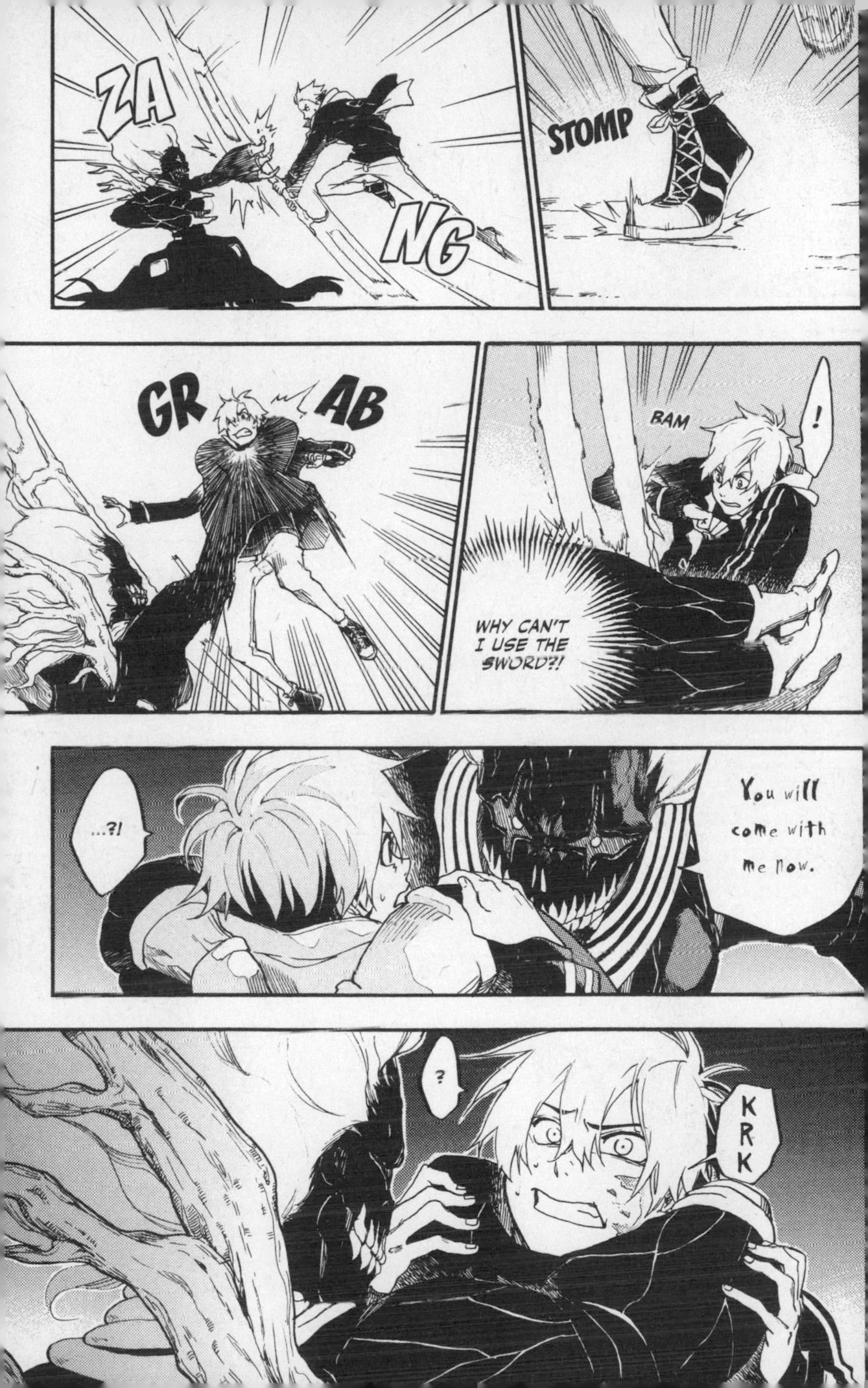
STOMP
ZA
NG
BAM
!
WHY CAN'T I USE THE SWORD?!
GR
AB
You will come with me now.
...?!
KRK
?

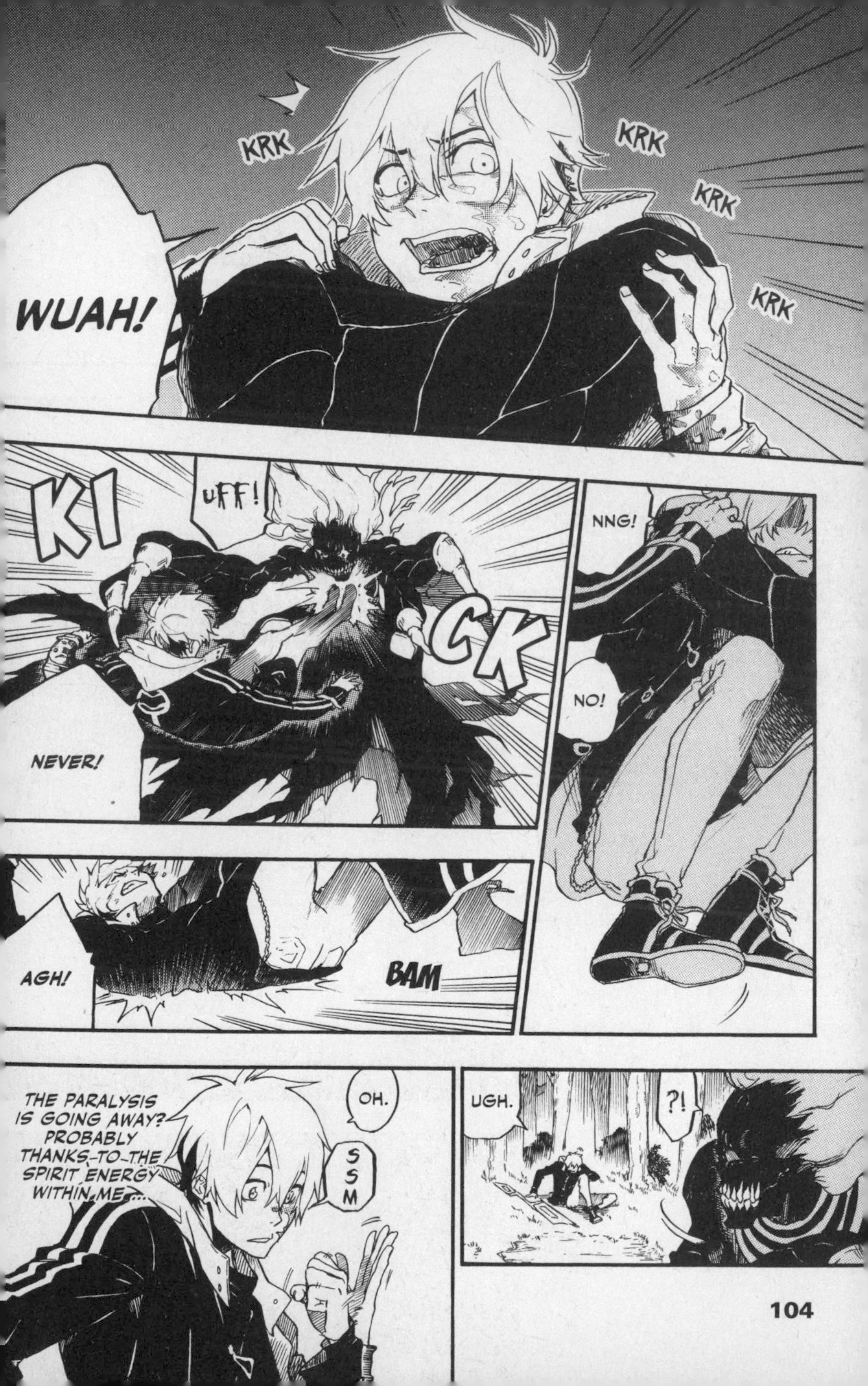
KRK
KRK
KRK
KRK
WUAH!
NNG!
NO!
UFF!
KI
CK
NEVER!
BAM
AGH!
?!
UGH.
OH.
SSM
THE PARALYSIS IS GOING AWAY? PROBABLY THANKS TO THE SPIRIT ENERGY WITHIN ME...

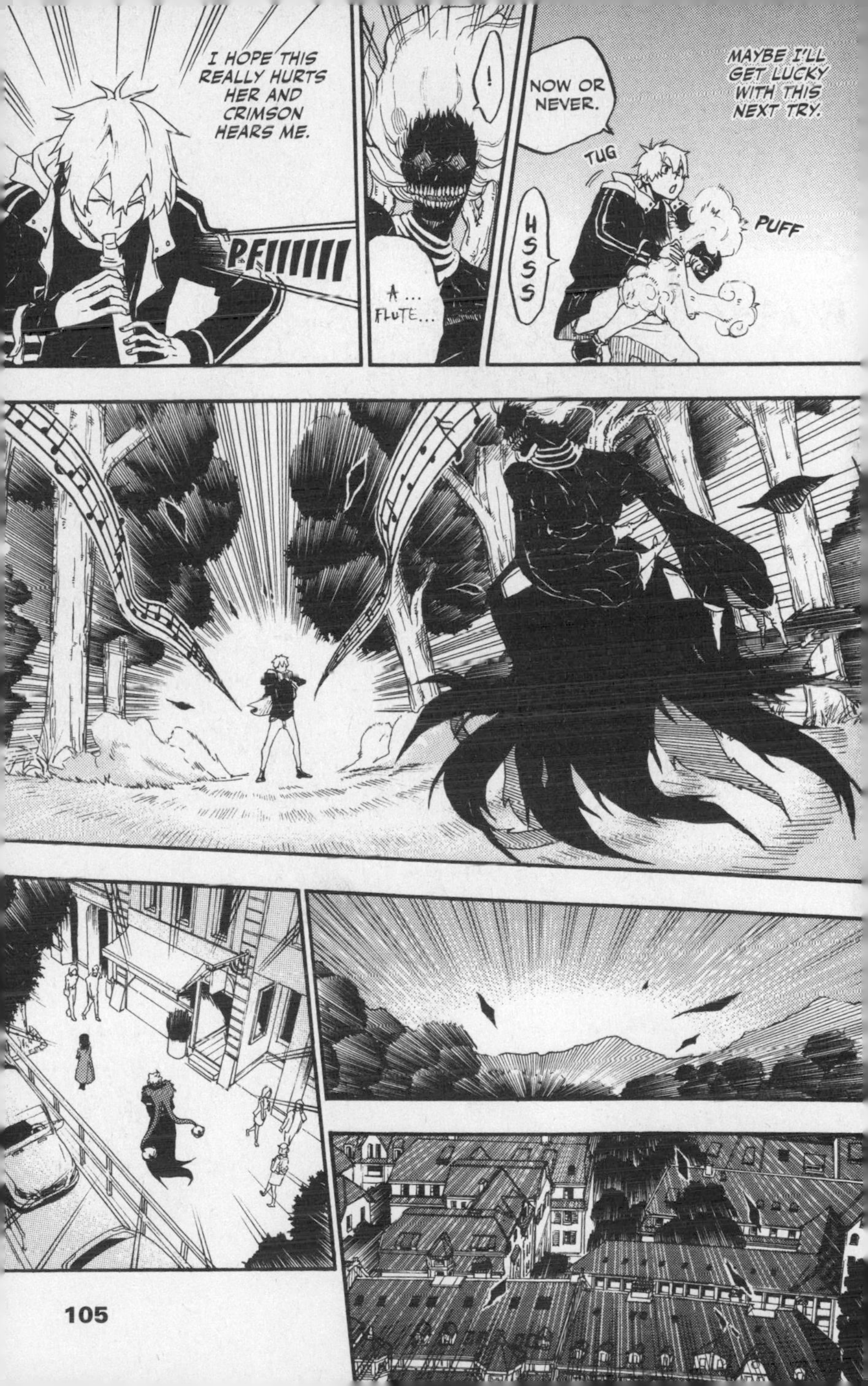
MAYBE I'LL GET LUCKY WITH THIS NEXT TRY.
NOW OR NEVER.
TUG
PUFF
!
HSSS
A... FLUTE...
I HOPE THIS REALLY HURTS HER AND CRIMSON HEARS ME.
PFIIIIIII

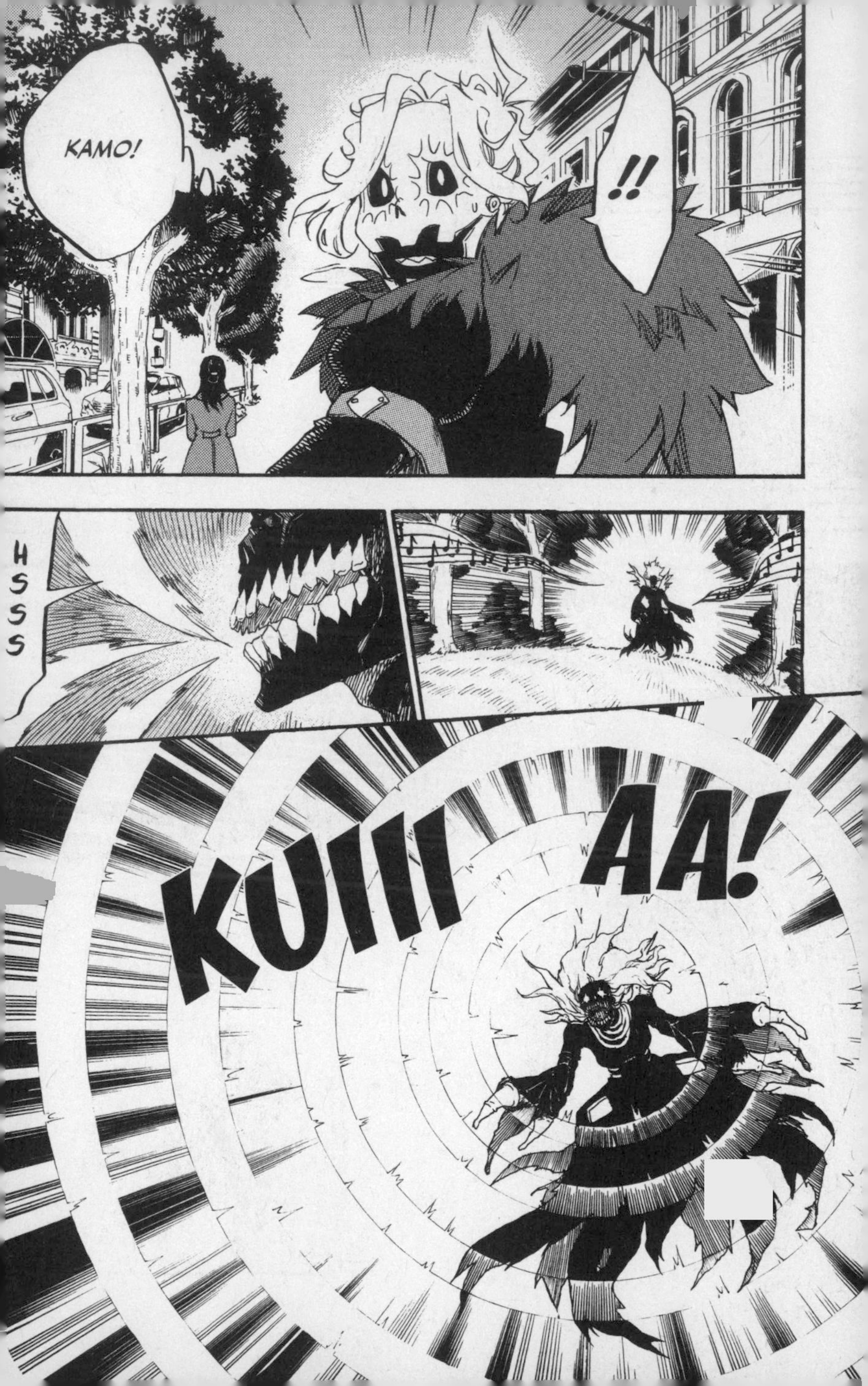
!!
KAMO!
HSSS
KUIII
AA!

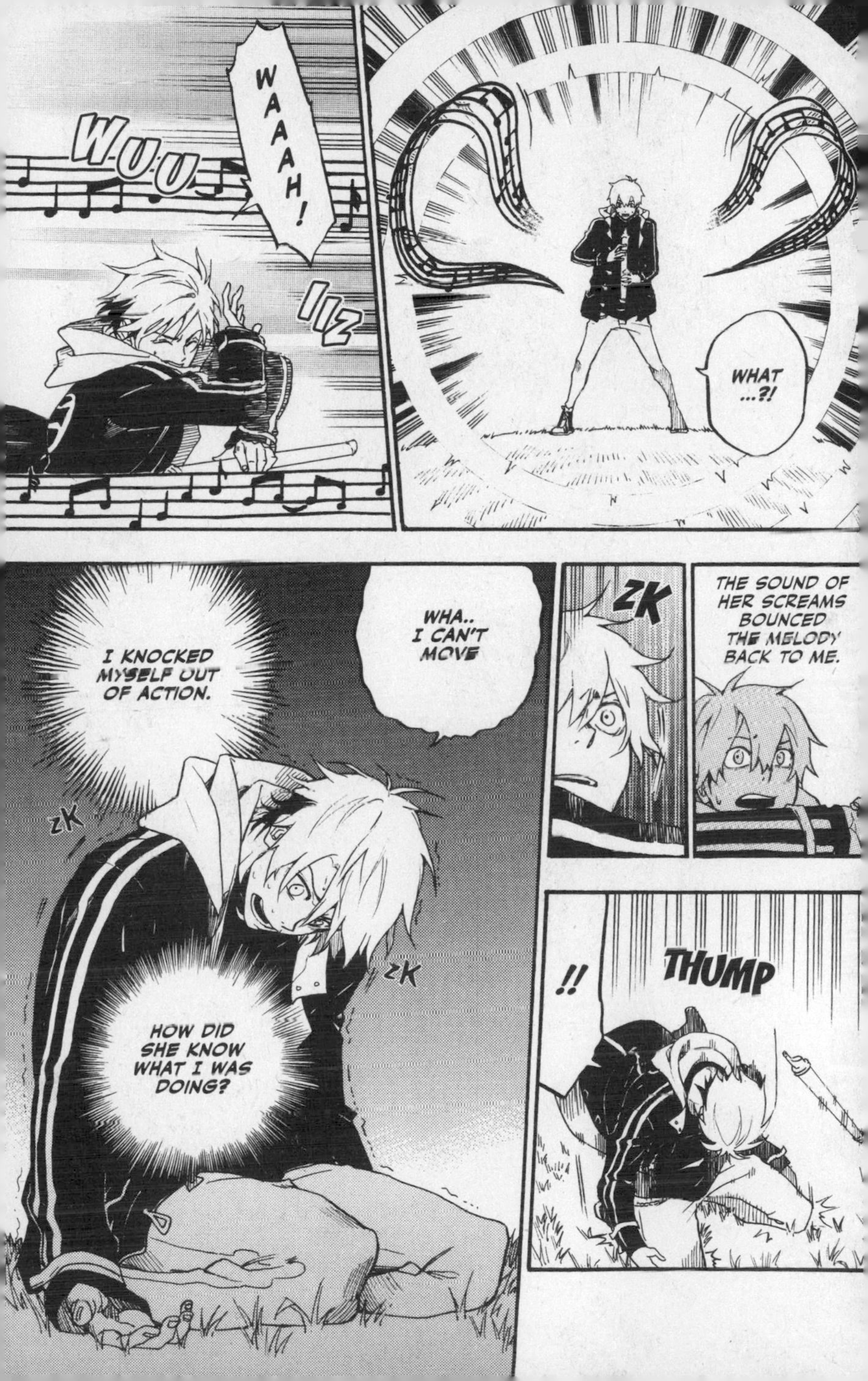
WHAT ...?!
WUUU
WAAAH!
IIZ
THE SOUND OF HER SCREAMS BOUNCED THE MELODY BACK TO ME.
ZK
!!
THUMP
WHA.. I CAN'T MOVE
I KNOCKED MYSELF OUT OF ACTION.
zK
zK
HOW DID SHE KNOW WHAT I WAS DOING?

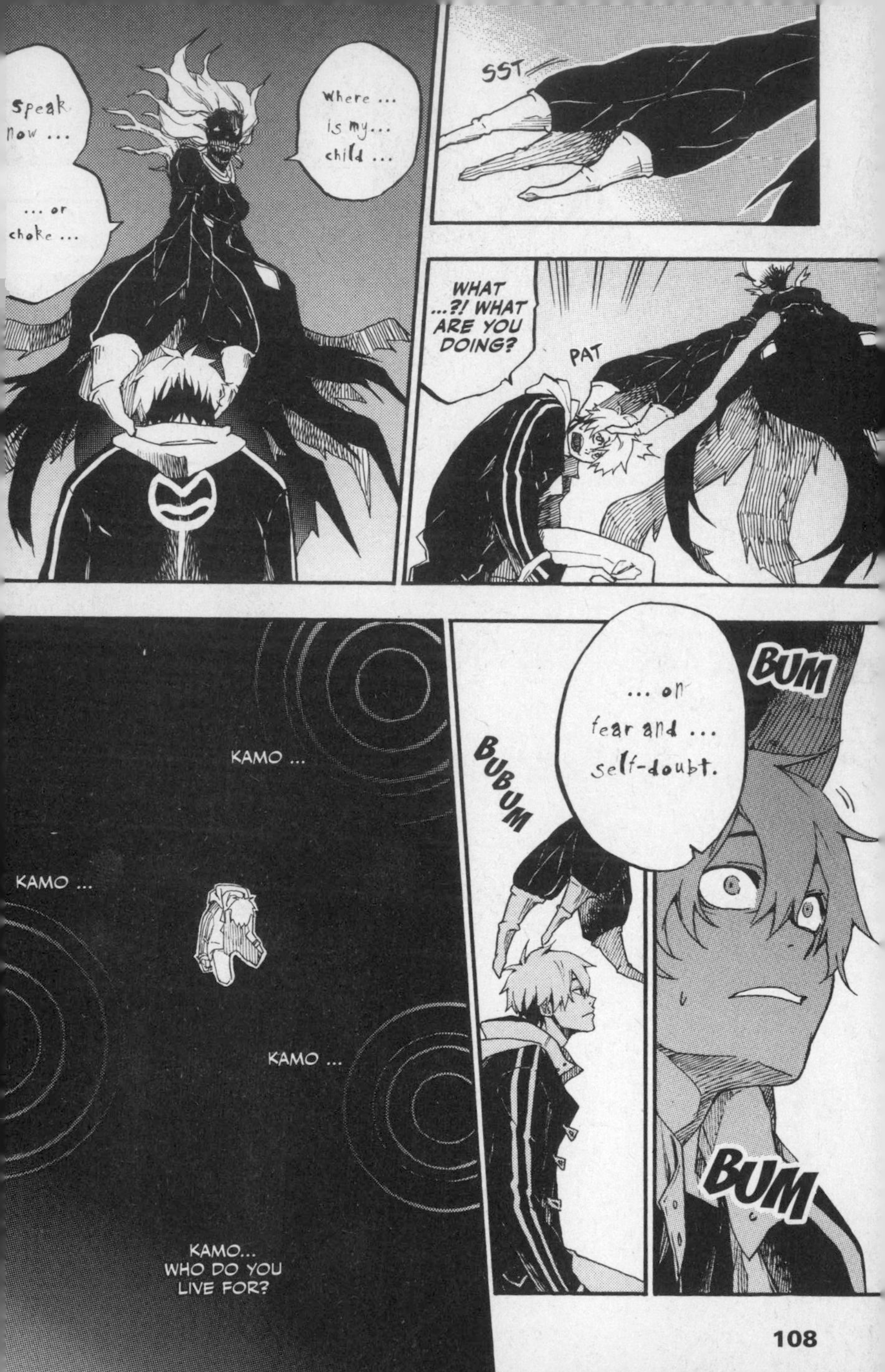
SST
WHAT ...?! WHAT ARE YOU DOING?
PAT
Where ... is my... child ...
Speak now ...
... or choke ...
BUM
... on fear and ... self-doubt.
BUBUM
BUM
KAMO ...
KAMO ...
KAMO ...
KAMO... WHO DO YOU LIVE FOR?

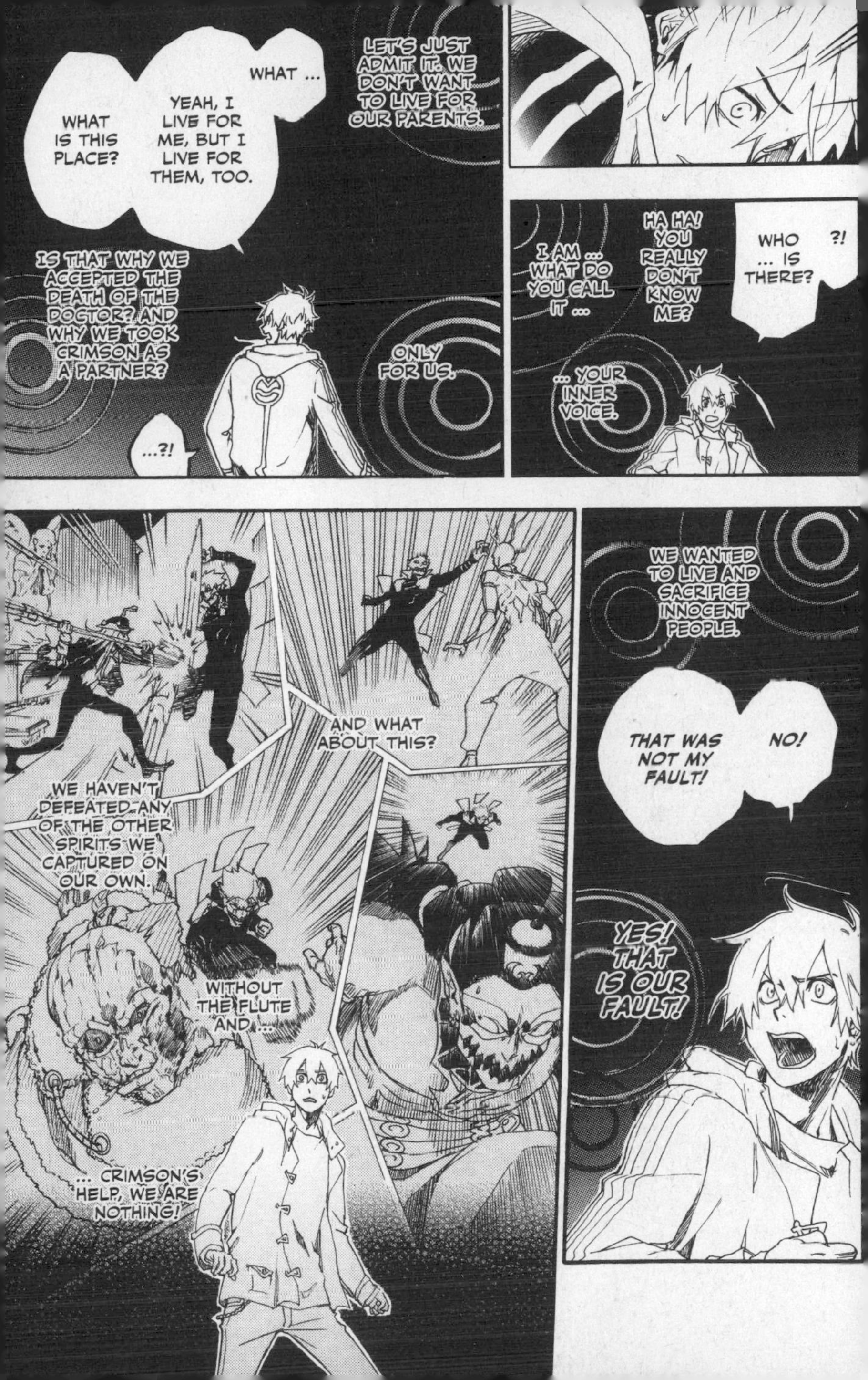
WHO ... IS THERE?!
HA HA! YOU REALLY DON'T KNOW ME?
I AM ... WHAT DO YOU CALL IT ...
... YOUR INNER VOICE.
LET'S JUST ADMIT IT. WE DON'T WANT TO LIVE FOR OUR PARENTS.
WHAT ...
YEAH, I LIVE FOR ME, BUT I LIVE FOR THEM, TOO.
WHAT IS THIS PLACE?
ONLY FOR US.
IS THAT WHY WE ACCEPTED THE DEATH OF THE DOCTOR? AND WHY WE TOOK CRIMSON AS A PARTNER?
...?!
WE WANTED TO LIVE AND SACRIFICE INNOCENT PEOPLE.
NO!
THAT WAS NOT MY FAULT!
YES! THAT IS OUR FAULT!
AND WHAT ABOUT THIS?
WE HAVEN'T DEFEATED ANY OF THE OTHER SPIRITS WE CAPTURED ON OUR OWN.
WITHOUT THE FLUTE AND ...
... CRIMSON'S HELP, WE ARE NOTHING!

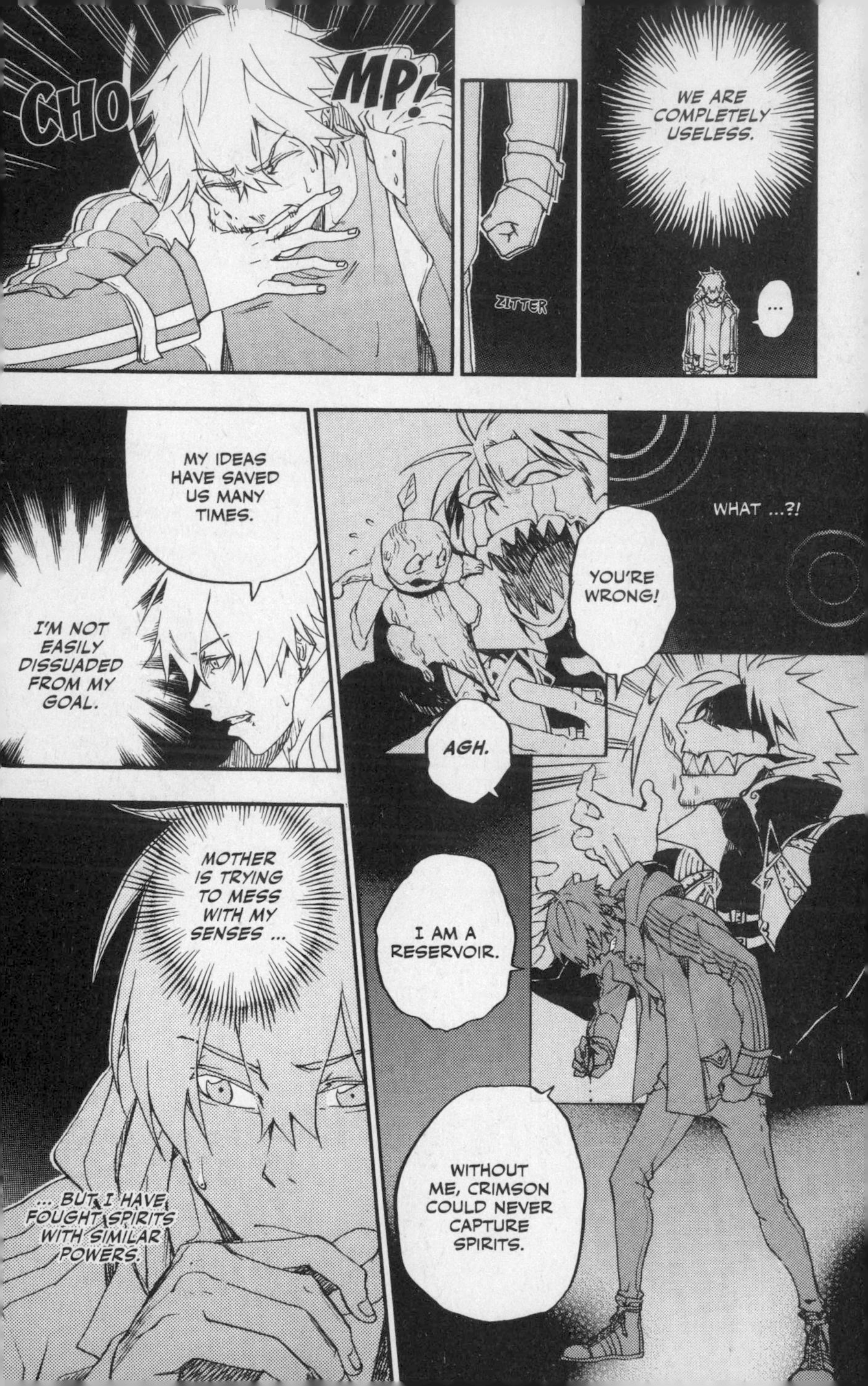
WE ARE COMPLETELY USELESS.
...
ZITTER
CHOMP!
WHAT ...?!
YOU'RE WRONG!
AGH.
I AM A RESERVOIR.
WITHOUT ME, CRIMSON COULD NEVER CAPTURE SPIRITS.
MY IDEAS HAVE SAVED US MANY TIMES.
I'M NOT EASILY DISSUADED FROM MY GOAL.
MOTHER IS TRYING TO MESS WITH MY SENSES ...
... BUT I HAVE FOUGHT SPIRITS WITH SIMILAR POWERS.

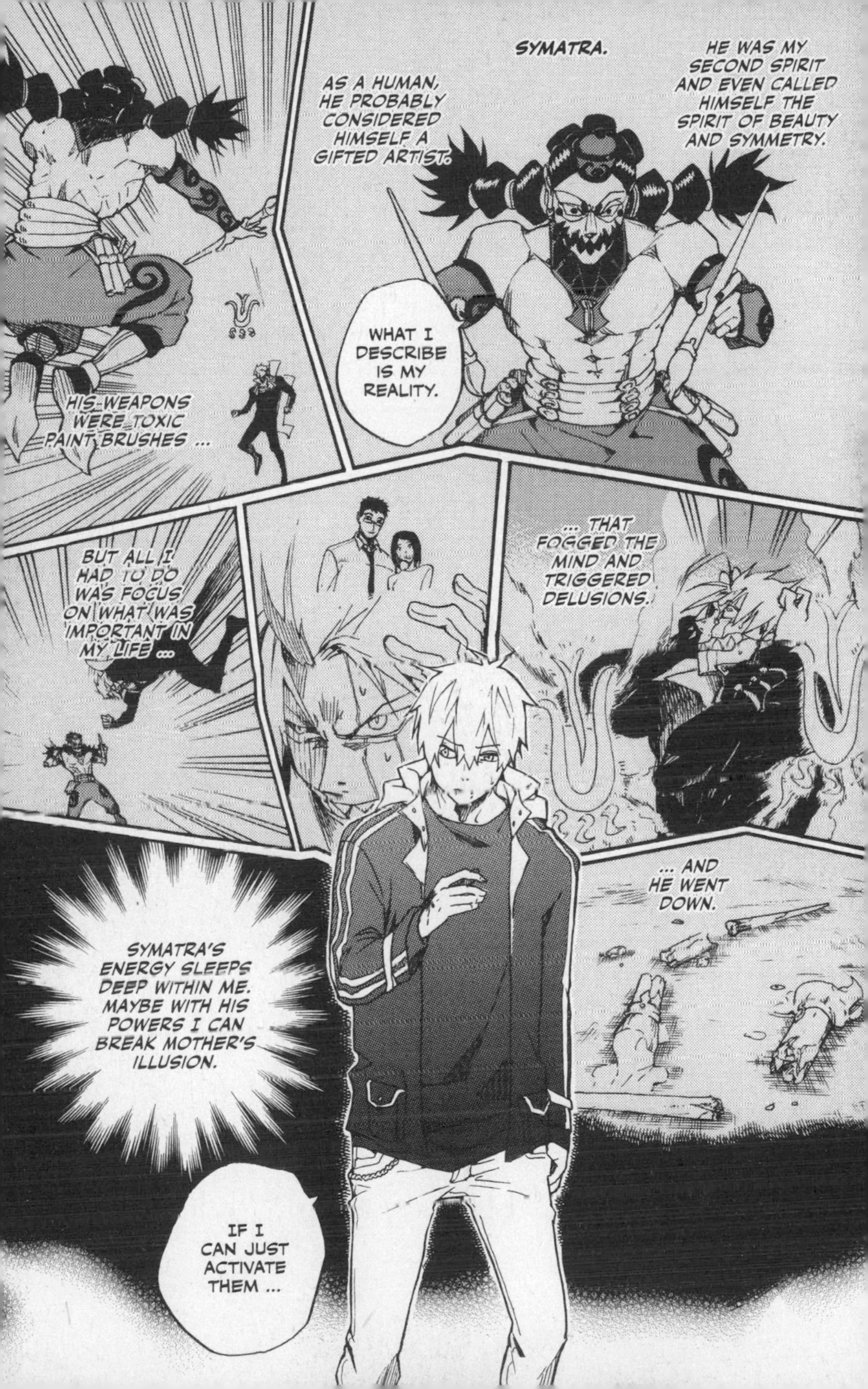
SYMATRA.
HE WAS MY SECOND SPIRIT AND EVEN CALLED HIMSELF THE SPIRIT OF BEAUTY AND SYMMETRY.
AS A HUMAN, HE PROBABLY CONSIDERED HIMSELF A GIFTED ARTIST.
WHAT I DESCRIBE IS MY REALITY.
HIS WEAPONS WERE TOXIC PAINT BRUSHES ...
... THAT FOGGED THE MIND AND TRIGGERED DELUSIONS.
BUT ALL I HAD TO DO WAS FOCUS ON WHAT WAS IMPORTANT IN MY LIFE ...
... AND HE WENT DOWN.
SYMATRA'S ENERGY SLEEPS DEEP WITHIN ME. MAYBE WITH HIS POWERS I CAN BREAK MOTHER'S ILLUSION.
IF I CAN JUST ACTIVATE THEM ...

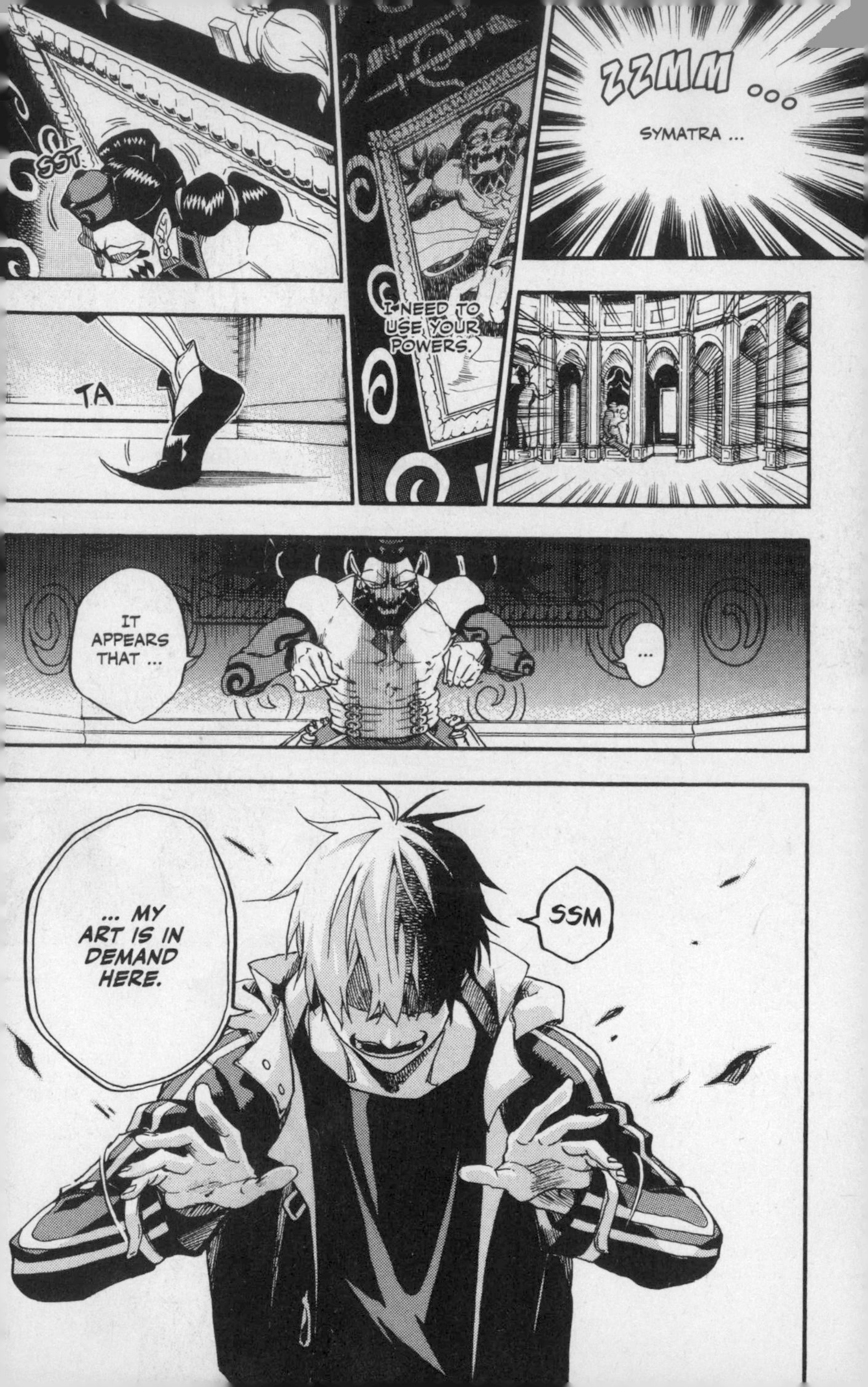
ZZMM ...
SYMATRA ...
I NEED TO USE YOUR POWERS.
SST
TA
...
IT APPEARS THAT ...
SSM
... MY ART IS IN DEMAND HERE.

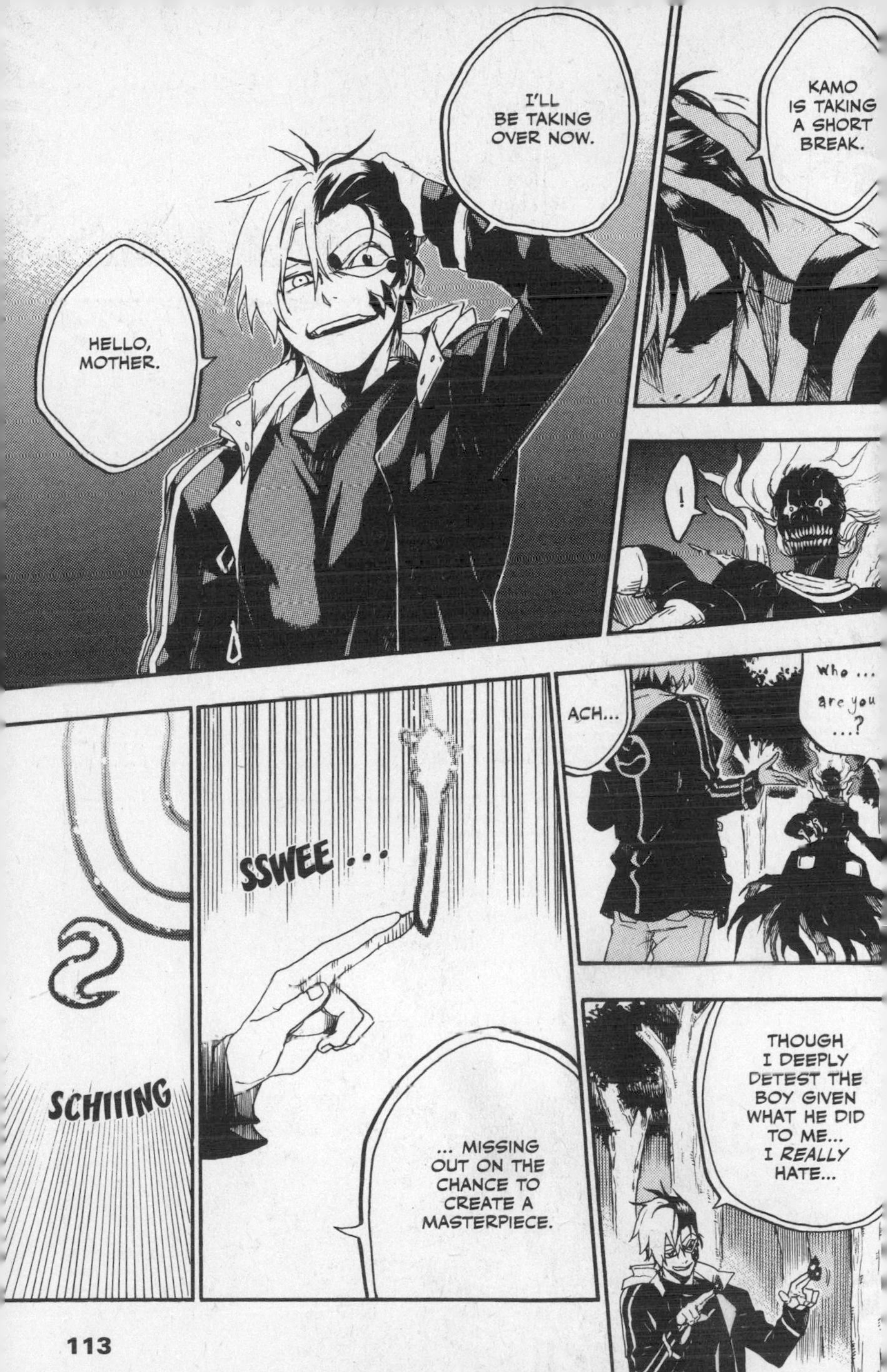
KAMO IS TAKING A SHORT BREAK.
!
I'LL BE TAKING OVER NOW.
HELLO, MOTHER.
Who ... are you ...?
ACH...
THOUGH I DEEPLY DETEST THE BOY GIVEN WHAT HE DID TO ME... I *REALLY* HATE...
SSWEE ...
... MISSING OUT ON THE CHANCE TO CREATE A MASTERPIECE.
SCHIIING

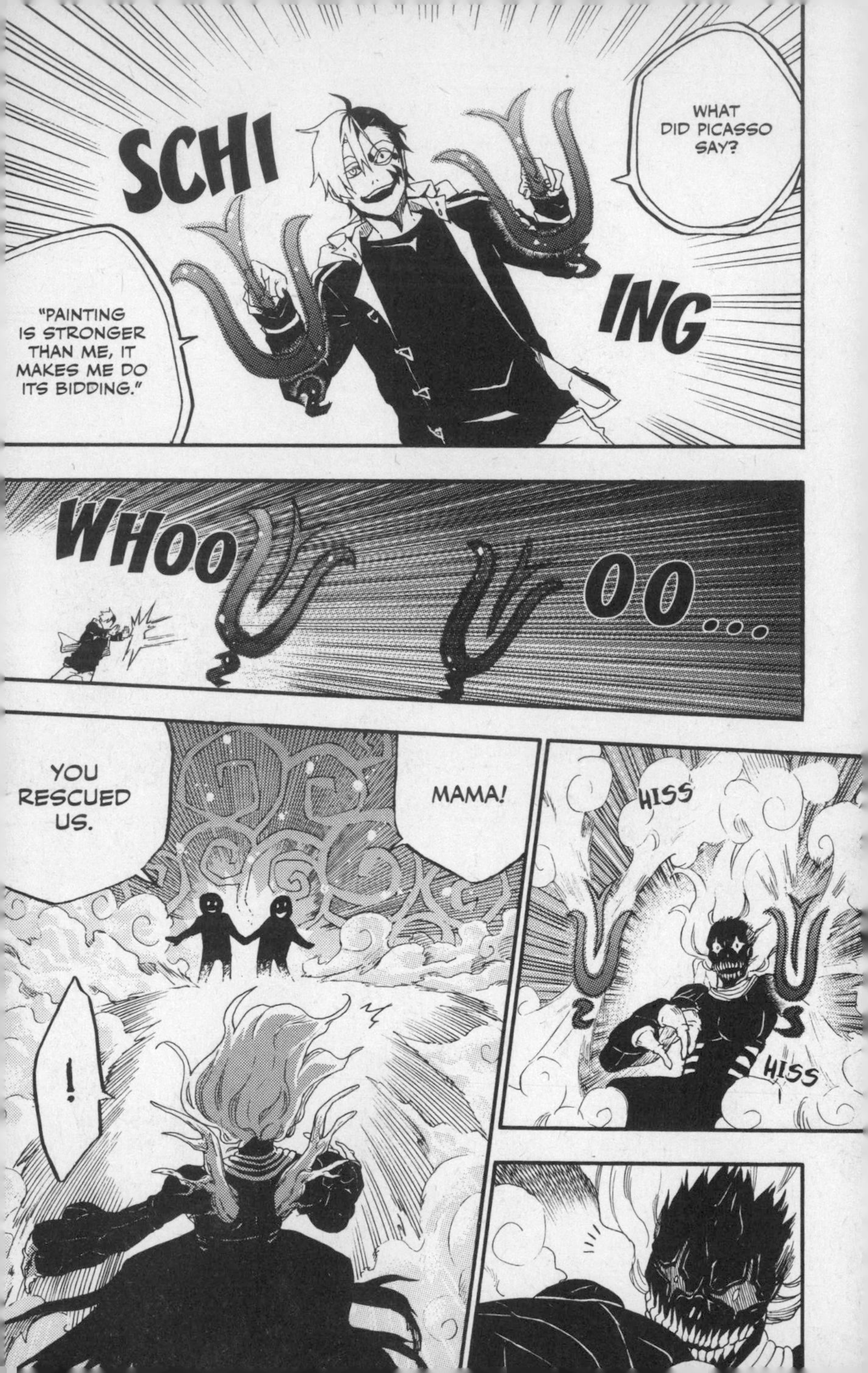
WHAT DID PICASSO SAY?
SCHI
ING
"PAINTING IS STRONGER THAN ME, IT MAKES ME DO ITS BIDDING."
WHOO
OO...
HISS
HISS
MAMA!
YOU RESCUED US.
!

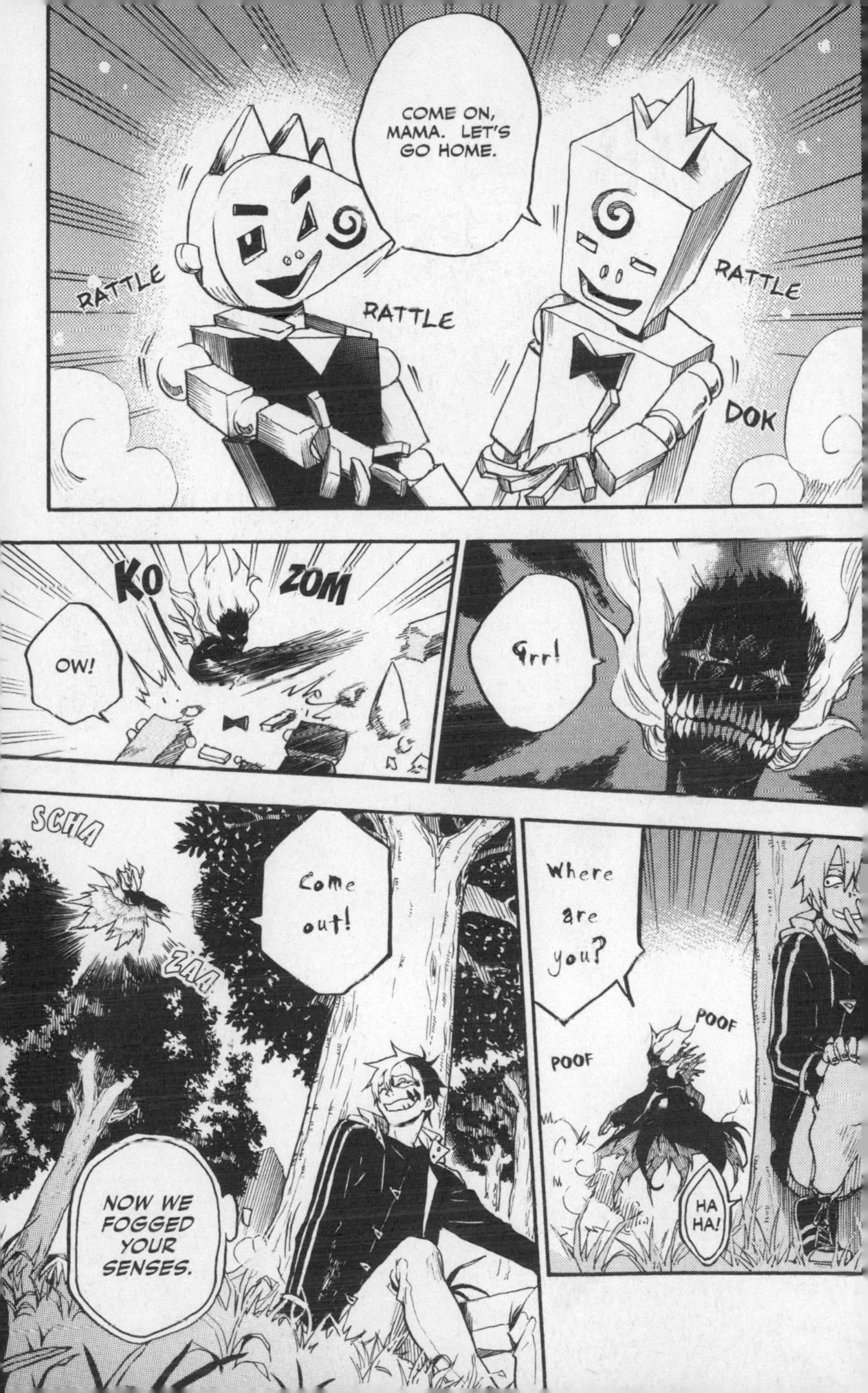

COME ON, MAMA. LET'S GO HOME.
RATTLE
RATTLE
RATTLE
DOK
Grr!
ZOM
KO
OW!
Where are you?
POOF
POOF
HA HA!
Come out!
SCHA
ZAA
NOW WE FOGGED YOUR SENSES.

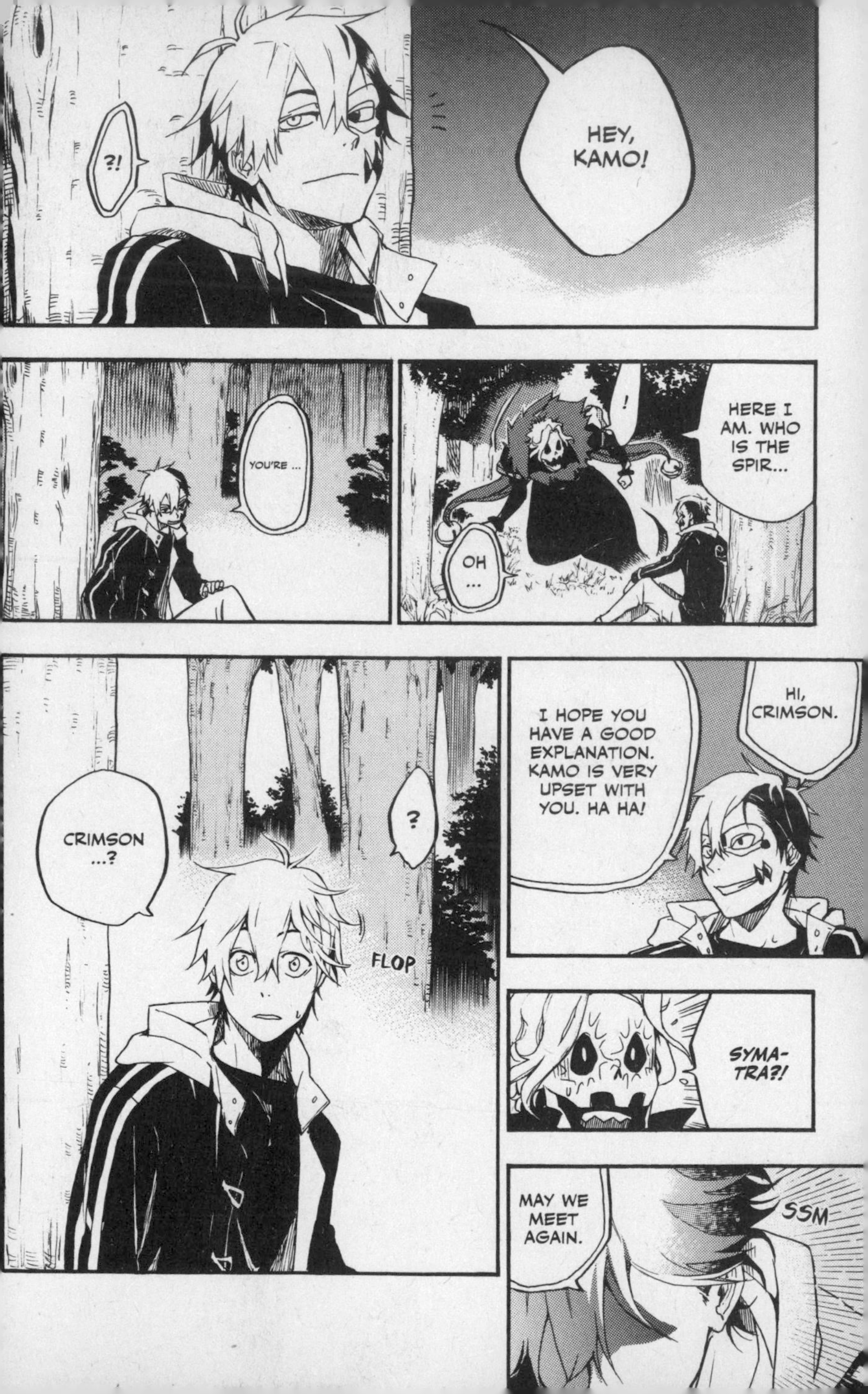
HEY, KAMO!
?!
HERE I AM. WHO IS THE SPIR...
!
OH ...
YOU'RE ...
HI, CRIMSON.
I HOPE YOU HAVE A GOOD EXPLANATION. KAMO IS VERY UPSET WITH YOU. HA HA!
SYMA-TRA?!
SSM
MAY WE MEET AGAIN.
?
CRIMSON ...?
FLOP

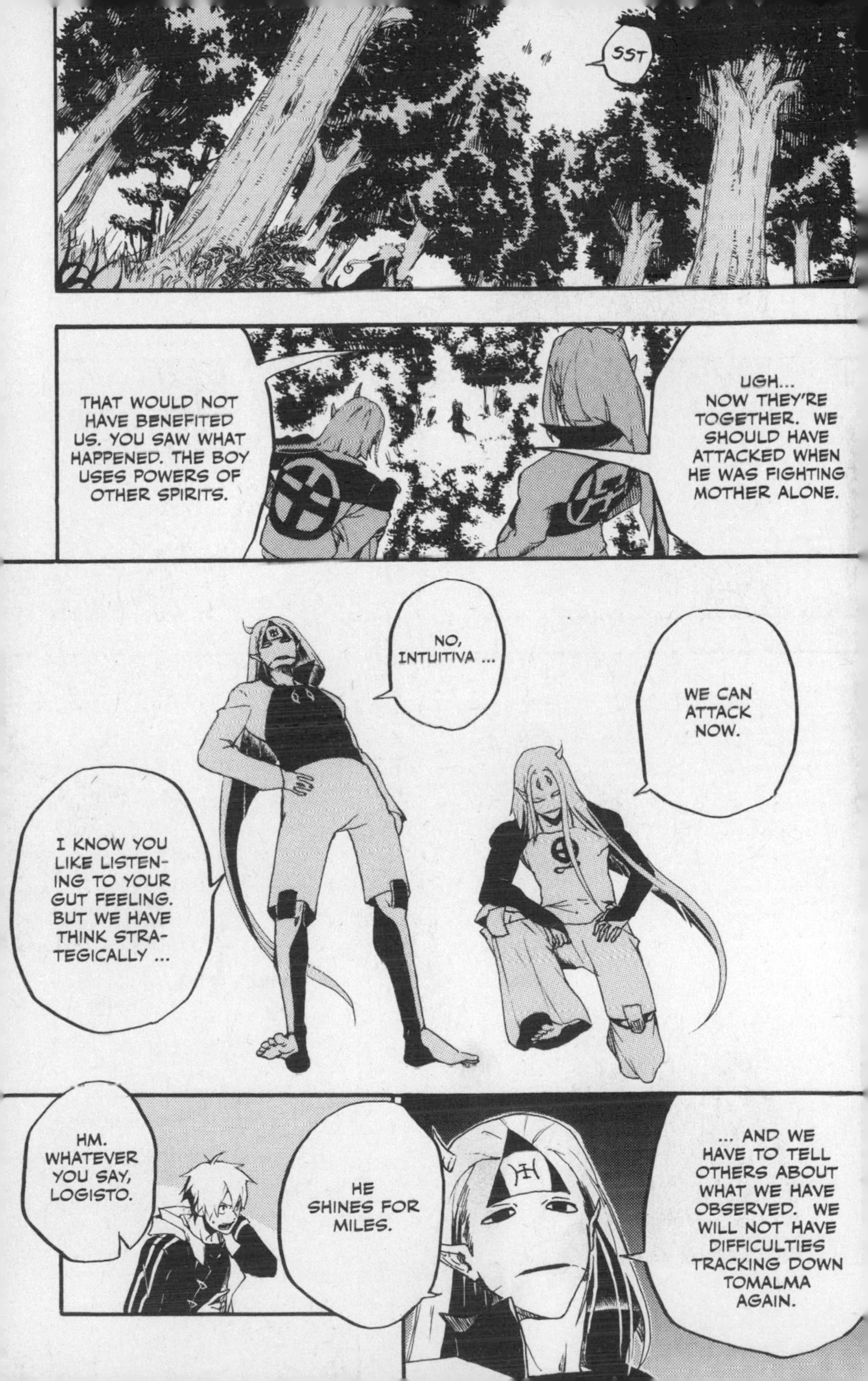
SST
UGH... NOW THEY'RE TOGETHER. WE SHOULD HAVE ATTACKED WHEN HE WAS FIGHTING MOTHER ALONE.
THAT WOULD NOT HAVE BENEFITED US. YOU SAW WHAT HAPPENED. THE BOY USES POWERS OF OTHER SPIRITS.
WE CAN ATTACK NOW.
NO, INTUITIVA ...
I KNOW YOU LIKE LISTEN-ING TO YOUR GUT FEELING. BUT WE HAVE THINK STRA-TEGICALLY ...
... AND WE HAVE TO TELL OTHERS ABOUT WHAT WE HAVE OBSERVED. WE WILL NOT HAVE DIFFICULTIES TRACKING DOWN TOMALMA AGAIN.
HE SHINES FOR MILES.
HM. WHATEVER YOU SAY, LOGISTO.

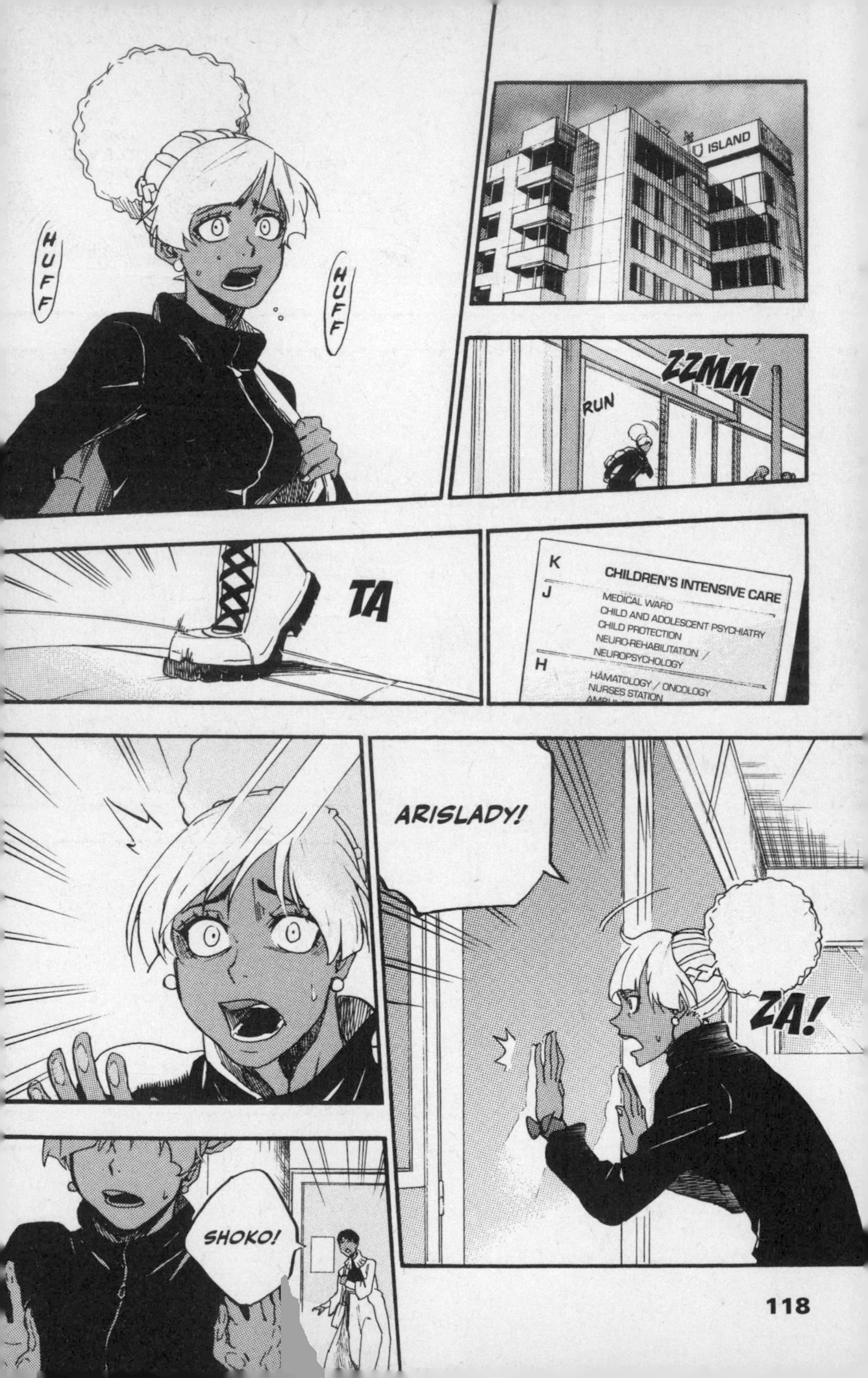
ISLAND
ZZMM
RUN
HUFF
HUFF
K
CHILDREN'S INTENSIVE CARE
J
MEDICAL WARD
CHILD AND ADOLESCENT PSYCHIATRY
CHILD PROTECTION
NEURO-REHABILITATION /
NEUROPSYCHOLOGY
H
HÄMATOLOGY / ONCOLOGY
NURSES STATION
TA
ARISLADY!
ZA!
SHOKO!

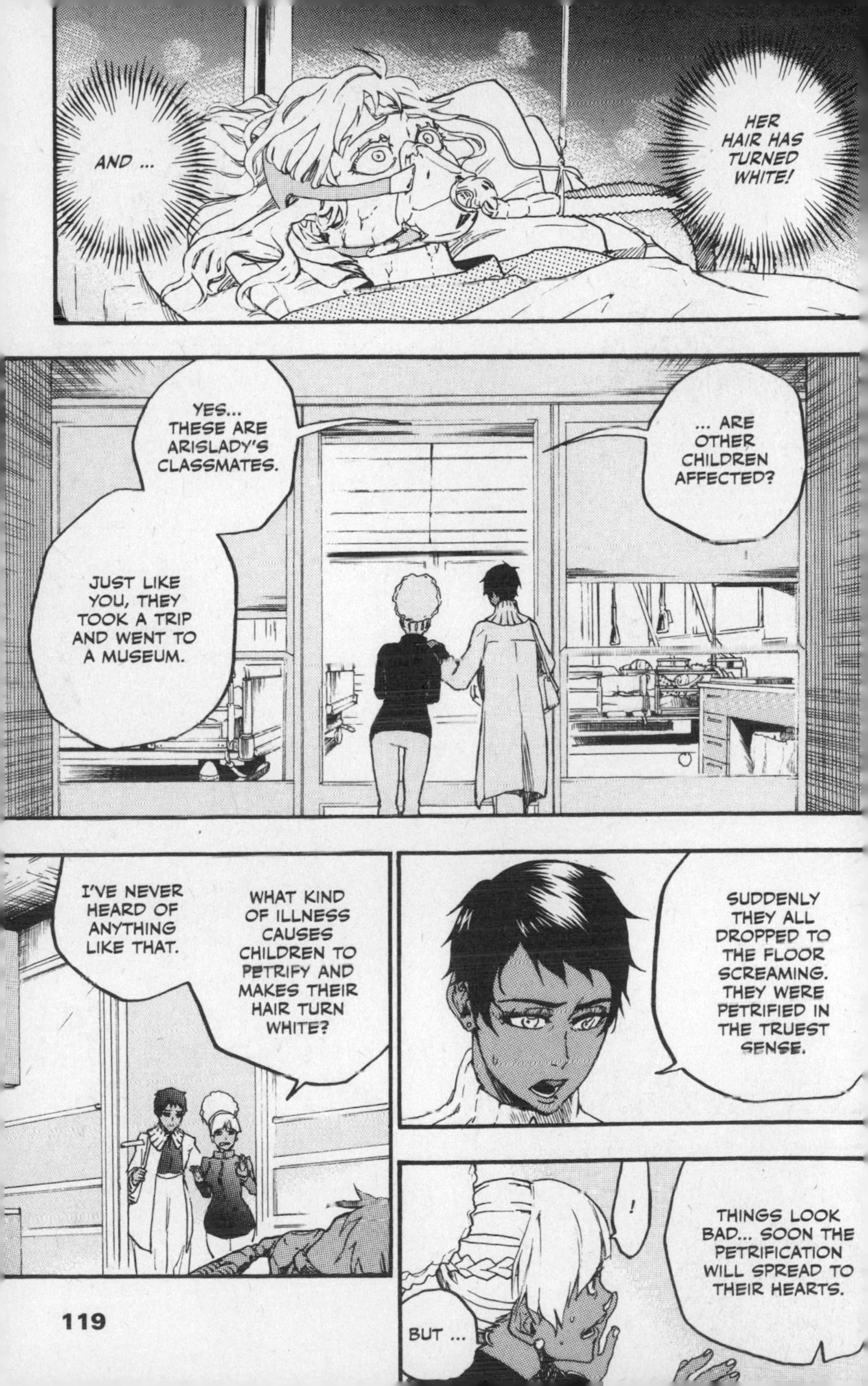
HER HAIR HAS TURNED WHITE!
AND ...
... ARE OTHER CHILDREN AFFECTED?
YES... THESE ARE ARISLADY'S CLASSMATES.
JUST LIKE YOU, THEY TOOK A TRIP AND WENT TO A MUSEUM.
SUDDENLY THEY ALL DROPPED TO THE FLOOR SCREAMING. THEY WERE PETRIFIED IN THE TRUEST SENSE.
!
THINGS LOOK BAD... SOON THE PETRIFICATION WILL SPREAD TO THEIR HEARTS.
BUT ...
WHAT KIND OF ILLNESS CAUSES CHILDREN TO PETRIFY AND MAKES THEIR HAIR TURN WHITE?
I'VE NEVER HEARD OF ANYTHING LIKE THAT.

MOM...

...?!

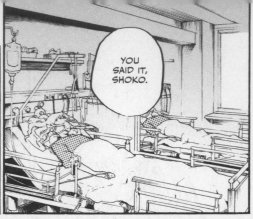

YOU SAID IT, SHOKO.

NOT REALLY...

SOMETHING IS NOT RIGHT HERE.

WHA...

YOU UNDERSTAND WHAT I MEAN.

SOMETHING WITH SPIRITS?!

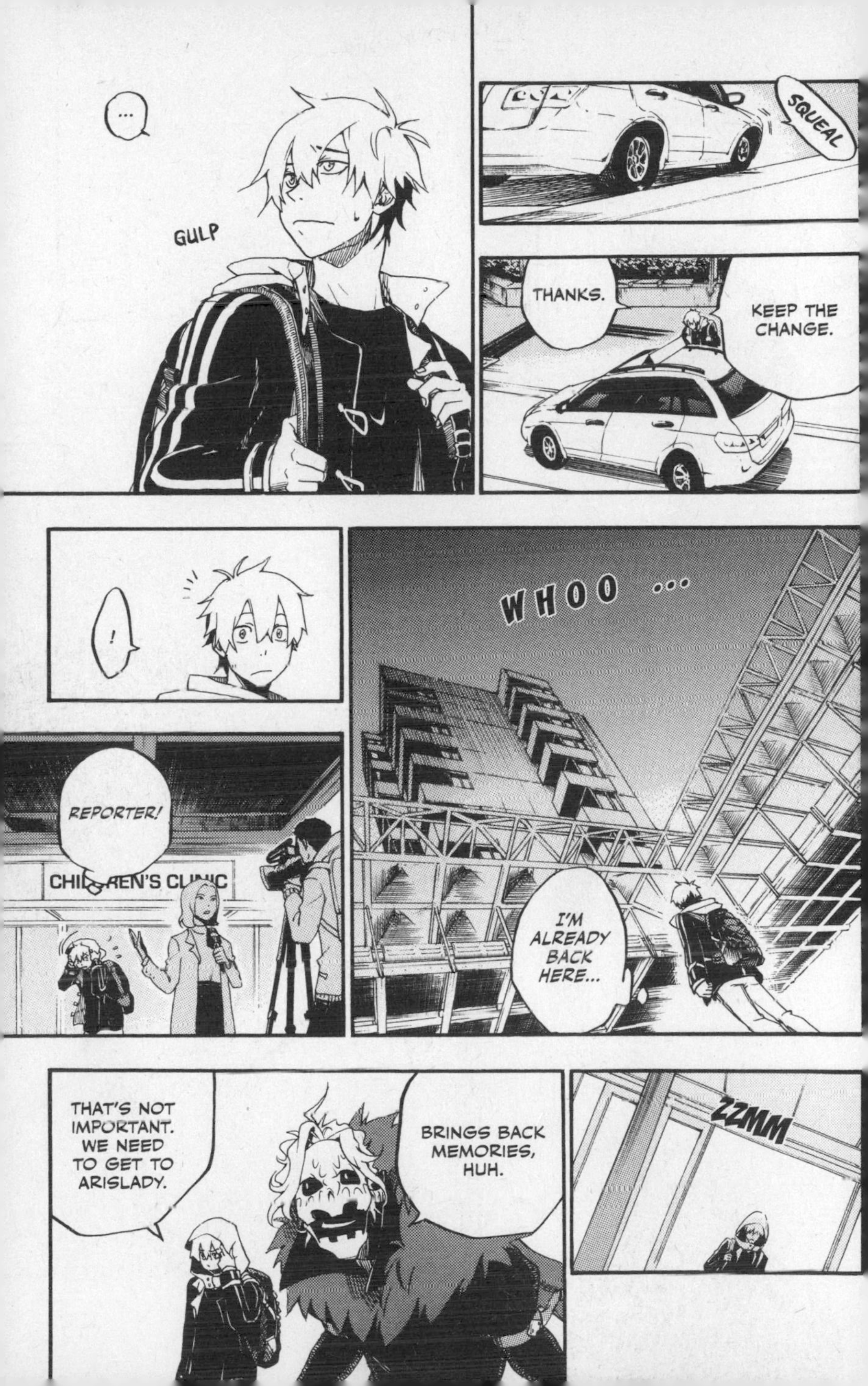
SQUEAL
KEEP THE CHANGE.
THANKS.
...
GULP
WHOO ...
I'M ALREADY BACK HERE...
!
REPORTER!
CHILDREN'S CLINIC
ZZMM
BRINGS BACK MEMORIES, HUH.
THAT'S NOT IMPORTANT. WE NEED TO GET TO ARISLADY.

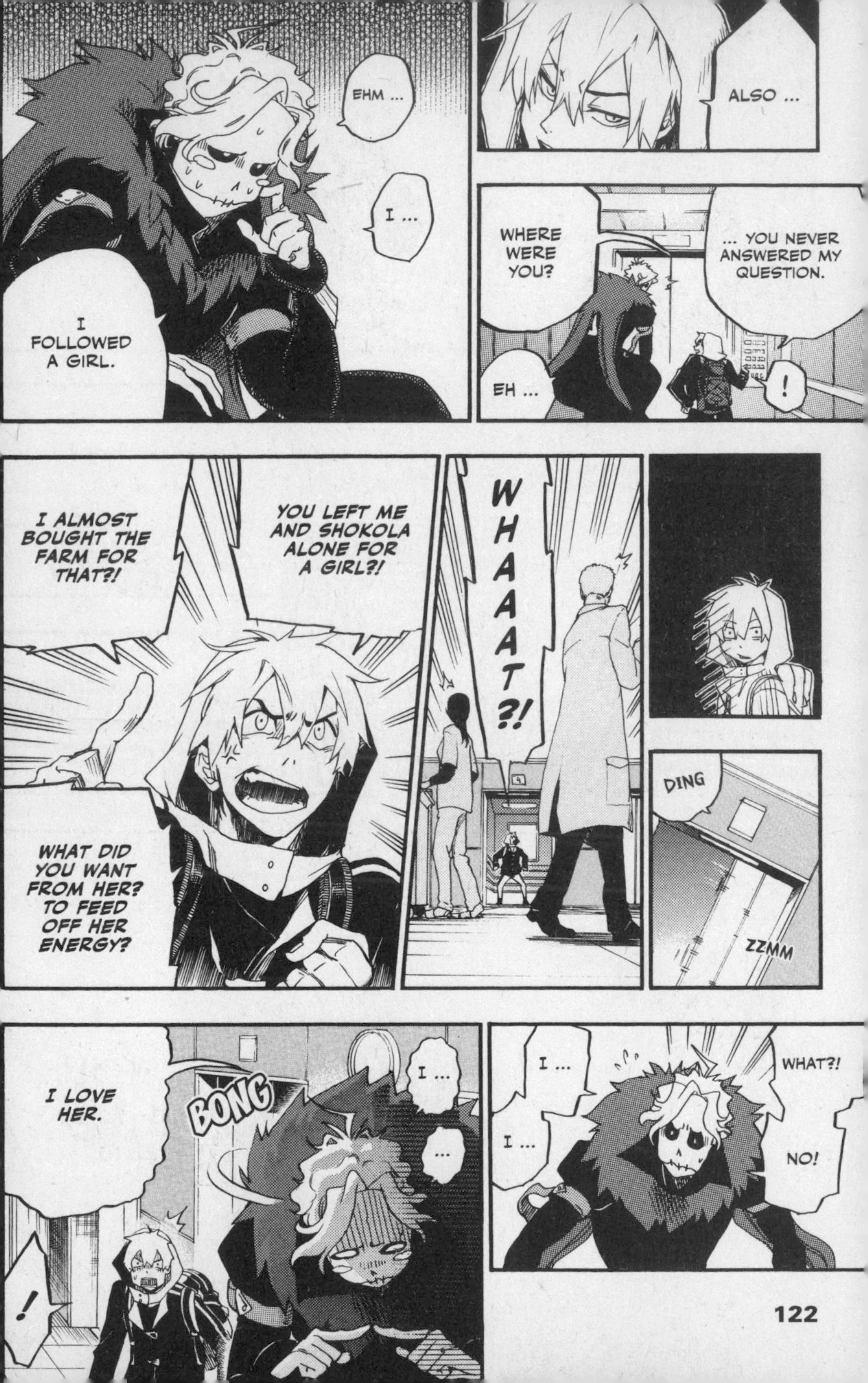
ALSO ...
... YOU NEVER ANSWERED MY QUESTION.
WHERE WERE YOU?
!
EH ...
EHM ...
I ...
I FOLLOWED A GIRL.
DING
ZZMM
WHAAAAT?!
YOU LEFT ME AND SHOKOLA ALONE FOR A GIRL?!
I ALMOST BOUGHT THE FARM FOR THAT?!
WHAT DID YOU WANT FROM HER? TO FEED OFF HER ENERGY?
WHAT?!
I ...
NO!
I ...
I ...
...
BONG
I LOVE HER.
!

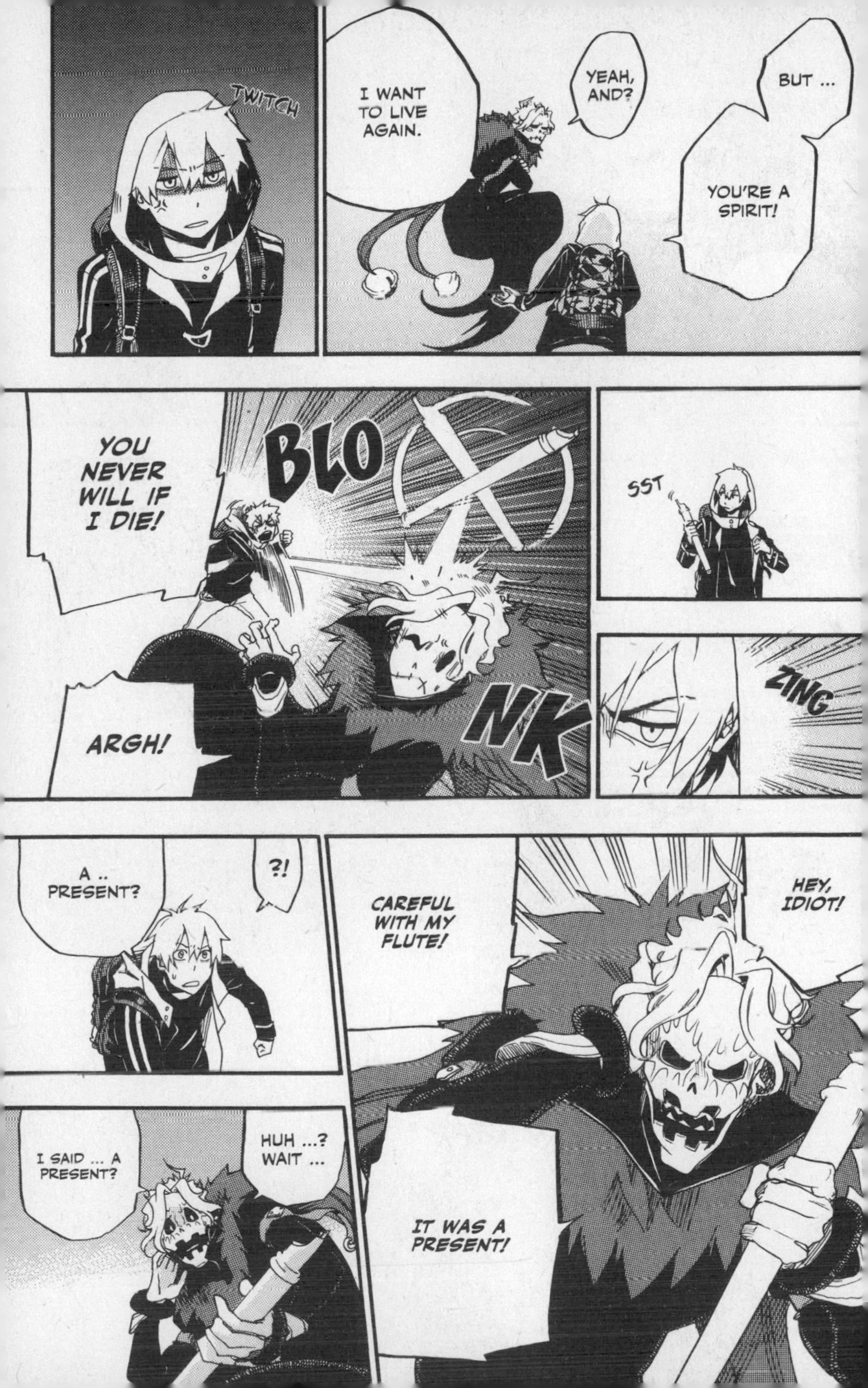
BUT ...
YOU'RE A SPIRIT!
YEAH, AND?
I WANT TO LIVE AGAIN.
TWITCH
SST
ZING
YOU NEVER WILL IF I DIE!
BLONK
ARGH!
HEY, IDIOT!
CAREFUL WITH MY FLUTE!
IT WAS A PRESENT!
?!
A .. PRESENT?
HUH ...? WAIT ...
I SAID ... A PRESENT?

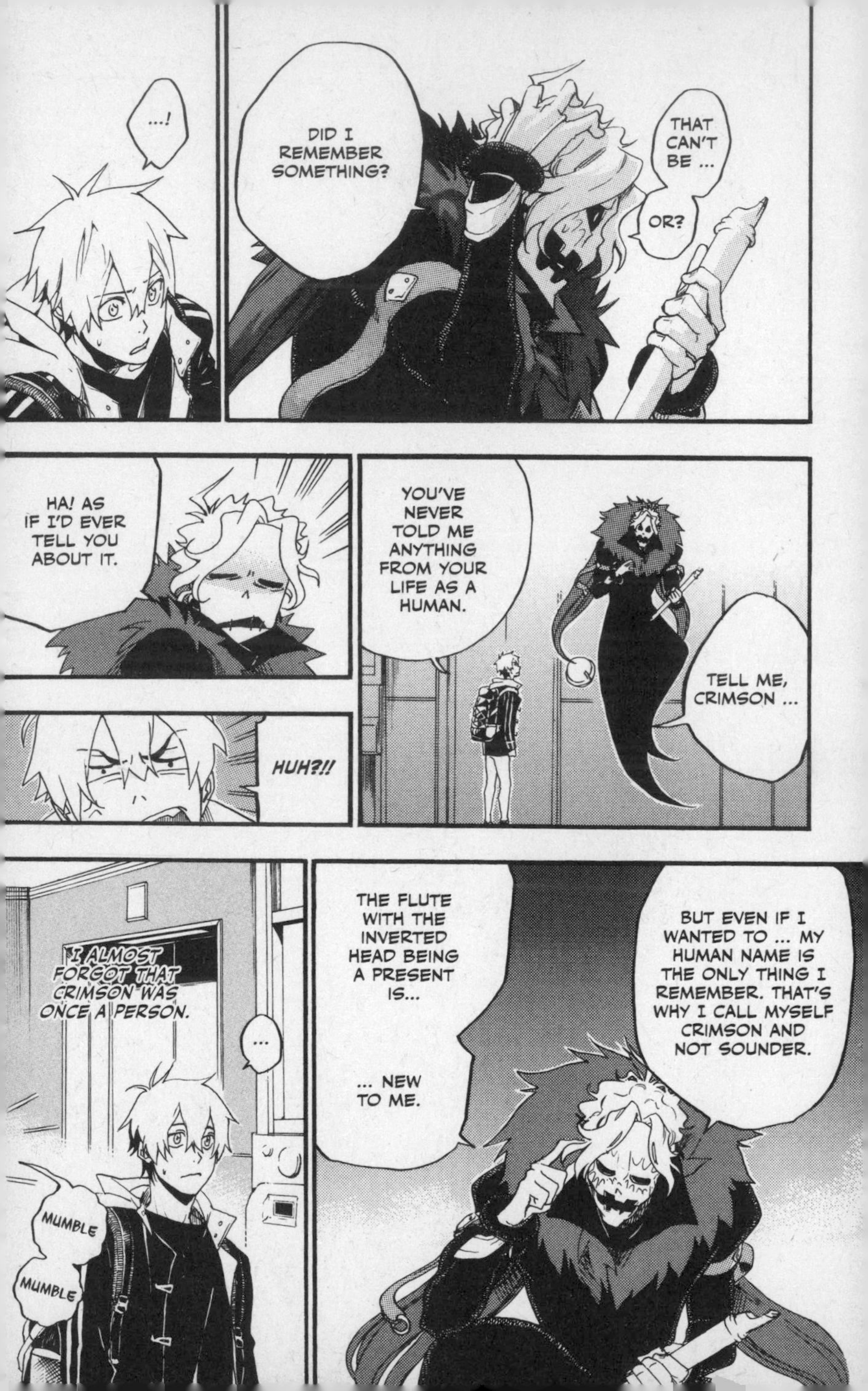
DID I REMEMBER SOMETHING?
THAT CAN'T BE ...
OR?
...!
YOU'VE NEVER TOLD ME ANYTHING FROM YOUR LIFE AS A HUMAN.
TELL ME, CRIMSON ...
HA! AS IF I'D EVER TELL YOU ABOUT IT.
HUH?!!
BUT EVEN IF I WANTED TO ... MY HUMAN NAME IS THE ONLY THING I REMEMBER. THAT'S WHY I CALL MYSELF CRIMSON AND NOT SOUNDER.
THE FLUTE WITH THE INVERTED HEAD BEING A PRESENT IS...
... NEW TO ME.
I ALMOST FORGOT THAT CRIMSON WAS ONCE A PERSON.
...
MUMBLE
MUMBLE

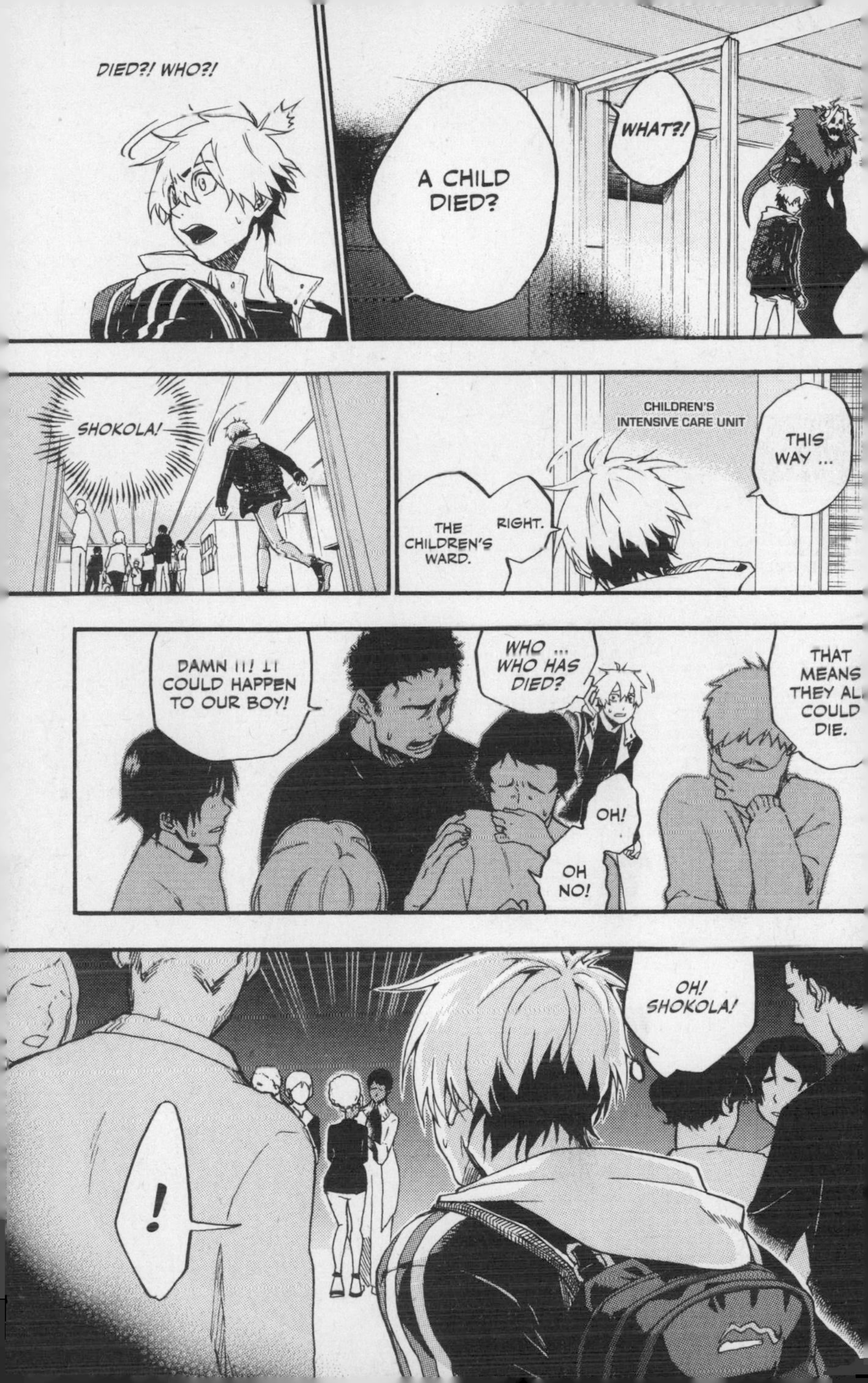
A CHILD DIED?
WHAT?!
DIED?! WHO?!
CHILDREN'S INTENSIVE CARE UNIT
THIS WAY ...
RIGHT.
THE CHILDREN'S WARD.
SHOKOLA!
THAT MEANS THEY AL COULD DIE.
WHO ... WHO HAS DIED?
DAMN IT! IT COULD HAPPEN TO OUR BOY!
OH!
OH NO!
OH! SHOKOLA!
!

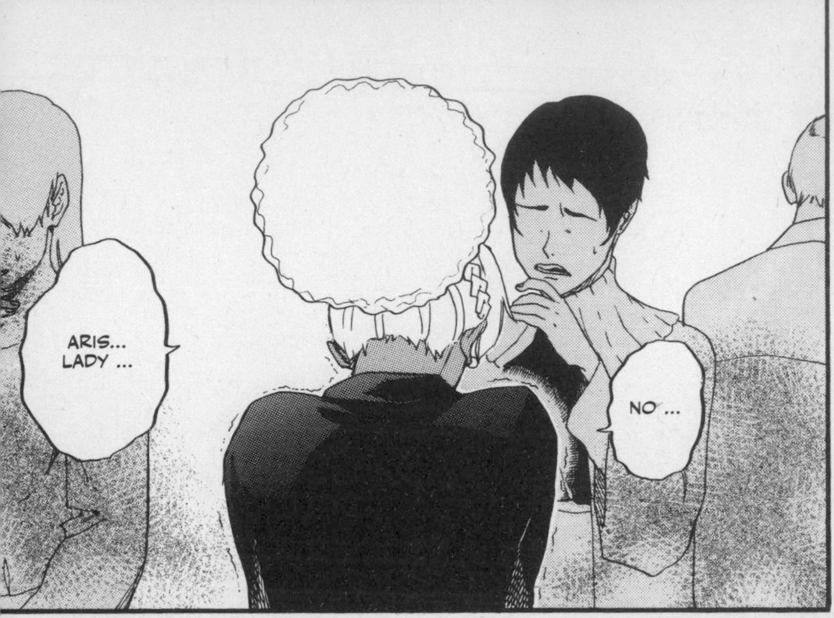
NO...
ARIS... LADY ...
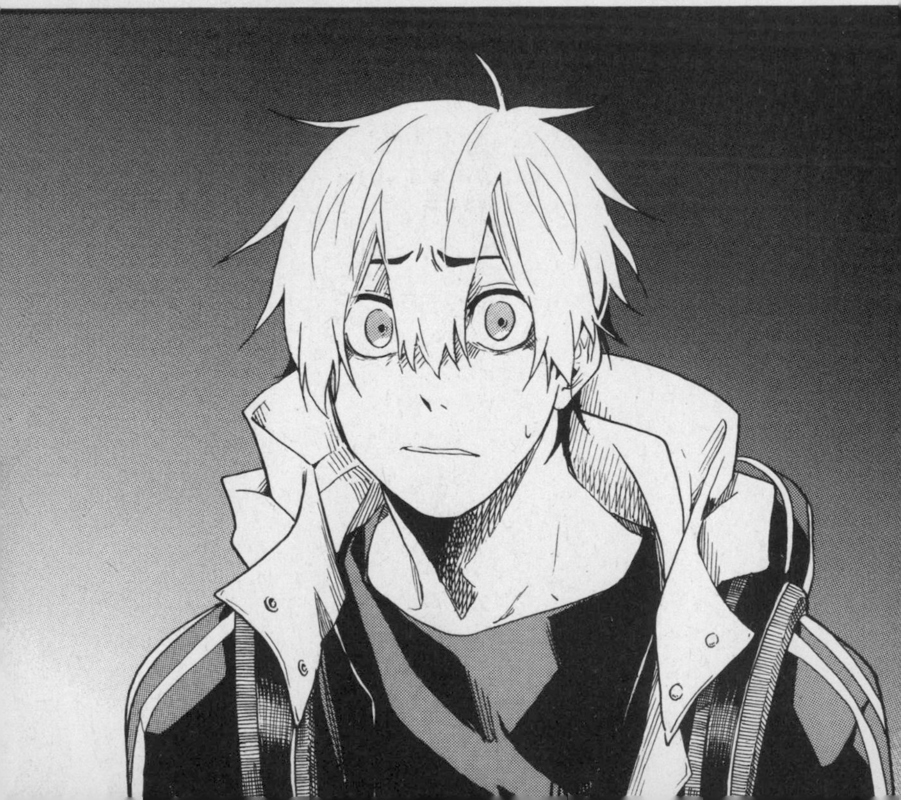

11
NO CHANCE

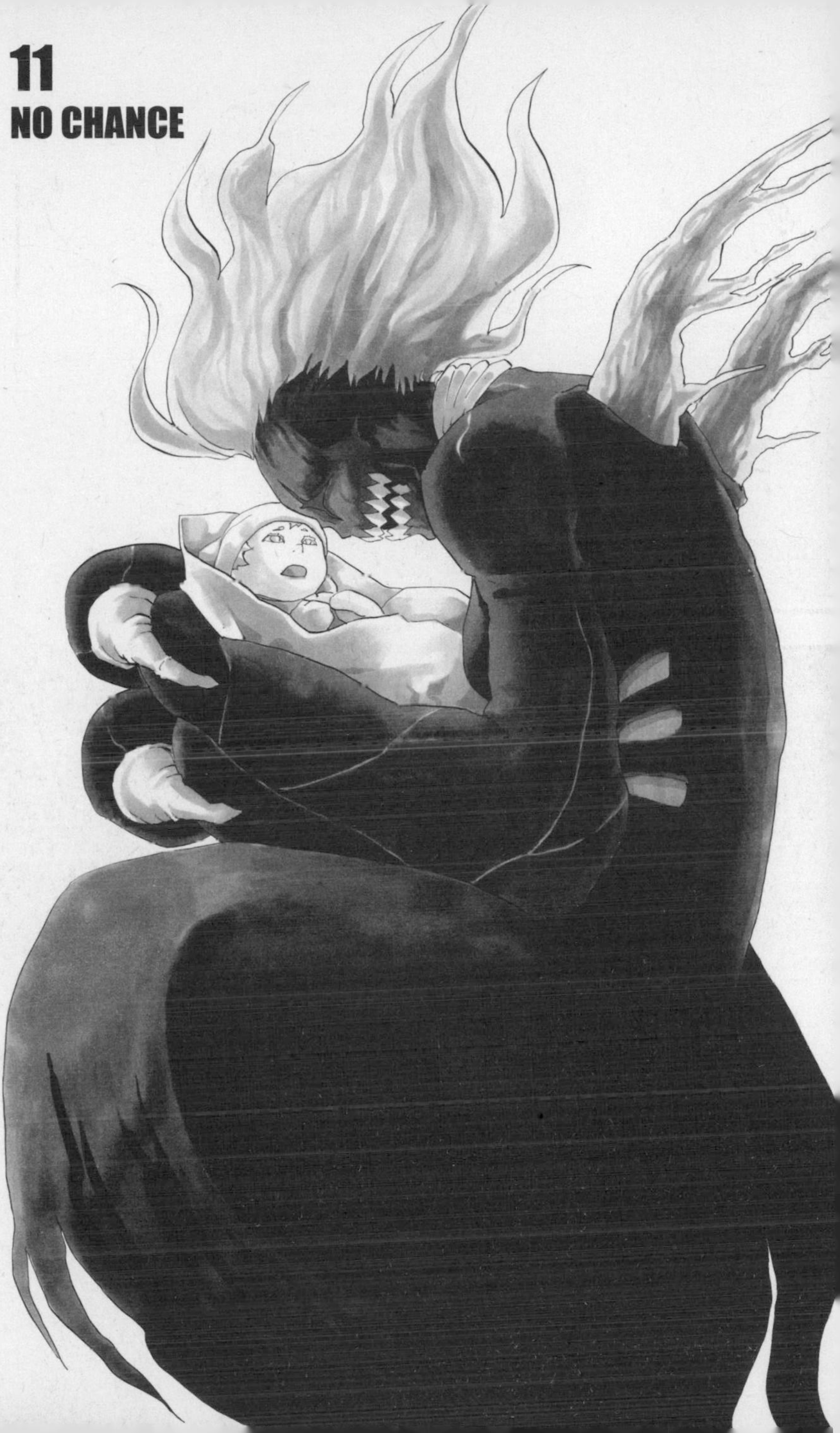

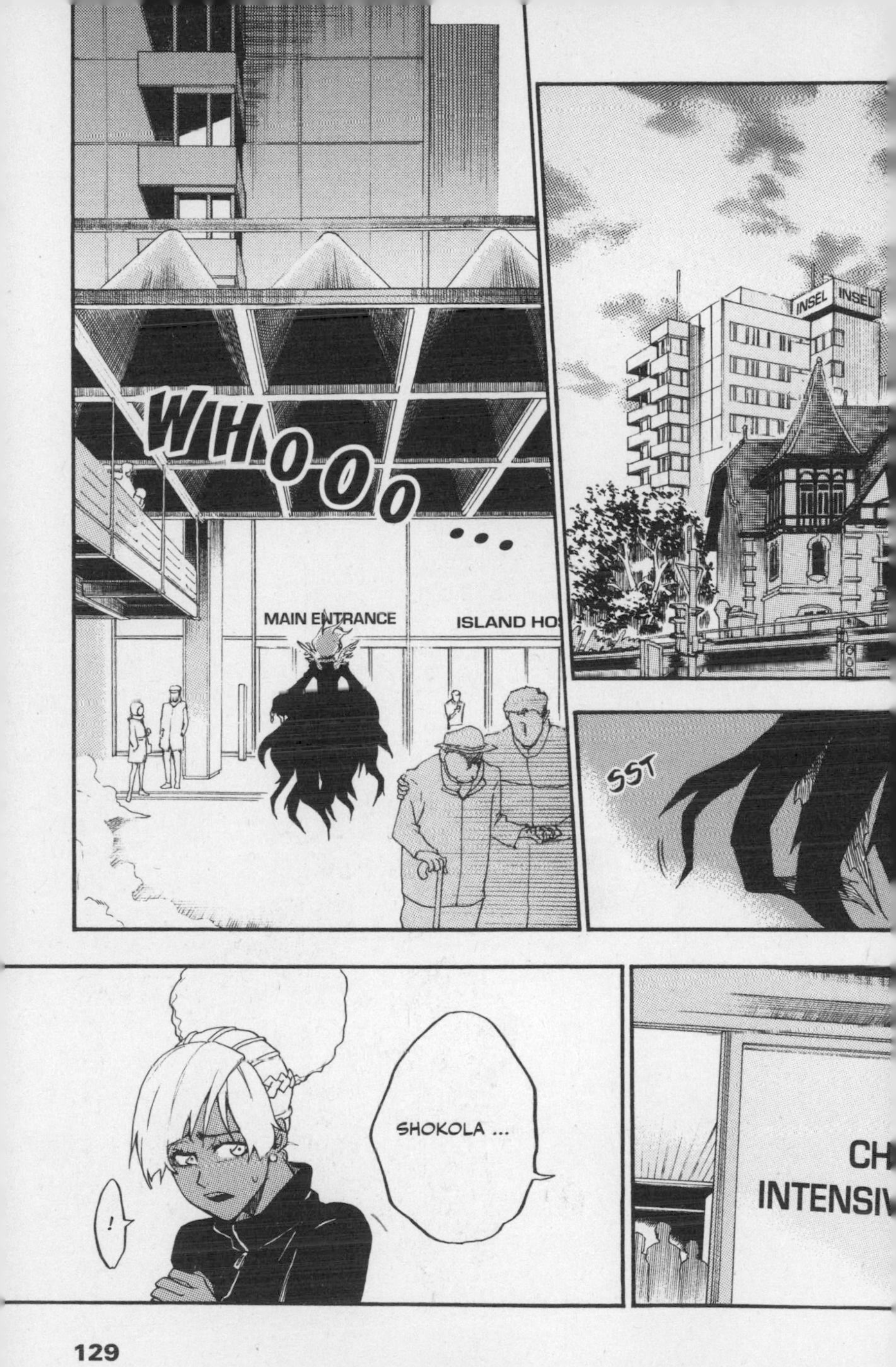
INSEL
INSEL
SST
WHOOOO...
MAIN ENTRANCE
ISLAND HOS
CH
INTENSIV
SHOKOLA ...
!

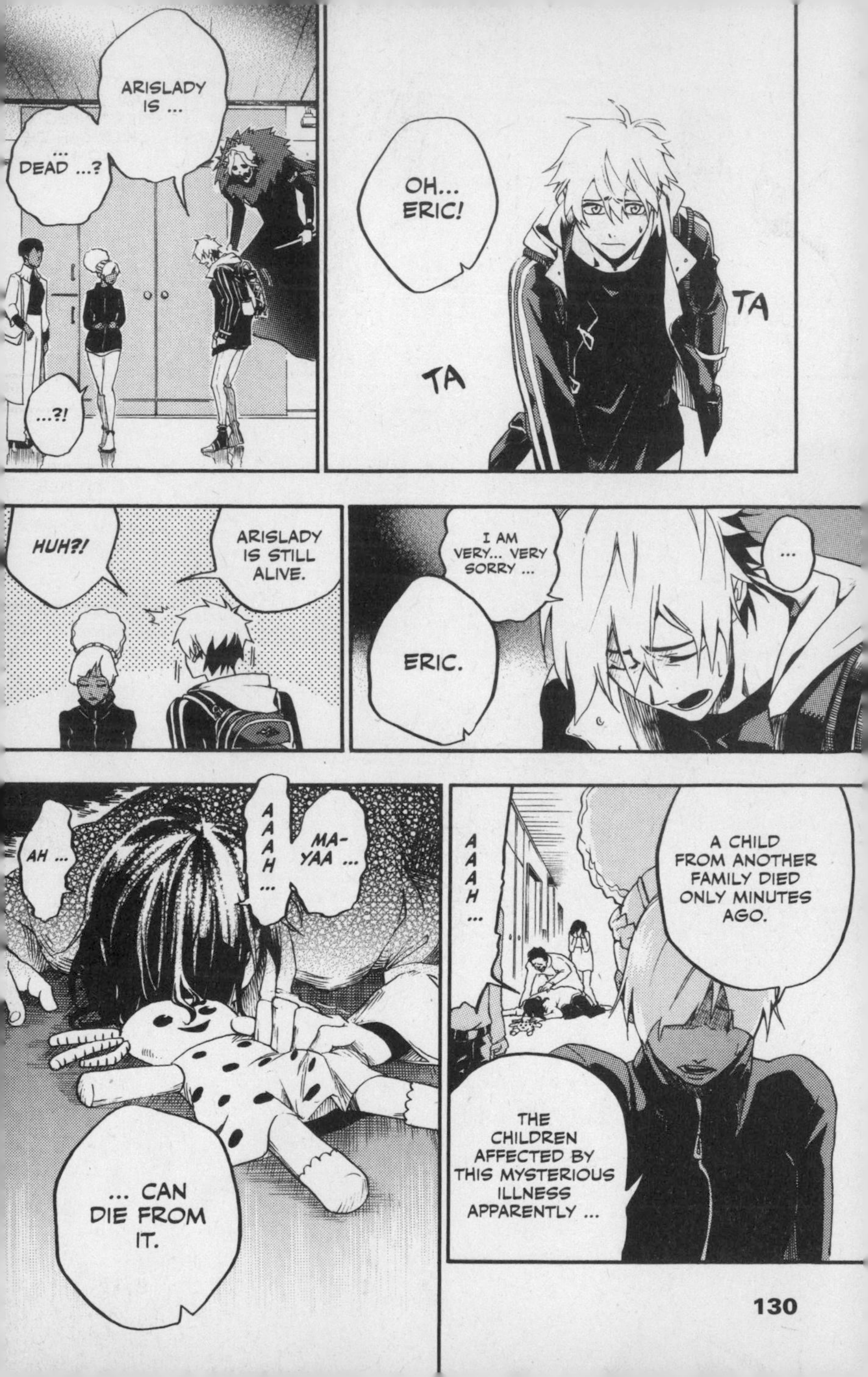
OH... ERIC!
TA
TA
ARISLADY IS ...
... DEAD ...?
...?!
...
I AM VERY... VERY SORRY ...
ERIC.
ARISLADY IS STILL ALIVE.
HUH?!
A CHILD FROM ANOTHER FAMILY DIED ONLY MINUTES AGO.
AAAAH ...
THE CHILDREN AFFECTED BY THIS MYSTERIOUS ILLNESS APPARENTLY ...
MA-YAA ...
AAAAH ...
AH ...
... CAN DIE FROM IT.

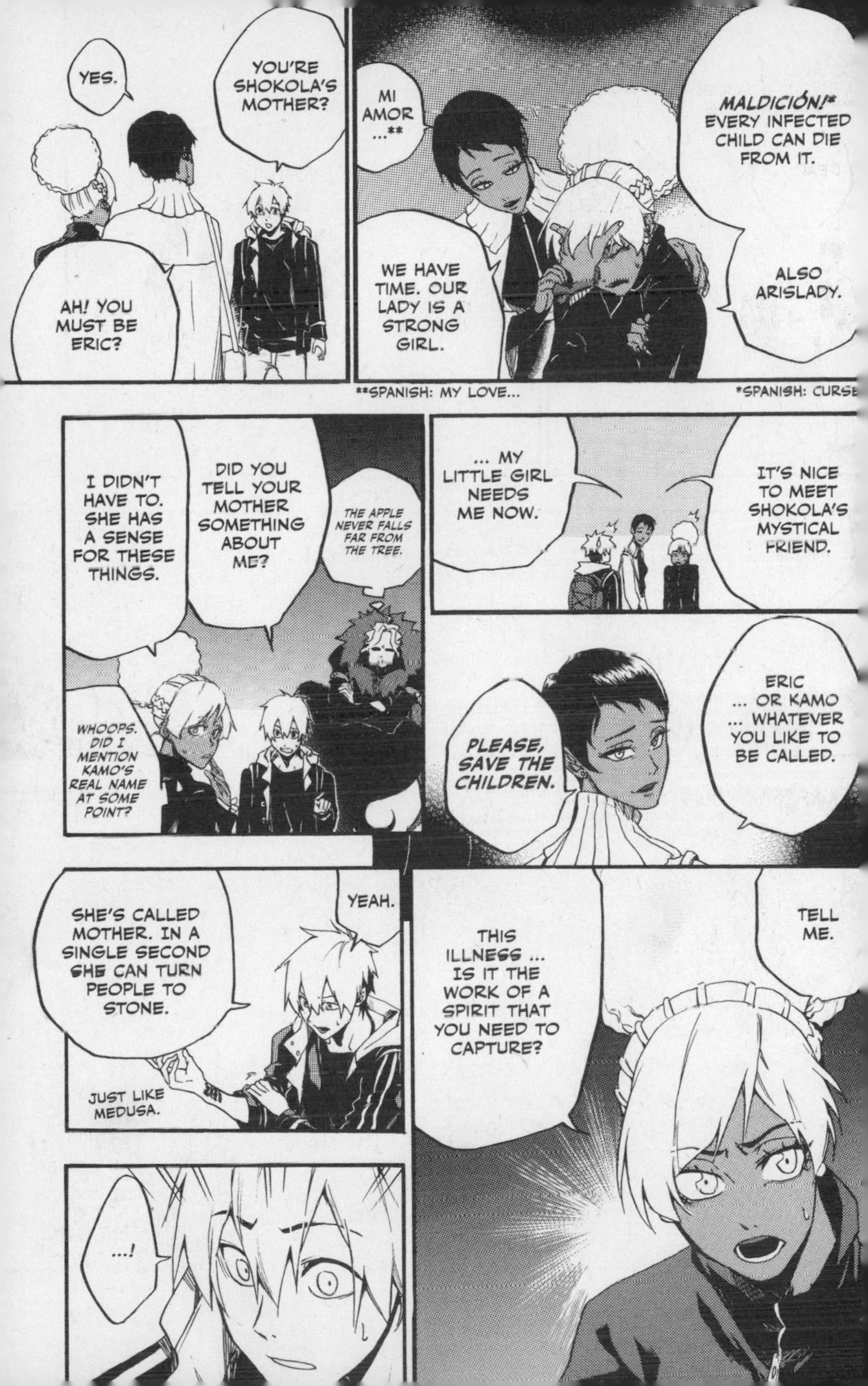
MALDICIÓN!* EVERY INFECTED CHILD CAN DIE FROM IT.
ALSO ARISLADY.
WE HAVE TIME. OUR LADY IS A STRONG GIRL.
MI AMOR ...**
YOU'RE SHOKOLA'S MOTHER?
YES.
AH! YOU MUST BE ERIC?
*SPANISH: CURSE
**SPANISH: MY LOVE...
IT'S NICE TO MEET SHOKOLA'S MYSTICAL FRIEND.
... MY LITTLE GIRL NEEDS ME NOW.
DID YOU TELL YOUR MOTHER SOMETHING ABOUT ME?
THE APPLE NEVER FALLS FAR FROM THE TREE.
I DIDN'T HAVE TO. SHE HAS A SENSE FOR THESE THINGS.
WHOOPS. DID I MENTION KAMO'S REAL NAME AT SOME POINT?
ERIC ... OR KAMO ... WHATEVER YOU LIKE TO BE CALLED.
PLEASE, SAVE THE CHILDREN.
TELL ME.
THIS ILLNESS ... IS IT THE WORK OF A SPIRIT THAT YOU NEED TO CAPTURE?
YEAH.
SHE'S CALLED MOTHER. IN A SINGLE SECOND SHE CAN TURN PEOPLE TO STONE.
JUST LIKE MEDUSA.
...!

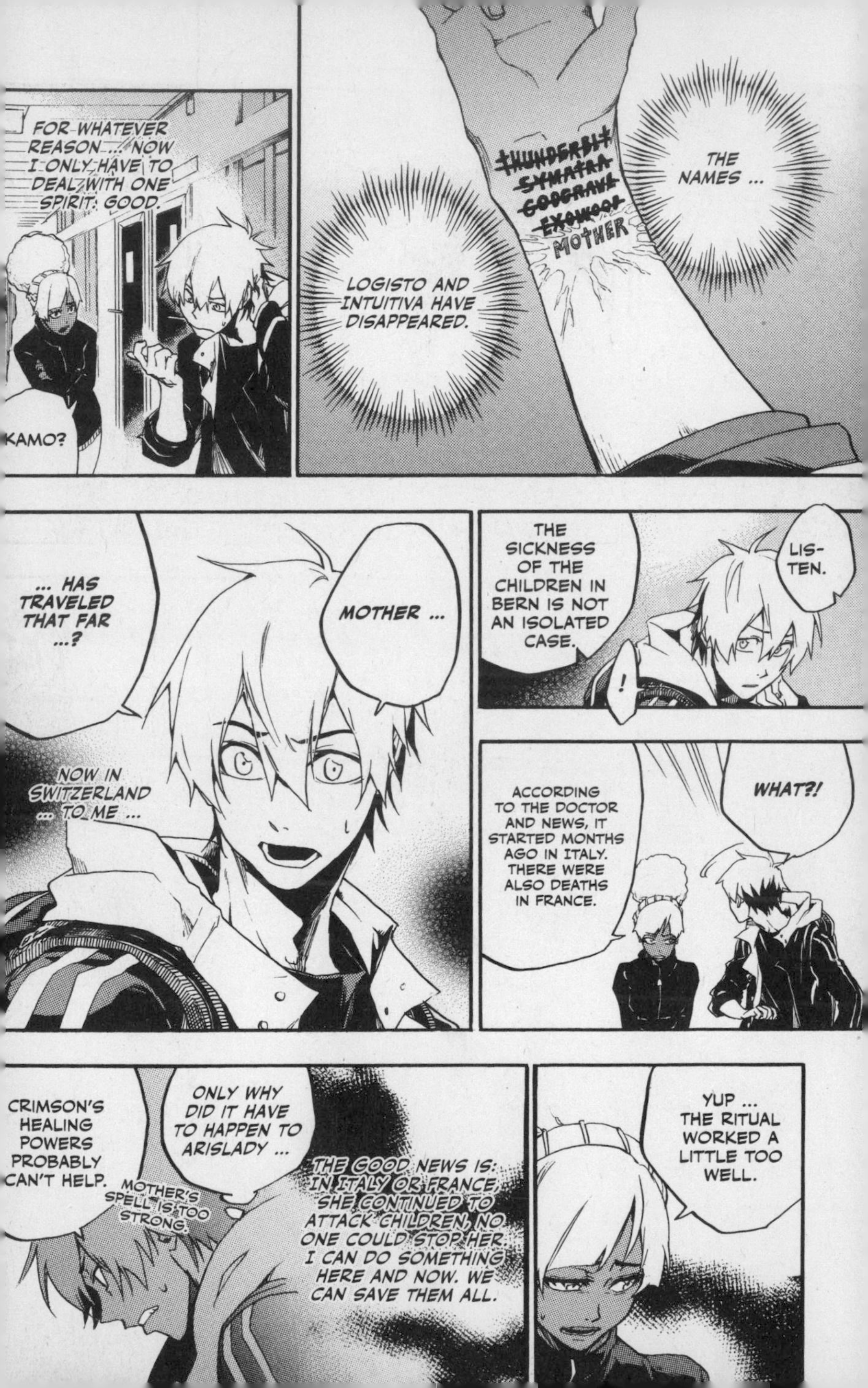
THE NAMES ...
MOTHER
LOGISTO AND INTUITIVA HAVE DISAPPEARED.
FOR WHATEVER REASON ... NOW I ONLY HAVE TO DEAL WITH ONE SPIRIT: GOOD.
KAMO?
LIS- TEN.
THE SICKNESS OF THE CHILDREN IN BERN IS NOT AN ISOLATED CASE.
!
WHAT?!
ACCORDING TO THE DOCTOR AND NEWS, IT STARTED MONTHS AGO IN ITALY. THERE WERE ALSO DEATHS IN FRANCE.
MOTHER ...
... HAS TRAVELED THAT FAR ...?
NOW IN SWITZERLAND ... TO ME ...
YUP ... THE RITUAL WORKED A LITTLE TOO WELL.
ONLY WHY DID IT HAVE TO HAPPEN TO ARISLADY ...
CRIMSON'S HEALING POWERS PROBABLY CAN'T HELP.
MOTHER'S SPELL IS TOO STRONG.
THE GOOD NEWS IS: IN ITALY OR FRANCE, SHE CONTINUED TO ATTACK CHILDREN, NO ONE COULD STOP HER. I CAN DO SOMETHING HERE AND NOW. WE CAN SAVE THEM ALL.

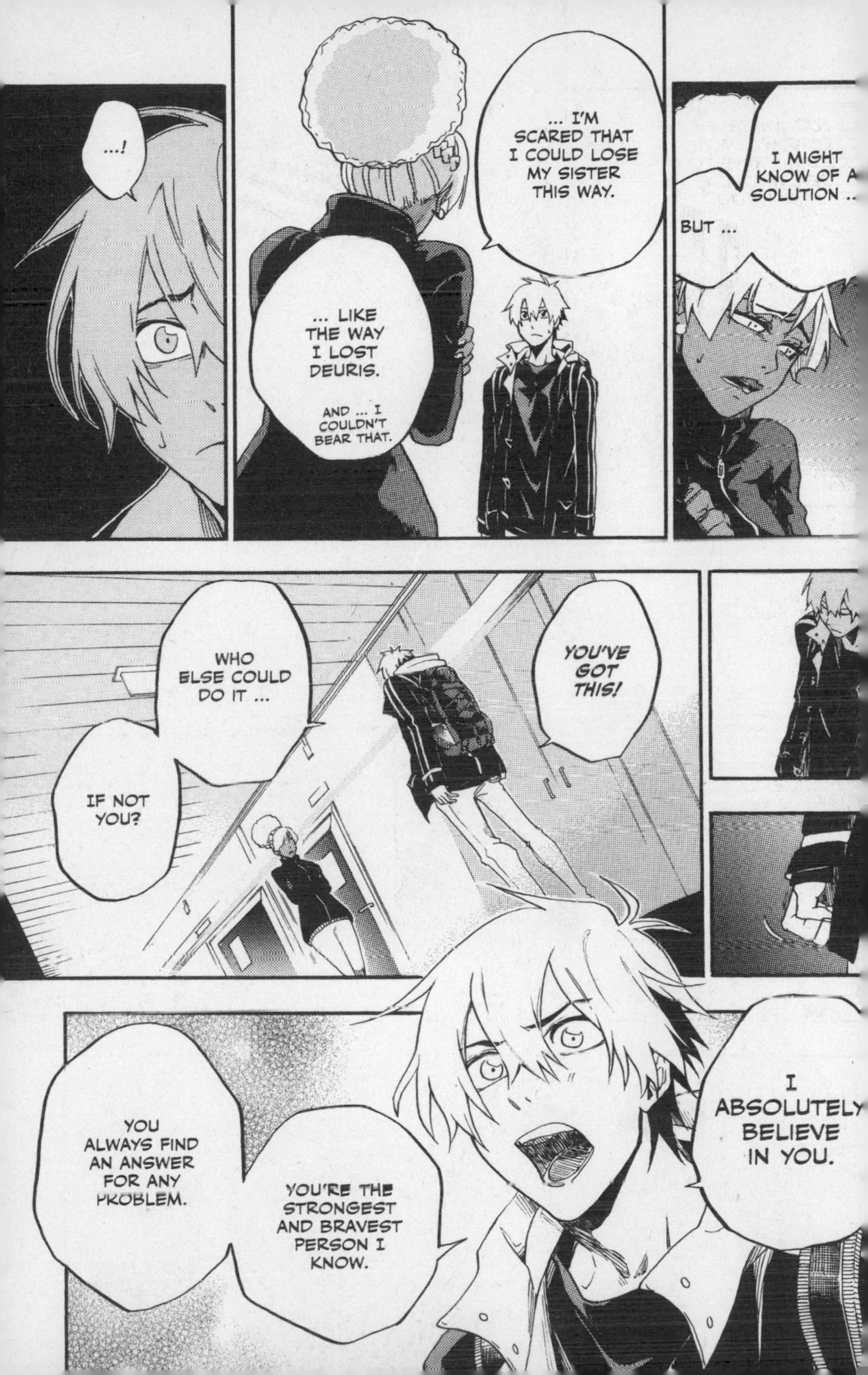
I MIGHT KNOW OF A SOLUTION ..
BUT ...
... I'M SCARED THAT I COULD LOSE MY SISTER THIS WAY.
... LIKE THE WAY I LOST DEURIS.
AND ... I COULDN'T BEAR THAT.
...!
YOU'VE GOT THIS!
WHO ELSE COULD DO IT ...
IF NOT YOU?
I ABSOLUTELY BELIEVE IN YOU.
YOU'RE THE STRONGEST AND BRAVEST PERSON I KNOW.
YOU ALWAYS FIND AN ANSWER FOR ANY PROBLEM.

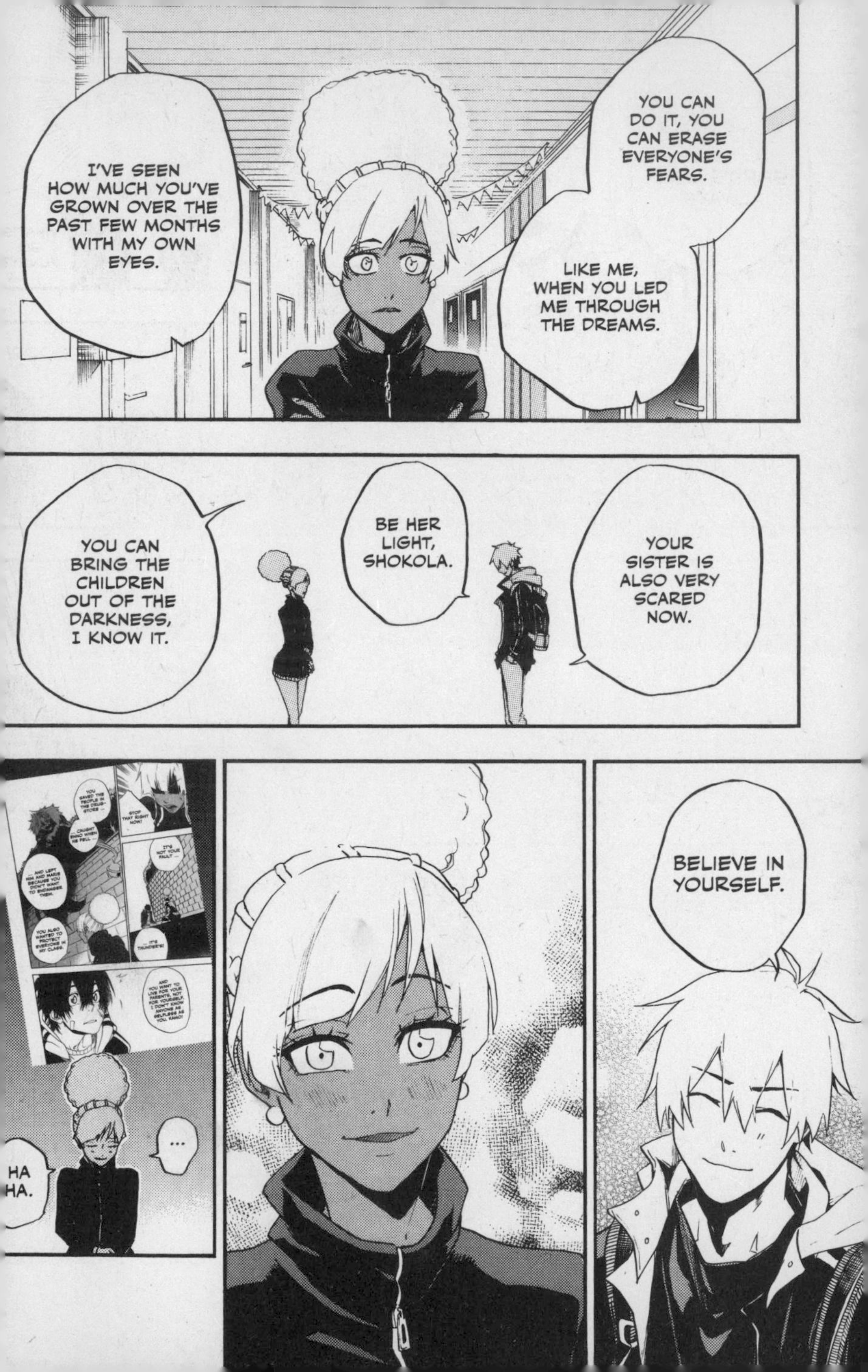
YOU CAN DO IT, YOU CAN ERASE EVERYONE'S FEARS.
LIKE ME, WHEN YOU LED ME THROUGH THE DREAMS.
I'VE SEEN HOW MUCH YOU'VE GROWN OVER THE PAST FEW MONTHS WITH MY OWN EYES.
YOUR SISTER IS ALSO VERY SCARED NOW.
BE HER LIGHT, SHOKOLA.
YOU CAN BRING THE CHILDREN OUT OF THE DARKNESS, I KNOW IT.
BELIEVE IN YOURSELF.
...
HA HA.

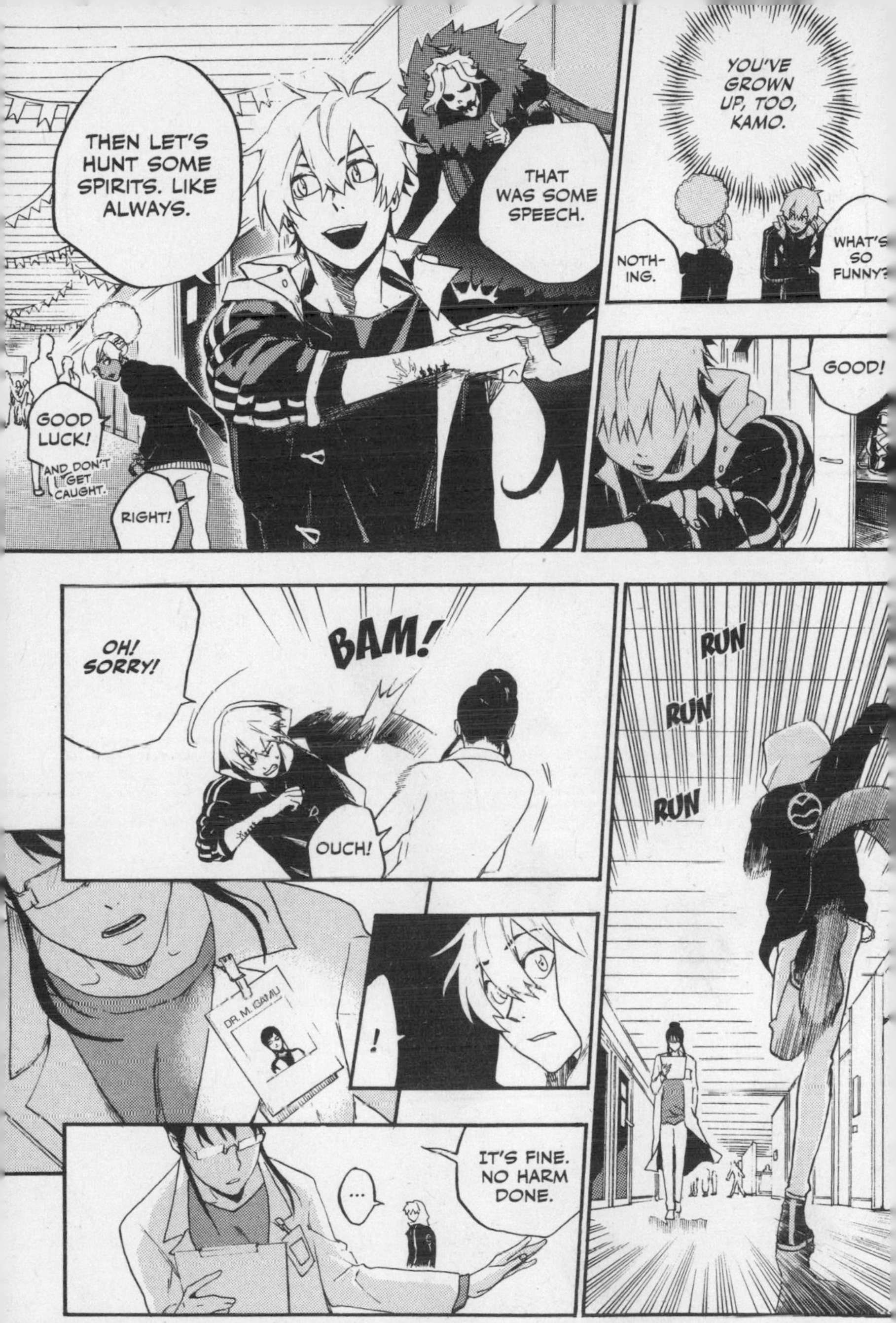
YOU'VE GROWN UP, TOO, KAMO.
WHAT'S SO FUNNY?
NOTHING.
GOOD!
THAT WAS SOME SPEECH.
THEN LET'S HUNT SOME SPIRITS. LIKE ALWAYS.
GOOD LUCK!
AND DON'T GET CAUGHT.
RIGHT!
RUN
RUN
RUN
BAM!
OH! SORRY!
OUCH!
DR. M. GAMU
!
...
IT'S FINE. NO HARM DONE.

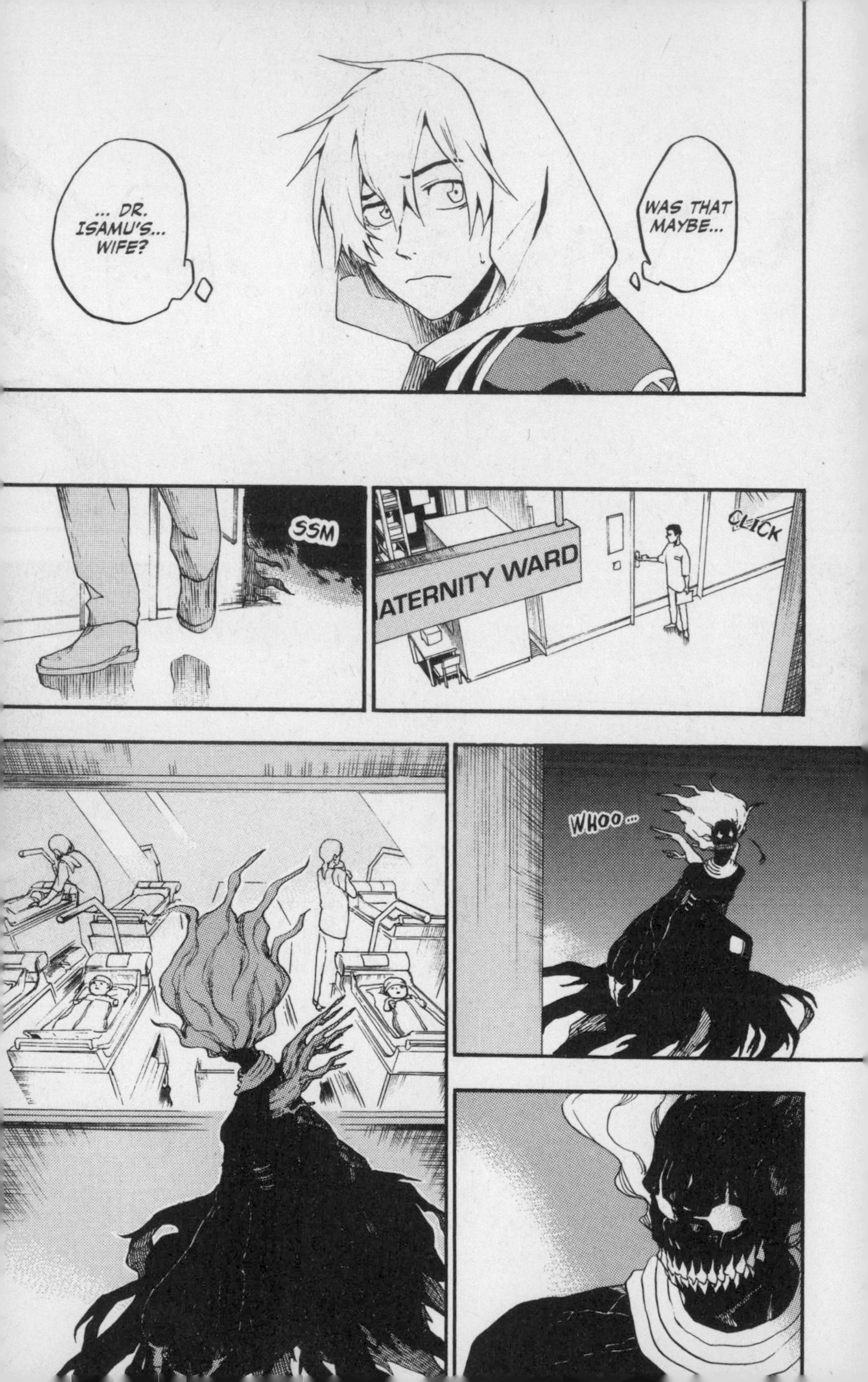
WAS THAT MAYBE...
... DR. ISAMU'S... WIFE?
ATERNITY WARD
CLICK
SSM
WHOO...

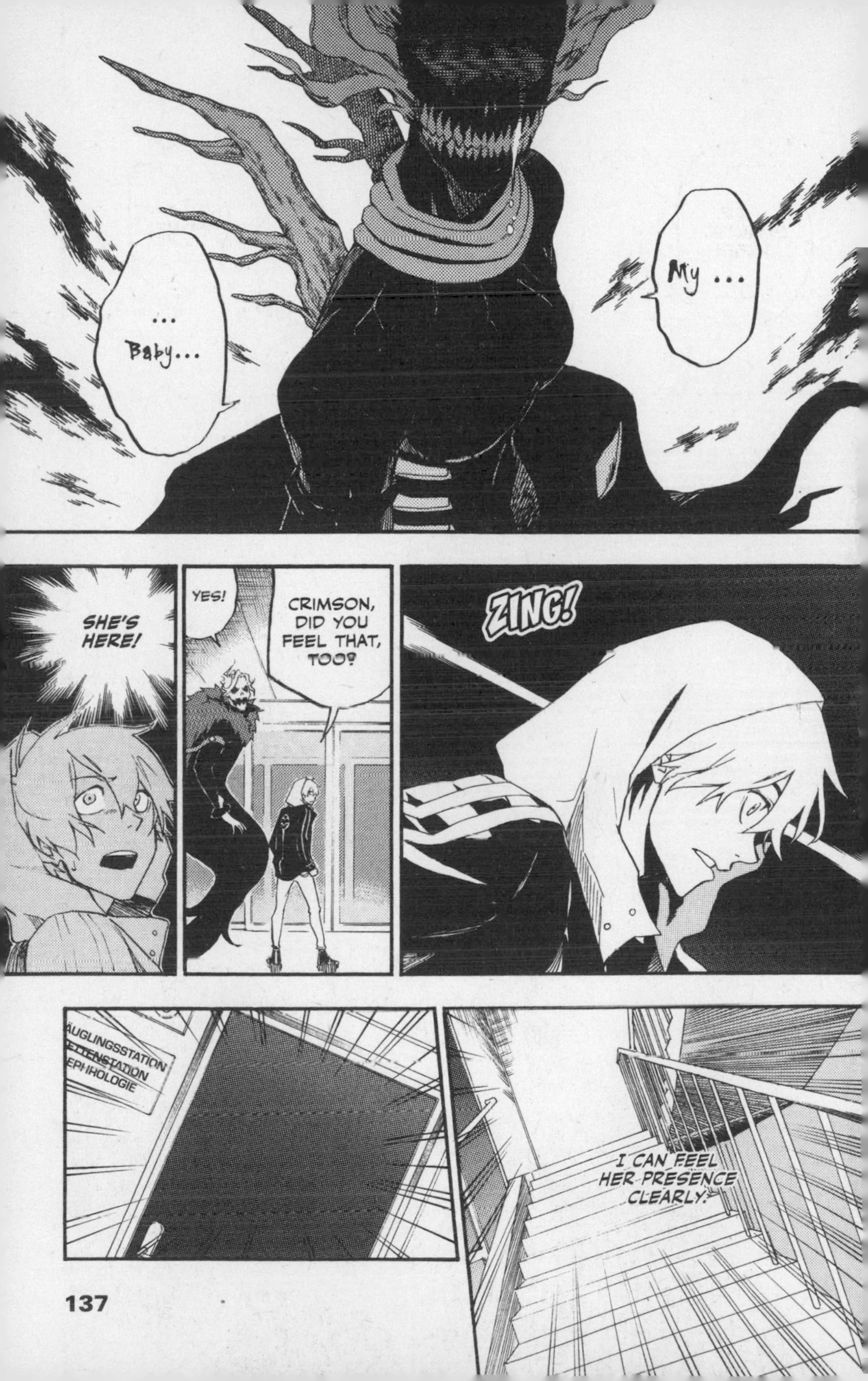
My ...
... Baby...
ZING!
CRIMSON, DID YOU FEEL THAT, TOO?
YES!
SHE'S HERE!
I CAN FEEL HER PRESENCE CLEARLY.
ÄUGLINGSSTATION
EPHROLOGIE

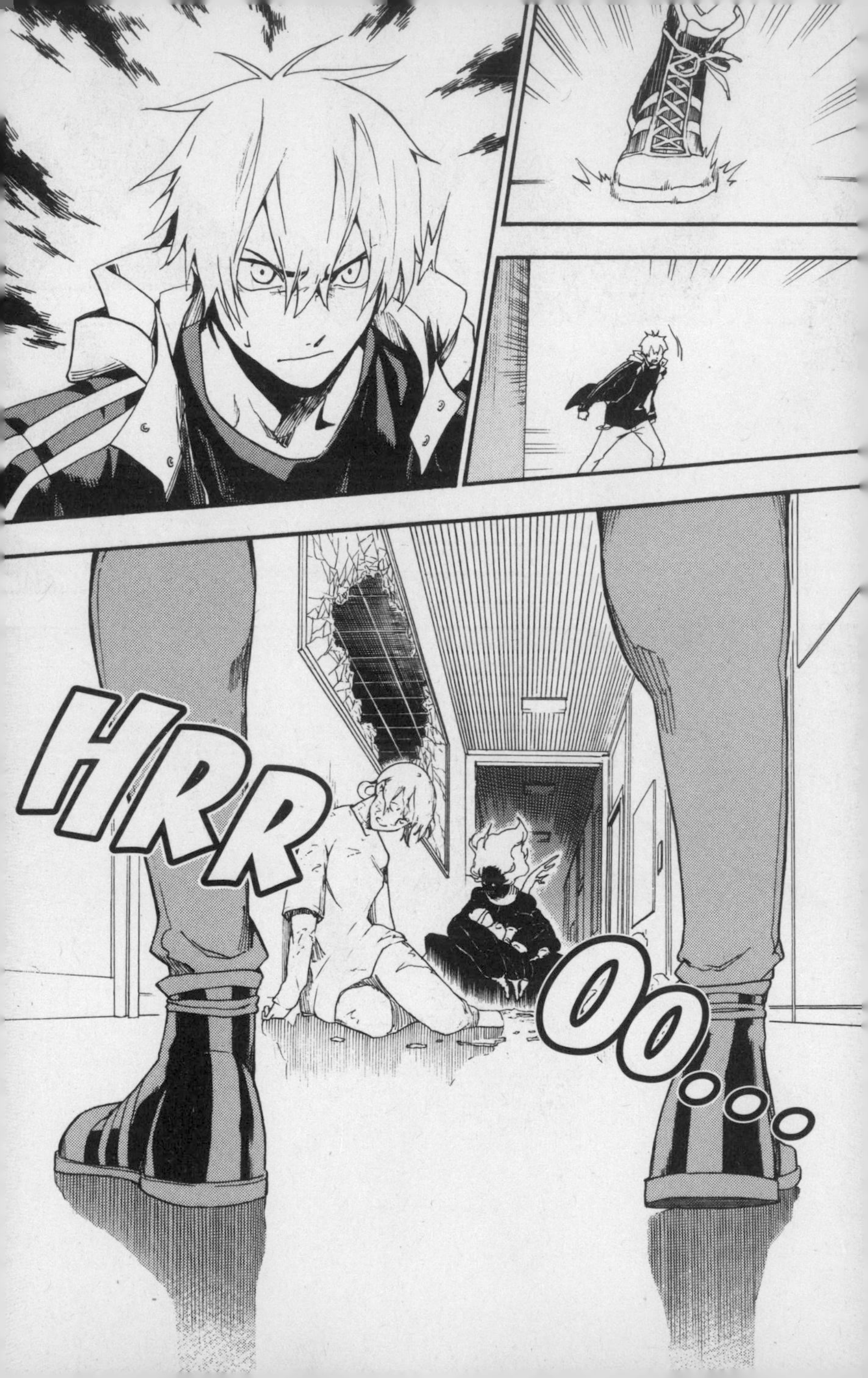
HRR
OO...

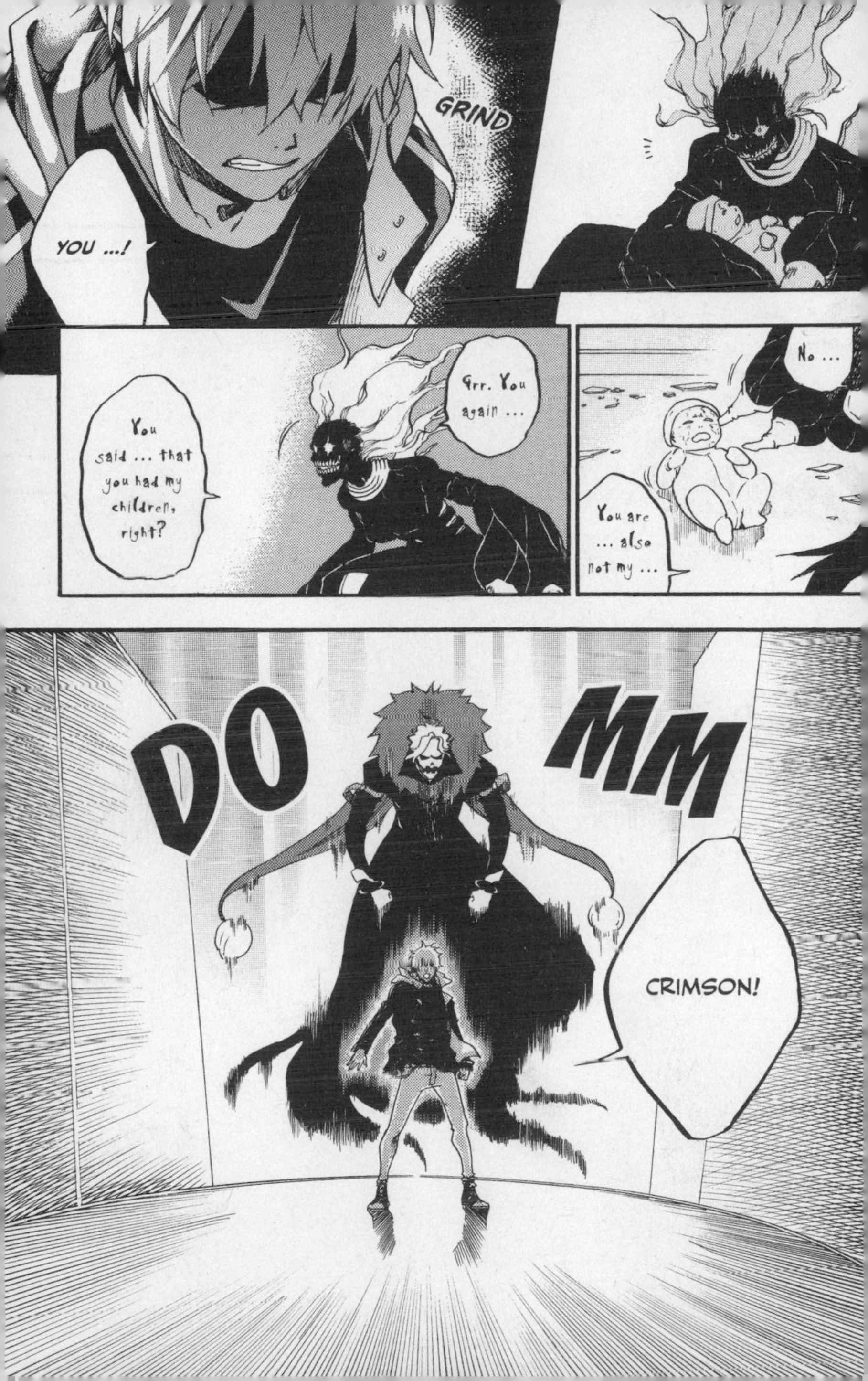
GRIND
YOU ...!
No ...
You are ... also not my ...
Grr. You again ...
You said ... that you had my children, right?
DO MM
CRIMSON!

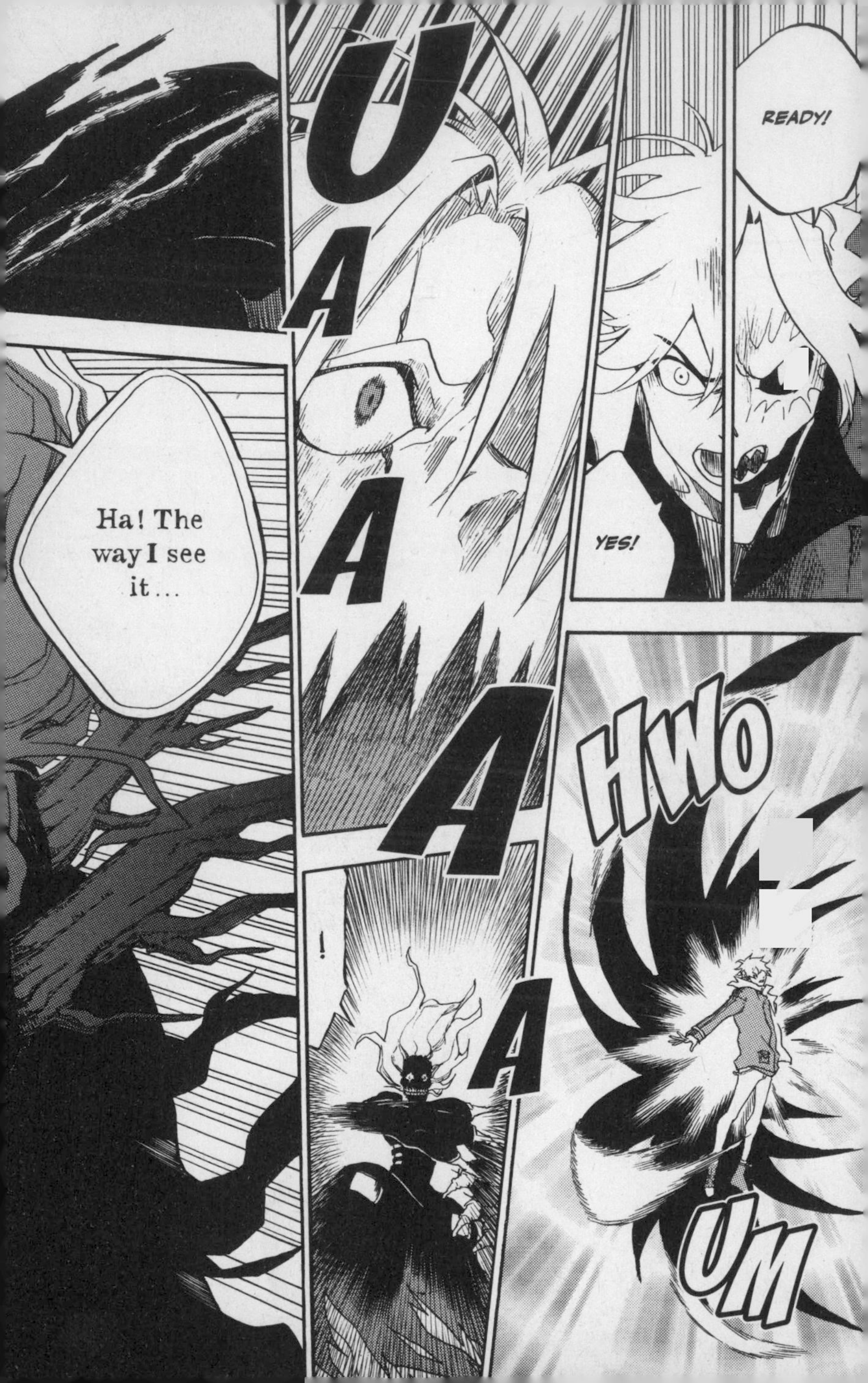
READY!
YES!
HWO
UM
UAAAAA
!
Ha! The way I see it...

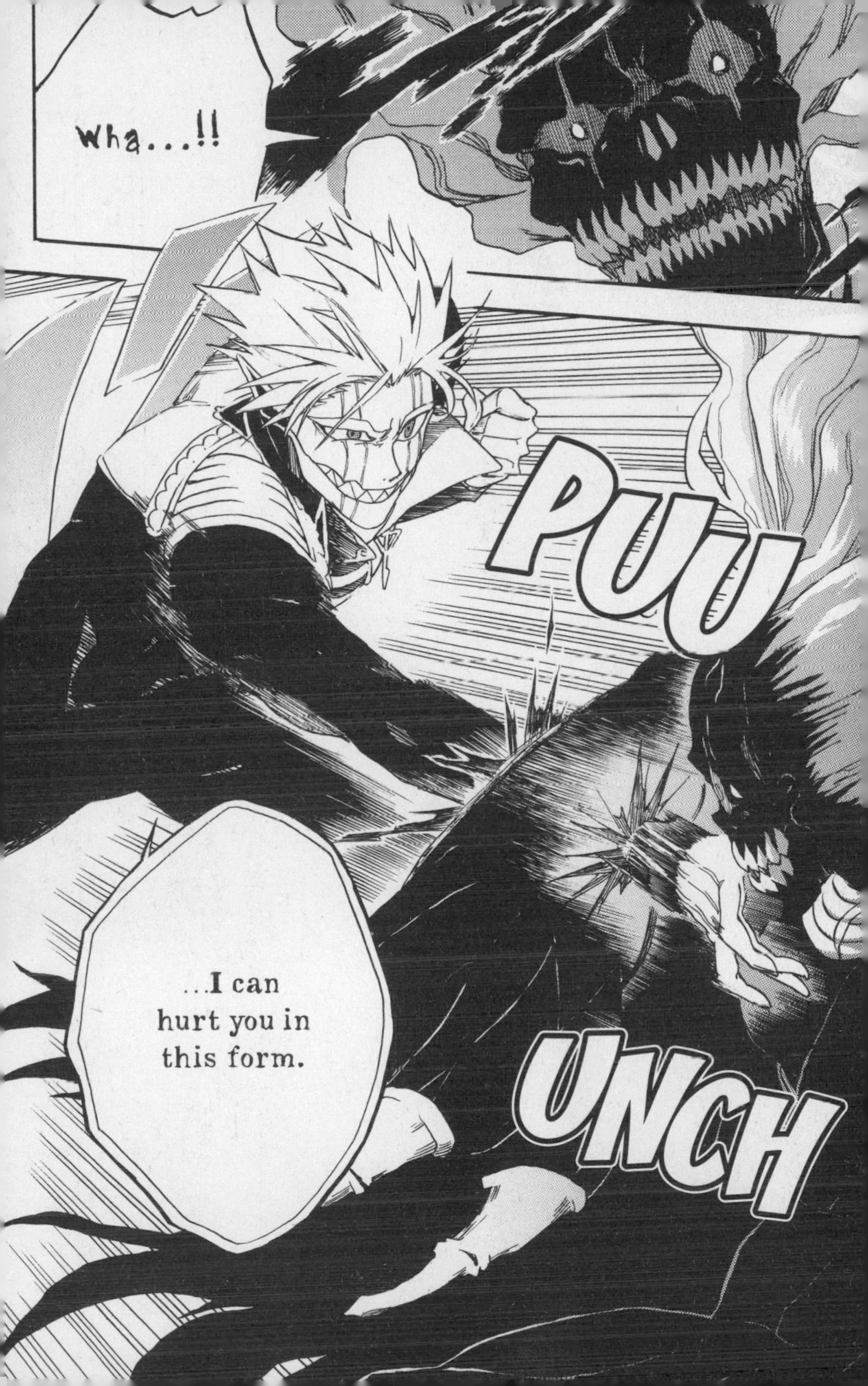
wha...!!
PUUUNCH
...I can hurt you in this form.

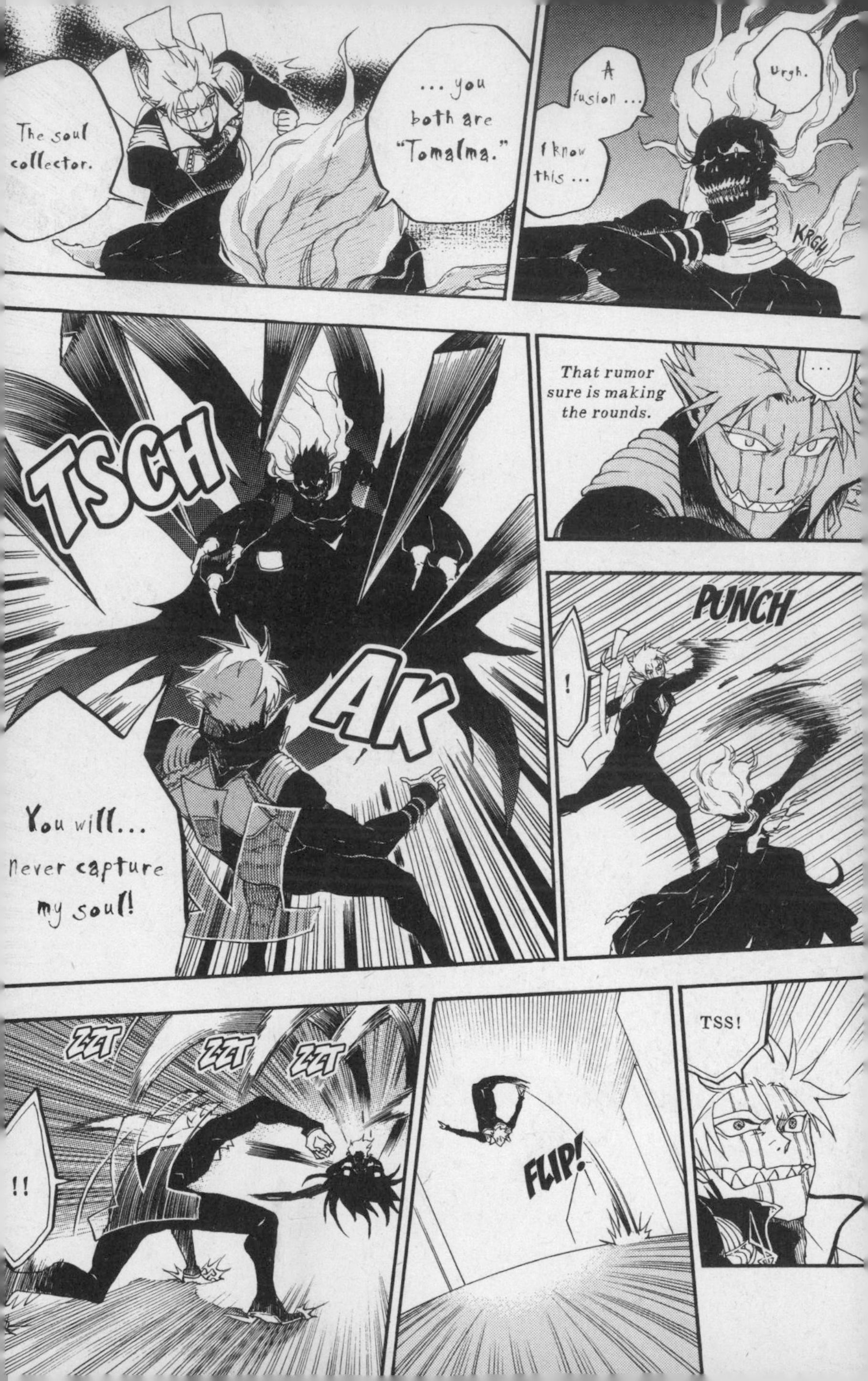
Urgh.
A fusion ...
I know this ...
KRGH
... you both are "Tomalma."
The soul collector.
...
That rumor sure is making the rounds.
PUNCH
!
TSCH
AK
You will... never capture my soul!
TSS!
FLIP!
ZZT
ZZT
ZZT
!!

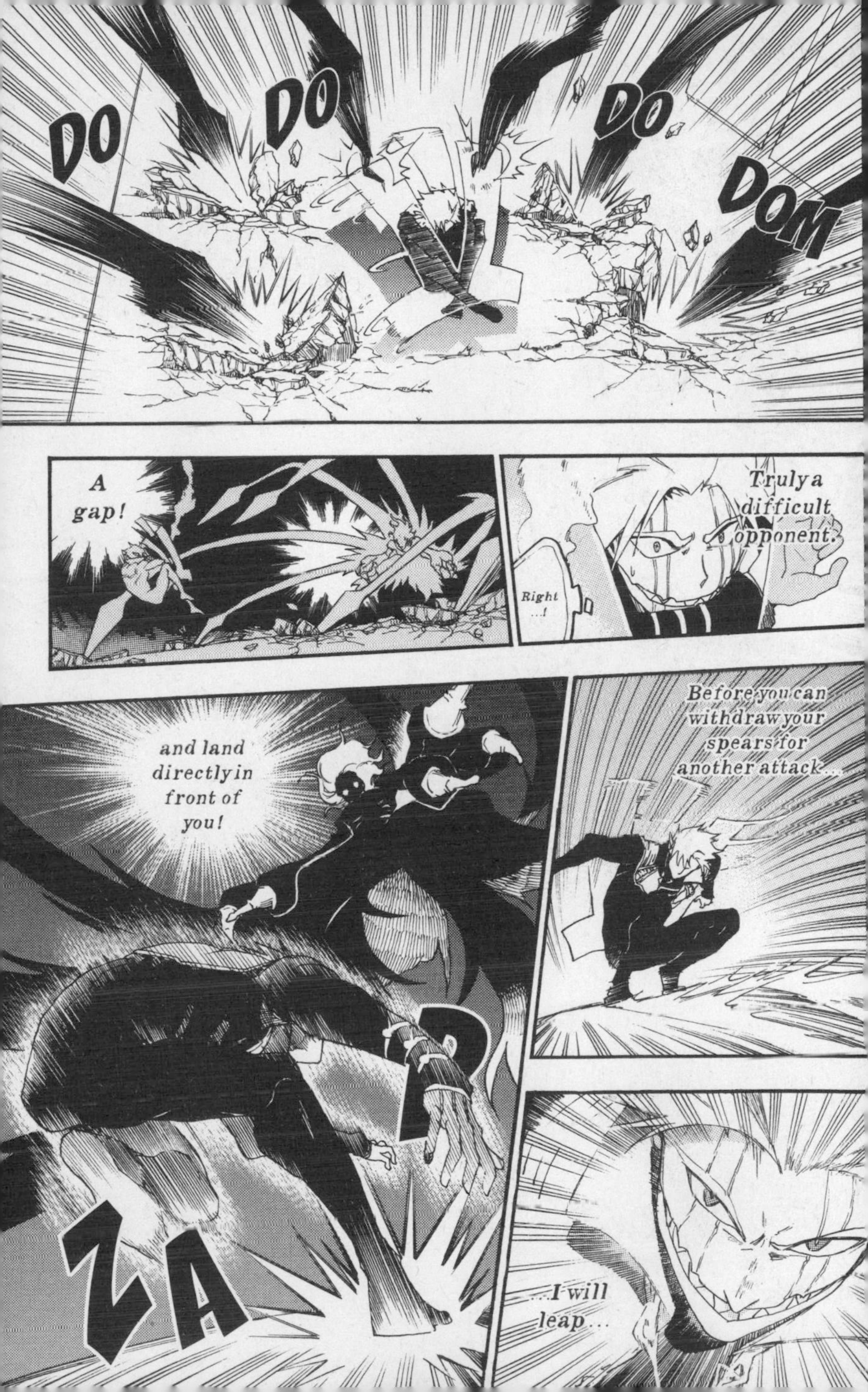
DO
DO
DO
DOM
Truly a difficult opponent.
Right ...!
A gap!
Before you can withdraw your spears for another attack...
...I will leap...
and land directly in front of you!
ZA

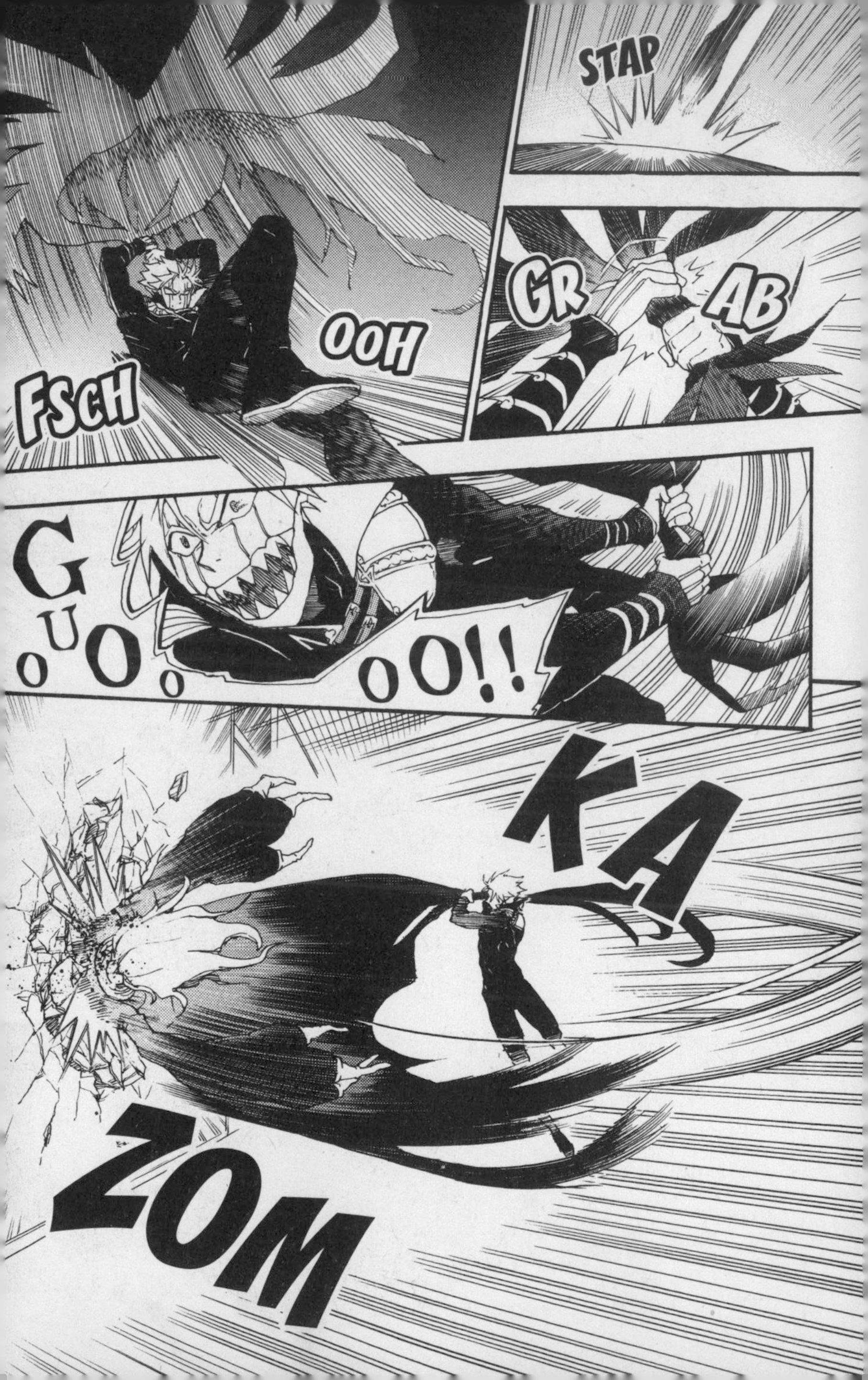
STAP
GR
AB
OOH
FSCH
GUoOooO!!
KA
ZOM

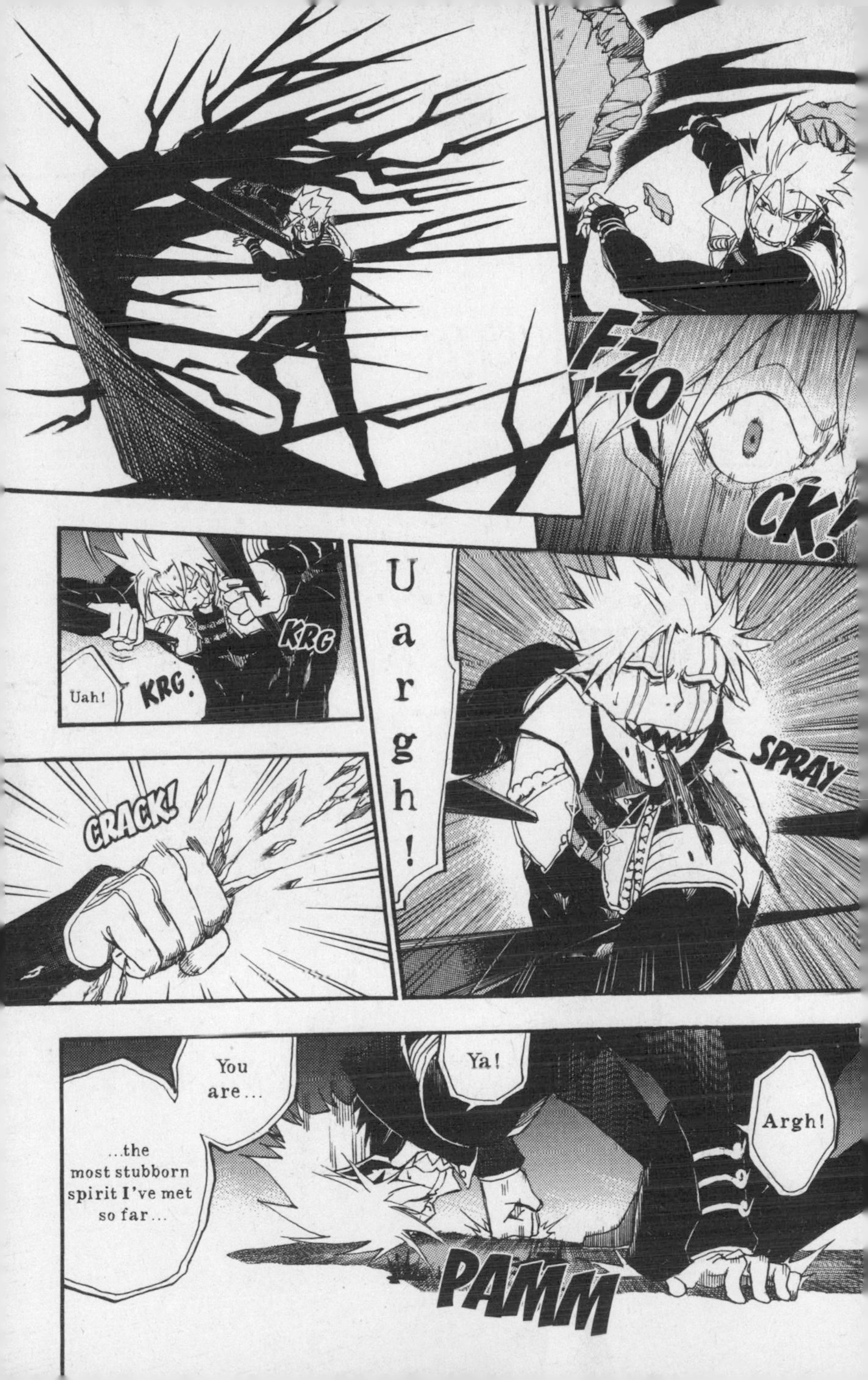
ZZOCK!
Uargh!
SPRAY
KRG
KRG
Uah!
CRACK!
Argh!
Ya!
You are...
...the most stubborn spirit I've met so far...
PAMM

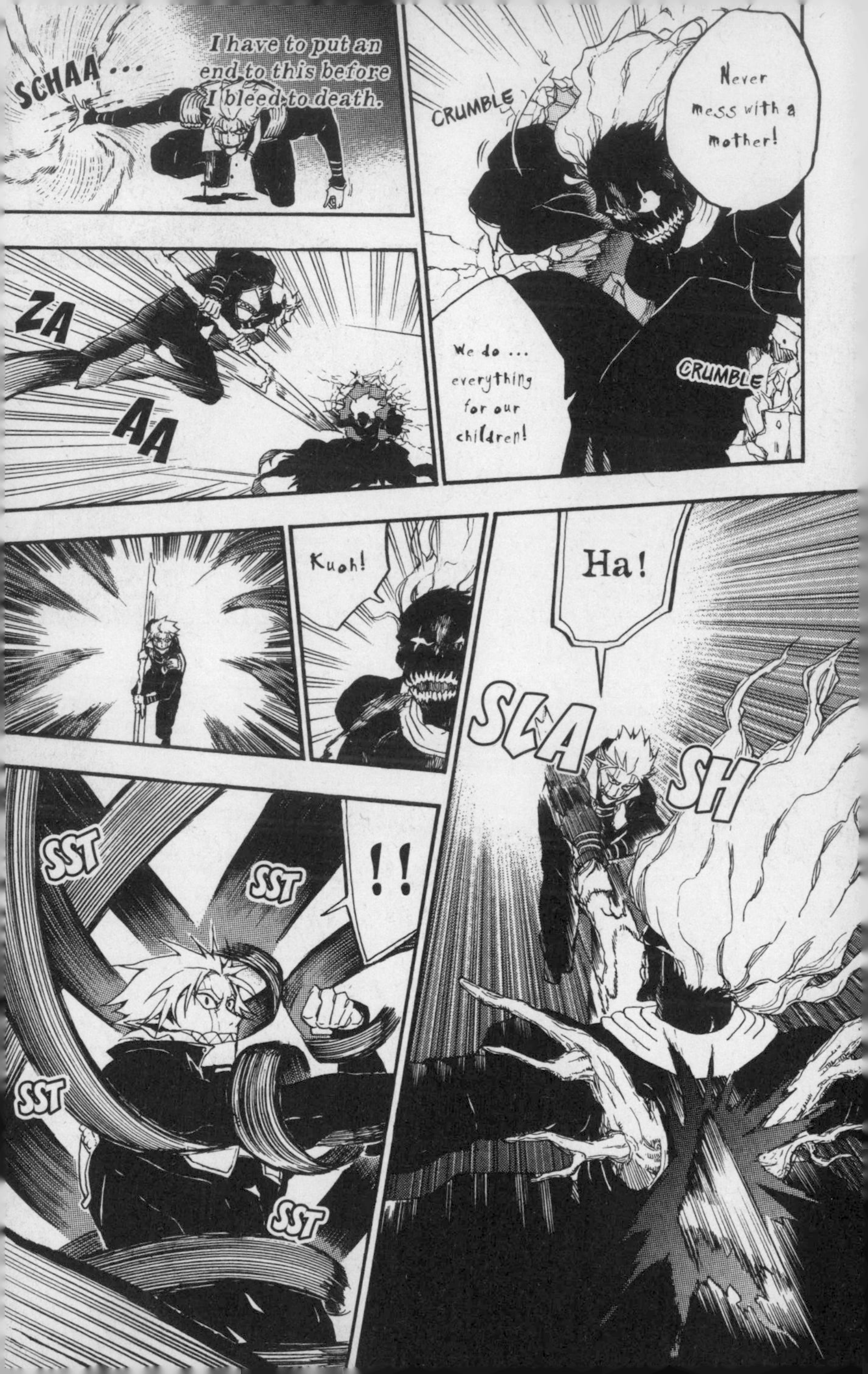
CRUMBLE
Never mess with a mother!
We do ... everything for our children!
CRUMBLE
SCHAA ...
I have to put an end to this before I bleed to death.
ZA
AA
Ha!
SLASH
Kuoh!
!!
SST
SST
SST
SST

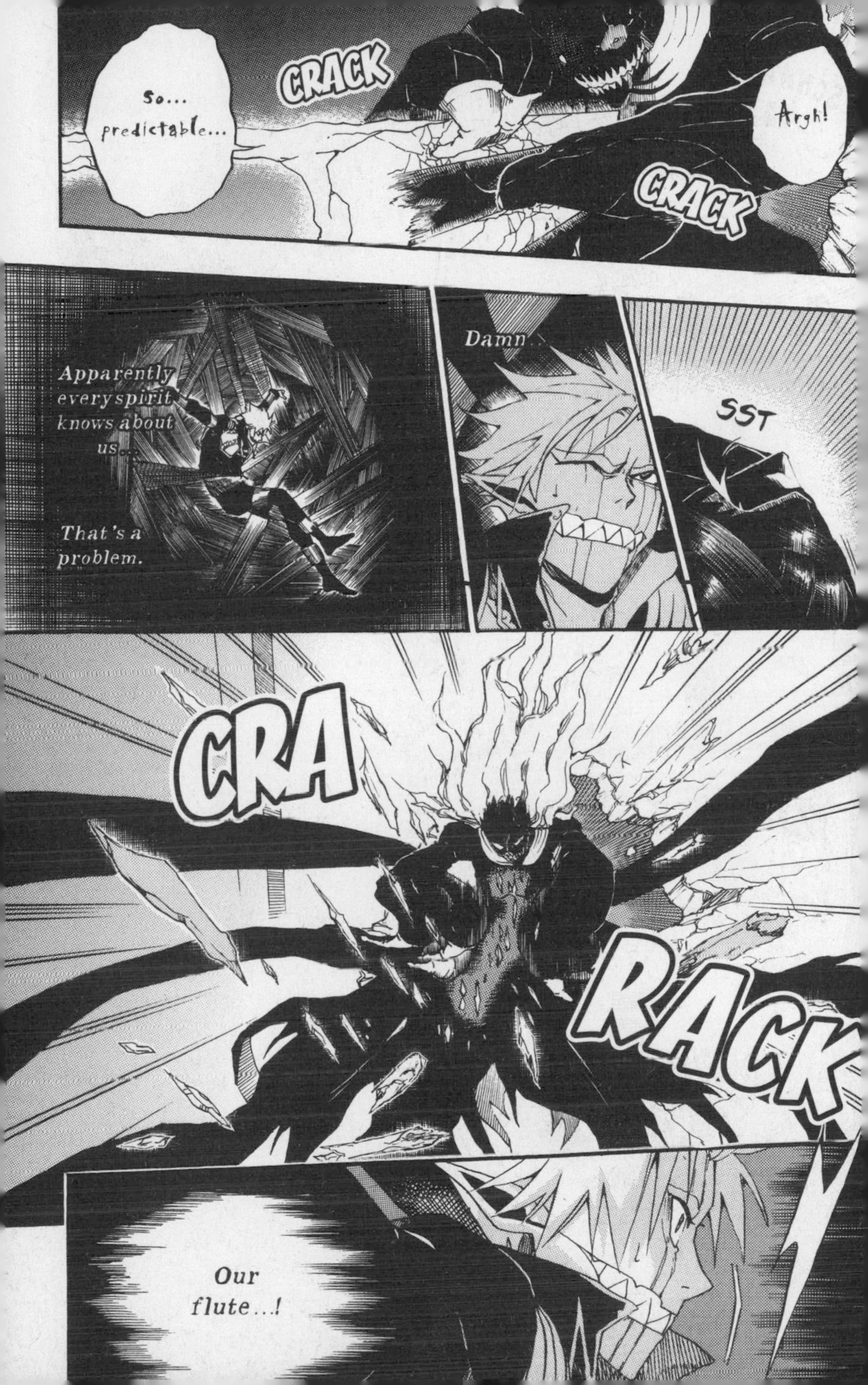
Argh!
CRACK
CRACK
So... predictable...
SST
Damn...
Apparently every spirit knows about us...
That's a problem.
CRA
RACK
Our flute...!

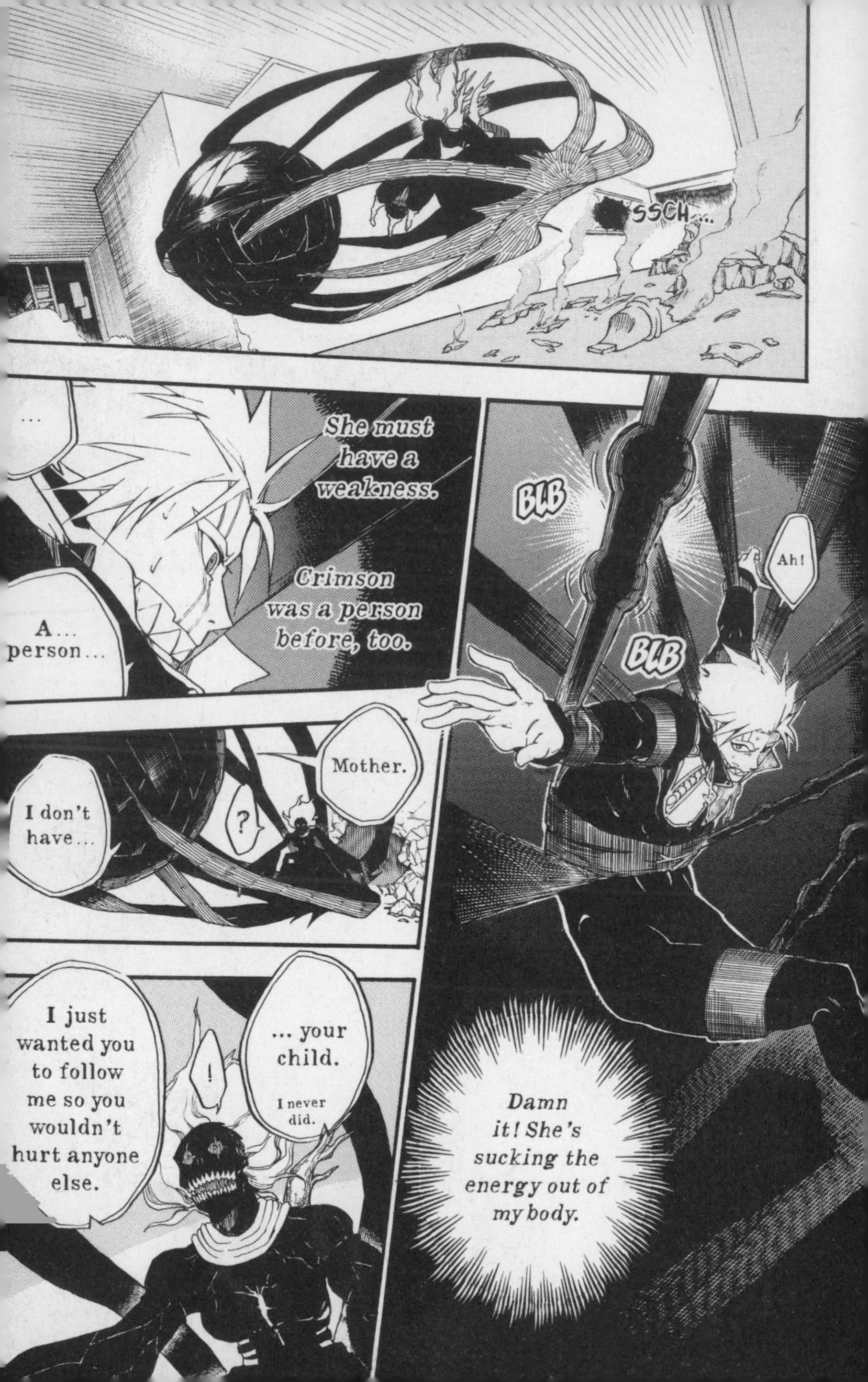
SSCH...
BLB
Ah!
BLB
Damn it! She's sucking the energy out of my body.
She must have a weakness.
Crimson was a person before, too.
...
A... person...
Mother.
?
I don't have...
... your child.
I never did.
!
I just wanted you to follow me so you wouldn't hurt anyone else.

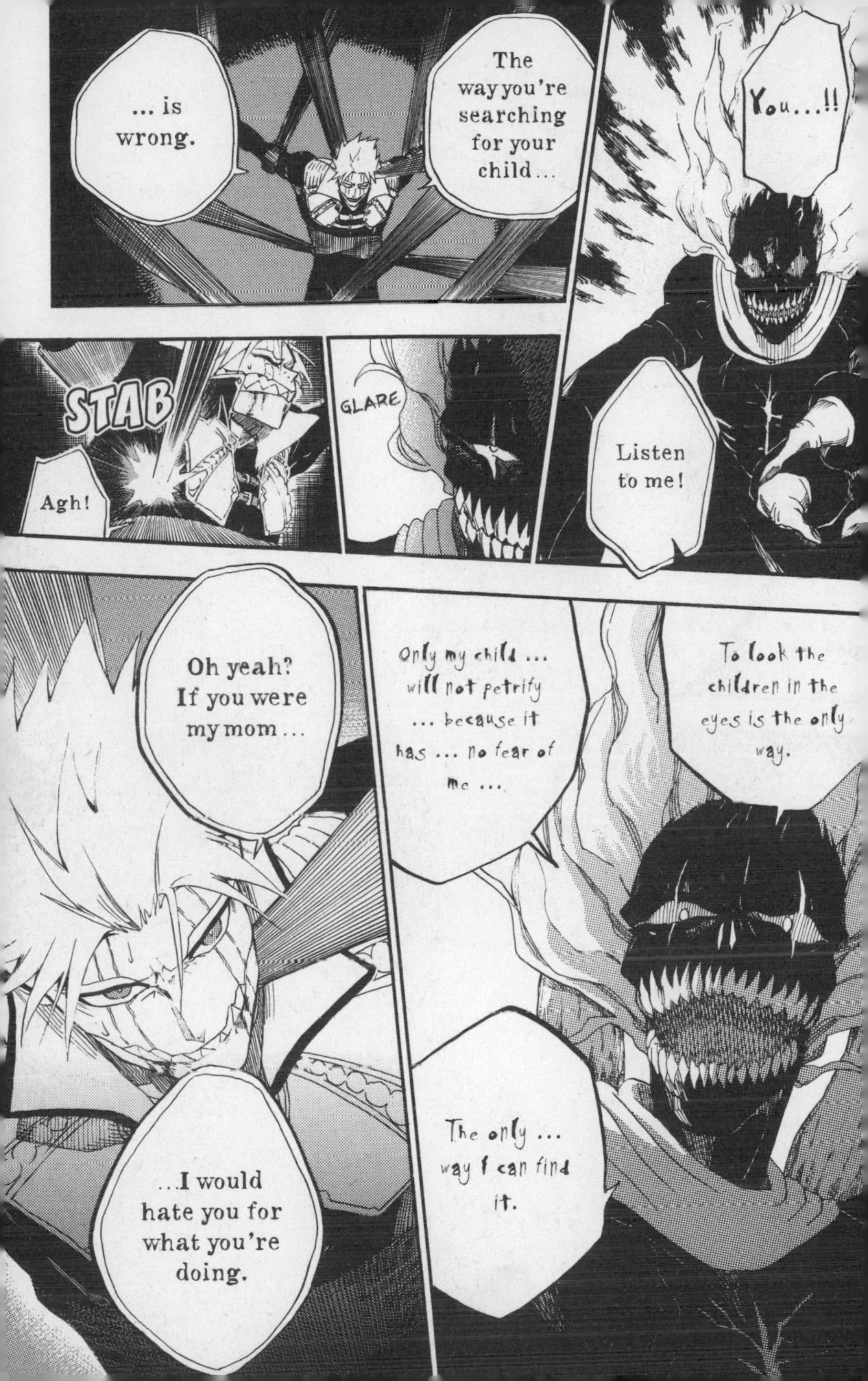
The way you're searching for your child...
... is wrong.
You...!!
Listen to me!
GLARE
STAB
Agh!
To look the children in the eyes is the only way.
Only my child ... will not petrify ... because it has ... no fear of me ...
The only ... way I can find it.
Oh yeah? If you were my mom...
...I would hate you for what you're doing.

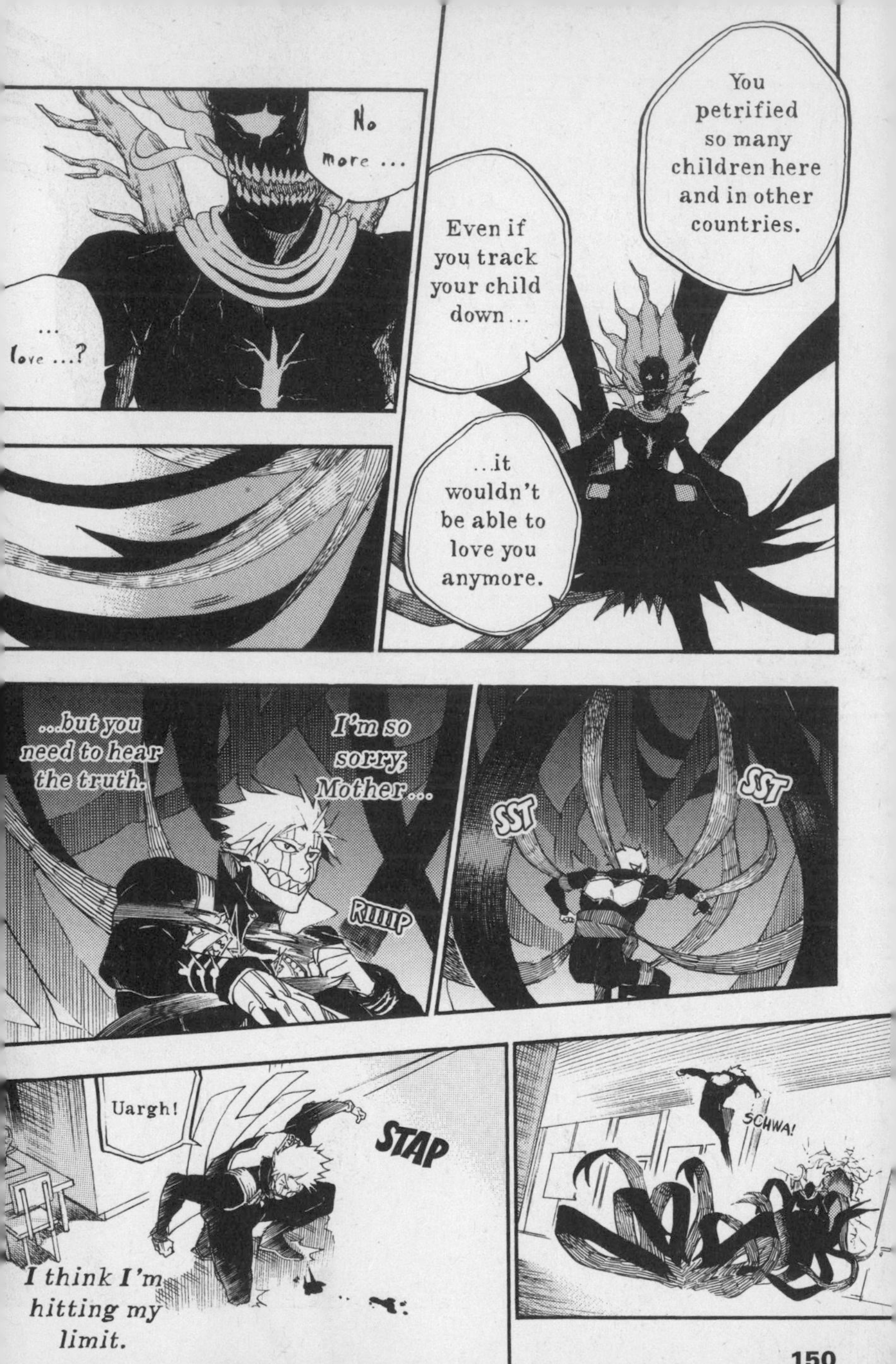
You petrified so many children here and in other countries.
Even if you track your child down…
…it wouldn't be able to love you anymore.
No more …
… love …?
SST
SST
I'm so sorry, Mother …
…but you need to hear the truth.
RIIIIP
SCHWA!
Uargh!
STAP
I think I'm hitting my limit.

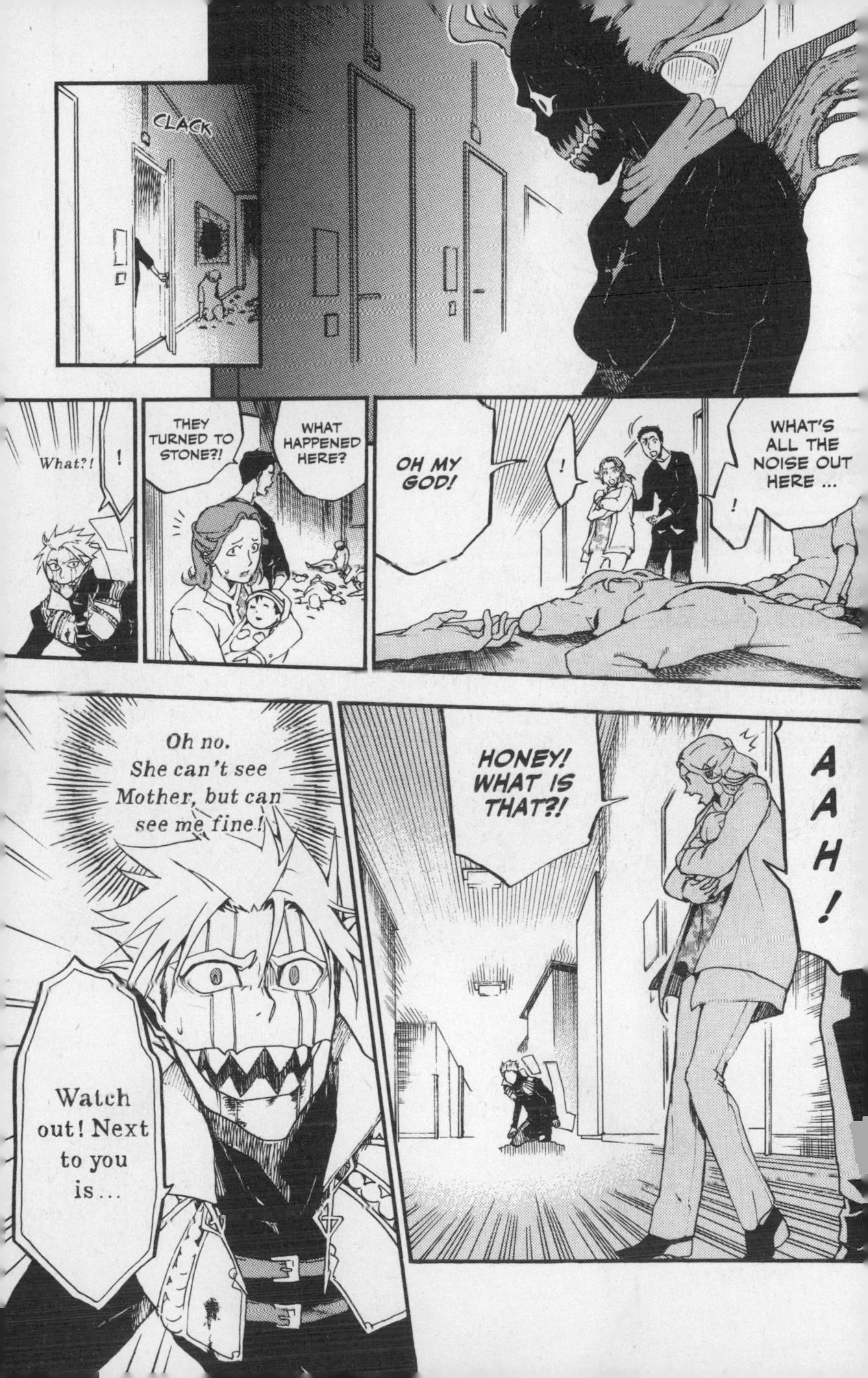
CLACK
WHAT'S ALL THE NOISE OUT HERE ...
!
!
OH MY GOD!
WHAT HAPPENED HERE?
THEY TURNED TO STONE?!
!
What?!
AAAH!
HONEY! WHAT IS THAT?!
Oh no. She can't see Mother, but can see me fine!
Watch out! Next to you is...

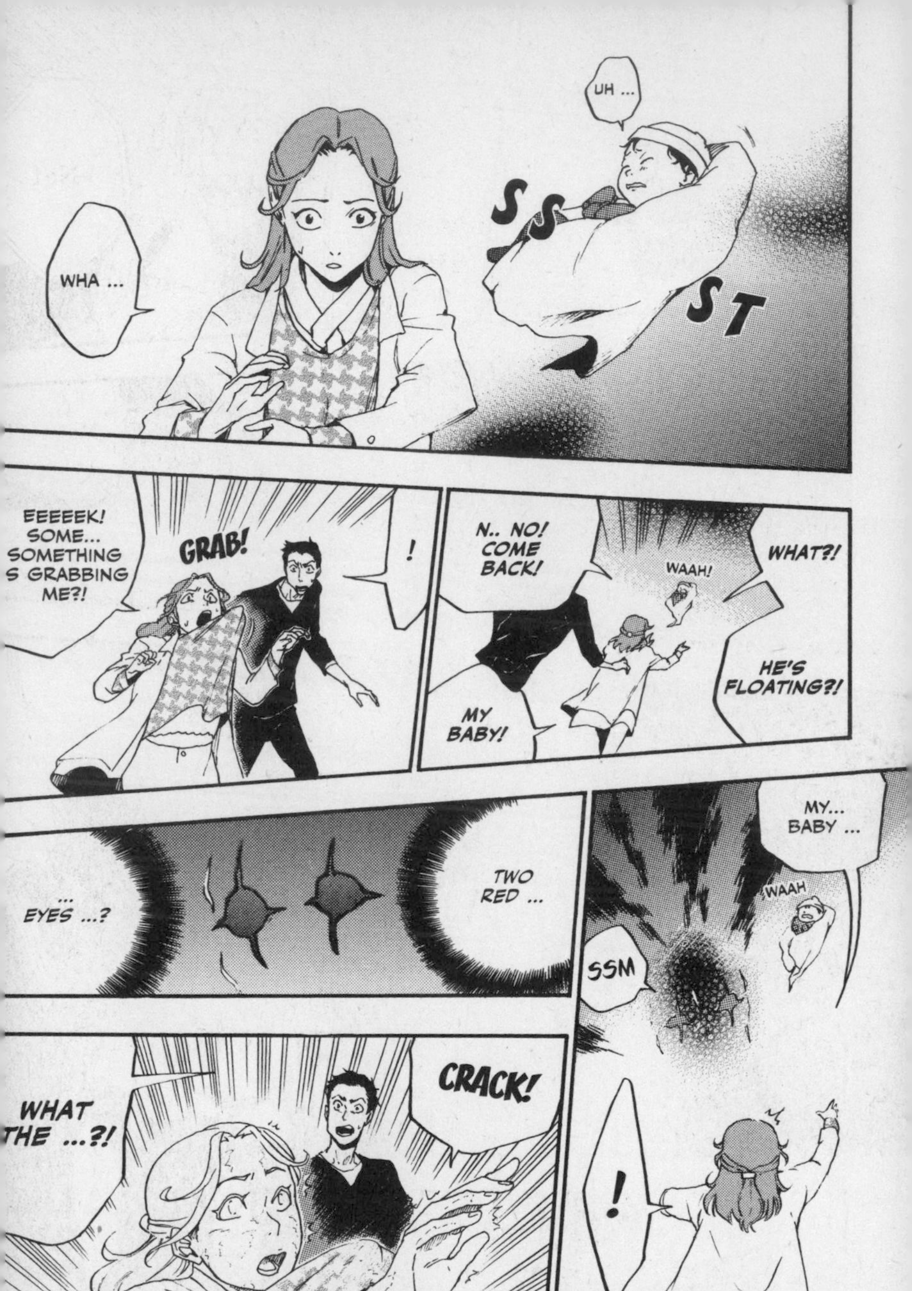
UH ...
S S S T
WHA ...
WHAT?!
N.. NO! COME BACK!
WAAH!
HE'S FLOATING?!
MY BABY!
!
GRAB!
EEEEEK! SOME... SOMETHING S GRABBING ME?!
MY... BABY ...
WAAH
SSM
!
TWO RED ...
... EYES ...?
CRACK!
WHAT THE ...?!

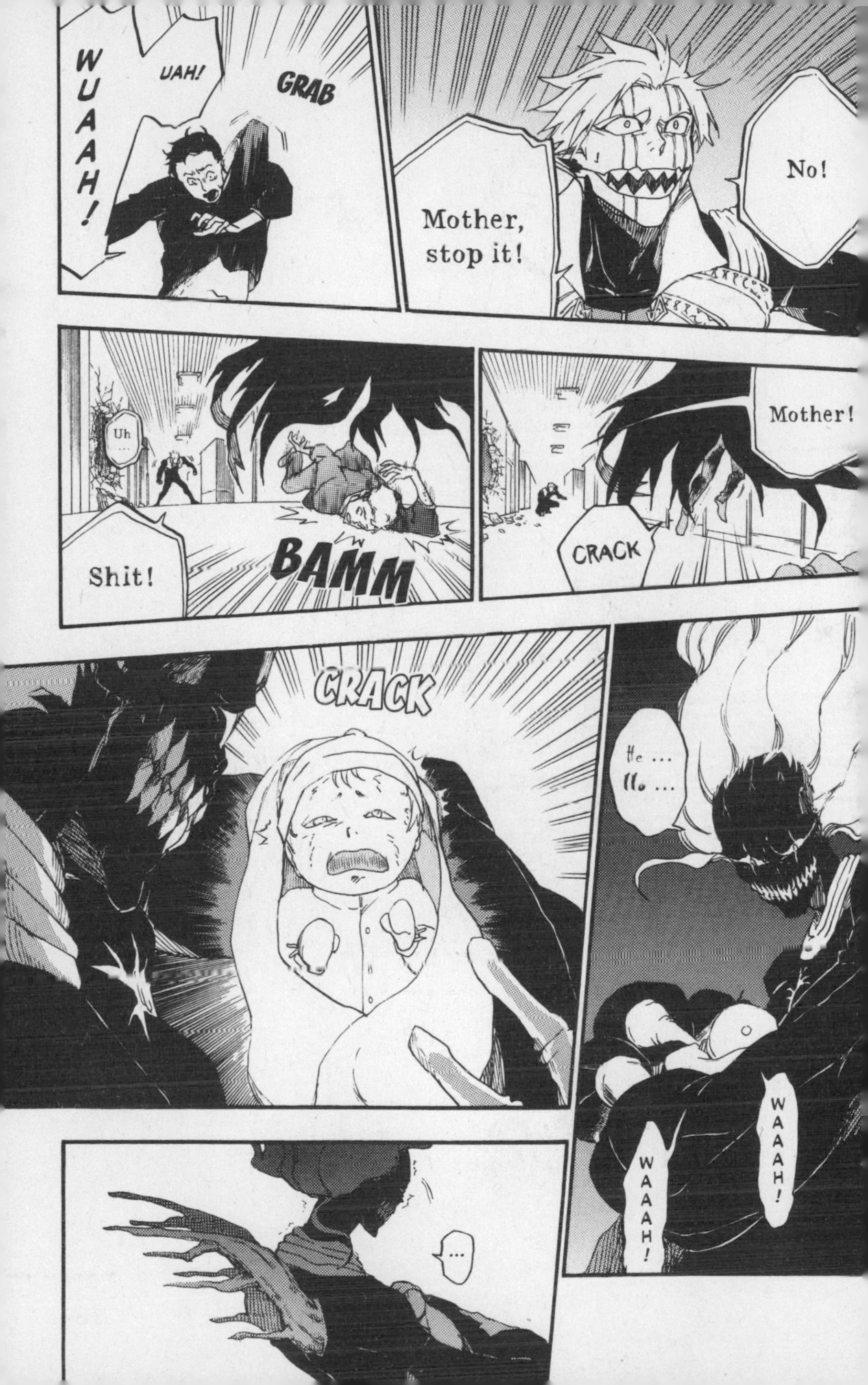
No!
Mother, stop it!
GRAB
UAH!
WUAAAH!
Mother!
CRACK
Uh ...
BAMM
Shit!
He ... llo ...
WAAAH!
WAAAH!
CRACK
...

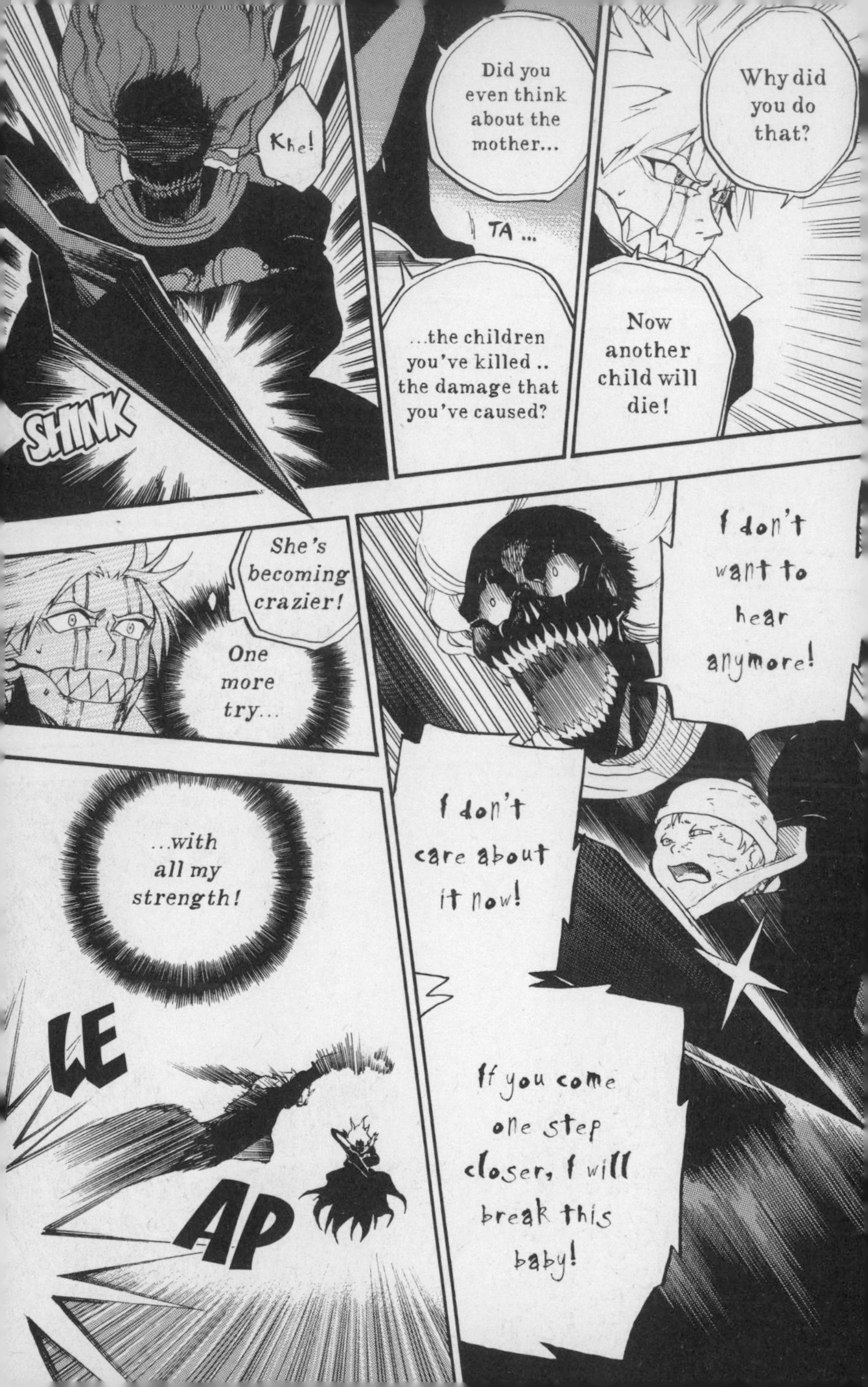
Why did you do that?
Now another child will die!
Did you even think about the mother...
TA ...
...the children you've killed .. the damage that you've caused?
Khe!
SHINK
I don't want to hear anymore!
I don't care about it now!
If you come one step closer, I will break this baby!
She's becoming crazier!
One more try...
...with all my strength!
LE
AP

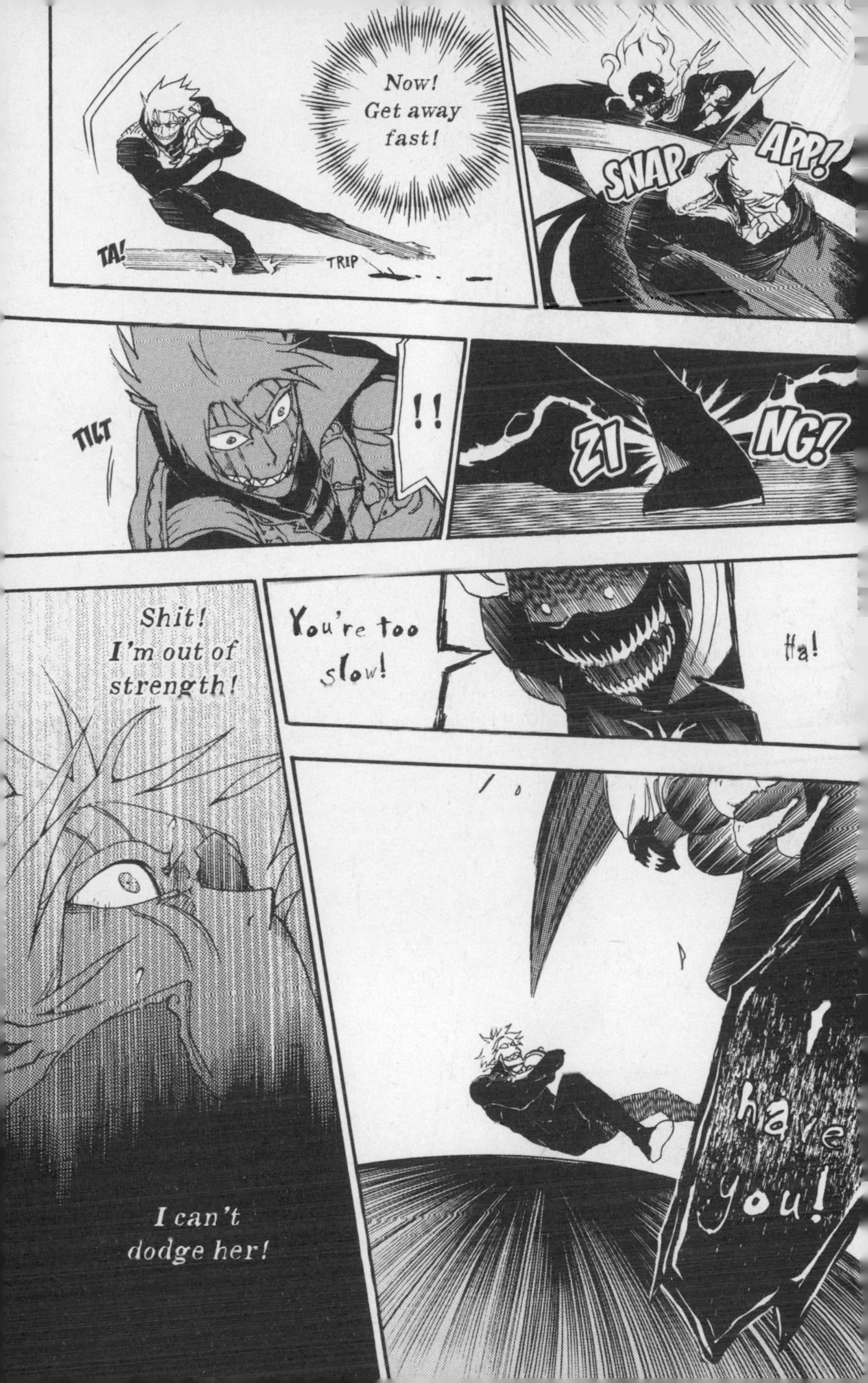
SNAP
APP!
Now! Get away fast!
TA!
TRIP
ZI
NG!
!!
TILT
You're too slow!
Ha!
I have you!
Shit! I'm out of strength!
I can't dodge her!

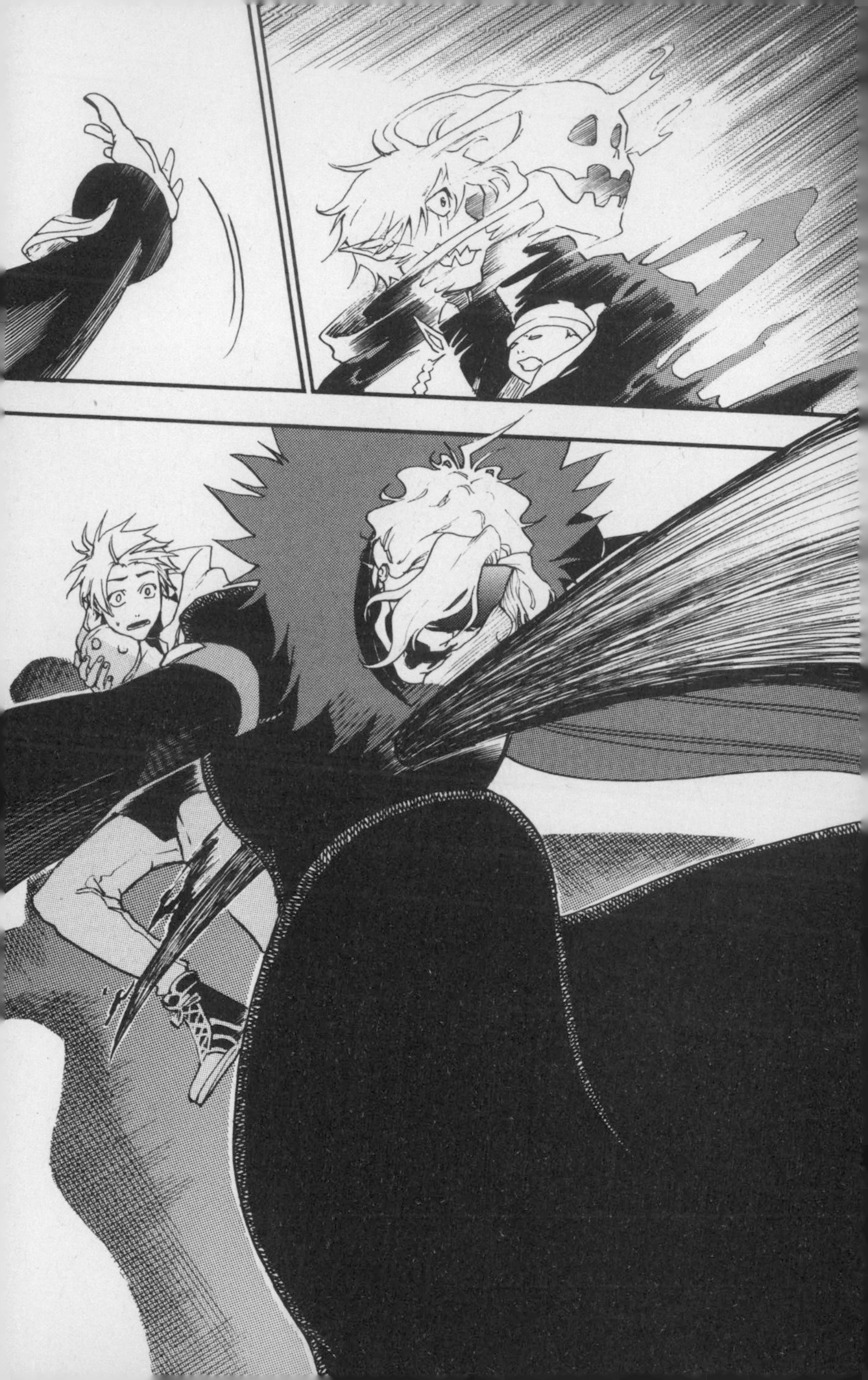

12
MOTHER'S PAIN

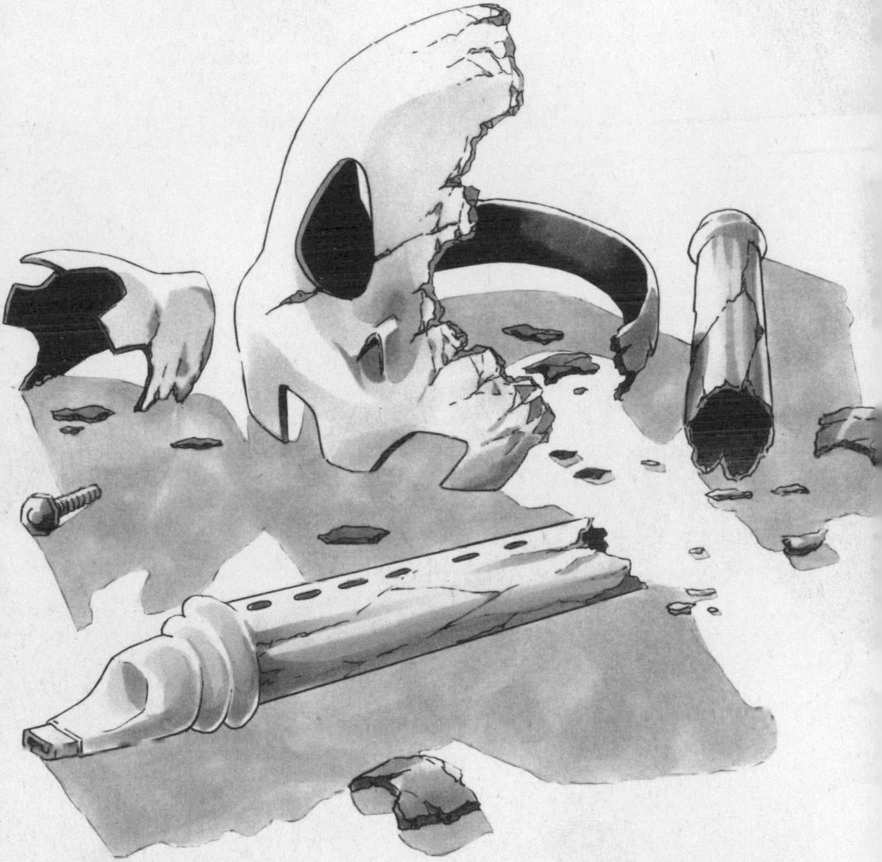

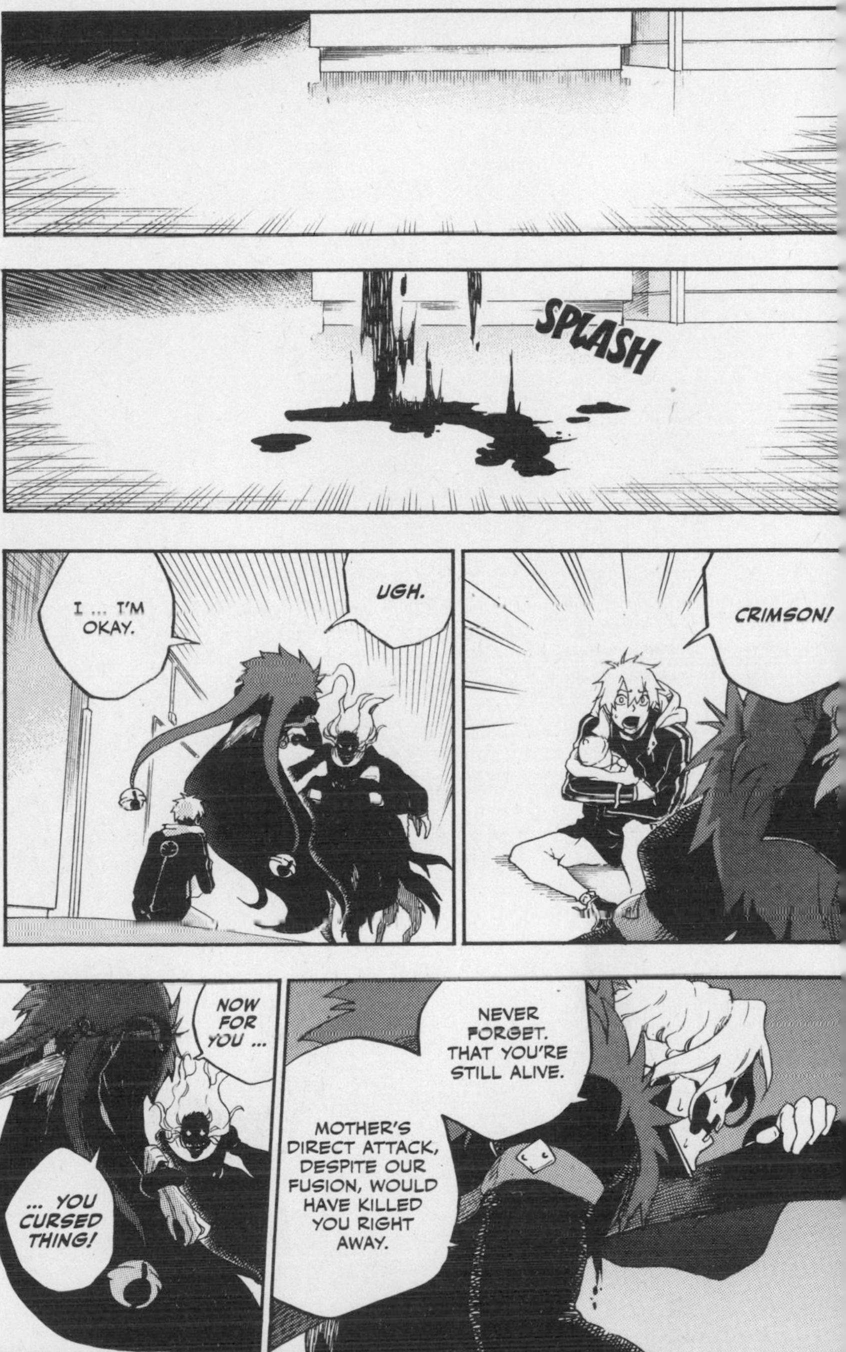
SPLASH
CRIMSON!
UGH.
I ... I'M OKAY.
NEVER FORGET. THAT YOU'RE STILL ALIVE.
MOTHER'S DIRECT ATTACK, DESPITE OUR FUSION, WOULD HAVE KILLED YOU RIGHT AWAY.
NOW FOR YOU ...
... YOU CURSED THING!

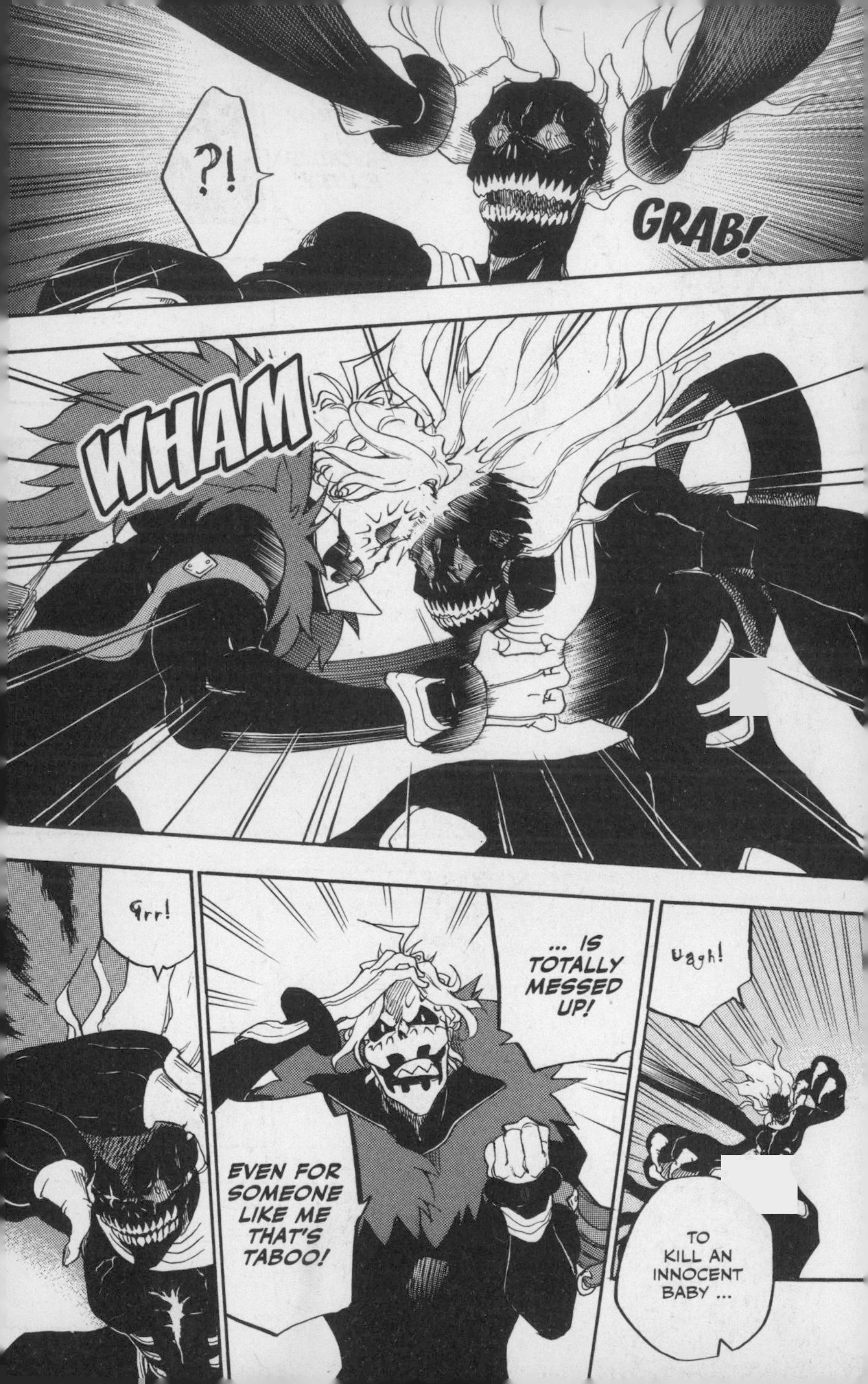
GRAB!
?!
WHAM
Uagh!
TO KILL AN INNOCENT BABY ...
... IS TOTALLY MESSED UP!
EVEN FOR SOMEONE LIKE ME THAT'S TABOO!
Grr!

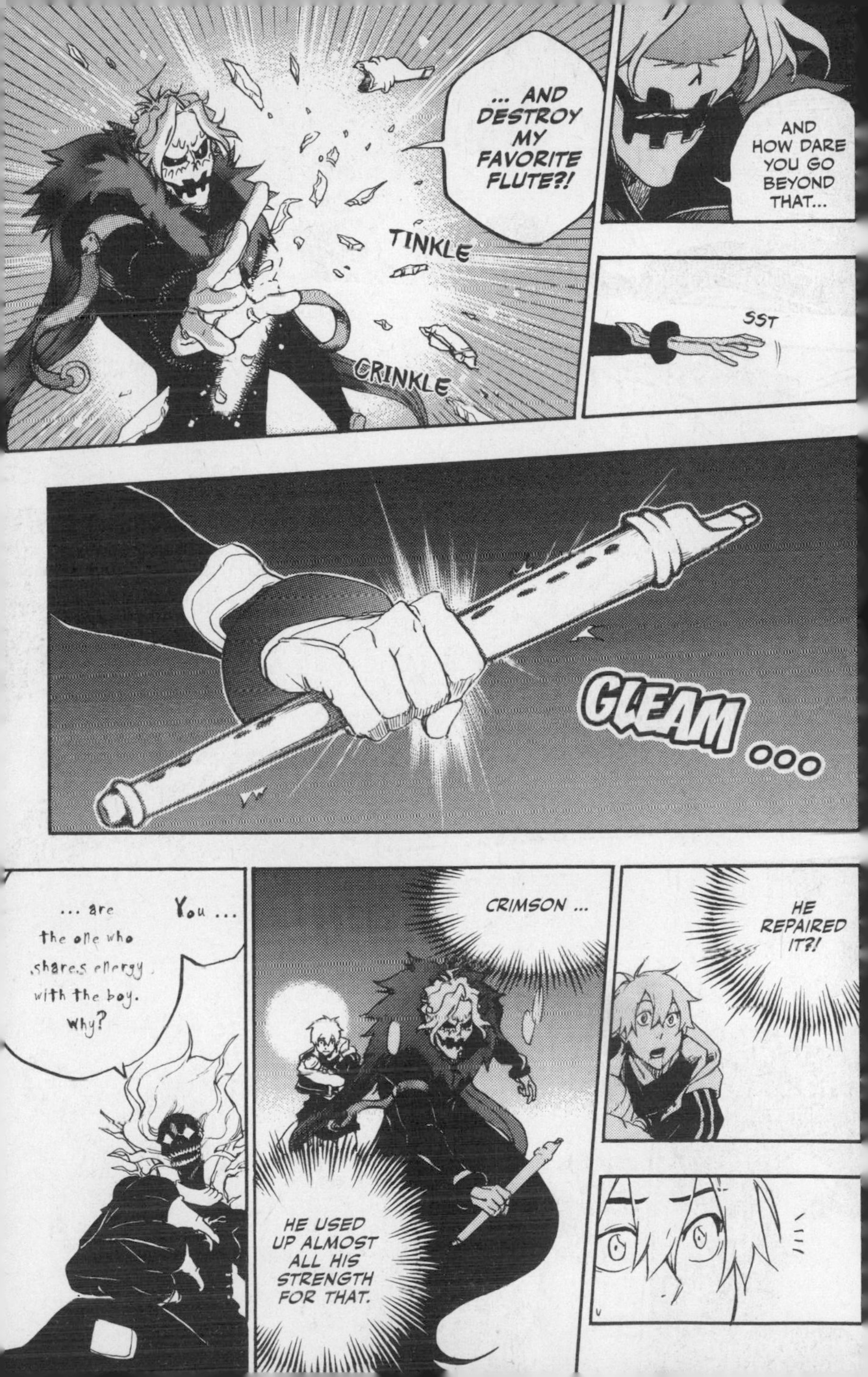
AND HOW DARE YOU GO BEYOND THAT...
SST
... AND DESTROY MY FAVORITE FLUTE?!
TINKLE
CRINKLE
GLEAM ooo
HE REPAIRED IT?!
CRIMSON ...
HE USED UP ALMOST ALL HIS STRENGTH FOR THAT.
You ...
... are the one who shares energy with the boy. Why?

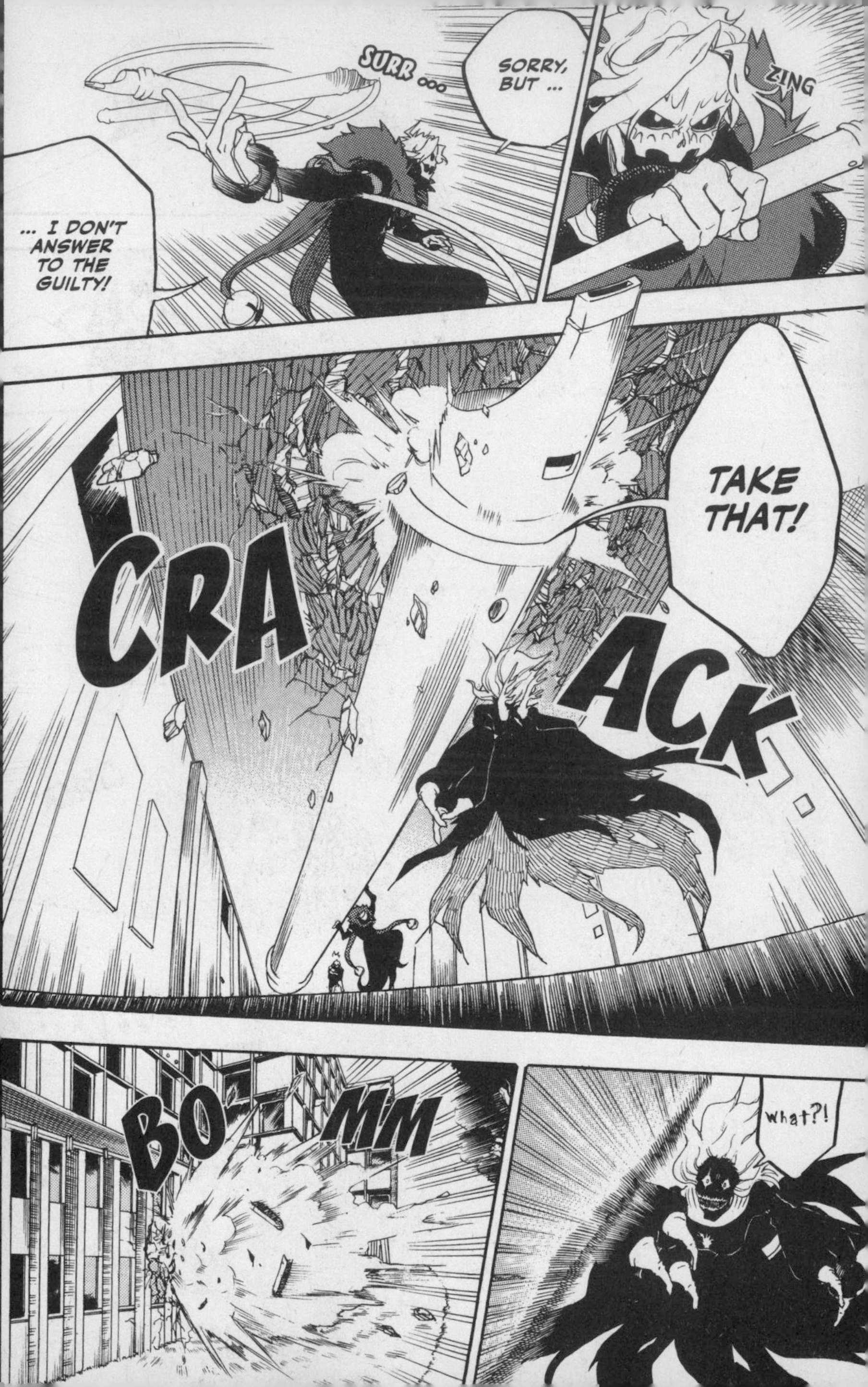
SORRY, BUT ...
ZING
SURR ...
... I DON'T ANSWER TO THE GUILTY!
TAKE THAT!
CRA
ACK
what?!
BO
MM

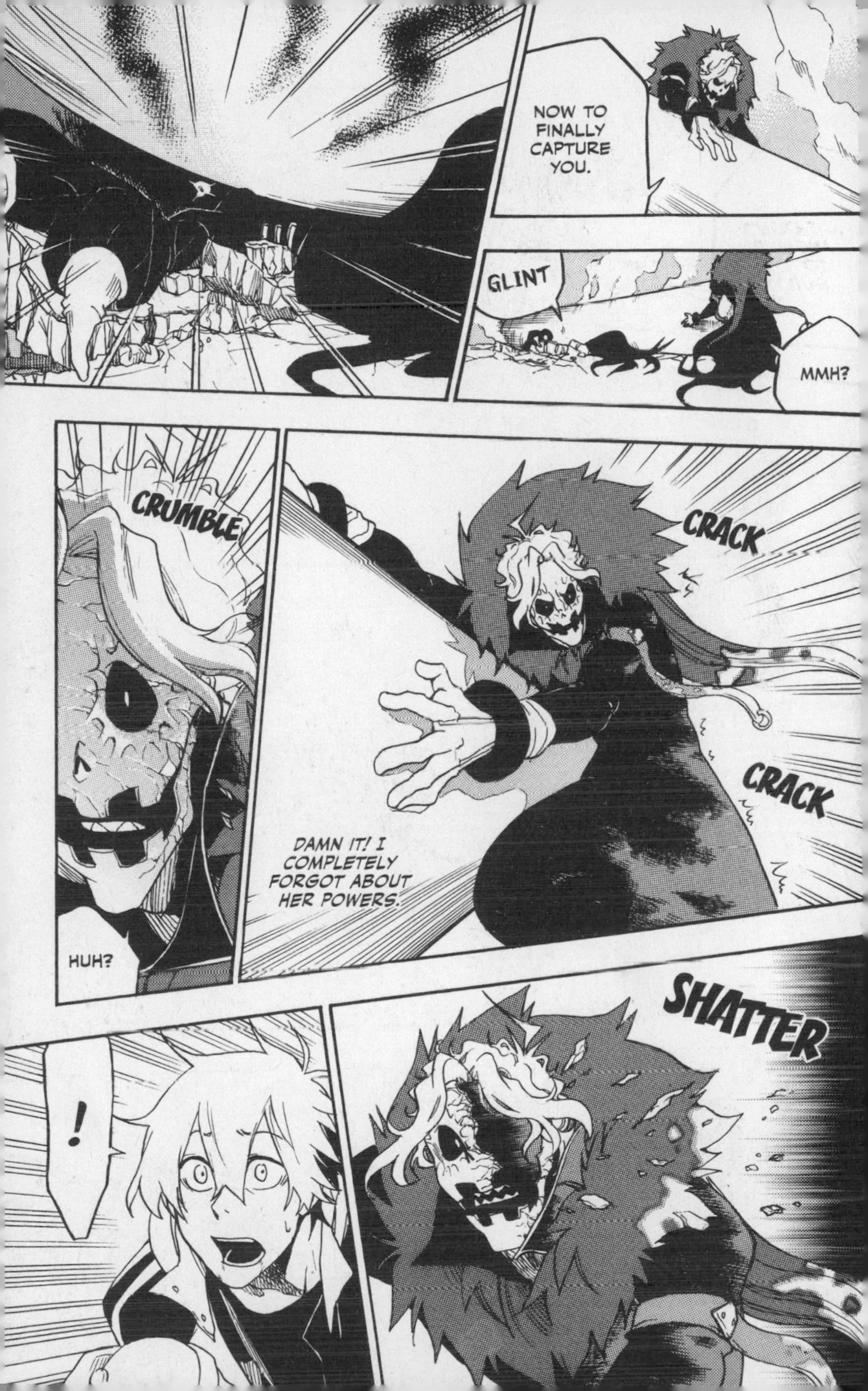
NOW TO FINALLY CAPTURE YOU.
GLINT
MMH?
CRACK
CRACK
DAMN IT! I COMPLETELY FORGOT ABOUT HER POWERS.
CRUMBLE
HUH?
SHATTER
!

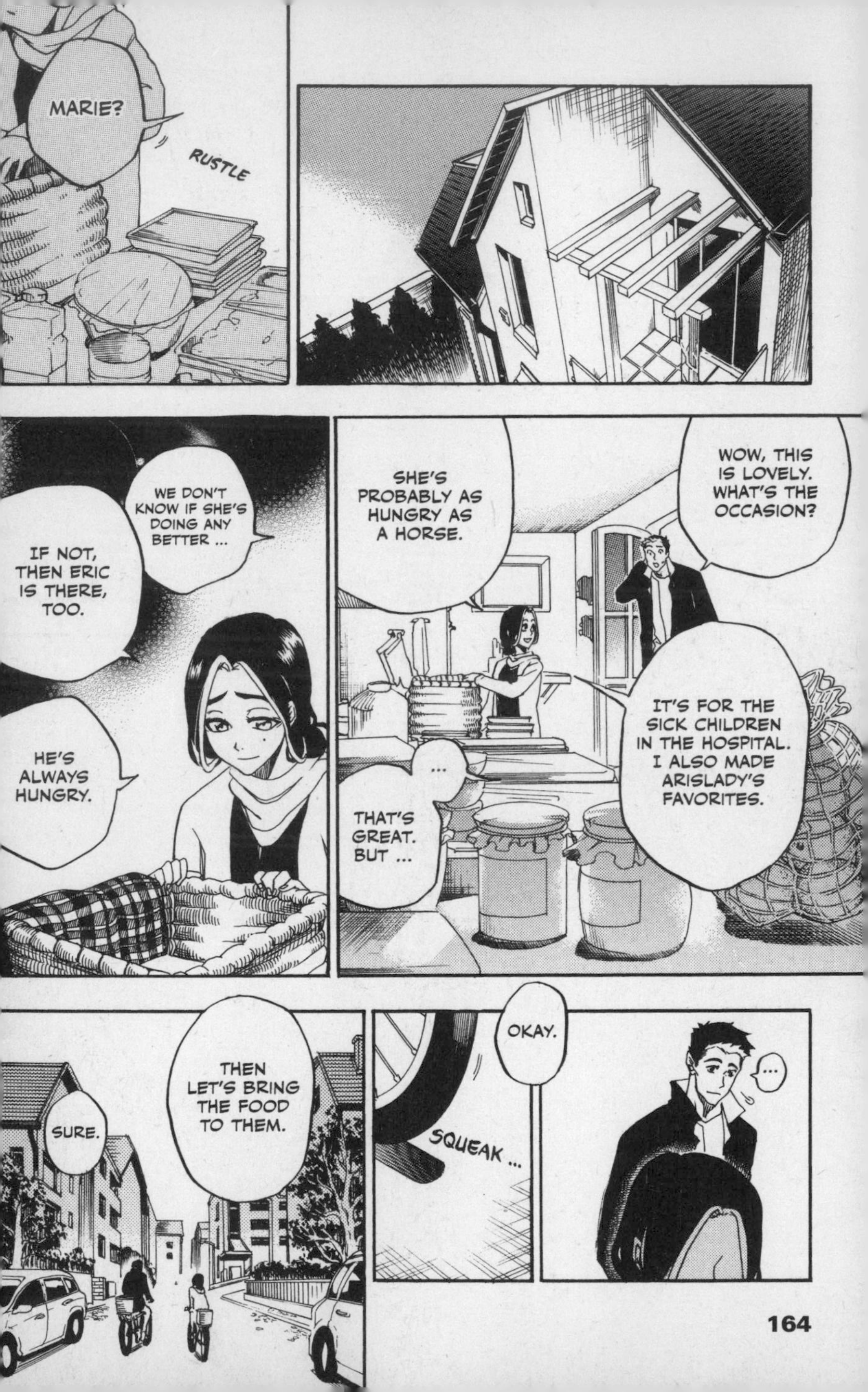
MARIE?
RUSTLE
WOW, THIS IS LOVELY. WHAT'S THE OCCASION?
IT'S FOR THE SICK CHILDREN IN THE HOSPITAL. I ALSO MADE ARISLADY'S FAVORITES.
SHE'S PROBABLY AS HUNGRY AS A HORSE.
...
THAT'S GREAT. BUT ...
WE DON'T KNOW IF SHE'S DOING ANY BETTER ...
IF NOT, THEN ERIC IS THERE, TOO.
HE'S ALWAYS HUNGRY.
...
OKAY.
SQUEAK ...
THEN LET'S BRING THE FOOD TO THEM.
SURE.

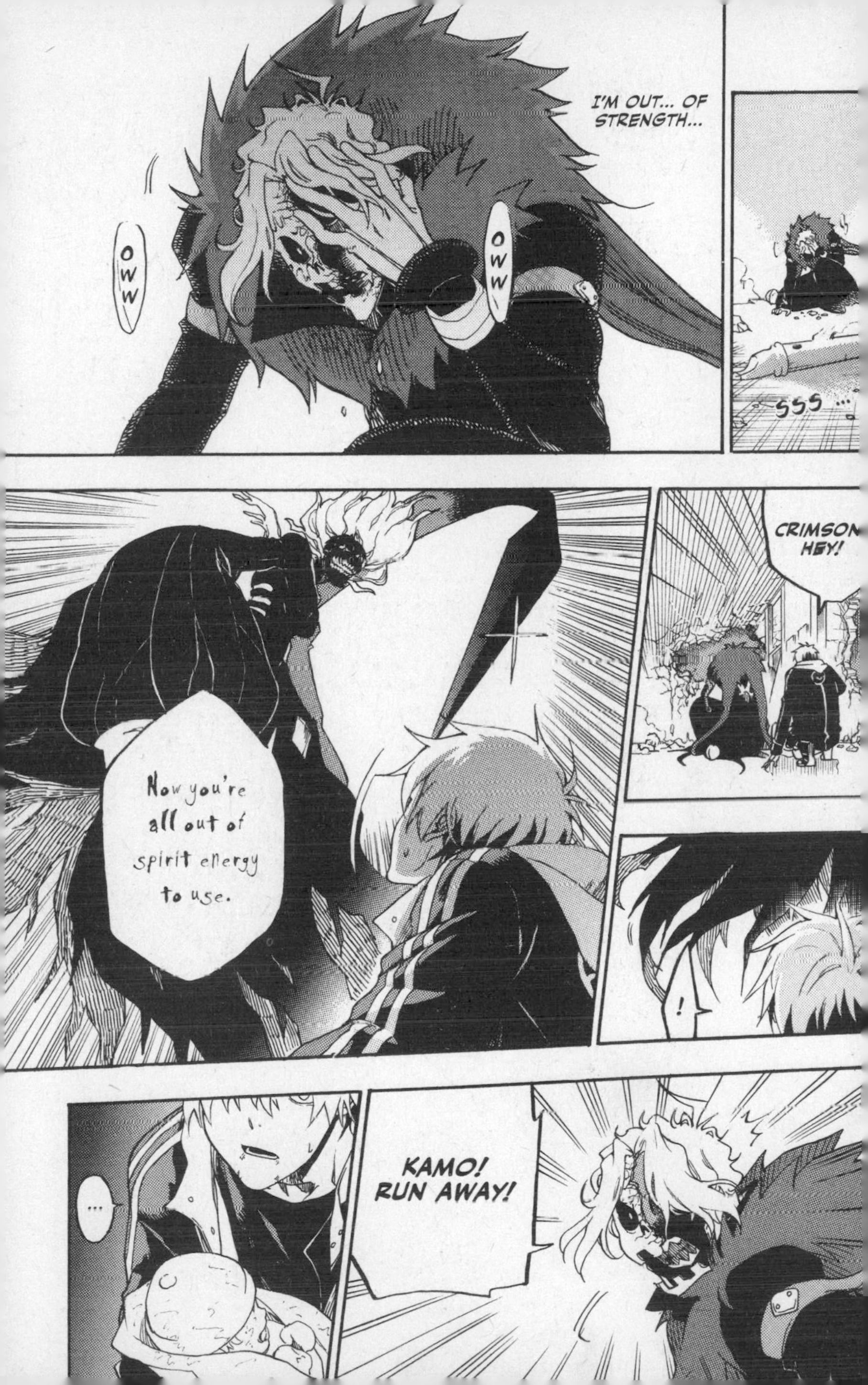
SSS...
I'M OUT... OF STRENGTH...
OWW
OWW
CRIMSON HEY!
!
Now you're all out of spirit energy to use.
KAMO! RUN AWAY!
...

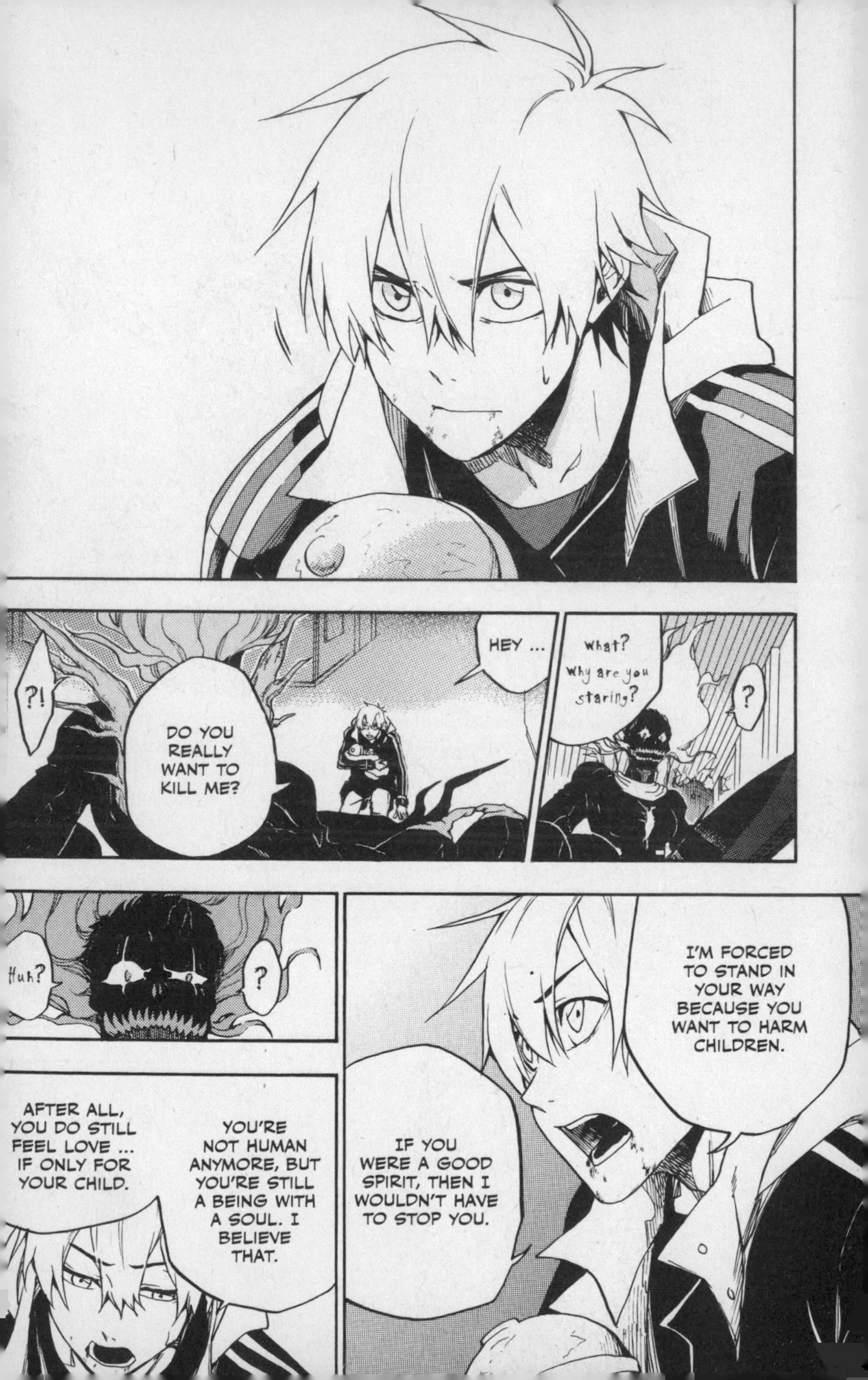
what? why are you staring?
?
HEY ...
DO YOU REALLY WANT TO KILL ME?
?!
I'M FORCED TO STAND IN YOUR WAY BECAUSE YOU WANT TO HARM CHILDREN.
IF YOU WERE A GOOD SPIRIT, THEN I WOULDN'T HAVE TO STOP YOU.
?
Huh?
YOU'RE NOT HUMAN ANYMORE, BUT YOU'RE STILL A BEING WITH A SOUL. I BELIEVE THAT.
AFTER ALL, YOU DO STILL FEEL LOVE ... IF ONLY FOR YOUR CHILD.

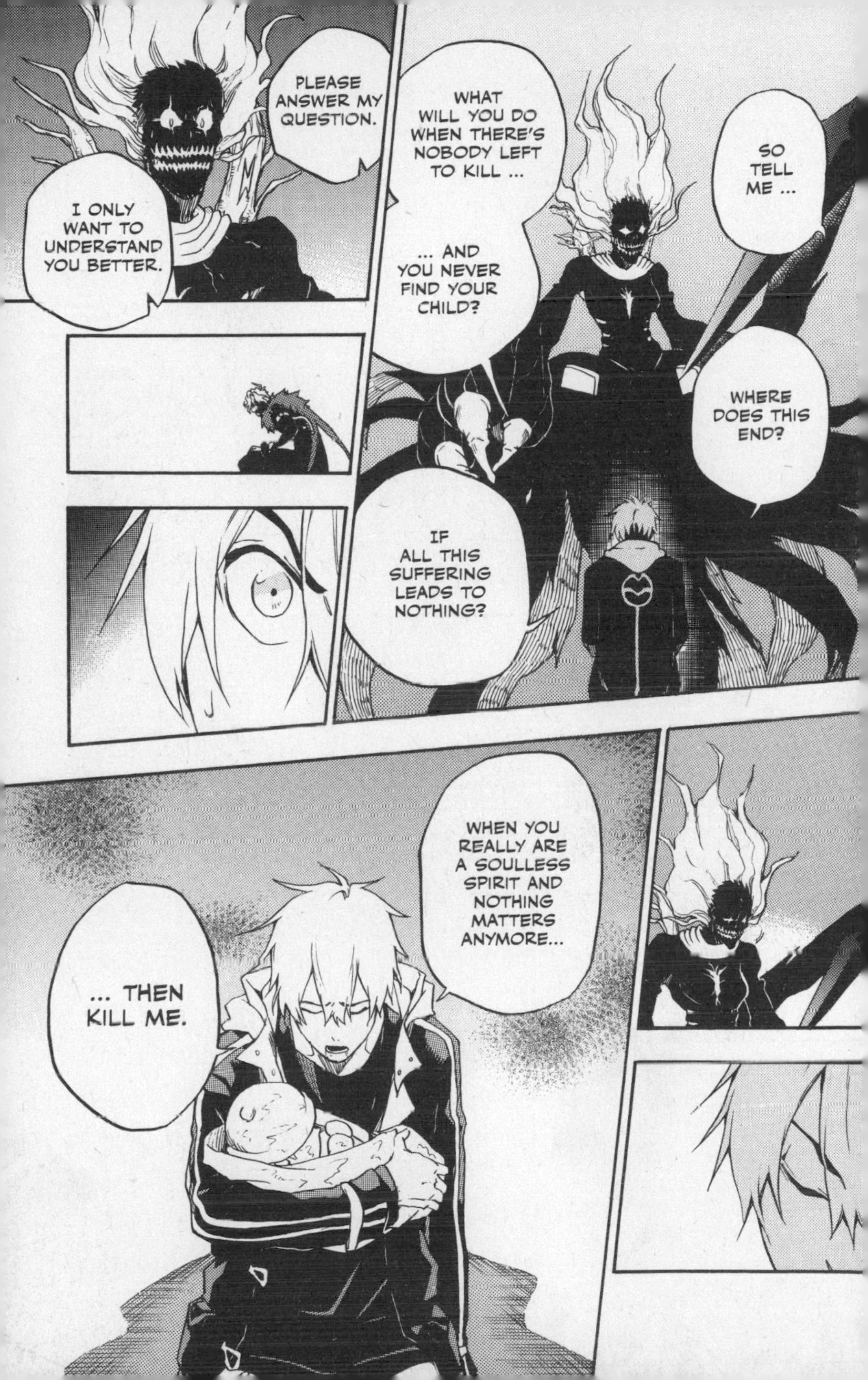
SO TELL ME ...
WHERE DOES THIS END?
WHAT WILL YOU DO WHEN THERE'S NOBODY LEFT TO KILL ...
... AND YOU NEVER FIND YOUR CHILD?
IF ALL THIS SUFFERING LEADS TO NOTHING?
PLEASE ANSWER MY QUESTION.
I ONLY WANT TO UNDERSTAND YOU BETTER.
WHEN YOU REALLY ARE A SOULLESS SPIRIT AND NOTHING MATTERS ANYMORE...
... THEN KILL ME.

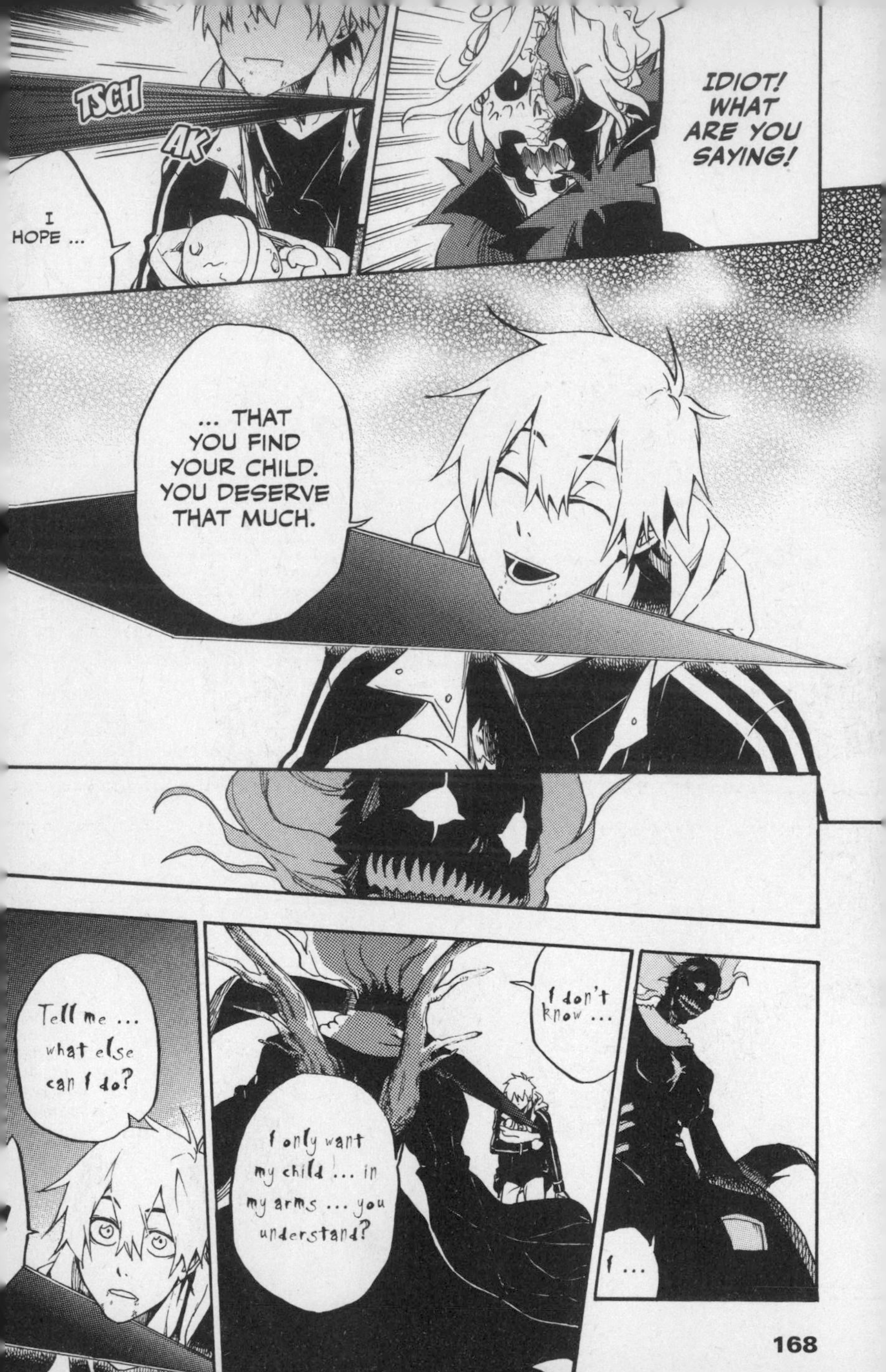
IDIOT! WHAT ARE YOU SAYING!
TSCH
AK
I HOPE ...
... THAT YOU FIND YOUR CHILD. YOU DESERVE THAT MUCH.
I ...
I don't know ...
I only want my child ... in my arms ... you understand?
Tell me ... what else can I do?

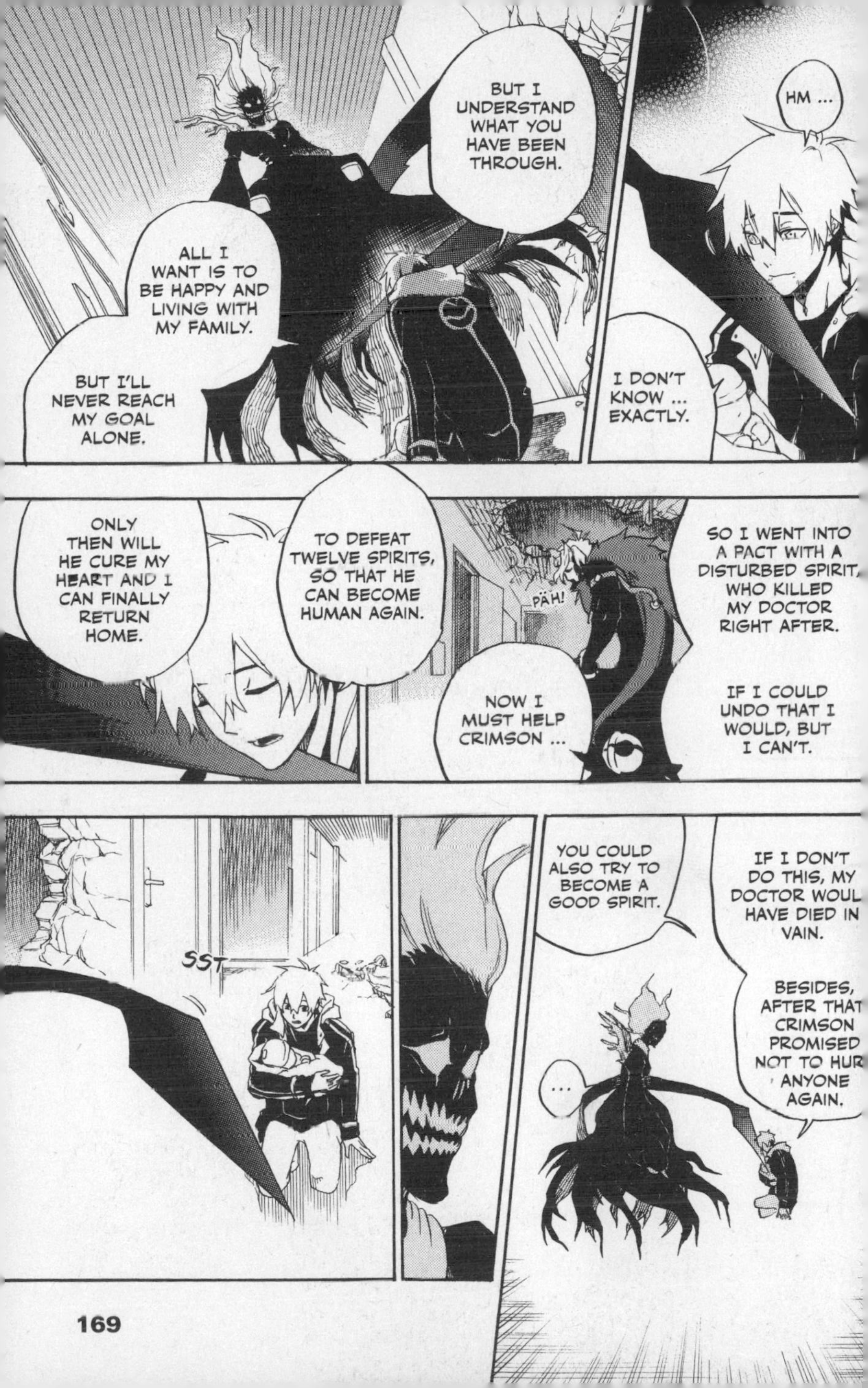
HM ...
I DON'T KNOW ... EXACTLY.
BUT I UNDERSTAND WHAT YOU HAVE BEEN THROUGH.
ALL I WANT IS TO BE HAPPY AND LIVING WITH MY FAMILY.
BUT I'LL NEVER REACH MY GOAL ALONE.
SO I WENT INTO A PACT WITH A DISTURBED SPIRIT, WHO KILLED MY DOCTOR RIGHT AFTER.
IF I COULD UNDO THAT I WOULD, BUT I CAN'T.
PÄH!
NOW I MUST HELP CRIMSON ...
TO DEFEAT TWELVE SPIRITS, SO THAT HE CAN BECOME HUMAN AGAIN.
ONLY THEN WILL HE CURE MY HEART AND I CAN FINALLY RETURN HOME.
IF I DON'T DO THIS, MY DOCTOR WOUL HAVE DIED IN VAIN.
BESIDES, AFTER THAT CRIMSON PROMISED NOT TO HUR ANYONE AGAIN.
YOU COULD ALSO TRY TO BECOME A GOOD SPIRIT.
...
SST

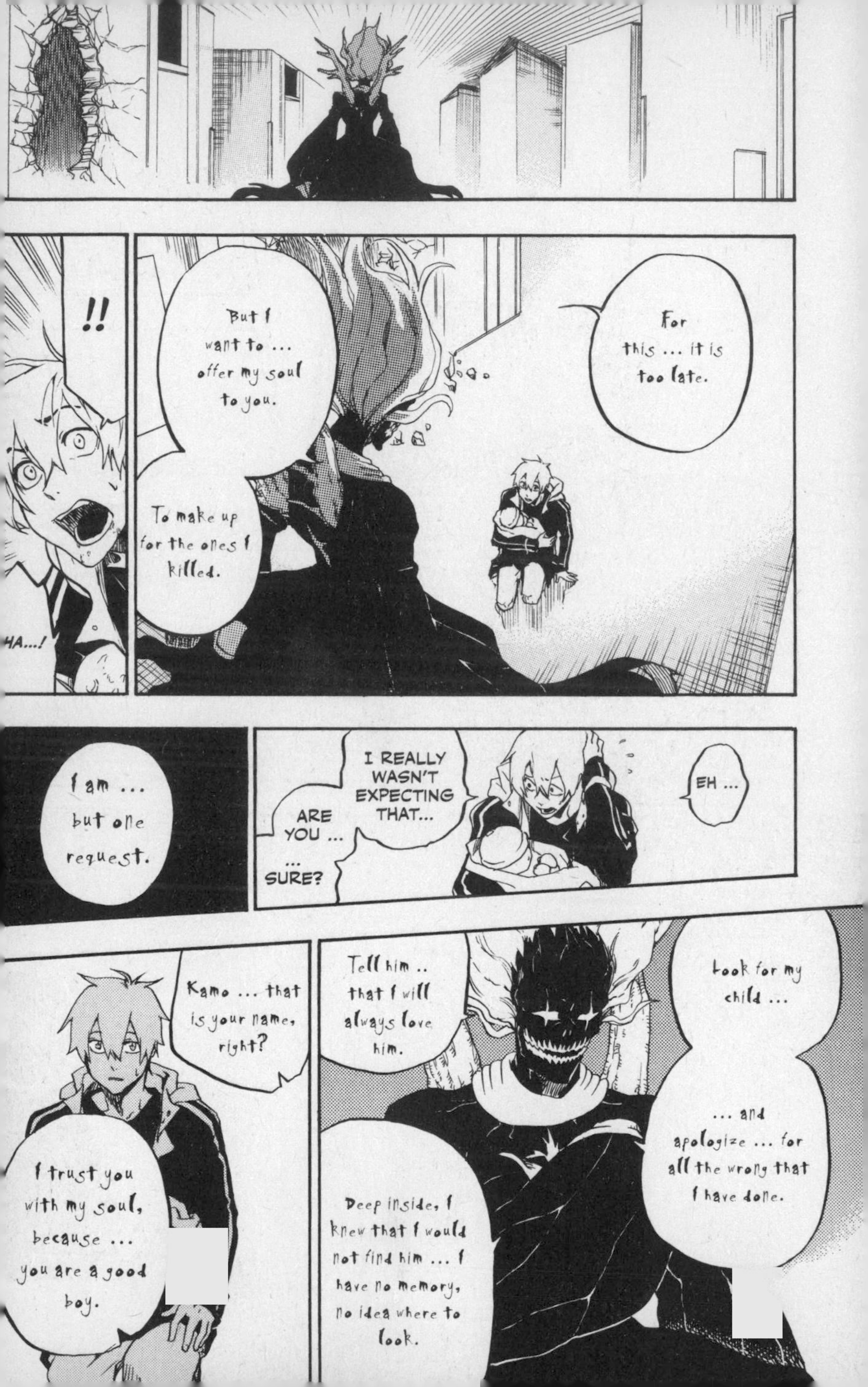
For this ... it is too late.
But I want to ... offer my soul to you.
To make up for the ones I killed.
!!
HA...!
EH ...
I REALLY WASN'T EXPECTING THAT...
ARE YOU ... ... SURE?
I am ... but one request.
Look for my child ...
... and apologize ... for all the wrong that I have done.
Tell him .. that I will always love him.
Deep inside, I knew that I would not find him ... I have no memory, no idea where to look.
Kamo ... that is your name, right?
I trust you with my soul, because ... you are a good boy.

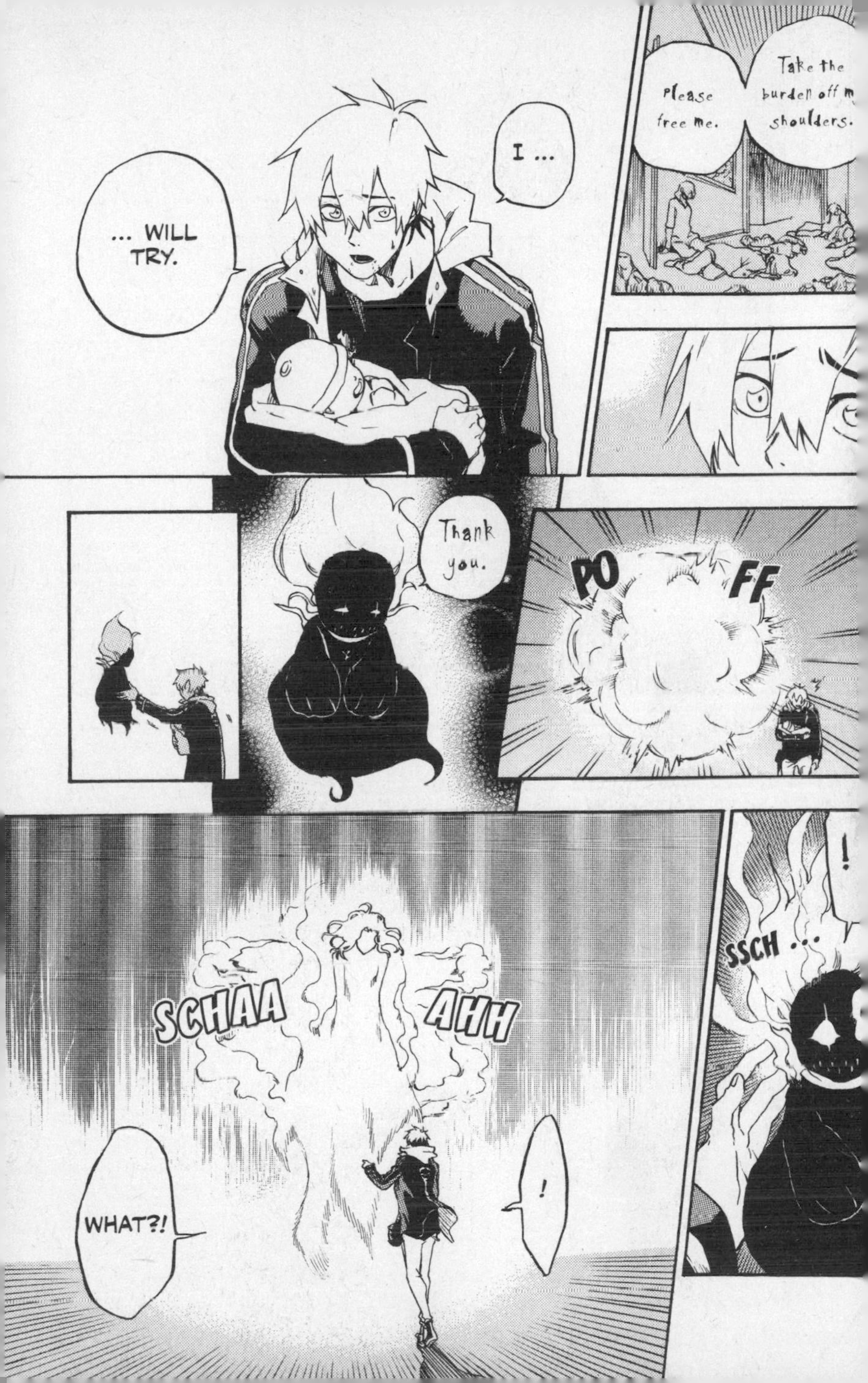
Take the burden off my shoulders.
Please free me.
I ...
... WILL TRY.
Thank you.
POFF
!
SSCH ...
!
SCHAAAHH
WHAT?!

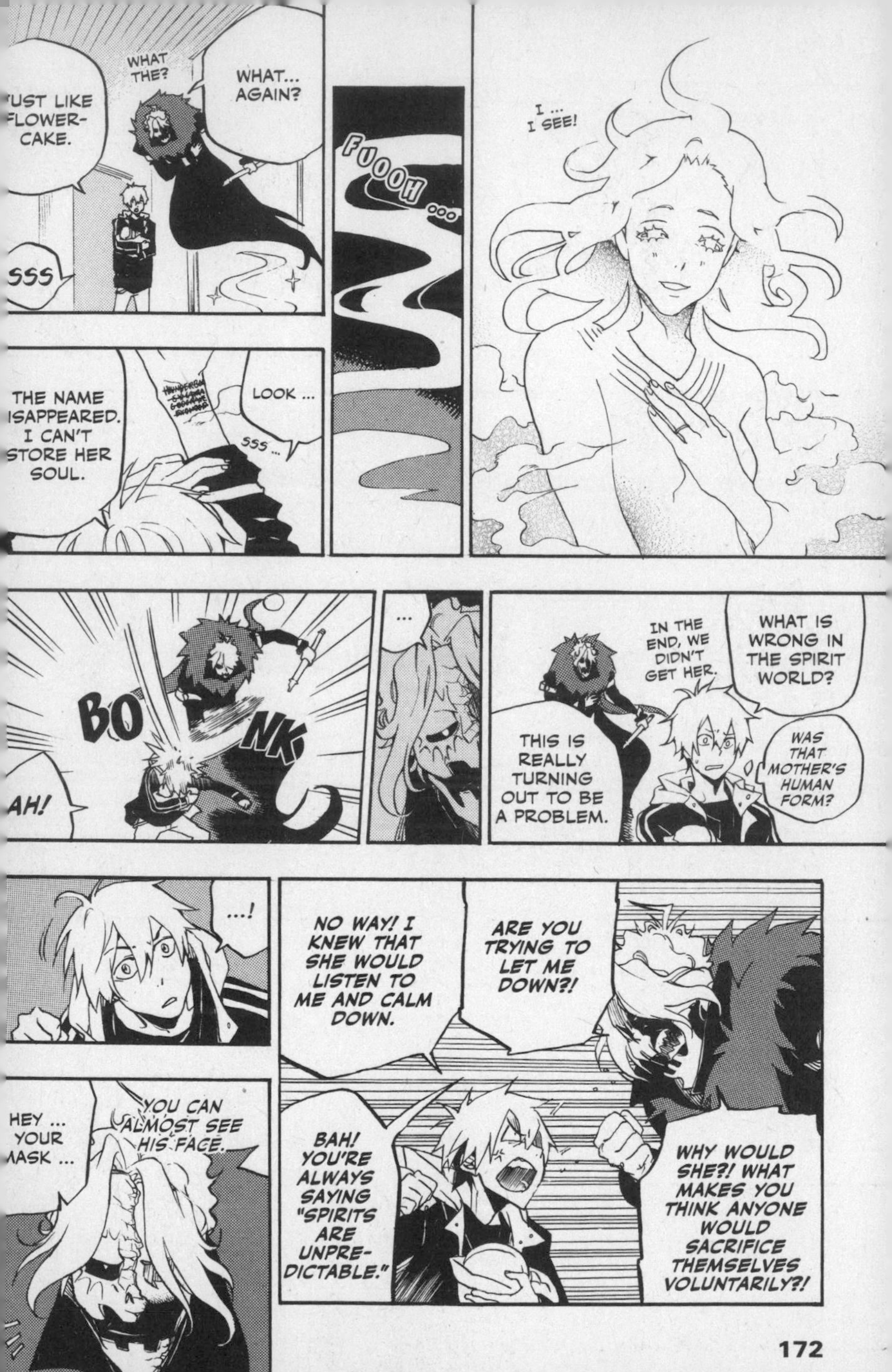
I ... I SEE!
FUOOH ...
WHAT... AGAIN?
WHAT THE?
JUST LIKE FLOWER-CAKE.
SSS
LOOK ...
THE NAME ISAPPEARED. I CAN'T STORE HER SOUL.
SSS ...
WHAT IS WRONG IN THE SPIRIT WORLD?
IN THE END, WE DIDN'T GET HER.
WAS THAT MOTHER'S HUMAN FORM?
THIS IS REALLY TURNING OUT TO BE A PROBLEM.
...
BONK
AH!
ARE YOU TRYING TO LET ME DOWN?!
NO WAY! I KNEW THAT SHE WOULD LISTEN TO ME AND CALM DOWN.
WHY WOULD SHE?! WHAT MAKES YOU THINK ANYONE WOULD SACRIFICE THEMSELVES VOLUNTARILY?!
BAH! YOU'RE ALWAYS SAYING "SPIRITS ARE UNPREDICTABLE."
...!
YOU CAN ALMOST SEE HIS FACE.
HEY ... YOUR MASK ...

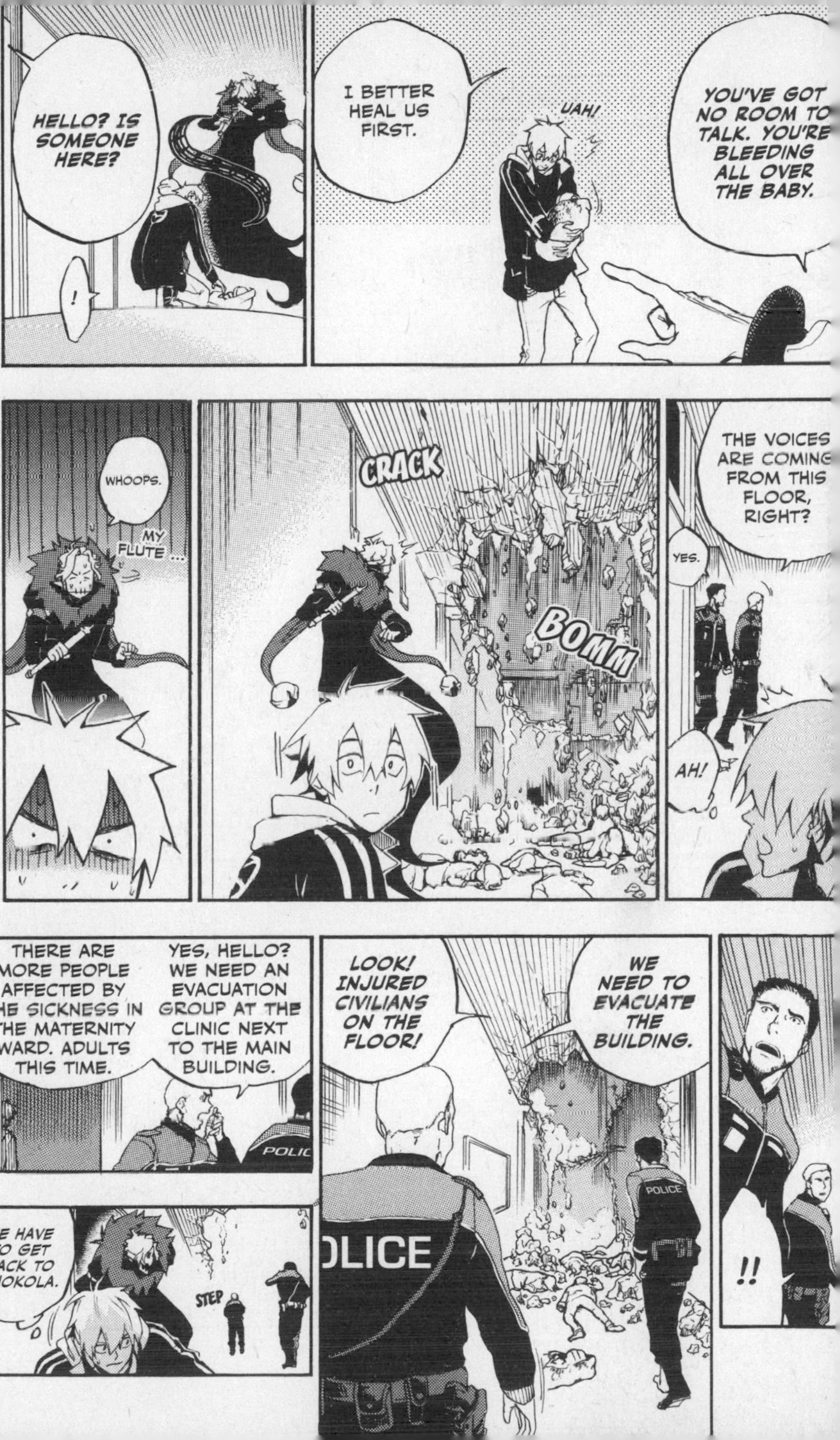
HELLO? IS SOMEONE HERE?
!
I BETTER HEAL US FIRST.
UAH!
YOU'VE GOT NO ROOM TO TALK. YOU'RE BLEEDING ALL OVER THE BABY.
WHOOPS.
MY FLUTE ...
CRACK
BOMM
THE VOICES ARE COMING FROM THIS FLOOR, RIGHT?
YES.
AH!
YES, HELLO? WE NEED AN EVACUATION GROUP AT THE CLINIC NEXT TO THE MAIN BUILDING.
THERE ARE MORE PEOPLE AFFECTED BY THE SICKNESS IN THE MATERNITY WARD. ADULTS THIS TIME.
POLIC
WE HAVE TO GET BACK TO SHOKOLA.
STEP
LOOK! INJURED CIVILIANS ON THE FLOOR!
WE NEED TO EVACUATE THE BUILDING.
OLICE
POLICE
!!

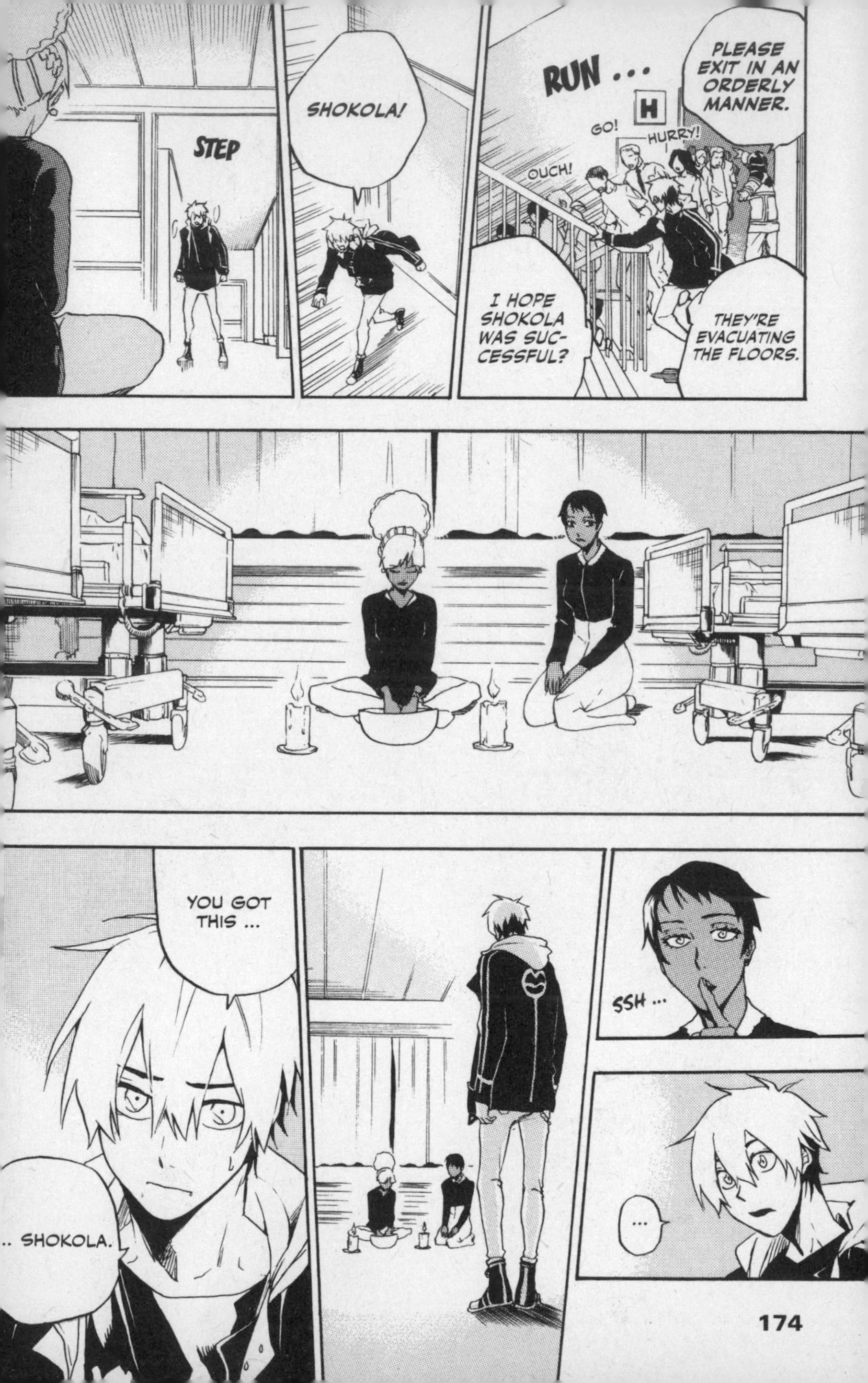

PLEASE EXIT IN AN ORDERLY MANNER.
RUN ...
H
HURRY!
GO!
OUCH!
THEY'RE EVACUATING THE FLOORS.
I HOPE SHOKOLA WAS SUC-CESSFUL?
SHOKOLA!
STEP
SSH ...
...
YOU GOT THIS ...
.. SHOKOLA.

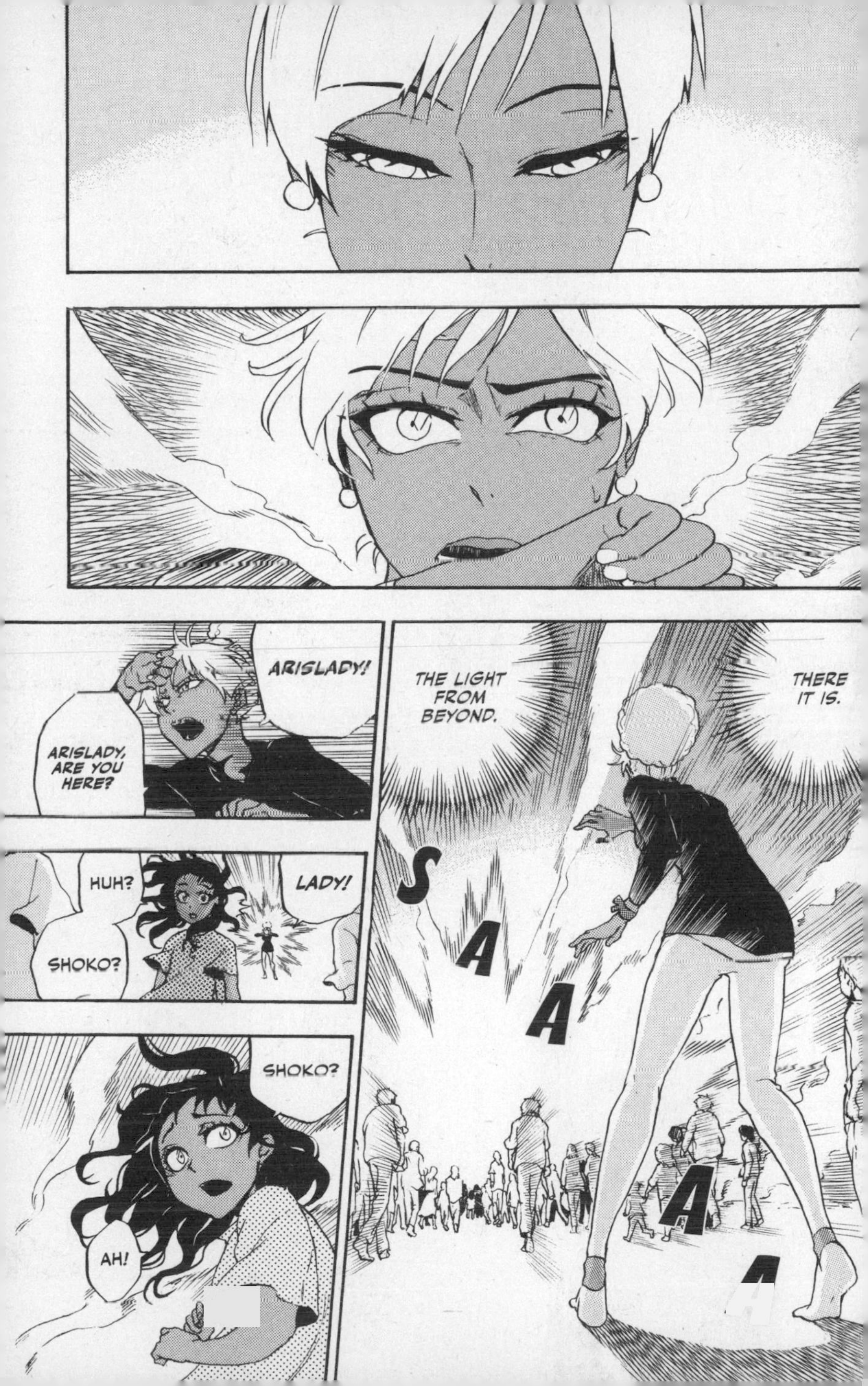
THERE IT IS.
THE LIGHT FROM BEYOND.
SAAAAA
ARISLADY!
ARISLADY, ARE YOU HERE?
LADY!
HUH?
SHOKO?
SHOKO?
AH!

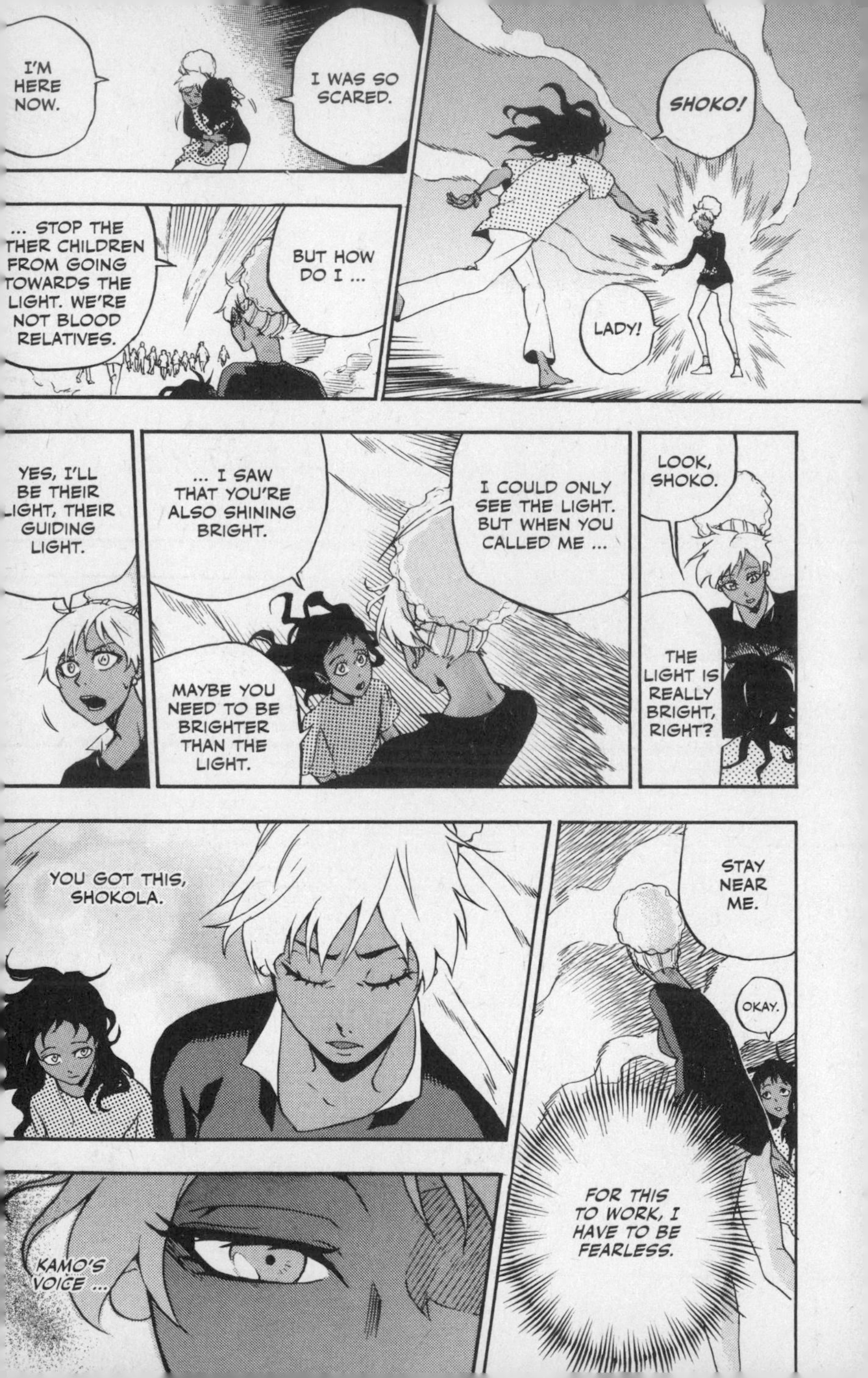
SHOKO!
LADY!
I WAS SO SCARED.
I'M HERE NOW.
BUT HOW DO I ...
... STOP THE THER CHILDREN FROM GOING TOWARDS THE LIGHT. WE'RE NOT BLOOD RELATIVES.
LOOK, SHOKO.
THE LIGHT IS REALLY BRIGHT, RIGHT?
I COULD ONLY SEE THE LIGHT. BUT WHEN YOU CALLED ME ...
... I SAW THAT YOU'RE ALSO SHINING BRIGHT.
MAYBE YOU NEED TO BE BRIGHTER THAN THE LIGHT.
YES, I'LL BE THEIR IGHT, THEIR GUIDING LIGHT.
STAY NEAR ME.
OKAY.
FOR THIS TO WORK, I HAVE TO BE FEARLESS.
YOU GOT THIS, SHOKOLA.
KAMO'S VOICE ...

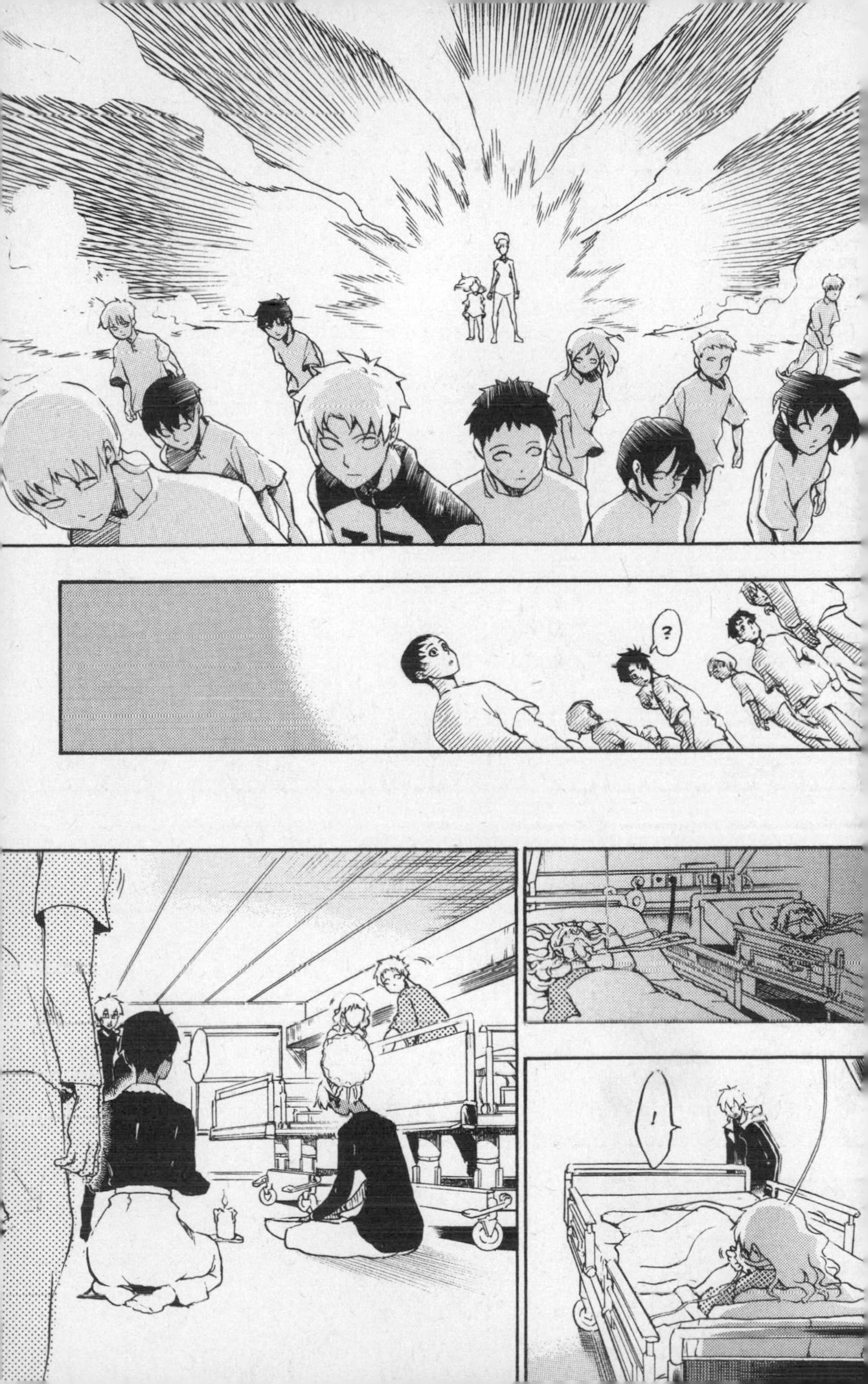
?
!

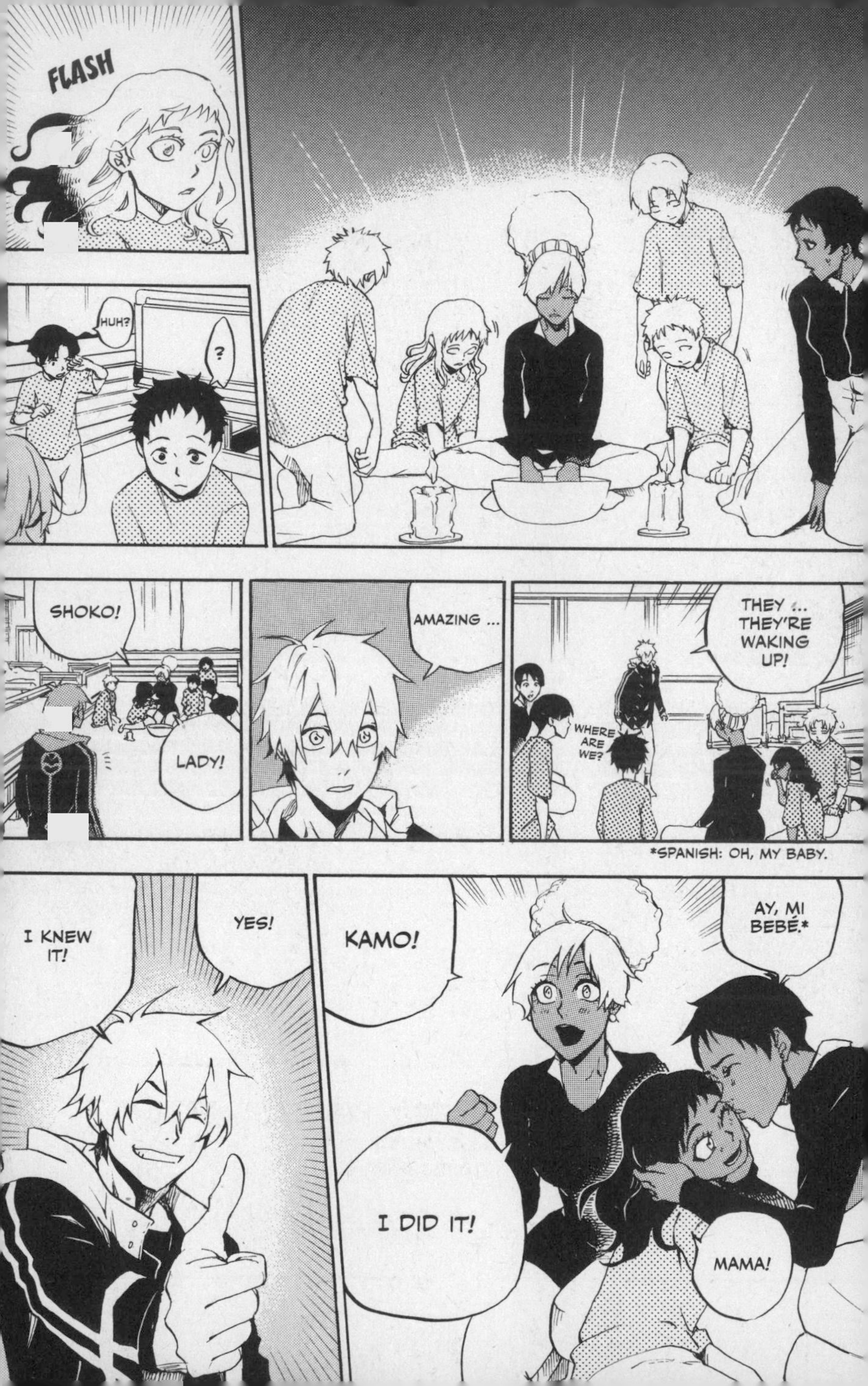
FLASH
HUH?
?
THEY ... THEY'RE WAKING UP!
WHERE ARE WE?
AMAZING ...
SHOKO!
LADY!
*SPANISH: OH, MY BABY.
AY, MI BEBÉ.*
KAMO!
MAMA!
I DID IT!
YES!
I KNEW IT!

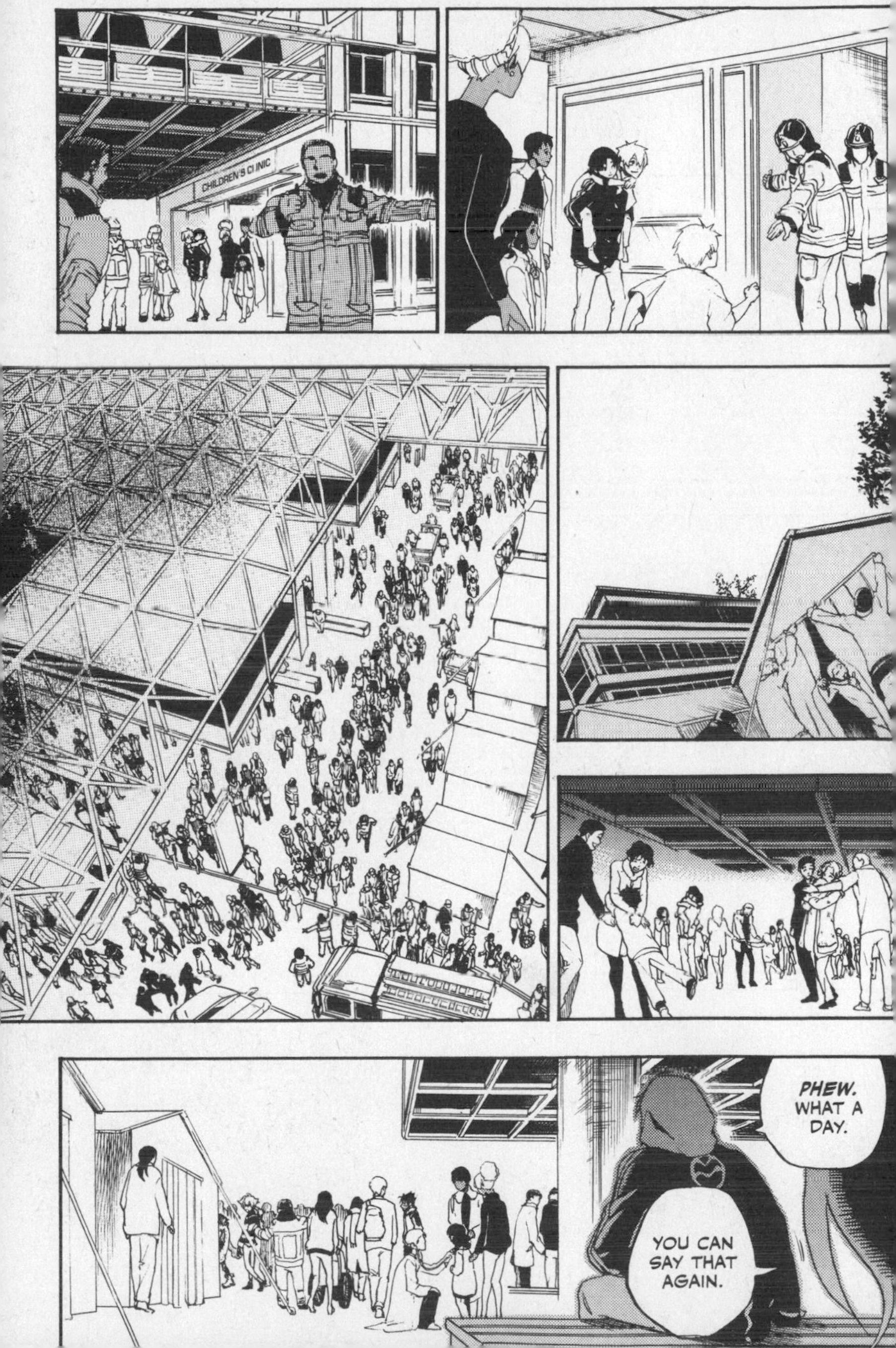
CHILDREN'S CLINIC
PHEW. WHAT A DAY.
YOU CAN SAY THAT AGAIN.

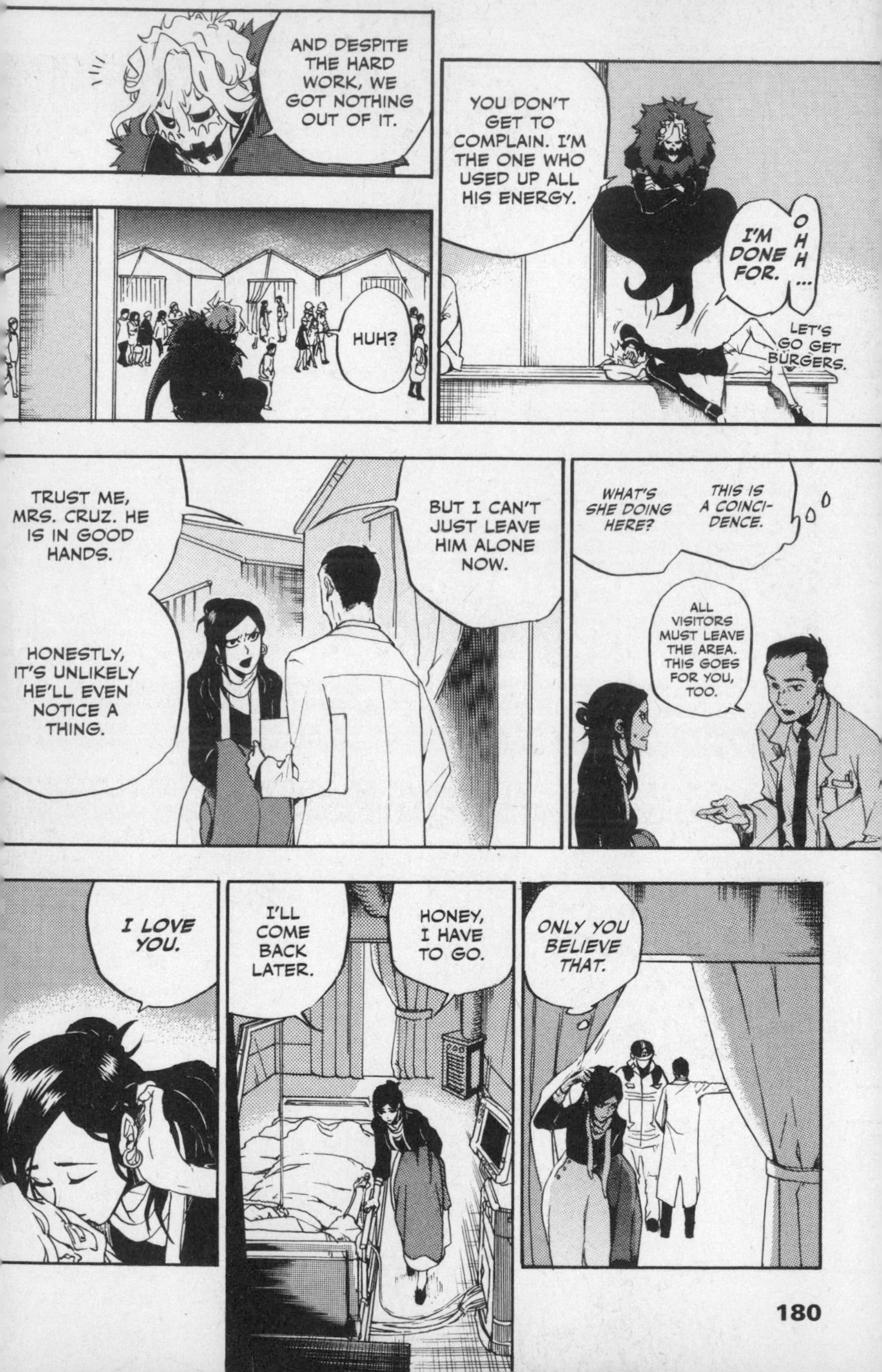

YOU DON'T GET TO COMPLAIN. I'M THE ONE WHO USED UP ALL HIS ENERGY.
OHH...
I'M DONE FOR.
LET'S GO GET BURGERS.
AND DESPITE THE HARD WORK, WE GOT NOTHING OUT OF IT.
HUH?
THIS IS A COINCIDENCE.
WHAT'S SHE DOING HERE?
ALL VISITORS MUST LEAVE THE AREA. THIS GOES FOR YOU, TOO.
BUT I CAN'T JUST LEAVE HIM ALONE NOW.
TRUST ME, MRS. CRUZ. HE IS IN GOOD HANDS.
HONESTLY, IT'S UNLIKELY HE'LL EVEN NOTICE A THING.
ONLY YOU BELIEVE THAT.
HONEY, I HAVE TO GO.
I'LL COME BACK LATER.
I LOVE YOU.

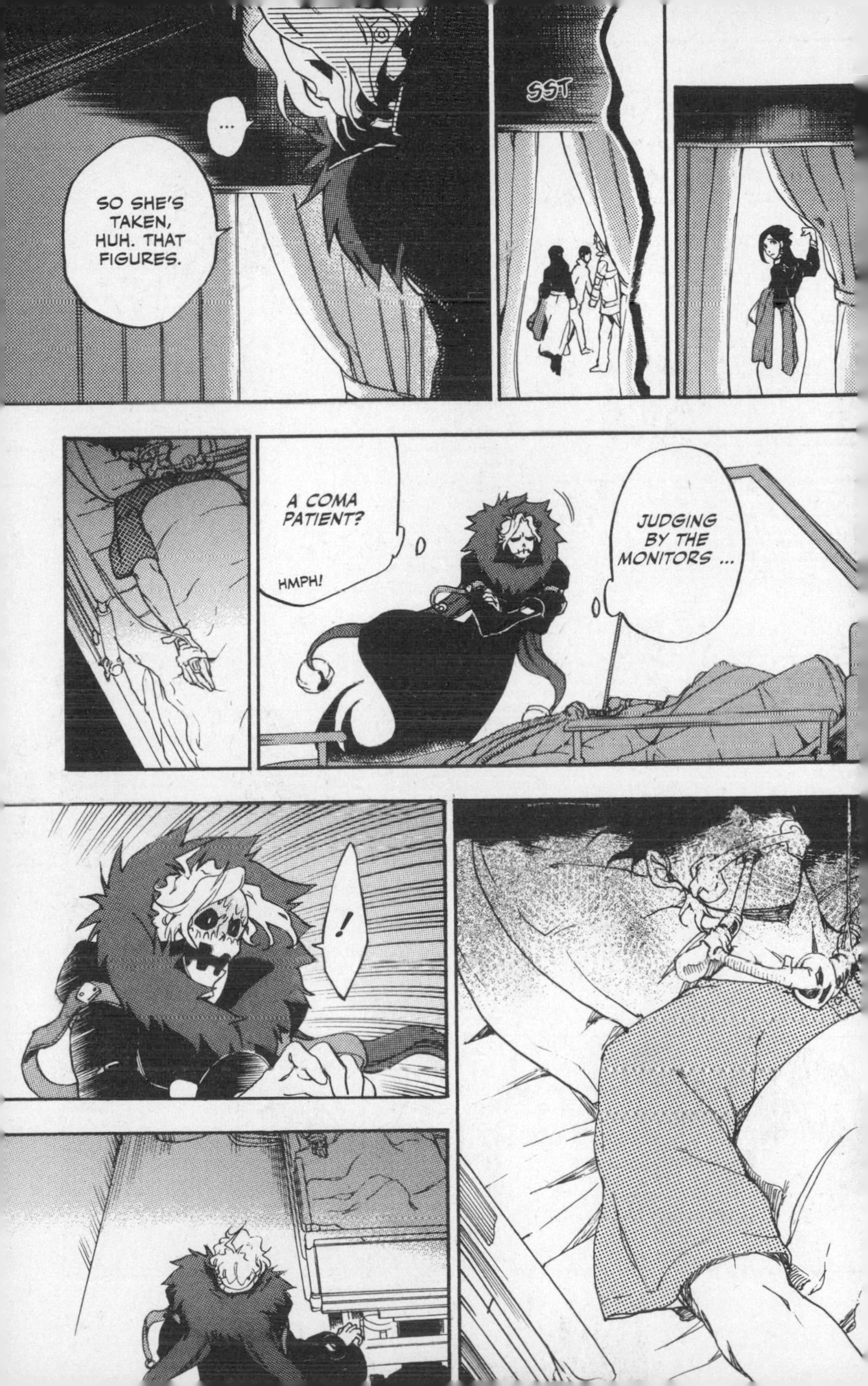
SST
...
SO SHE'S TAKEN, HUH. THAT FIGURES.
JUDGING BY THE MONITORS ...
A COMA PATIENT?
HMPH!
!

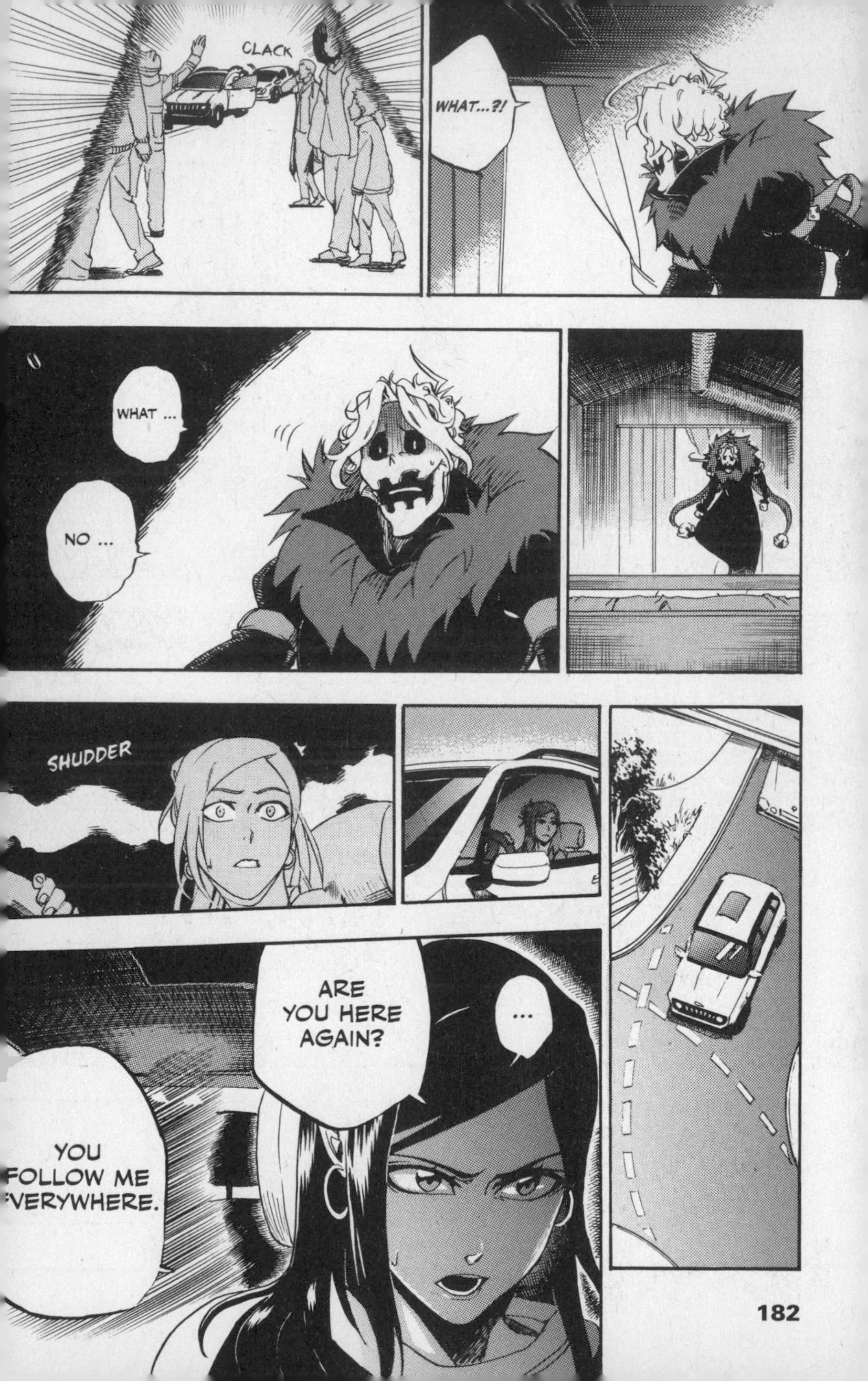
WHAT...?!
CLACK
WHAT ...
NO ...
SHUDDER
...
ARE YOU HERE AGAIN?
YOU FOLLOW ME EVERYWHERE.

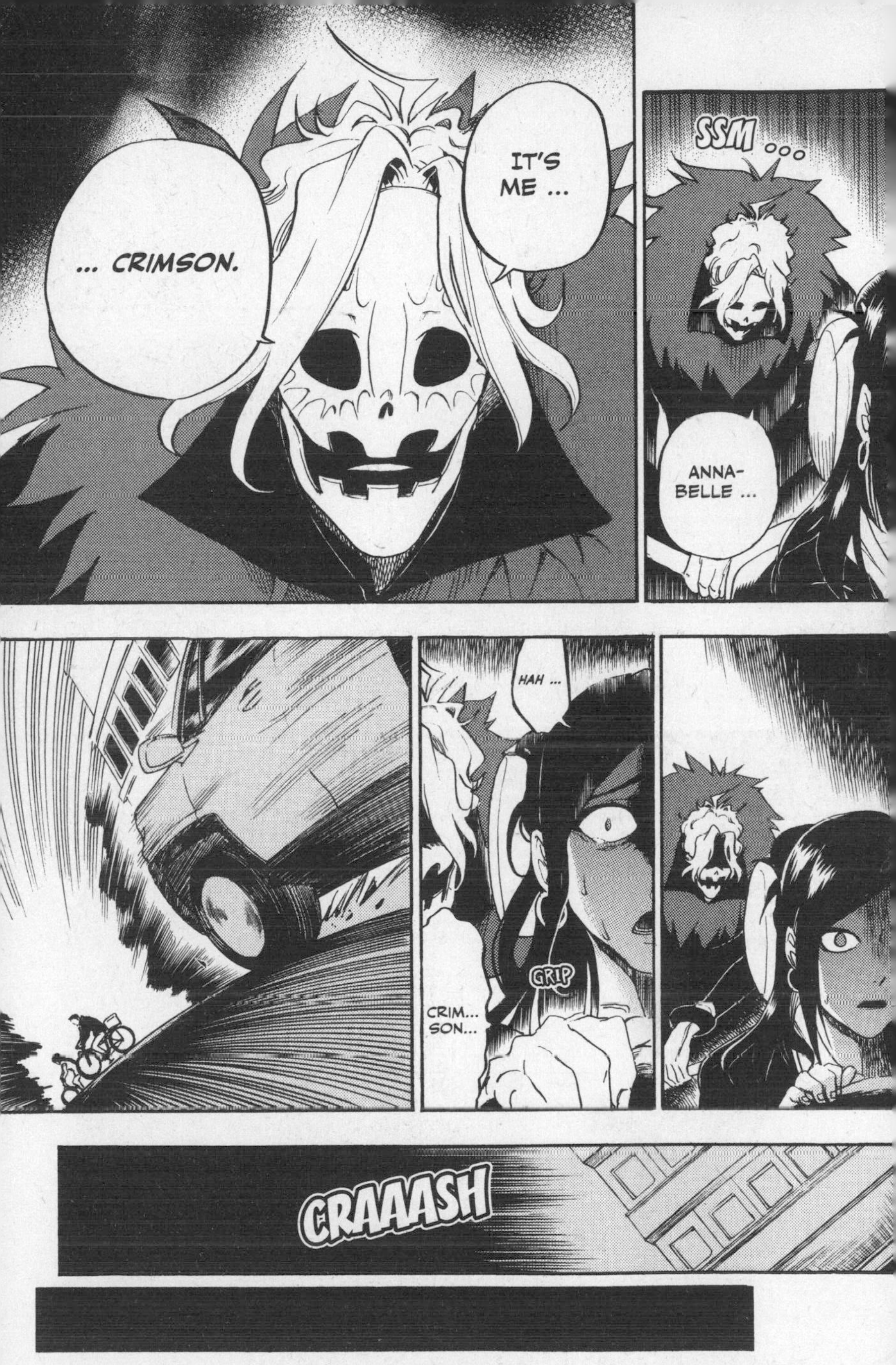
SSM ...
ANNA-BELLE ...
IT'S ME ...
... CRIMSON.
HAH ...
GRIP
CRIM... SON...
CRAAASH

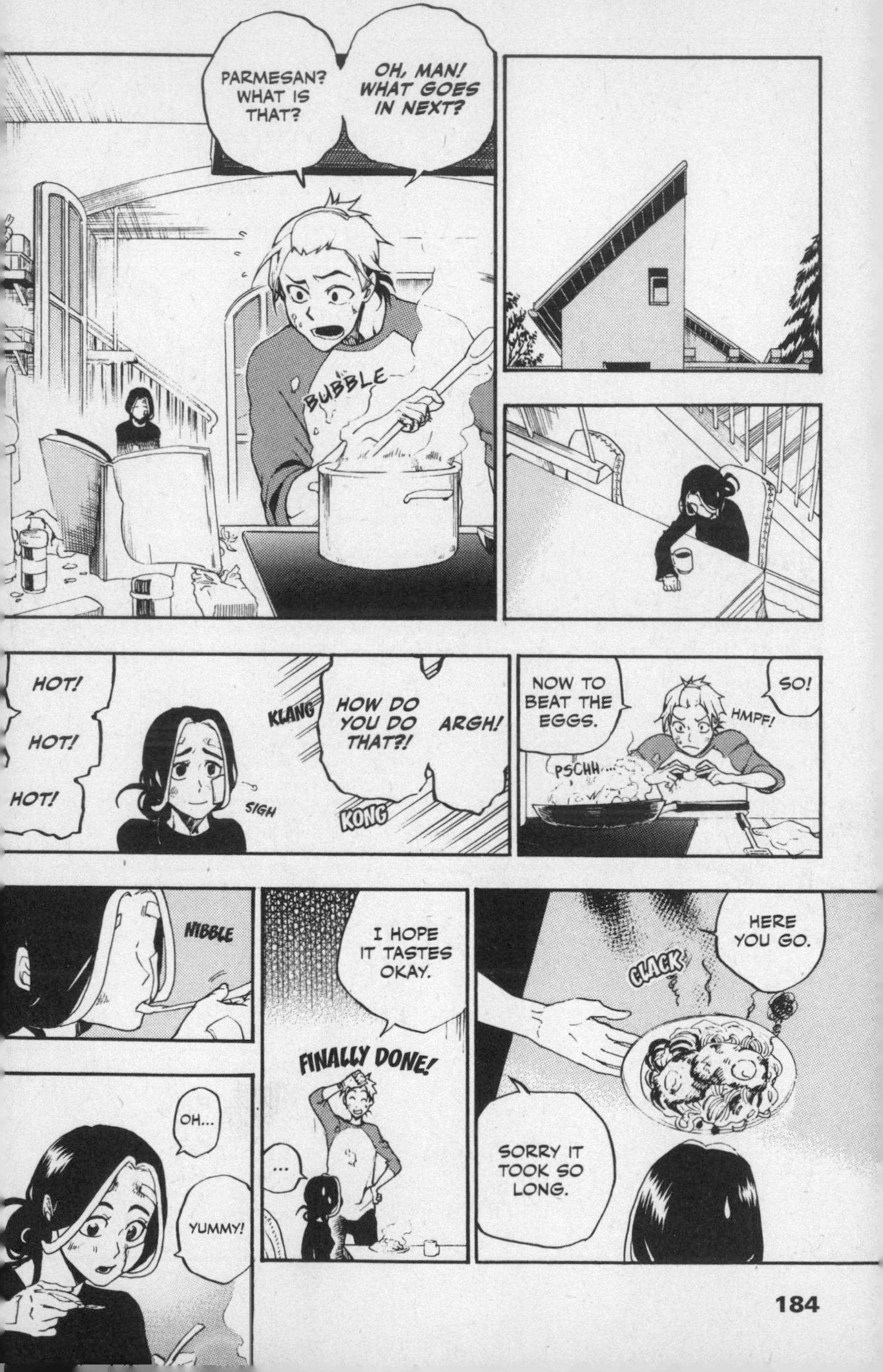
OH, MAN! WHAT GOES IN NEXT?
PARMESAN? WHAT IS THAT?
BUBBLE
SO!
HMPF!
NOW TO BEAT THE EGGS.
PSCHH...
ARGH!
HOW DO YOU DO THAT?!
KLANG
KONG
HOT!
HOT!
HOT!
SIGH
HERE YOU GO.
CLACK
SORRY IT TOOK SO LONG.
I HOPE IT TASTES OKAY.
FINALLY DONE!
...
NIBBLE
OH...
YUMMY!

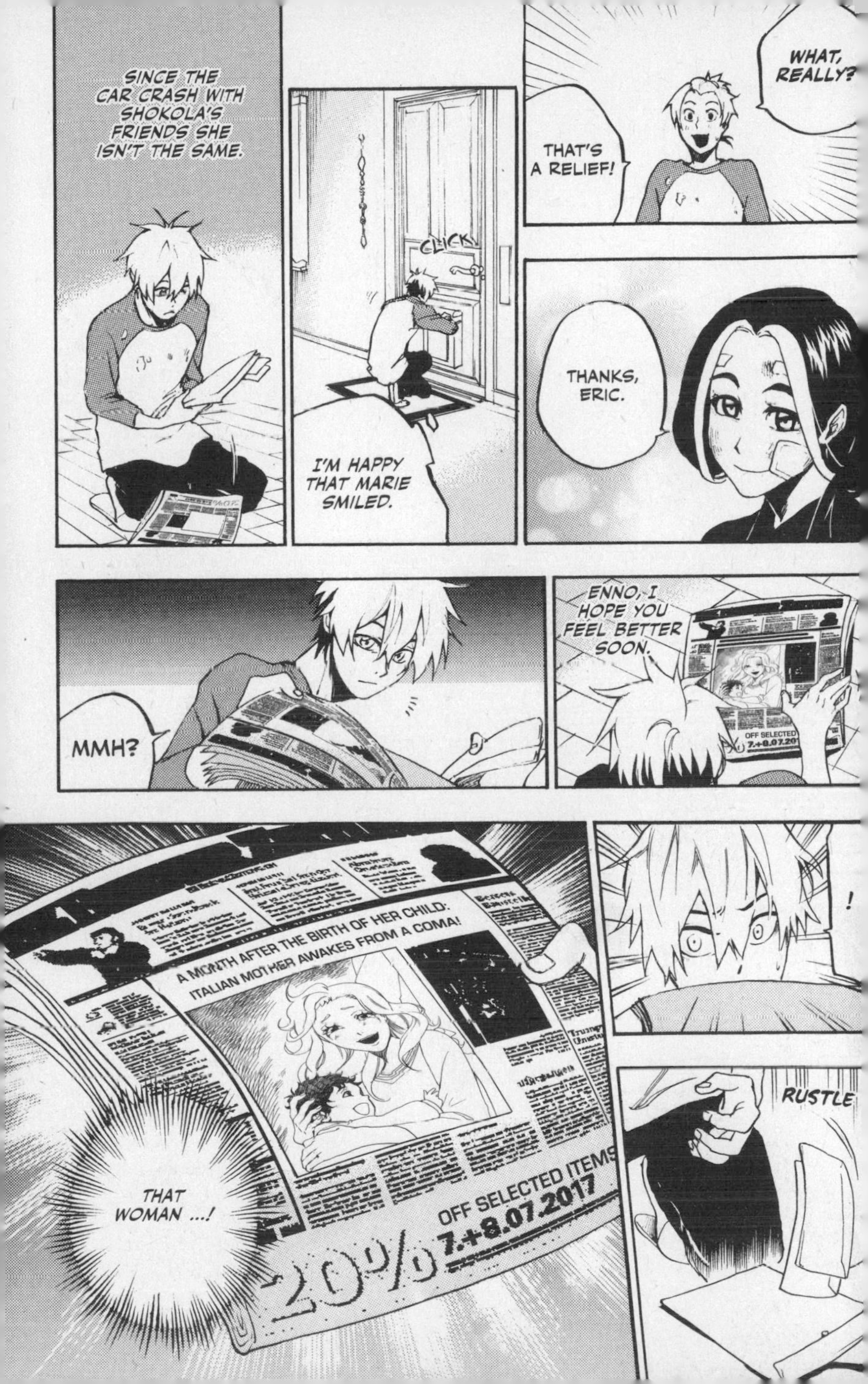

SINCE THE CAR CRASH WITH SHOKOLA'S FRIENDS SHE ISN'T THE SAME.
CLICK
I'M HAPPY THAT MARIE SMILED.
WHAT, REALLY?
THAT'S A RELIEF!
THANKS, ERIC.
MMH?
ENNO, I HOPE YOU FEEL BETTER SOON.
A MONTH AFTER THE BIRTH OF HER CHILD: ITALIAN MOTHER AWAKES FROM A COMA!
OFF SELECTED ITEMS
7.+8.07.2017
20%
THAT WOMAN ...!
!
RUSTLE

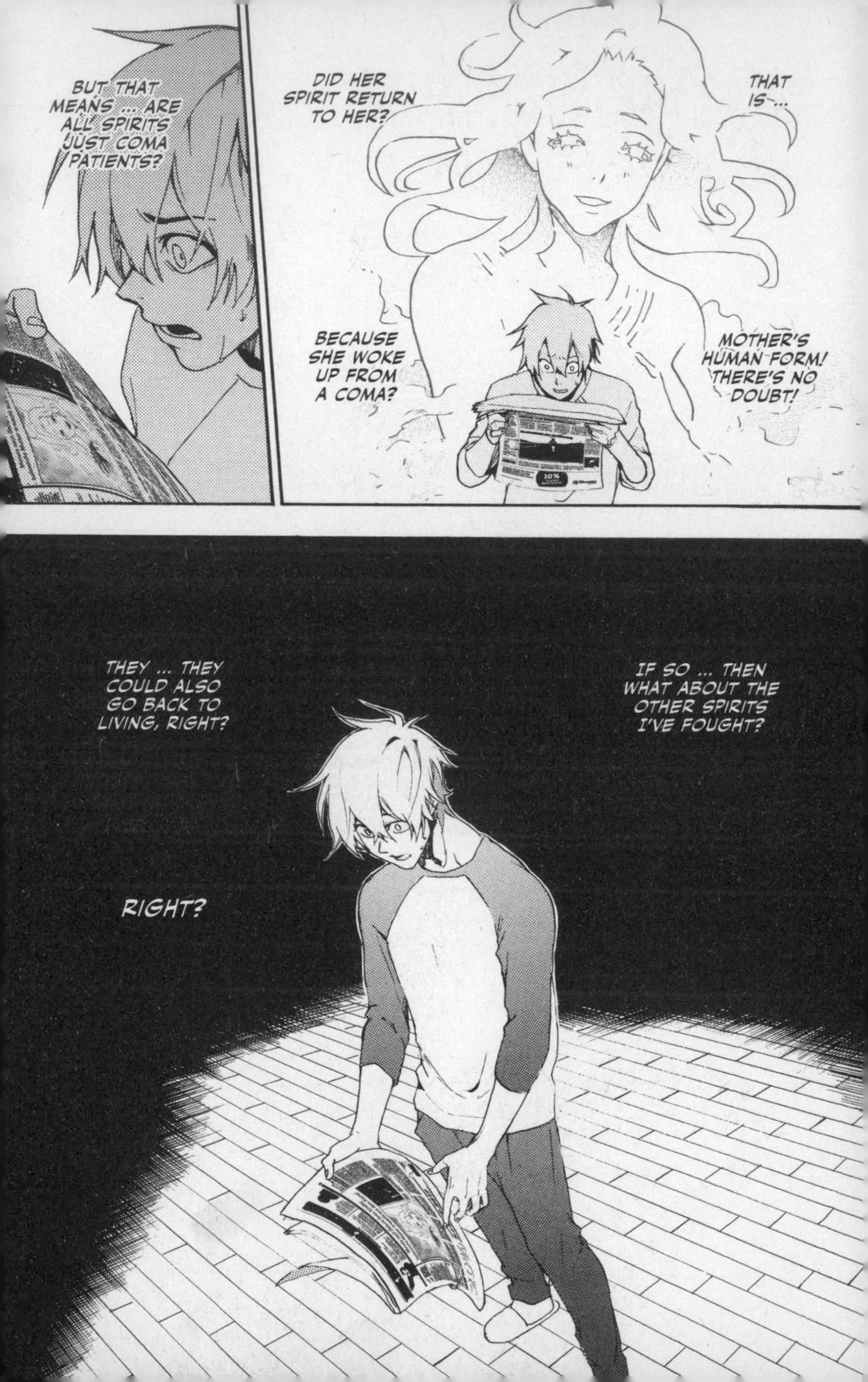
THAT IS-...
DID HER SPIRIT RETURN TO HER?
MOTHER'S HUMAN FORM! THERE'S NO DOUBT!
BECAUSE SHE WOKE UP FROM A COMA?
BUT THAT MEANS ... ARE ALL SPIRITS JUST COMA PATIENTS?
IF SO ... THEN WHAT ABOUT THE OTHER SPIRITS I'VE FOUGHT?
THEY ... THEY COULD ALSO GO BACK TO LIVING, RIGHT?
RIGHT?

KAMO

PACT WITH THE SPIRIT WORLD

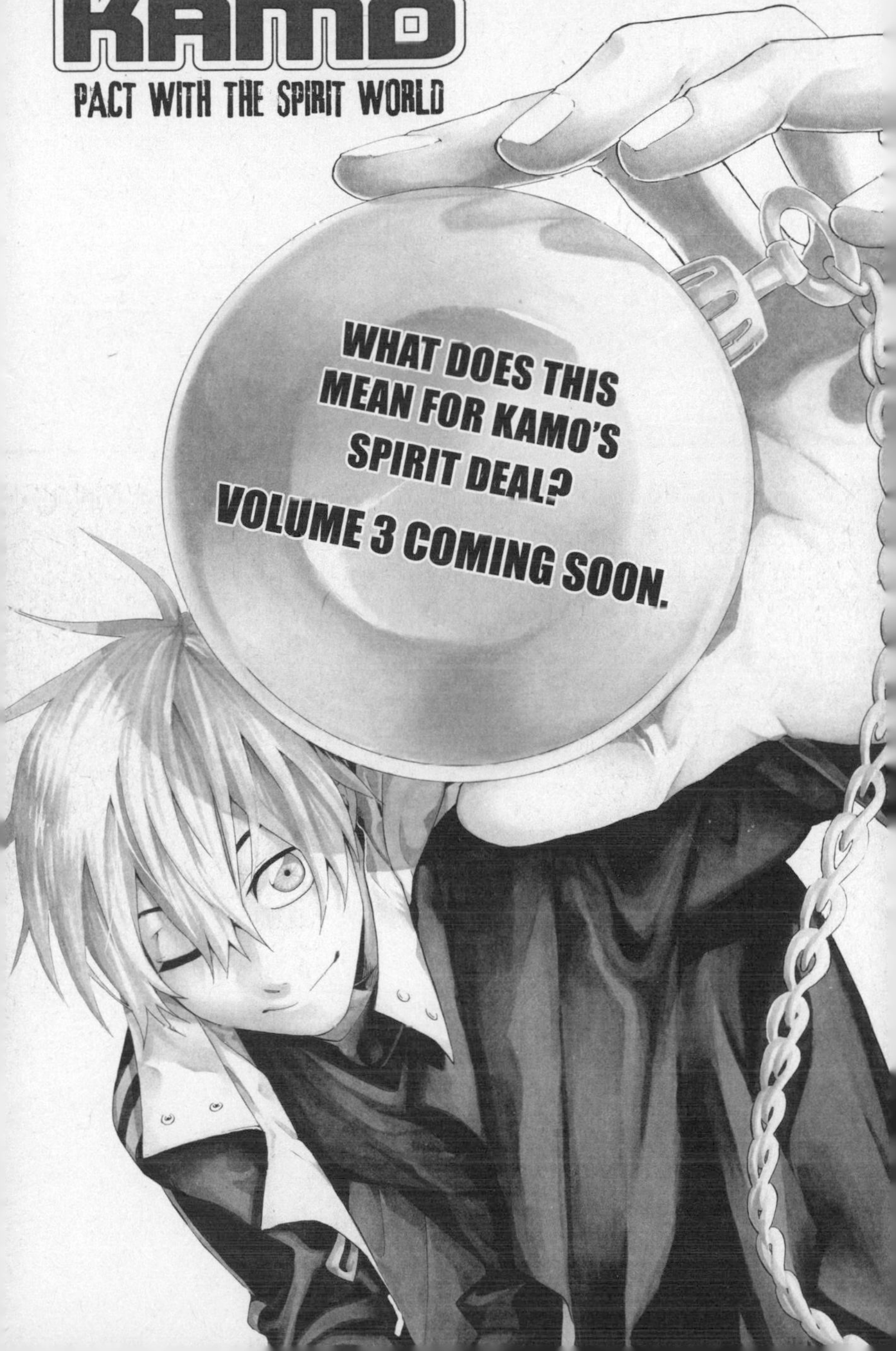
WHAT DOES THIS MEAN FOR KAMO'S SPIRIT DEAL?
VOLUME 3 COMING SOON.

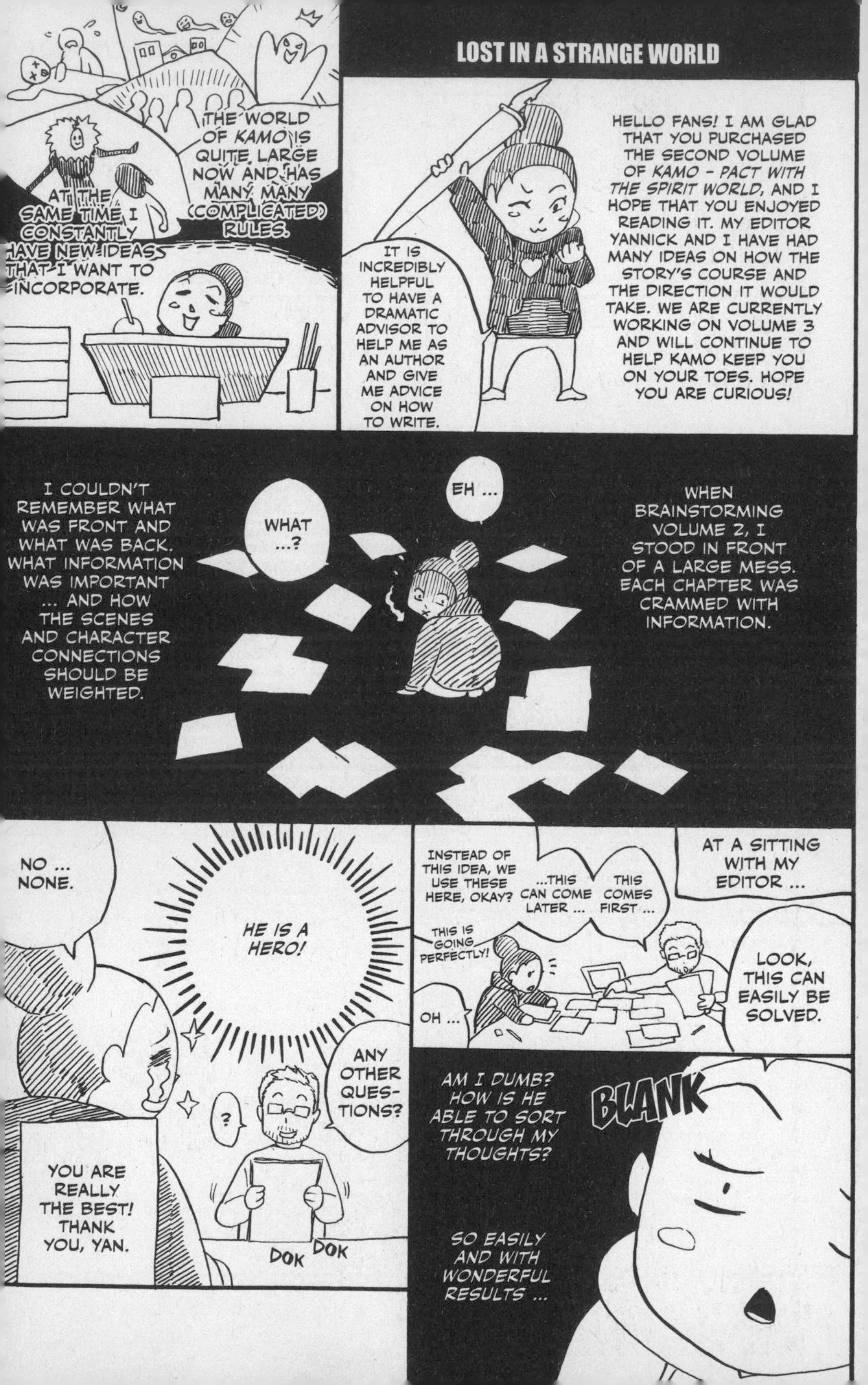
LOST IN A STRANGE WORLD
HELLO FANS! I AM GLAD THAT YOU PURCHASED THE SECOND VOLUME OF *KAMO - PACT WITH THE SPIRIT WORLD*, AND I HOPE THAT YOU ENJOYED READING IT. MY EDITOR YANNICK AND I HAVE HAD MANY IDEAS ON HOW THE STORY'S COURSE AND THE DIRECTION IT WOULD TAKE. WE ARE CURRENTLY WORKING ON VOLUME 3 AND WILL CONTINUE TO HELP KAMO KEEP YOU ON YOUR TOES. HOPE YOU ARE CURIOUS!
IT IS INCREDIBLY HELPFUL TO HAVE A DRAMATIC ADVISOR TO HELP ME AS AN AUTHOR AND GIVE ME ADVICE ON HOW TO WRITE.
THE WORLD OF *KAMO* IS QUITE LARGE NOW AND HAS MANY, MANY (COMPLICATED) RULES.
AT THE SAME TIME, I CONSTANTLY HAVE NEW IDEAS THAT I WANT TO INCORPORATE.
WHEN BRAINSTORMING VOLUME 2, I STOOD IN FRONT OF A LARGE MESS. EACH CHAPTER WAS CRAMMED WITH INFORMATION.
EH ...
WHAT ...?
I COULDN'T REMEMBER WHAT WAS FRONT AND WHAT WAS BACK. WHAT INFORMATION WAS IMPORTANT ... AND HOW THE SCENES AND CHARACTER CONNECTIONS SHOULD BE WEIGHTED.
AT A SITTING WITH MY EDITOR ...
THIS COMES FIRST ...
...THIS CAN COME LATER ...
INSTEAD OF THIS IDEA, WE USE THESE HERE, OKAY?
THIS IS GOING PERFECTLY!
LOOK, THIS CAN EASILY BE SOLVED.
OH ...
BLANK
AM I DUMB? HOW IS HE ABLE TO SORT THROUGH MY THOUGHTS?
SO EASILY AND WITH WONDERFUL RESULTS ...
ANY OTHER QUES-TIONS?
?
HE IS A HERO!
NO ... NONE.
YOU ARE REALLY THE BEST! THANK YOU, YAN.
DOK
DOK

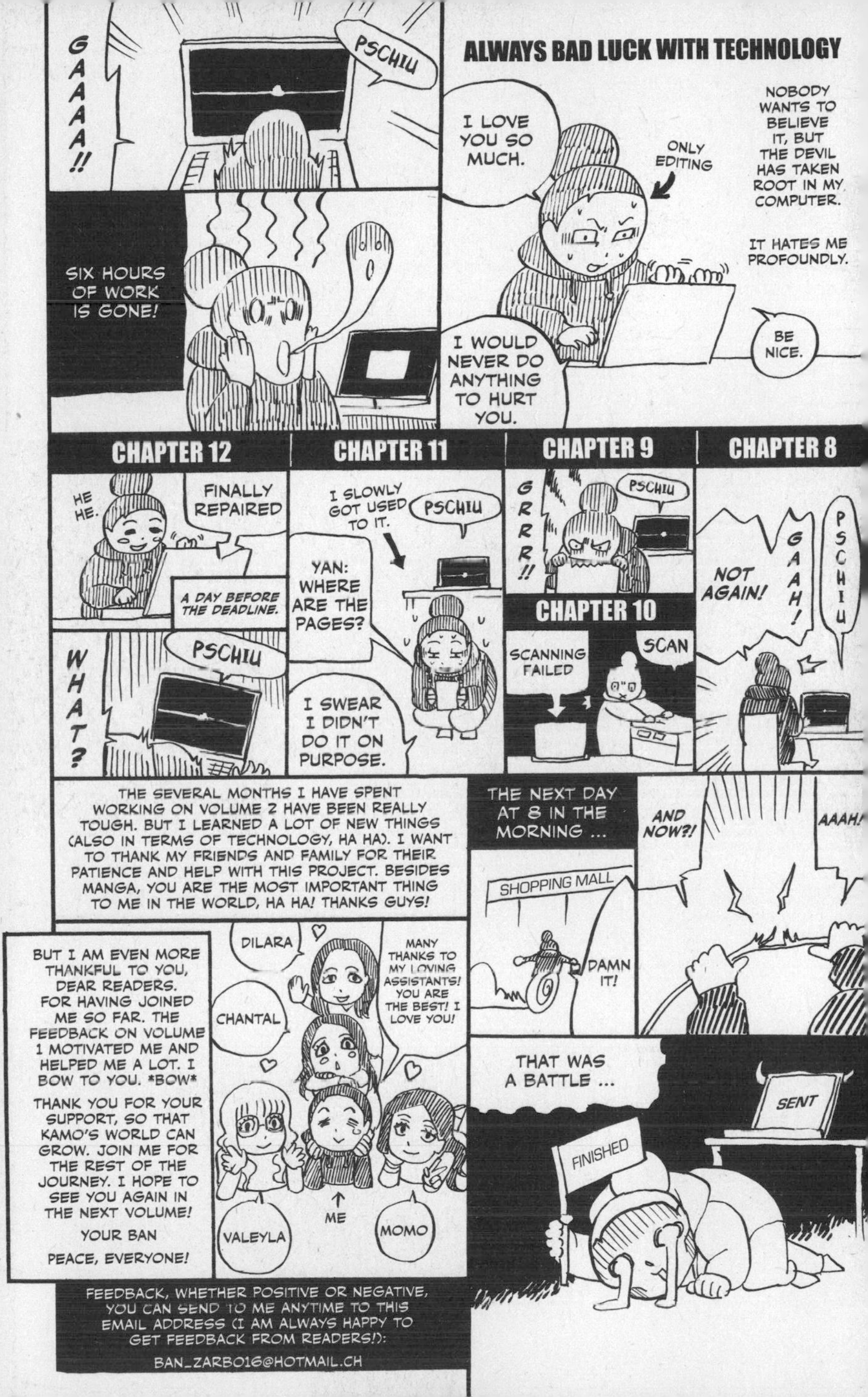
ALWAYS BAD LUCK WITH TECHNOLOGY
NOBODY WANTS TO BELIEVE IT, BUT THE DEVIL HAS TAKEN ROOT IN MY COMPUTER.
IT HATES ME PROFOUNDLY.
I LOVE YOU SO MUCH.
ONLY EDITING
I WOULD NEVER DO ANYTHING TO HURT YOU.
BE NICE.
PSCHIU
GAAAAA!!
SIX HOURS OF WORK IS GONE!
CHAPTER 8
PSCHIU
GAAH!
NOT AGAIN!
CHAPTER 9
PSCHIU
GRRR!!
CHAPTER 10
SCAN
SCANNING FAILED
CHAPTER 11
I SLOWLY GOT USED TO IT.
PSCHIU
YAN: WHERE ARE THE PAGES?
I SWEAR I DIDN'T DO IT ON PURPOSE.
CHAPTER 12
FINALLY REPAIRED
HE HE.
A DAY BEFORE THE DEADLINE.
PSCHIU
WHAT?
AAAH!
AND NOW?!
THE NEXT DAY AT 8 IN THE MORNING ...
SHOPPING MALL
DAMN IT!
THE SEVERAL MONTHS I HAVE SPENT WORKING ON VOLUME 2 HAVE BEEN REALLY TOUGH. BUT I LEARNED A LOT OF NEW THINGS (ALSO IN TERMS OF TECHNOLOGY, HA HA). I WANT TO THANK MY FRIENDS AND FAMILY FOR THEIR PATIENCE AND HELP WITH THIS PROJECT. BESIDES MANGA, YOU ARE THE MOST IMPORTANT THING TO ME IN THE WORLD, HA HA! THANKS GUYS!
THAT WAS A BATTLE ...
SENT
FINISHED
MANY THANKS TO MY LOVING ASSISTANTS! YOU ARE THE BEST! I LOVE YOU!
DILARA
CHANTAL
MOMO
ME
VALEYLA
BUT I AM EVEN MORE THANKFUL TO YOU, DEAR READERS. FOR HAVING JOINED ME SO FAR. THE FEEDBACK ON VOLUME 1 MOTIVATED ME AND HELPED ME A LOT. I BOW TO YOU. *BOW*
THANK YOU FOR YOUR SUPPORT, SO THAT KAMO'S WORLD CAN GROW. JOIN ME FOR THE REST OF THE JOURNEY. I HOPE TO SEE YOU AGAIN IN THE NEXT VOLUME!
YOUR BAN
PEACE, EVERYONE!
FEEDBACK, WHETHER POSITIVE OR NEGATIVE, YOU CAN SEND TO ME ANYTIME TO THIS EMAIL ADDRESS (I AM ALWAYS HAPPY TO GET FEEDBACK FROM READERS!):
BAN_ZARBO16@HOTMAIL.CH

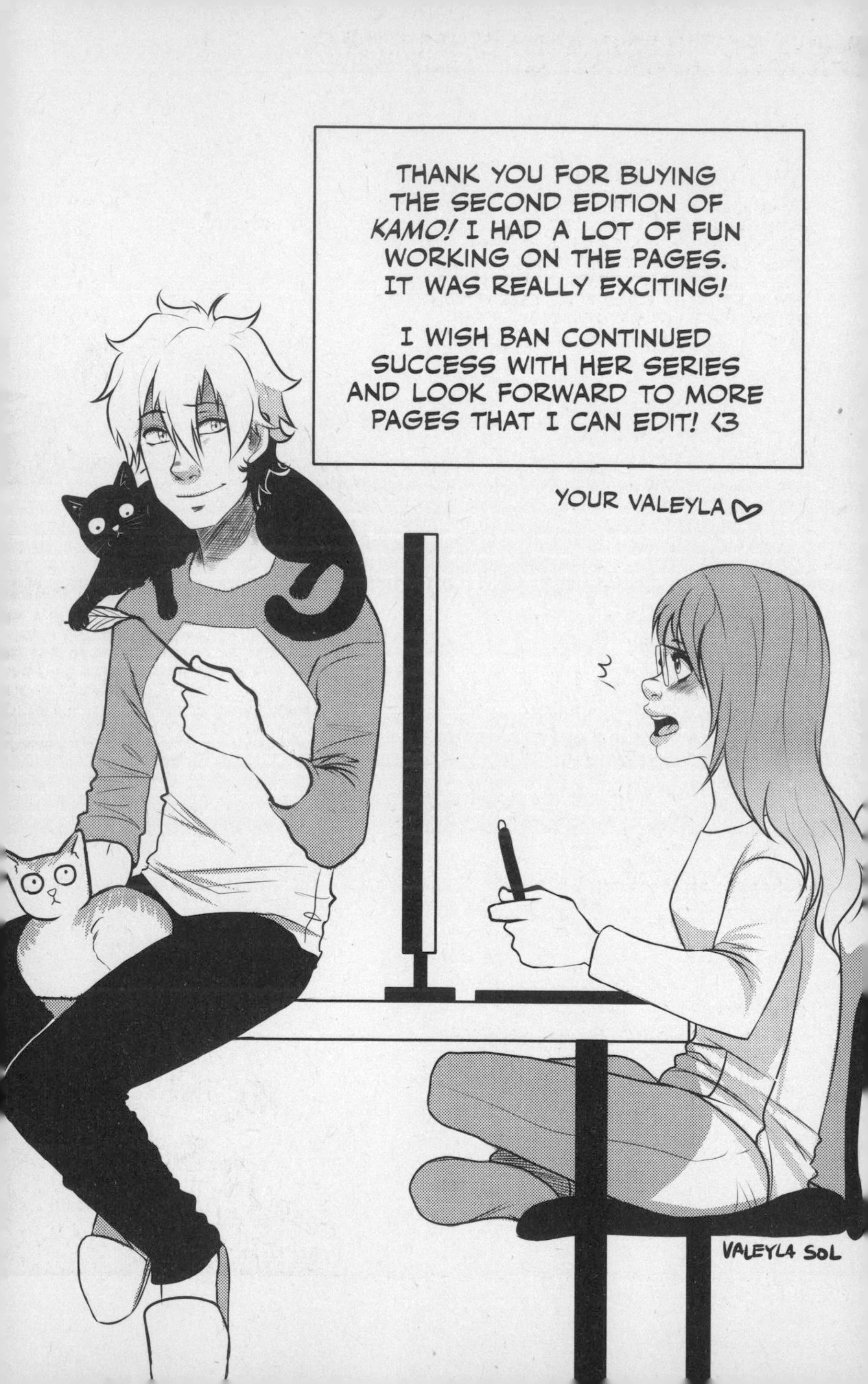
THANK YOU FOR BUYING THE SECOND EDITION OF *KAMO!* I HAD A LOT OF FUN WORKING ON THE PAGES. IT WAS REALLY EXCITING!

I WISH BAN CONTINUED SUCCESS WITH HER SERIES AND LOOK FORWARD TO MORE PAGES THAT I CAN EDIT! <3
YOUR VALEYLA ♡
VALEYLA SOL

MAIN CHARACTERS -- CONTINUED FROM VOLUME 1

KAMO

KAMO HAS REALLY GROWN SINCE MERGING WITH CRIMSON AT THE END OF THE FIRST VOLUME. WHILE IN VOLUME 1, HE WAS STILL CARRIED AWAY BY THE EVENTS AND BASICALLY JUST REACTED, IT WAS IMPORTANT FOR ME THAT IN VOLUME 2 HE SEEM MORE DETERMINED AND MATURE. EVEN SELF-REFLECTION IS A BIG THEME FOR HIM.

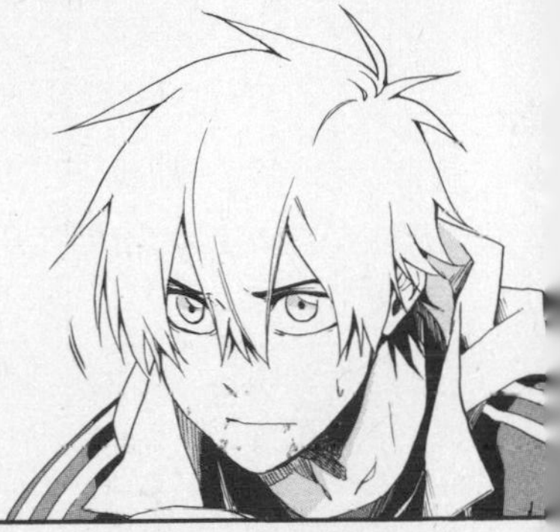

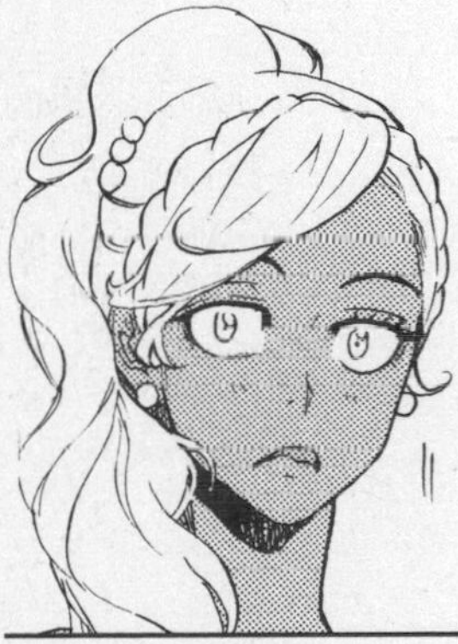

SHOKOL

SHOKOLA HAS FINALLY OPENED UP A BI
TO KAMO AND ENTRUSTED HIM WITH
BIG SECRET FROM HER PAST. I'M S
PROUD OF MY GIRL, HA HA. THAT DOESN'
MEAN THAT WE KNOW EVERYTHING ABOU
HER CHARACTER - SHOKOLA STIL
HIDES MANY SECRETS THAT KAMO WIL
(HOPEFULLY) DISCOVER AT SOME POIN

CRIMSON

FINALLY SINCE THE DOUJINSHI VERSION OF KAMO, I WAS LOOKING FORWARD TO ILLUMINATE CRIMSON'S BACKSTORY. THERE ARE ONLY A FEW HINTS IN VOLUME 2, BUT IN VOLUME 3 YOU GET MORE ANSWERS.

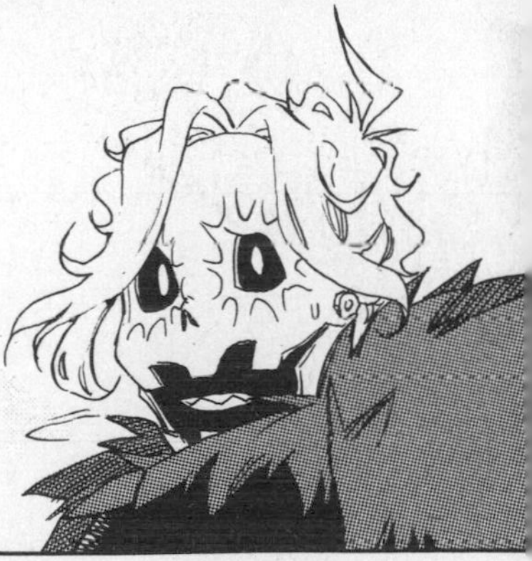

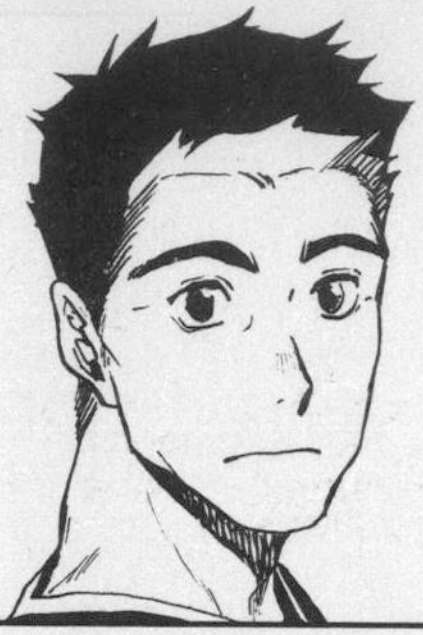

NNO

O REVEAL THAT ENNO HAS KNOWN
HE WHOLE TIME WHO KAMO REALLY IS
ELT QUITE NATURAL. ENNO IS A REALLY
ONDERFUL PERSON WHO WOULD DO
VERYTHING FOR THE GOOD OF HIS FAMILY
ND FRIENDS AND AT THE SAME TIME
LLOWS THEM TO DO THINGS FREELY.

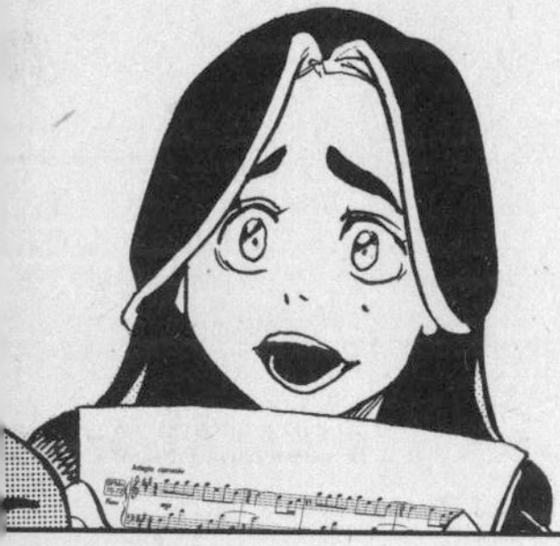

MARIE

EVEN AFTER VOLUME 2, MARIE IS STILL YOUNG. BUT AT SOME POINT SHE HAS TO GROW UP AND STEP OUT OF HER FATHER'S SHADOW. IT WILL BE EXCITING TO SEE HOW SHE MOVES FORWARD.

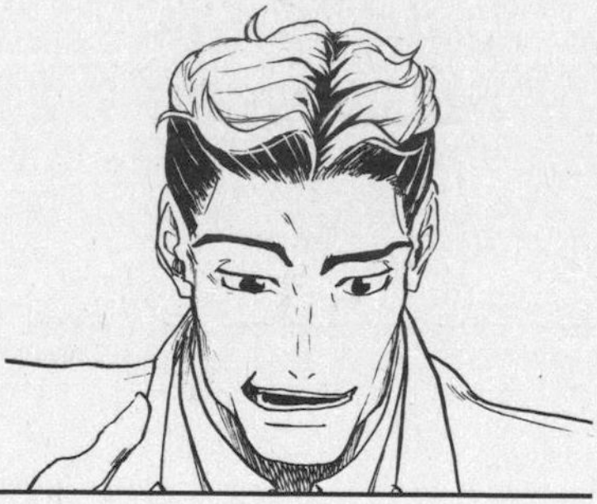

HUNDERBOLT/ ALVIN DORNACH

KNEW FROM THE BEGINNING THAT
WANTED THUNDERBOLT TO COME
ACK, BECAUSE I LOVED HIM IN VOLUME
HIS HUMAN FORM IS VERY DIFFERENT
CHARACTER FROM HIS SPIRIT FORM.

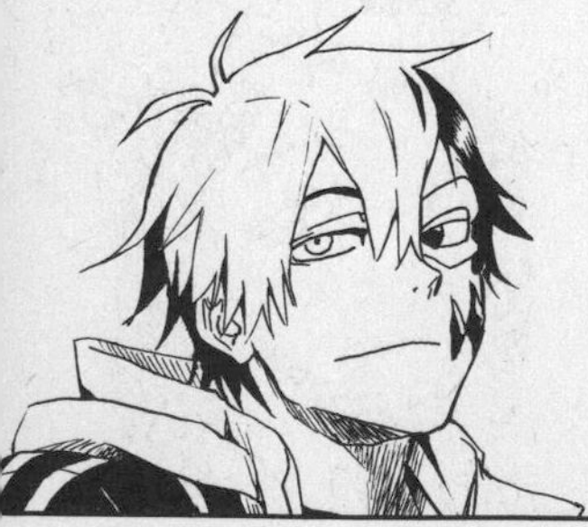

SYMATRA/KAMO

THE FACT THAT KAMO SHOULD BE ABLE TO UTILIZE THE POWERS OF THE GHOSTS STORED IN HIMSELF WAS ALREADY A FIXED IDEA BEFORE I WORKED ON VOLUME 1. HE'S LUCKY THAT SYMATRA HELPED HIM, NEXT TIME IT WON'T BE AS EASY TO CONVINCE THE SPIRITS TO DO SO.

NEW MINOR CHARACTERS

ARISLADY

THE SIX YEAR OLD SISTER OF SHOKOLA, WHO ALWAYS SAYS WHAT SHE THINKS. SHOKOLA HAS OTHER SIBLINGS, BUT NOT ALL LIVE WITH HER AND HER MOTHER.

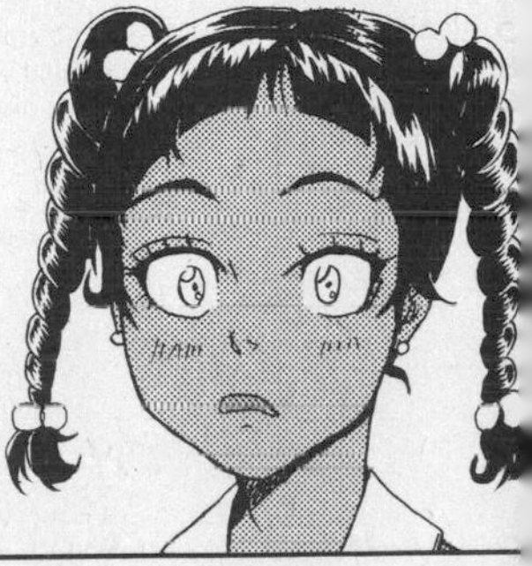

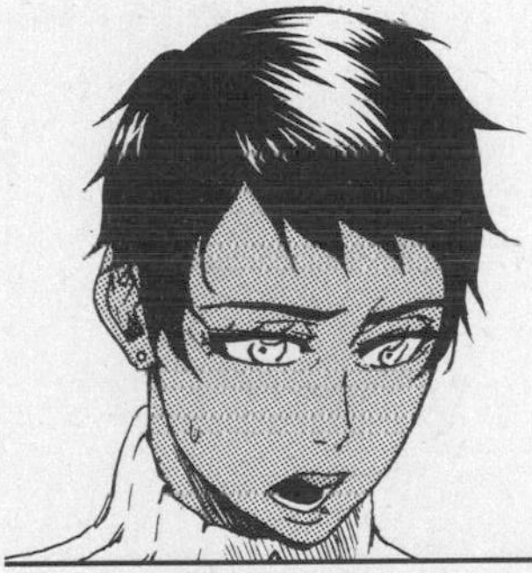

SHOKOLA'S MOTHE

LIKE SHOKOLA, SHE KNOWS ABOUT TH EXISTENCE OF SPIRITS (IN FACT, EVERYONE I OR FROM THE DOMINICAN REPUBLIC BELIEVE IN SPIRITS). HER TRENDY HAIRCUT SET HE APART FROM CLASSIC LATIN MOTHER

ANNABELLE

ANNABELLE IS ALSO LATIN AND COMES FROM THE SAME COMMUNITY AS SHOKOLA AND HER FAMILY. THERE IS A SPECIAL CONNECTION BETWEEN HER AND CRIMSON. YOU WILL LEARN MORE ABOUT THIS IN THE NEXT VOLUME.

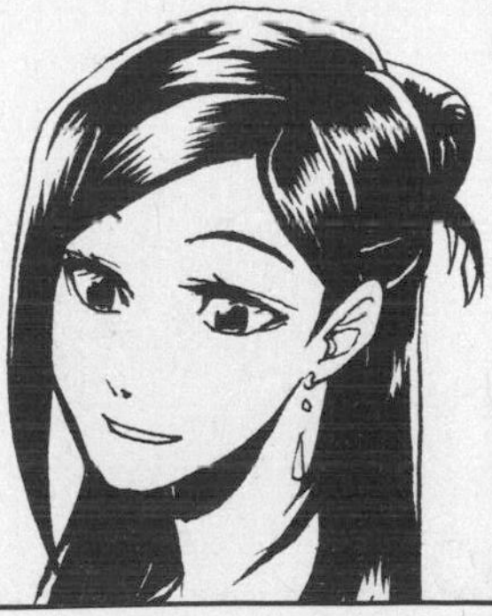

NEW SPIRITS

LOWERCAKE

RR ... I DON'T LIKE CLOWNS (OR PORCELAIN
OLLS), BUT IT WAS STILL FUN DRAWING
IM BECAUSE UNLIKE OTHER SPIRITS HE
AS A VERY DETAILED AND WRINKLY FACE.

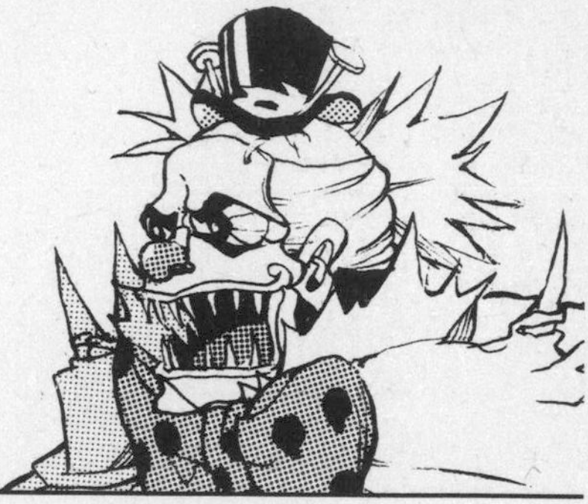

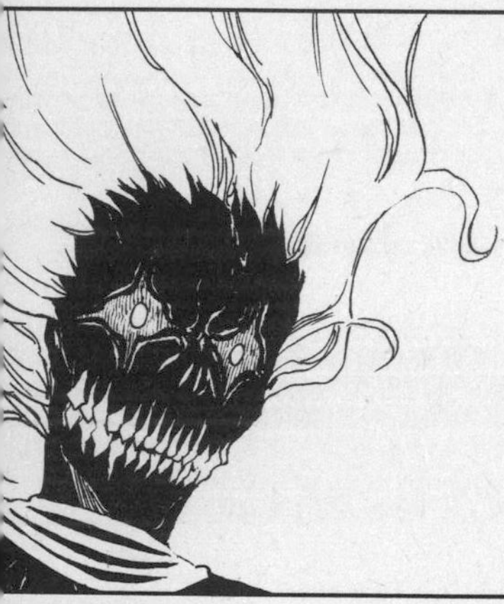

MOTHER

SINCE SHE IS COMPLETELY BLACK, THE COMPLETION OF THIS CHAPTER TOOK ME TWICE AS LONG AND WAS DIFFICULT TO INK. I COULD HAVE SMACKED MYSELF FOR DOING THAT. LUCKILY MY ASSISTANTS HELPED ME WITH INKING HER.

OGISTO & INTUITIVA

HOST TWINS (I FEEL SO CONNECTED
) THEM, HA HA). THEIR APPEARANCE
AS SHORT AND AS OF NOW WE ONLY
NOW THAT THEY ARE ACTING AS
FORMANTS FOR THE SPIRIT WORLD...

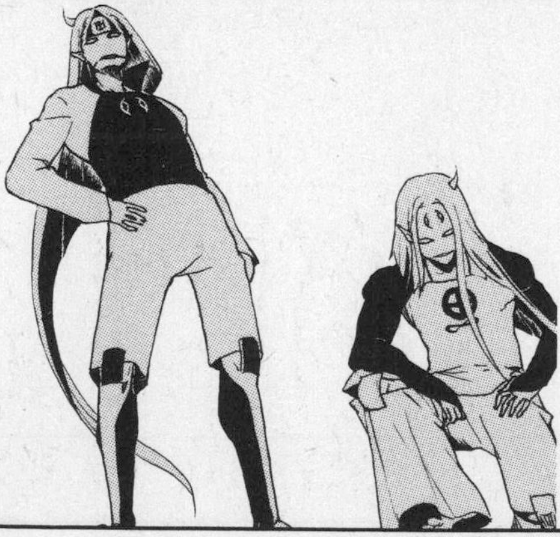

THIS WAS THE FIRST SKETCH FOR THE COVER OF VOLUME 2.

THE IDEA WAS TO SHOW KAMO (WITH HIS NEW LOOK) ALONG WITH SHOKOLA AND CRIMSON. SHOKOLA WAS ESPECIALLY IN FOCUS, AS SHE PLAYS A BIGGER ROLE IN VOLUME 2. HOWEVER, IT ULTIMATELY PUT TOO MUCH EMPHASIZE ON HER. THAT IS WHY I DECIDED TO GO WITH ANOTHER LAYOUT AND TO USE COLOR ILLUSTRATIONS.

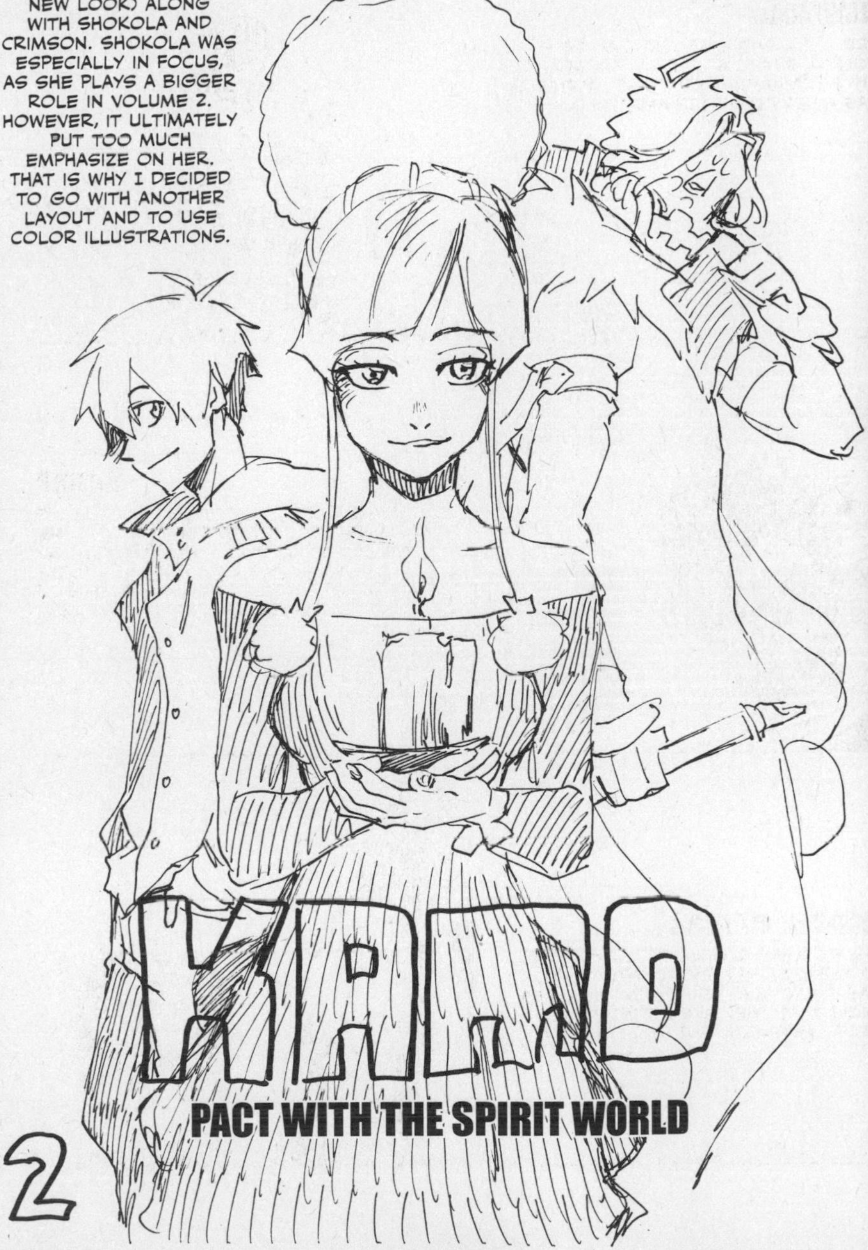
KAMO
PACT WITH THE SPIRIT WORLD
2

ANOTHER POSSIBLE SKETCH FOR THE COVER OF VOLUME 2.

A NEW ATTEMPT, WITH LUCK: KAMO STANDS OUT AS THE MAIN CHARACTER. SHOKOLA IS SEEN AS THE SECOND MOST IMPORTANT CHARACTER. HOWEVER, I WAS NOT 100% SATISFIED WITH THIS.

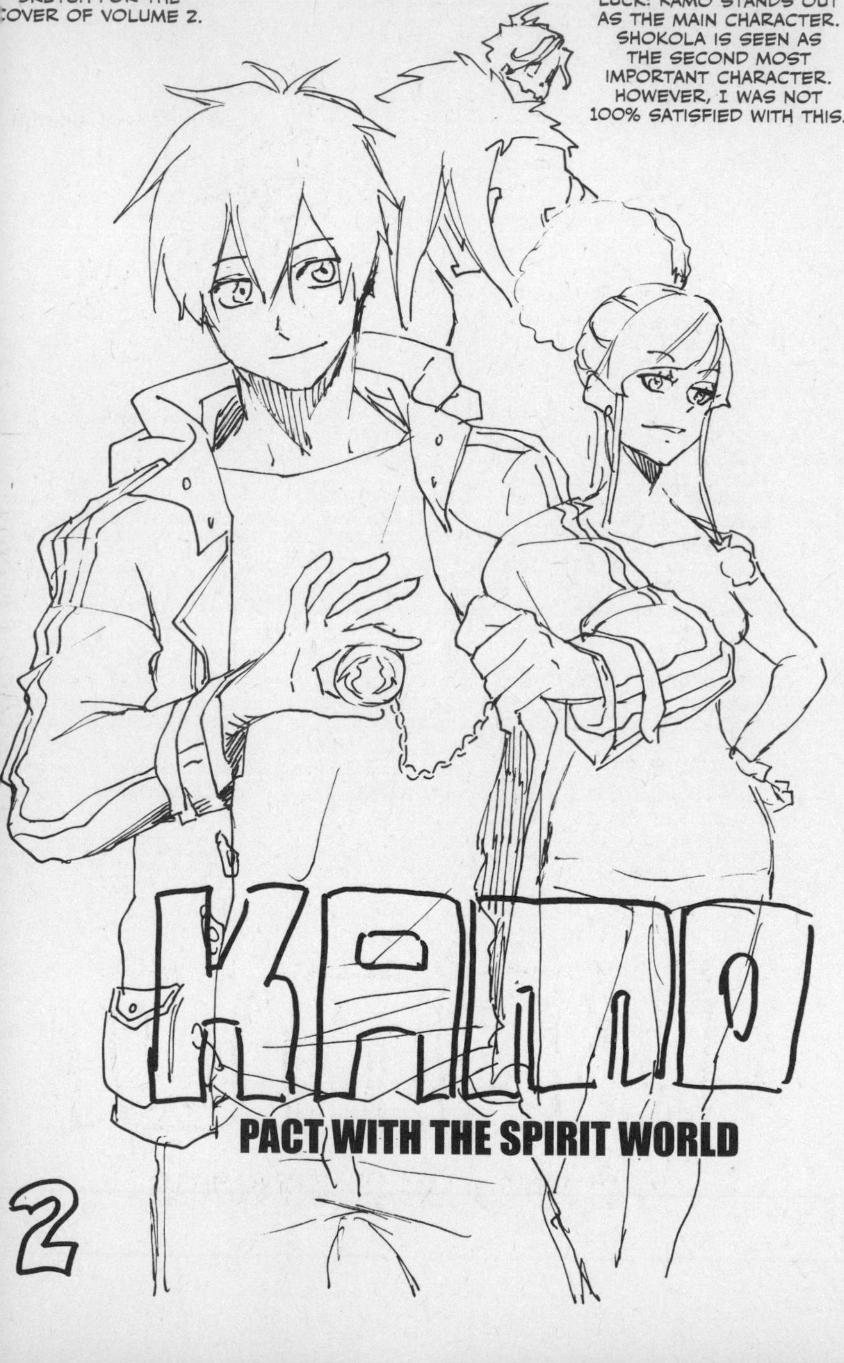
KAMO
PACT WITH THE SPIRIT WORLD
2

THIS BECAME THE FINAL LAYOUT. WELL, ALMOST. I FINISHED COLORING ALL THREE FIGURES ON THE TOKYOPOP PREVIEW FOR THE DEALERS, BUT A COLLEAGUE FROM THE MARKETING DEPARTMENT THOUGHT THAT I SHOULD DELETE CRIMSON COMPLETELY. A GOOD IDEA, I THINK, BECAUSE NOW THE COVER IS NOT AS CLUTTERED AND KAMO AND SHOKOLA ARE CLEARLY THE FOCUS.

THE FINAL SKETCH

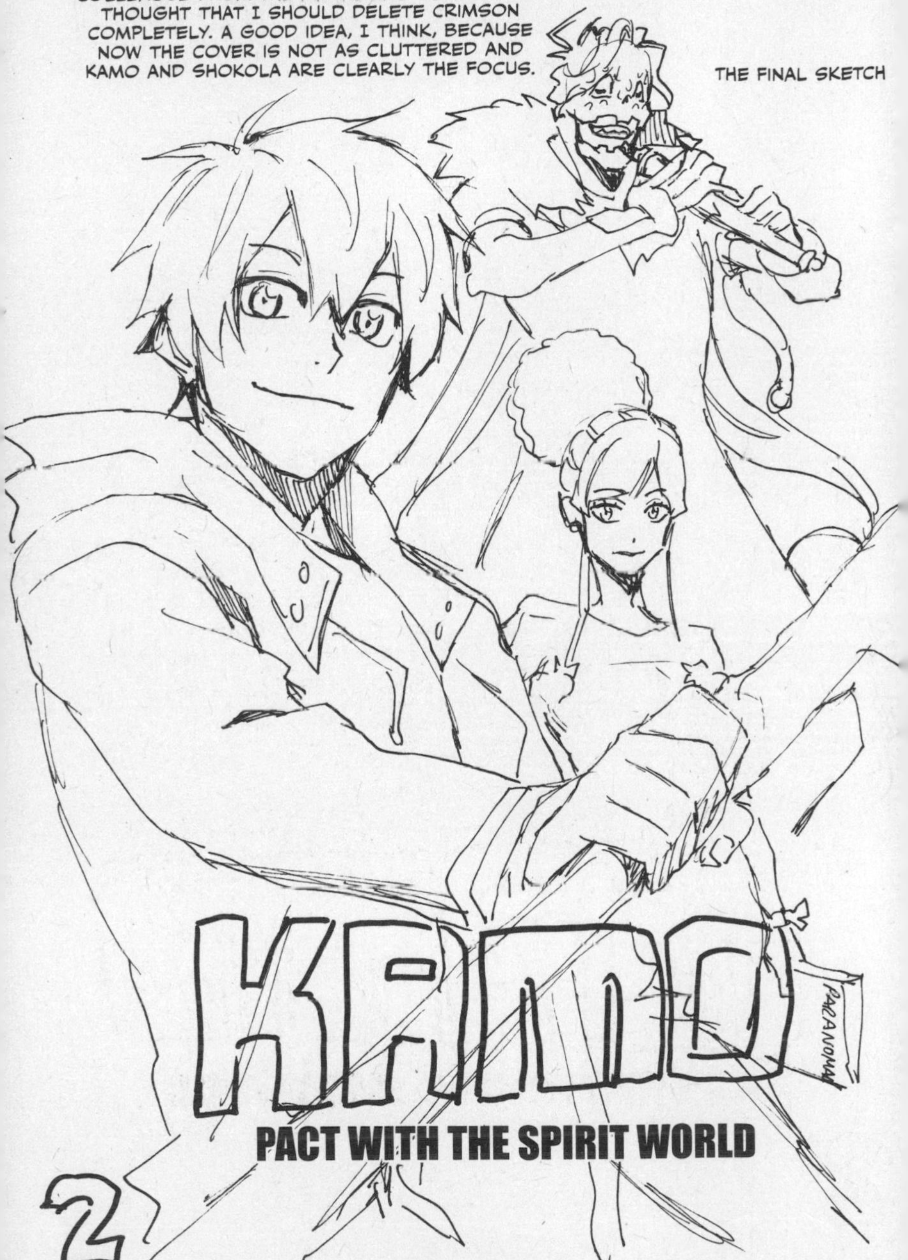
KAMO
PACT WITH THE SPIRIT WORLD
2

UNDEAD
MESSIAH

UNDEAD
MESSIAH

1

Gin Zarbo

ZOMBIE APOCALYPSES
ARE SO LAST YEAR!

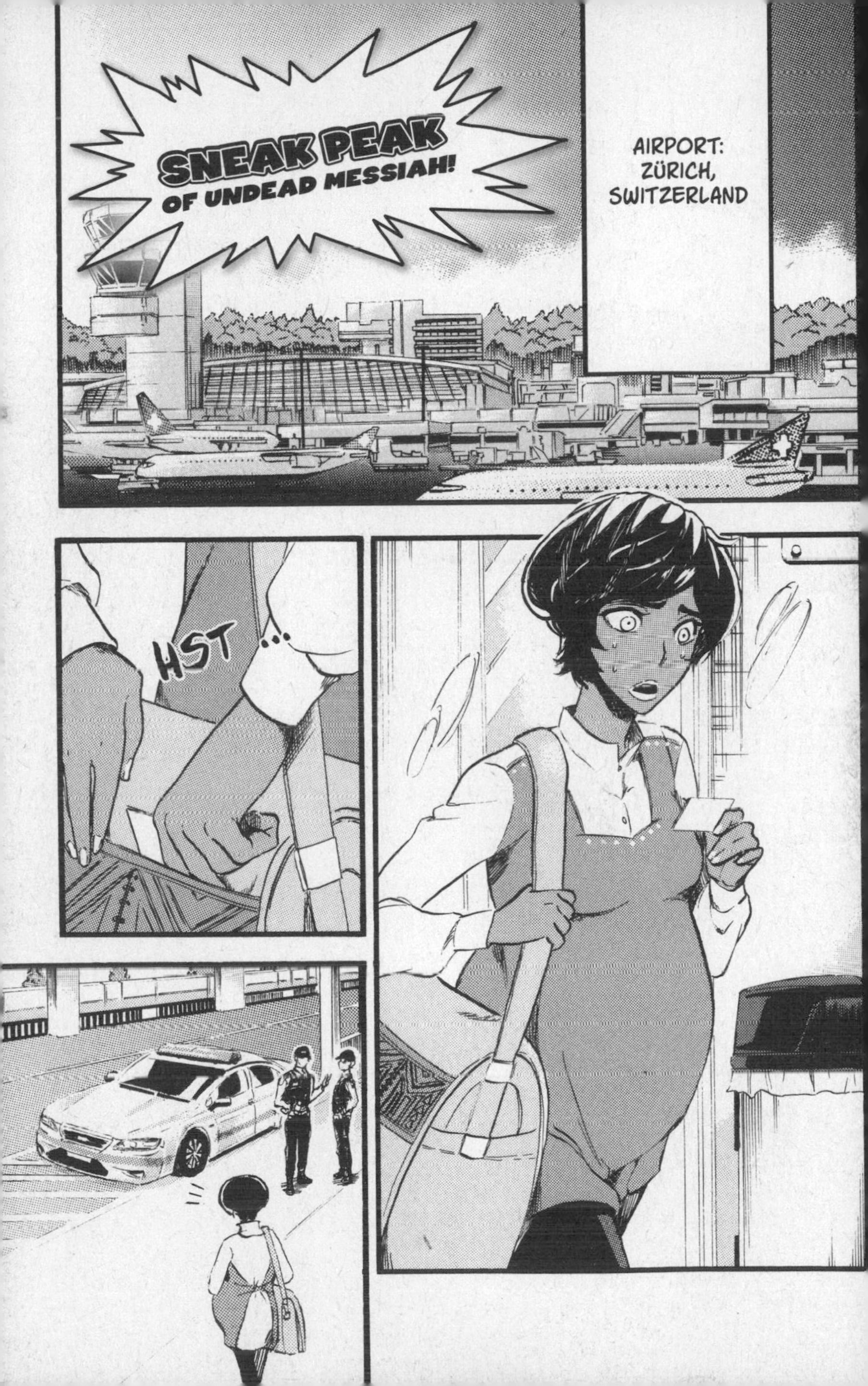
SNEAK PEAK
OF UNDEAD MESSIAH!
AIRPORT: ZÜRICH, SWITZERLAND
HST

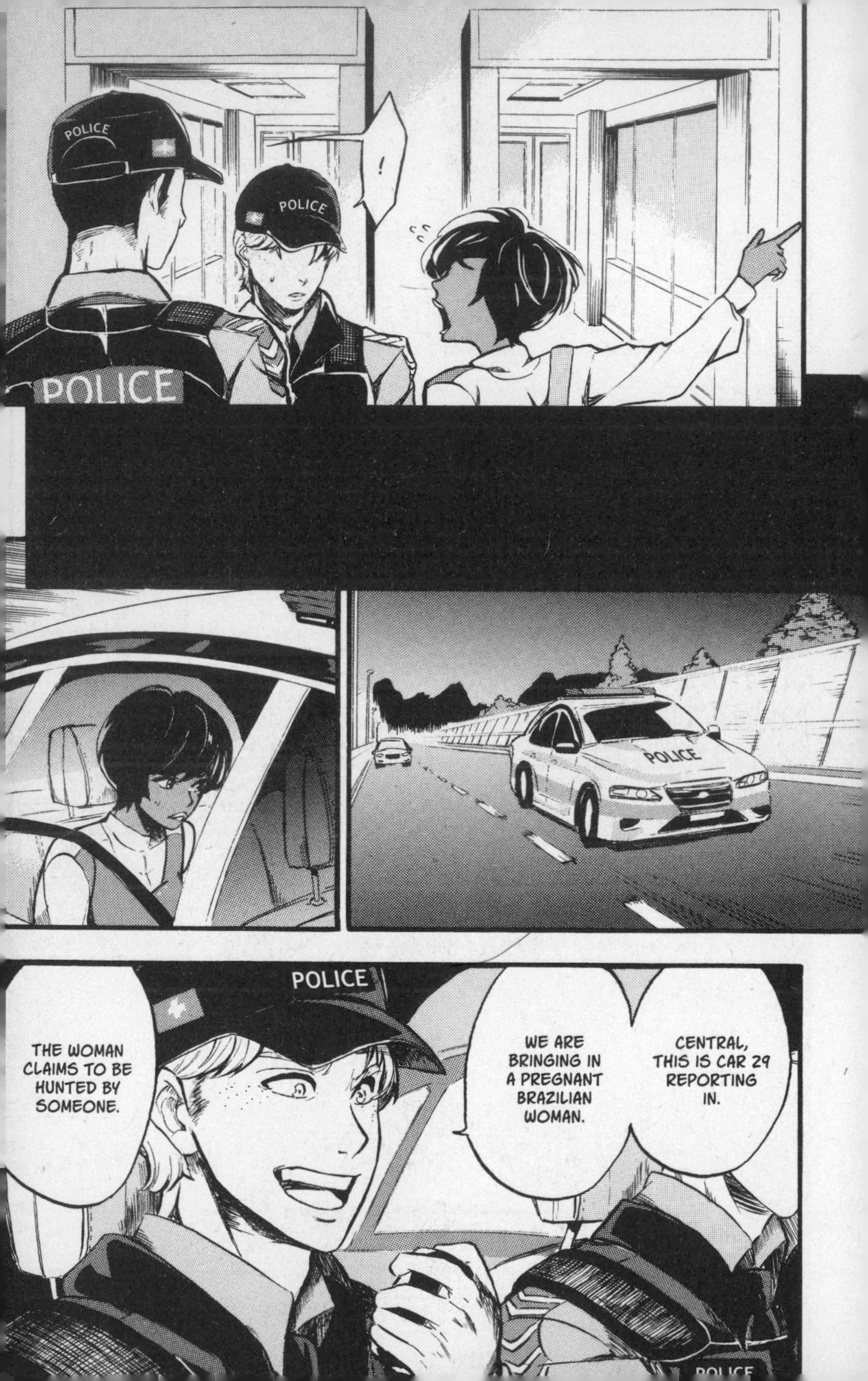
!
CENTRAL, THIS IS CAR 29 REPORTING IN.
WE ARE BRINGING IN A PREGNANT BRAZILIAN WOMAN.
THE WOMAN CLAIMS TO BE HUNTED BY SOMEONE.

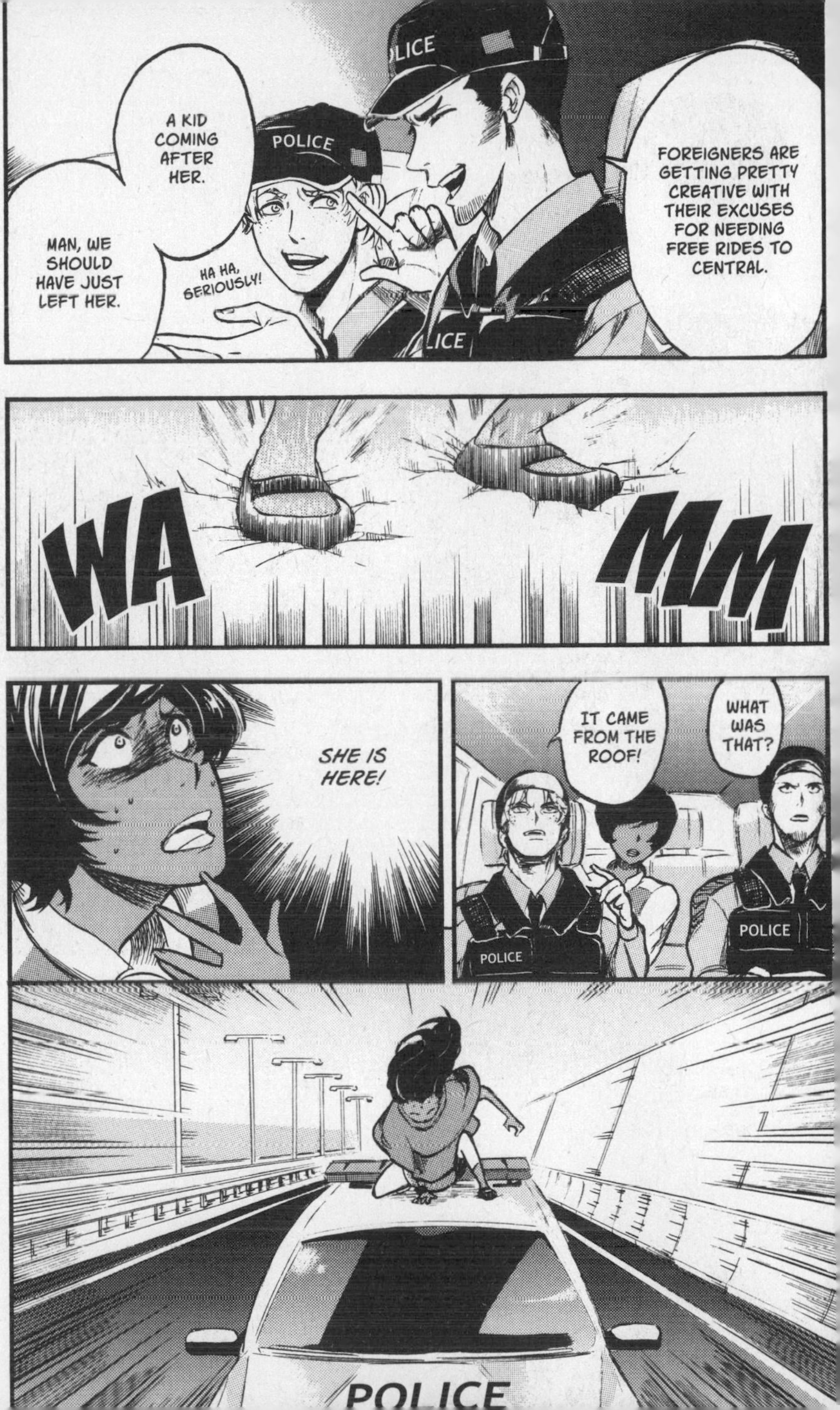

POLICE
POLICE
FOREIGNERS ARE GETTING PRETTY CREATIVE WITH THEIR EXCUSES FOR NEEDING FREE RIDES TO CENTRAL.
A KID COMING AFTER HER.
HA HA, SERIOUSLY!
MAN, WE SHOULD HAVE JUST LEFT HER.
WA
MM
WHAT WAS THAT?
IT CAME FROM THE ROOF!
POLICE
POLICE
SHE IS HERE!
POLICE

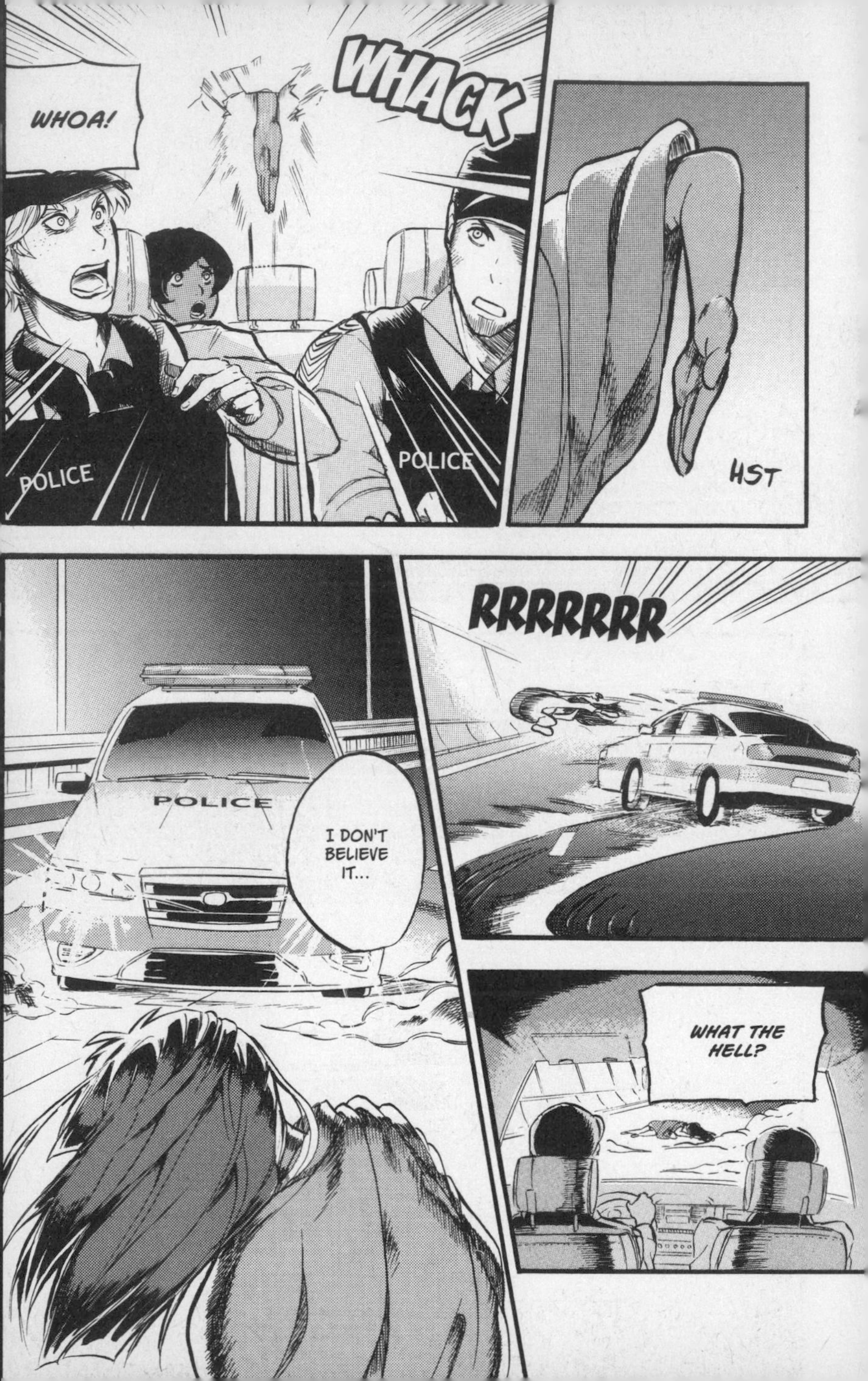
HST
WHACK
WHOA!
POLICE
POLICE
RRRRRRR
WHAT THE HELL?
POLICE
I DON'T BELIEVE IT...

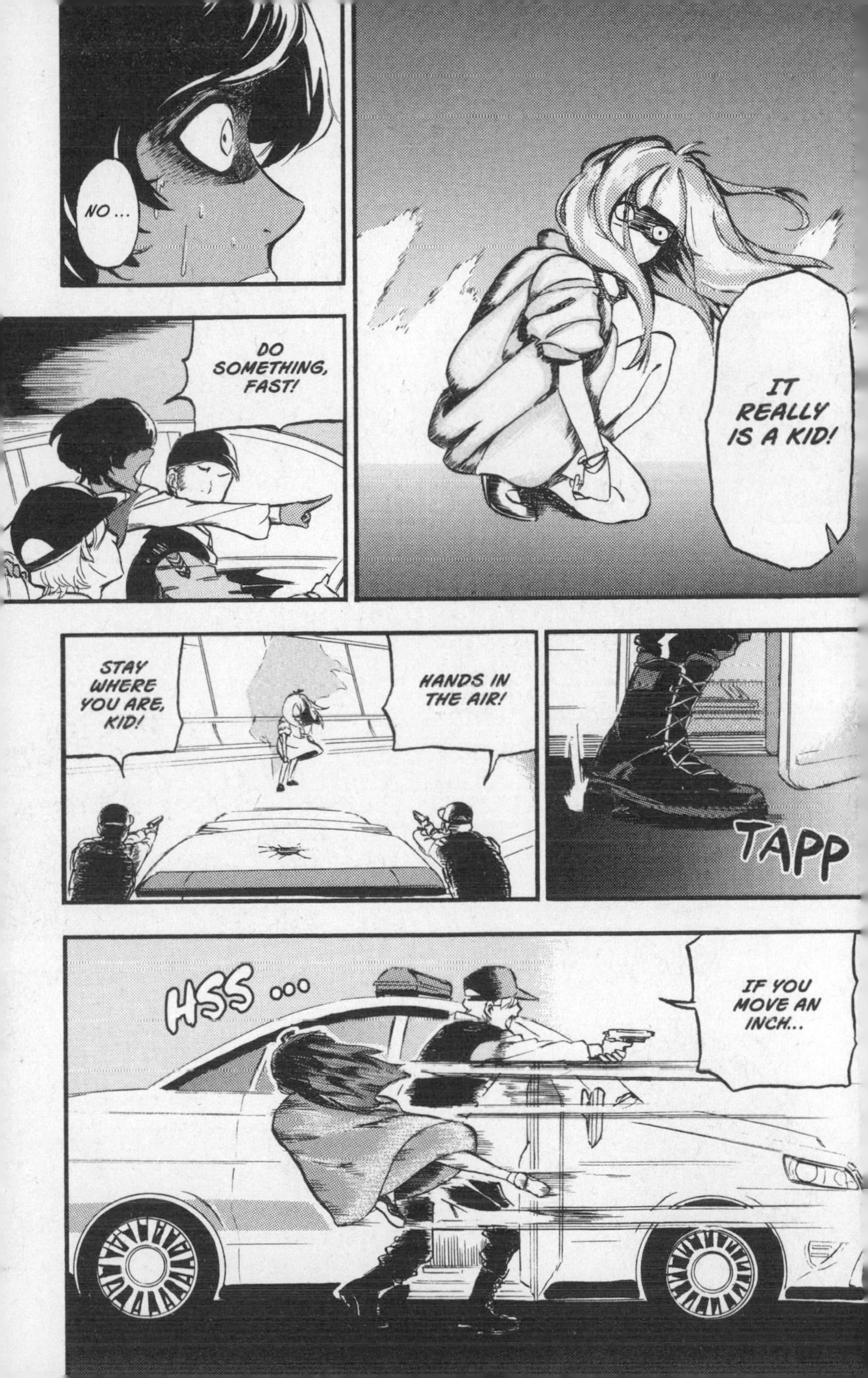
IT REALLY IS A KID!
NO ...
DO SOMETHING, FAST!
TAPP
HANDS IN THE AIR!
STAY WHERE YOU ARE, KID!
IF YOU MOVE AN INCH...
HSS ...

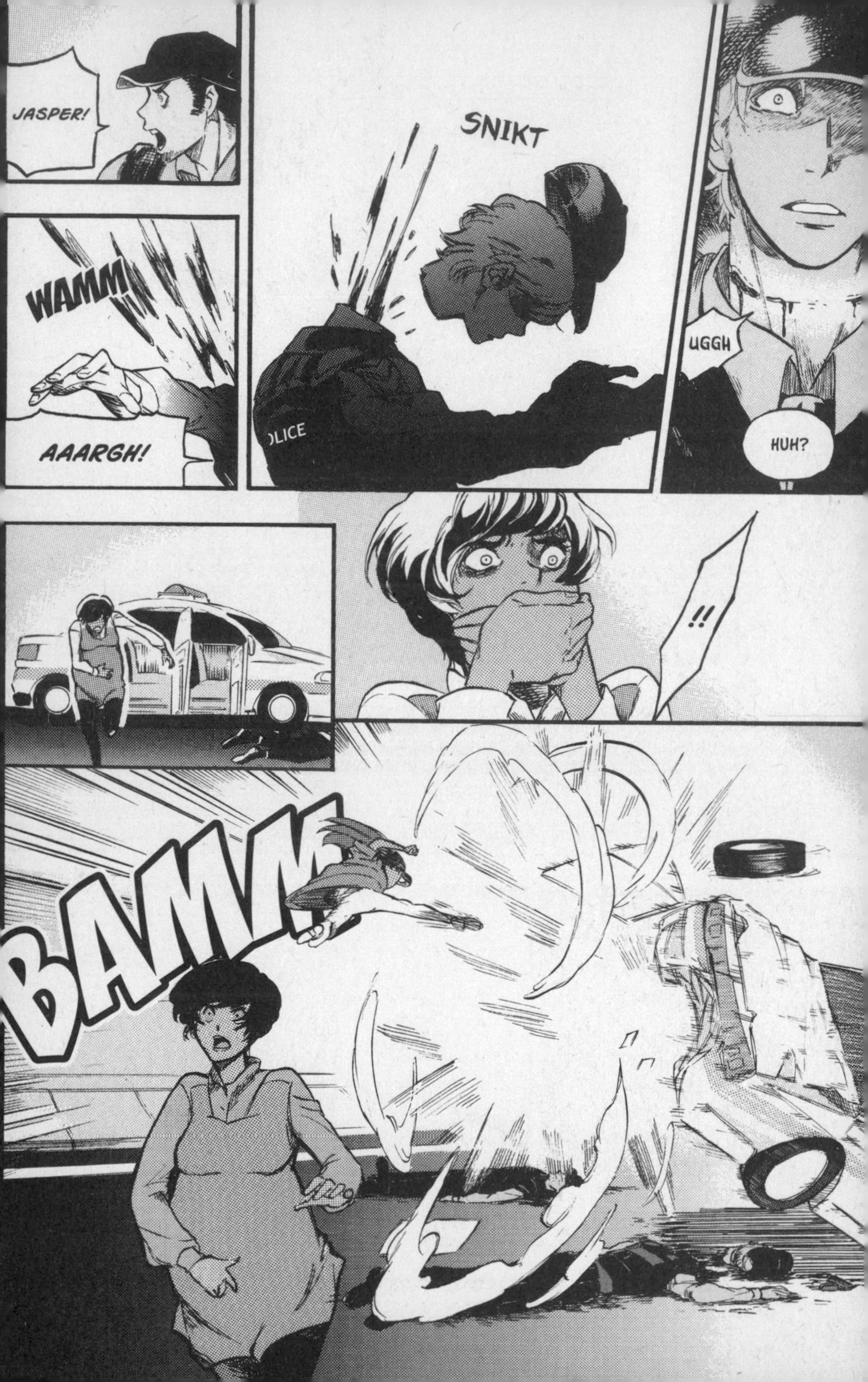

JASPER!
WAMM
AAARGH!
SNIKT
UGGH
HUH?
!!
BAMM

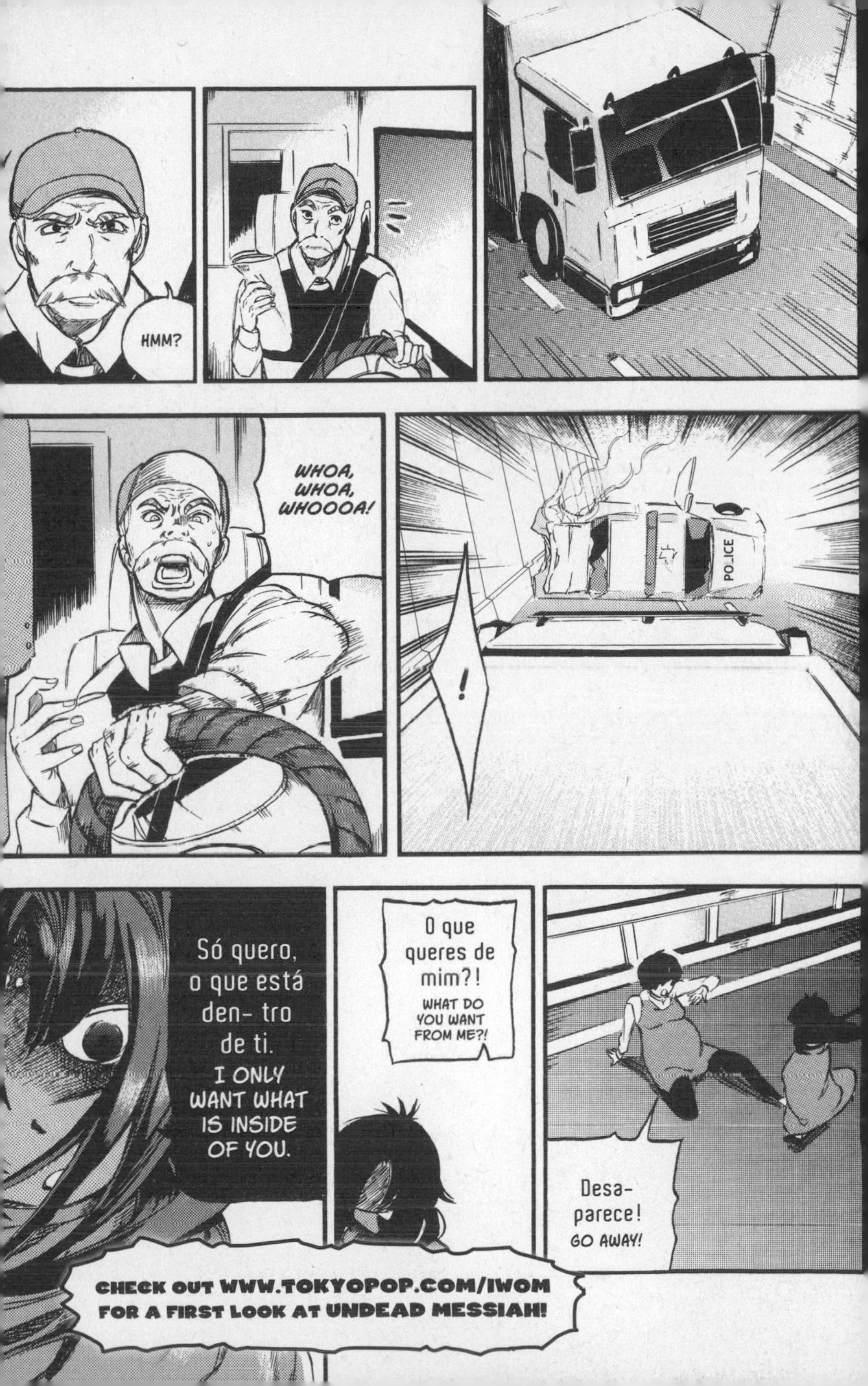
HMM?
WHOA, WHOA, WHOOOA!
!
Desaparece!
GO AWAY!
O que queres de mim?!
WHAT DO YOU WANT FROM ME?!
Só quero, o que está den- tro de ti.
I ONLY WANT WHAT IS INSIDE OF YOU.
CHECK OUT WWW.TOKYOPOP.COM/IWOM FOR A FIRST LOOK AT UNDEAD MESSIAH!

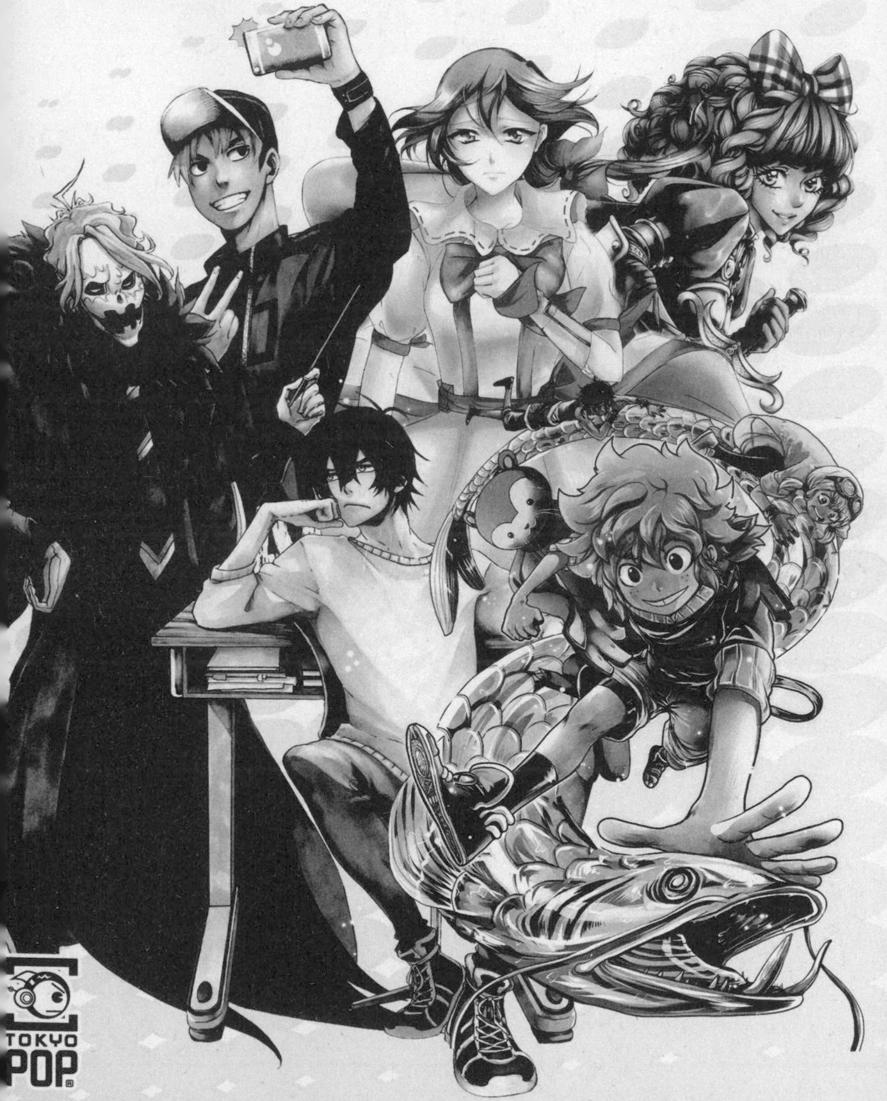

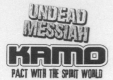

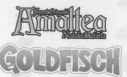

TOKYOPOP
· PRESENTS ·

INTERNATIONAL
WOMEN *of* MANGA

Nana Yaa

GOLDFISCH

Popular German manga artist who won her first award at age 17.

Sophie-Chan

Ocean
of
Secrets

A self-taught manga artist from the Middle East, with a huge YouTube following!

Ban Zarbo

KAMO
PACT WITH THE SPIRIT WORLD

A lifelong manga fan from Switzerland, she and her twin sister take inspiration from their Dominican roots!

Gin Zarbo

UNDEAD MESSIAH

An aspiring manga artist since she was a child, along with her twin sister she's releasing her debut title!

Natalia Batista

Sword Princess
Amaltea
Natalia Batista

A Swedish creator whose popular manga has already been published in Sweden, Italy and the Czech Republic!

TO LEARN MORE PLEASE VISIT OUR WEBSITE

www.TOKYOPOP.com

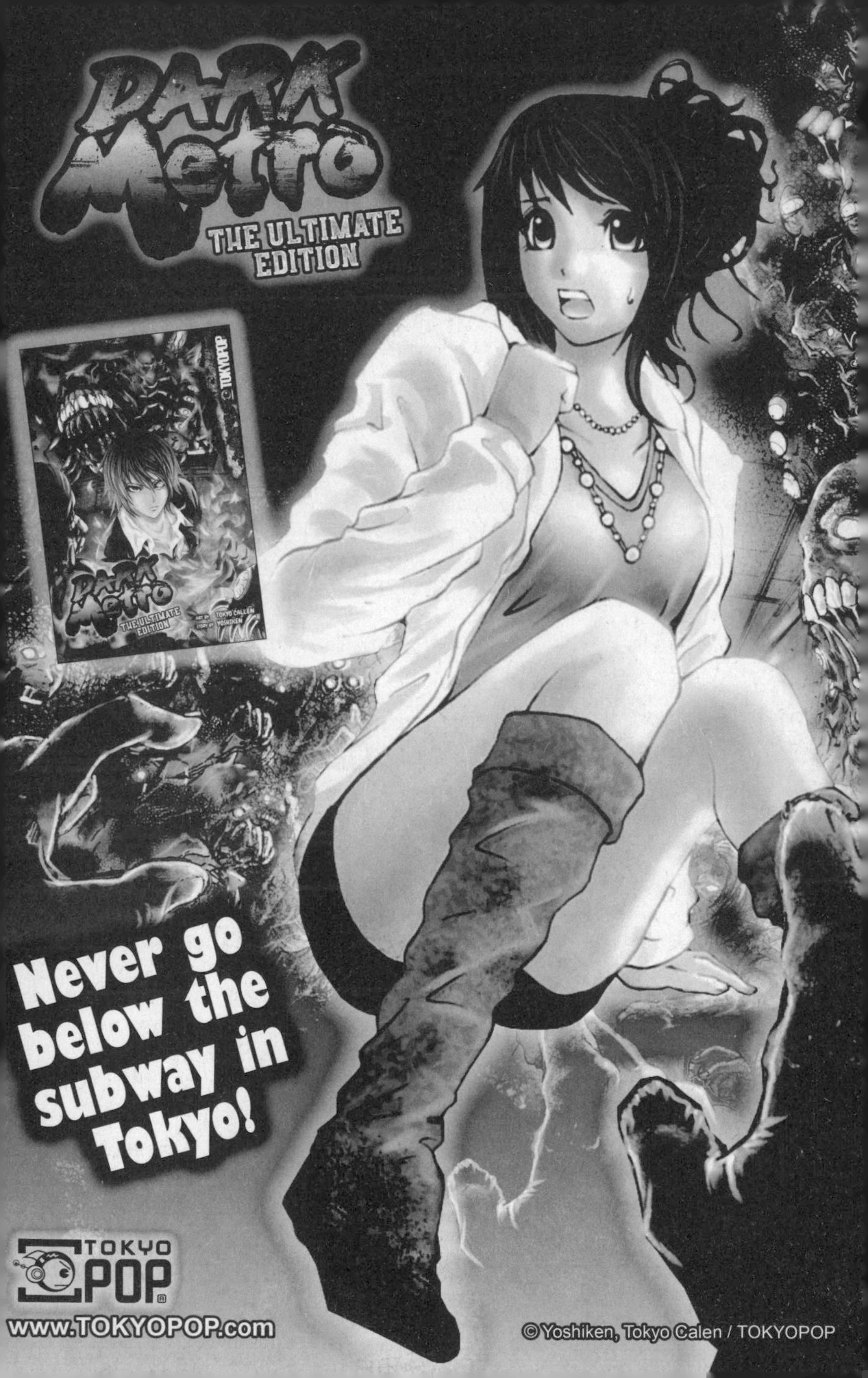
DARK METRO
THE ULTIMATE EDITION
TOKYOPOP
DARK METRO
THE ULTIMATE EDITION
Never go below the subway in Tokyo!
TOKYOPOP
www.TOKYOPOP.com
© Yoshiken, Tokyo Calen / TOKYOPOP

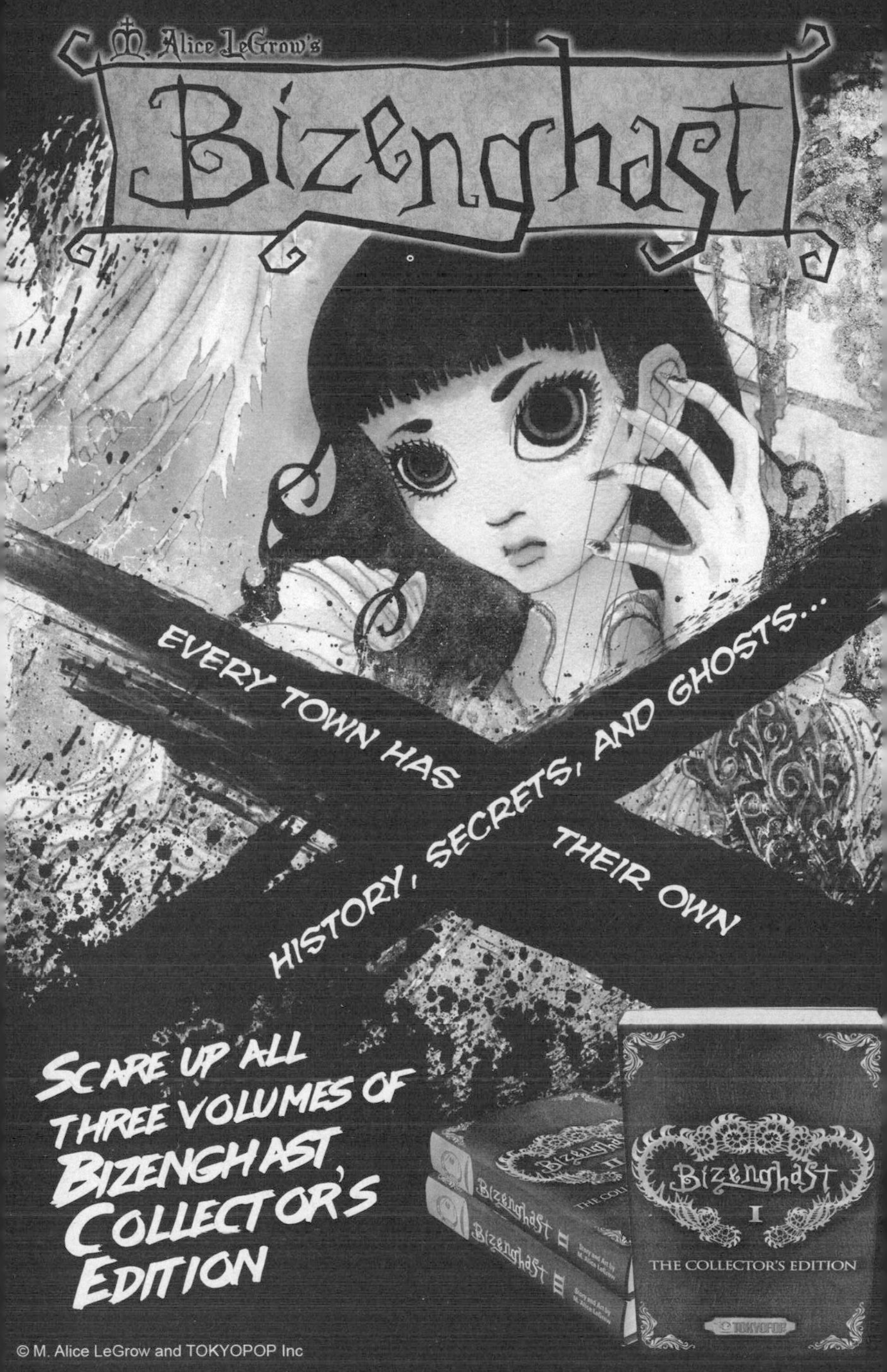
M. Alice LeGrow's
Bizenghast
EVERY TOWN HAS
HISTORY, SECRETS, AND GHOSTS...
THEIR OWN
SCARE UP ALL THREE VOLUMES OF BIZENGHAST, COLLECTOR'S EDITION
Bizenghast
I
THE COLLECTOR'S EDITION
TOKYOPOP

THE AUTHOR

IT WAS HER MOTHER WHO INTRODUCED BAN TO ANIME
AND MANGA AS A YOUNG GIRL. EVEN BACK THEN,
BAN KNEW THAT SHE WANTED TO ONE DAY BECOME
A MANGAKA. BORN IN 1993, SHE IS A SWISS NATIVE
WITH DOMINICAN AND ITALIAN ROOTS. MANY YEARS
LATER, SHE REACHED HER GOAL: *KAMO – PACT WITH
THE SPIRIT WORLD* WAS HER FIRST PUBLICATION WITH
A PUBLISHER AND IS BASED ON THE DOUJINSHI KA-
MO, WHICH SHE SELF-PUBLISHED IN 2014. INSPIRATION
FOR HER MOSTLY SUPERNATURAL STORIES COME FROM
CARIBBEAN SAGAS AND MYTHS. BAN'S TWIN SISTER, GIN,
IS ALSO A MANGAKA. TOGETHER, THEY SHARE A STUDY
IN THE SWISS TOWN OF LANGENDORF, WHERE THEY
ALSO HAVE A MASSIVE MANGA COLLECTION.

FACEBOOK: BANZARBO
TWITTER: BANZARBO
INSTAGRAM: BAN_ZARBO

Kamo Volume 2
Manga By: Ban Zarbo

Editorial Associate - Janae Young
Marketing Associate - Kae Winters
Technology and Digital Media Assistant - Phillip Hong
Digital Media Coordinator - Rico Brenner-Quiñonez
Licensing Specialist - Arika Yanaka
Translator - Kenneth Shinabery
Editor - M. Cara Carper
Graphic Designer - Phillip Hong
Retouching and Lettering - Vibrraant Publishing Studio
Editor-in-Chief & Publisher - Stu Levy

A  Manga

TOKYOPOP and 🐢 are trademarks or registered trademarks of TOKYOPOP Inc.

TOKYOPOP inc.
5200 W Century Blvd
Suite 705
Los Angeles, CA 90045 USA

E-mail: info@TOKYOPOP.com
Come visit us online at www.TOKYOPOP.com

f www.facebook.com/TOKYOPOP
🐦 www.twitter.com/TOKYOPOP
▶ www.youtube.com/TOKYOPOPTV
📌 www.pinterest.com/TOKYOPOP
📷 www.instagram.com/TOKYOPOP

ISBN: 978-1-4278-5871-9
First TOKYOPOP Printing: September 2018
10 9 8 7 6 5 4 3 2 1
Printed in CANADA

STOP

THIS IS THE BACK OF THE BOOK!

How do you read manga-style? It's simple! Let's practice -- just start in the top right panel and follow the numbers below!

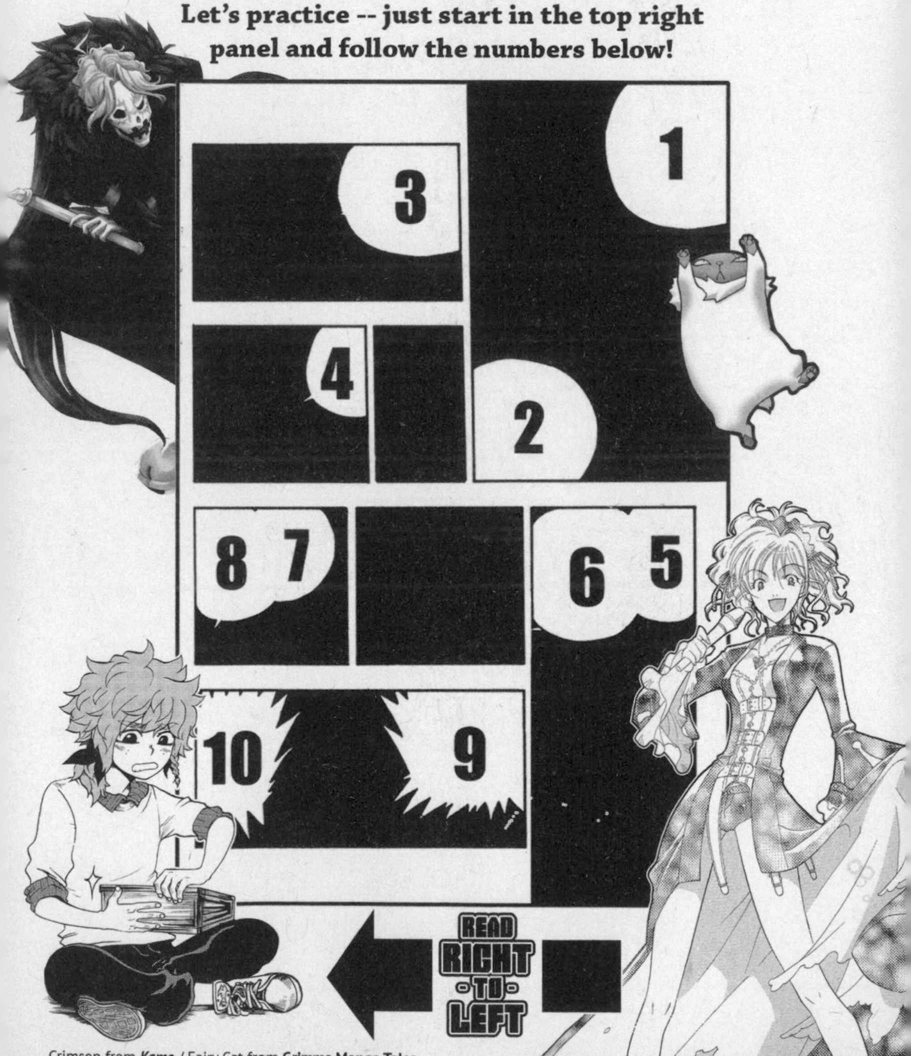
1
2
3
4
5
6
7
8
9
10
READ
RIGHT
-TO-
LEFT

Crimson from *Kamo* / Fairy Cat from **Grimms Manga Tales**
Morrey from *Goldfisch* / Princess Ai from *Princess Ai*